After the Mating

His fangs retracted as his mouth crushed hers. Anger rode his kiss, and he plundered deep, showing her in no uncertain terms who was stronger. Not only physically, but as he softened his assault, as he shot fire through her until her ears rang, he showed her true strength. After one night with him, he controlled her responses. He could make her want on demand. Possibly from the mating, from the marking ... but more likely from Jase himself. The man was sex, danger, and fire combined.

She whimpered in her throat, her eyes fluttering shut. Desire slashed with jagged edges as it ripped into her.

His kiss held nothing back. No smoothness—no persuasion. He took everything she had and then demanded more. Demanded everything. The male wasn't taking no for an answer.

Shadowed

REBECCA ZANETTI

LYRICAL PRESS
Kensington Publishing Corp.
www.kensingtonbooks.com

LYRICAL PRESS BOOKS are published by

Kensington Publishing Corp.
119 West 40th Street
New York, NY 10018

Copyright © 2013 Rebecca Zanetti

All Kensington titles, imprints, and distributed lines are available at special quantity discounts for bulk purchases for sales promotions, premiums, fund-raising, educational, or institutional use. Special book excerpts or customized printings can also be created to fit specific needs. For details, write or phone the office of the Kensington special sales manager: Kensington Publishing Corp., 119 West 40th Street, New York, NY 10018, attn: Special Sales Department; phone 1-800-221-2647.

Lyrical Press and Lyrical Press logo Reg. U.S. Pat. & TM Off.

First electronic edition: October 2013

ISBN-13: 978-1-60183-152-1
ISBN-10: 1-60183-152-8

First print edition: October 2013

ISBN-13: 978-1-60183-216-0
ISBN-10: 1-60183-216-8

This book is dedicated to my mom, Gail Cornell English. She has always been the "room mom," the softball coach, and the one person who can take a bad day and make us laugh about it. She taught me to love reading, and more important, she taught me that I could do anything I wanted to do . . . even create wild characters like the ones we found in books. Now, as Gaga, she's passing those lessons down to my kids, and she's definitely their soft place to land. Thank you, Mom. I love you.

ACKNOWLEDGMENTS

I have many people to thank for help in getting this book to readers, and I sincerely apologize for anyone I've forgotten.

Thank you to Tony, Gabe, and Karlina Zanetti, my very patient family, for giving me time and space to write, as well as lots of love and excitement. Also, congrats to Gabe for the undefeated arena football season, and to Karly for first place in the KGSA softball minor's division this year;

Thank you to my talented agent, Caitlin Blasdell, who works so very hard for her authors. I am so grateful to be working with you. Thanks also to Liza Dawson and everyone at Liza Dawson Associates for the hard work and encouragement.

Thank you to my amazing editor, Alicia Condon, who has such wonderful insight into characters and motivation . . . and is one of the kindest people I've ever had the privilege of working with;

Thank you to all the folks at Kensington Publishing, especially Alexandra Nicolajsen and Vida Engstrand because they're such a joy to work with, and I'm always so happy to see them at conferences. Thanks also to Arthur Maisel for the excellent copy edits.

Thank you to my critique partner Jennifer Dorough—who one day said . . . "I think Jase should be with Brenna Dunne, don't you?"

Thank you to Deb Stewart for her very generous donation to the Excel Foundation last year;

Thank you to Kim Killion and her colleagues at Hot Damn Designs—your covers are spectacular;

And thanks also to my constant support system: Gail and Jim English, Debbie and Travis Smith, Stephanie and Don West, Brandie and Mike Chapman, Jessica and Jonah Namson, and Kathy and Herb Zanetti.

Chapter 1

"There's a vampire here to see you," said a chipper voice from the office doorway.

Brenna Dunne glanced up from the stack of ledgers toward her best friend. "I don't have any appointments today."

Deb shrugged a delicate shoulder. "Since when do vampires make appointments?"

Good point. Brenna pushed her glasses up her nose. She was the only witch in existence who required reading glasses. "Did you see who it was?"

"Nope." Deb Stewart had never been much of a vampire fan. "They all look alike to me." She mock-shrugged. "Though, when I passed by the conference room, vibrations of some seriously strong energy made the air heavy."

"Huh." Brenna folded her glasses to tuck in her pocket before standing. The room swayed.

Deb frowned, and lines of concern fanned out from her brown eyes. "How did your treatment go this morning?"

"Terrible." Brenna grimaced. "The treatments have stopped doing any good." In fact, having the doctors replace her blood was just a waste of time at this point.

"That's what I thought." Deb shuffled the stack of papers in her hands. "Maybe it's time to tell the council."

"Aye." The room stopped tilting, so Brenna skirted the desk. "I'll need to submit my resignation soon." She could barely stand up, much less participate on the Council of the Coven Nine, the ruling body for witches the world over.

Deb tilted her dark head toward the pile of paperwork on the desk. "Any marriage proposals?"

"Three proposals and two death threats this week." Brenna's legs wobbled as she reached the doorway.

"The usual, huh?" Deb said.

Brenna paused to regain her bearings. "Yes. Man, I need to get my strength back."

Deb patted her arm. "The doctors will find a cure. I'm sure of it."

"I know." Brenna forced a smile as they both lied.

Deb swallowed. "I'll take the afternoon meeting with the Dublin economic group for you."

Relief and gratitude swept Brenna. "Thanks. I owe you once again." She slid into the hallway. "Wish me luck with the vampire."

"Luck," Deb muttered as she bustled in the other direction.

Good thing Deb had fallen in love with and married a witch. She and a vampire would've been a disaster.

Brenna eyed the wall of windows as she walked. Lightning flashed outside the windows, and the Liffey threw up whitecaps. Nothing like a December snowstorm in Ireland to get things interesting. With her diminishing vision, the world morphed into different shades of gray outside.

She carefully picked her way along the hallway to push open the door to the small meeting room.

Her breath caught. "Jase."

Jase Kayrs sprawled in one of three overstuffed chairs, reading a stack of papers neatly attached inside a manila file folder. A fire crackled behind him, while the storm raged outside the full wall of windows to his left. At her entry, he flipped the file shut and stood. "Brenna."

She swallowed and fought the urge to step back. At one time, Jase had been the most charming male she'd ever met. Now, a predatory danger cascaded off him in waves. Dressed in a dark shirt, faded jeans, and combat boots, the vampire was anything but a typical soldier. He even looked different, having cut his brown hair short in contrast to the wild mane he used to sport.

Deep copper eyes glowed from his chiseled face and illustrated a torment he apparently hadn't triumphed over.

Mindful of manners, she hastened forward and held out a hand. "How are you?"

"Fine." His hand swallowed hers in heat as they shook. A wicked scar had faded to a long white strip above his right cheekbone, making him look even more dangerous than before. For a vampire to scar, he must've been near death when sustaining the injury. Considering the demons had tortured him for five years before nearly cutting off his head, he had been as close to death as possible without succumbing. "Not as crazy as everyone thinks. How are you?"

"Fine. Not as odd as everyone thinks." Her knees wobbled, and not just from her illness. The vampire had presence. All male, all danger. Her heart sped up even as it broke from that deadly scar on his immortal face.

"I never thought you odd." He released her and gestured toward the chair facing his.

Brenna sat and smoothed her hands down her pencil skirt, suddenly grateful she'd dressed up. There was a time she'd had a colossal crush on the youngest Kayrs brother. "Ah, Moira didn't mention you'd be visiting Ireland." Moira was Brenna's older sister who had mated Jase's brother, Conn. They mainly lived in Oregon at the vampire headquarters.

"She and Conn are chasing a witch who's abusing physics up in Canada. I didn't tell them I was heading over here." Jase's gaze raked Brenna. "You're pale."

Irritation and an odd hurt warmed her chest. She slowly ran her gaze from his boots to his head. Hard, ripped muscle showed clearly through his clothing. Cut angles made up his handsome face, leaving shadowed hollows matching those in his eyes. "You're, ah, fit. Been working out?"

"Something like that." His gaze intensified, but she couldn't read his thoughts.

She cleared her throat. "Why are you here?"

The door swept open. "He's here because I asked him." Councilwoman Northcutt, the head of the Coven Nine, glided into the room. She wore a long maroon skirt and matching top, and had pinned her dark hair up in a business-casual look. As the ruler of the witches for the last five centuries, the woman could dress.

Brenna straightened her posture. "Hi, Aunt Viv. Did you want me in on this, or shall I attend the economic meetings?"

Viv settled herself on the third seat. "I want you here."

"All right." Brenna eyed her aunt.

Viv's dark eyes narrowed, and she clasped her hands together before focusing on Jase. "Did you read the file?"

"Yes." He handed the manila folder to Viv.

Brenna glanced at the folder. "What file?"

Viv met her gaze. "Your medical records."

A ball of dread slammed into Brenna's stomach. "Excuse me?"

Viv sighed. "Did you really think we wouldn't notice your deteriorating health?"

Panic wanted to rise to the surface. "My medical records are private," said Brenna.

"Bollocks." Red spun across Viv's high cheekbones. "Not only are we family and should've been told, but I'm also your boss. The council needs to be aware if you're too ill to work."

"I'm perfectly fine." A very rare temper tickled at the base of Brenna's neck.

"No, you're not. The planekite has been slowly poisoning you from the inside for a decade." Fury and helplessness filled Viv's eyes. "The blood treatments aren't working any longer."

So much for living in denial for another week. Brenna flashed back to the moment ten years previous when a male witch who'd kidnapped her poured the vile concoction down her throat. The liquid had burned like acid, firing her veins into pinpricks of pain. Her limbs had weakened, and her blood had thickened in an effort to expel the poison.

In that moment, she'd known the planekite would kill her. The only question was when.

Yanking herself back to the present, she plastered on her best dignitary expression. "Replacing my blood with clean blood worked for the first eight years, but the poison has leaked into my tissues and muscles now," she murmured. Planekite harmed witches, and most of it had been destroyed or locked away by armed guards to be used in research. Unfortunately, there didn't seem to be an antidote to the poison. "I'll submit my resignation tonight." Then she frowned and glanced at Jase. "Why are you reading my medical records?"

No expression crossed his face. "I'm your cure."

The world narrowed. Wait a minute. Brenna angled away from him. "Excuse me?"

Viv's shoulders went back. "I contacted the king and requested an arranged mating between you and a member of the Kayrs royal family. Jase has kindly agreed."

A roaring filled Brenna's head. She opened her mouth, but no sound emerged. Her head jerked in a shaky motion. Mating meant sex. Crazy, dangerous, vampire sex. "Mate?"

Viv leaned forward. "The doctors think you have less than six months to live, so mating is your only option."

Well, that was true. Mating an immortal would give Brenna the male's health and gifts by altering not only her chromosomal pairs but her immune system. She'd be able to counter the planekite— probably. "Why a vampire?" She didn't look at Jase as she asked the question.

Viv cleared her throat. "Unfortunately, you can't mate a witch because the planekite will also poison your mate. You need another immortal. We're at war with the demons and Kurjans, so that leaves either a shifter or a vampire. A vampire is better than an animal."

Jase's eyebrow rose. "Thank you."

Viv sniffed. "You know what I mean."

"I know exactly what you mean." An ominous tone filtered through his words. "Please leave us, Councilwoman Northcutt. I'd like to speak with Brenna. Alone."

For the first time, indecision wavered across Viv's face. Even so, she gracefully stood. "If you do mate, then we need to discuss the winter solstice."

Brenna shook her head. "You're kidding, right?"

"Not at all." Viv glided toward the door. "There's more to the issue than you know."

Brenna blinked. She'd worry about the solstice later. "Aunt Viv? Do my parents know about the illness?" Her mother was on the council, and her parents were on a monthlong cruise.

"No. You need to call them tonight." Viv slipped into the hallway, and the door closed.

Brenna took a deep breath, her gaze turning on the vampire. Her heart slammed against her ribs hard enough to bruise. He was damaged, and he was dangerous. Even so, heat uncoiled in her abdomen at the thought of becoming his. Her body flared to life, but her mind screamed caution. "My answer is no."

He held himself perfectly still, somehow on alert and in perfect control. In fact, the man barely seemed to breathe. "If you don't mate, you'll die."

"That's my problem." She shook her head. "Besides, why would you want to mate me? All of your brothers have mated for love, and look how much stronger they've become."

Shadows cascaded over Jase's face to be ruthlessly smoothed out. "I don't want love."

Awareness pricked up her back. "What do you want?" she asked quietly.

"Revenge." His copper eyes morphed into an angry, sizzling green and then back again.

She'd wondered about his secondary color—the eye color that emerged when a vampire was angry or aroused. "I see. If we mate, you'll get my skills."

"Yes."

She shook her head. "I don't have skills to use against demons."

"You're a witch with a strong command of quantum physics." Jase leaned forward, elbows on his knees. "Being able to alter matter will come in handy when fighting demons." Vulnerability flashed in his eyes for the tiniest of seconds. "Besides, your skills will help me regain mine."

"Regain yours?" She bit her lip, memories swamping her. Jase used to command the elements. "You can't control the elements any longer?"

"No." His angled jaw hardened.

She flashed back to a Realm picnic twenty years ago when the Kayrs brothers had competed fiercely in an obstacle course that would've killed most humans. Jase and his brother Talen had ended up trying to tackle each other on a rope stretched over a river. They'd crashed into the water, both swearing and throwing punches.

Jase had waved his hand, and a wall of ice had risen from the rushing water. Talen had broken his hand trying to punch through.

Then, in typical Kayrs fashion, they'd laughed their asses off. Jase had been charming, fun, and free, and she'd instantly been in love. In fact, she'd angled close to him at dinner that night, and he'd tried to teach her how to control the air. That was when she could still create fire, so she'd popped his oxygen molecules.

His sexy smile had stayed with her for years.

She returned to the present, wondering when he'd last smiled. Her heart clutched. What the demons must've done to him to destroy his gifts with the elements. "I'm sorry."

"I don't want your sympathy."

Her head jerked up. "No. You just want to mate me, brand me like an animal, and then use my gifts."

"That's exactly what I want." No apology, no expression sat on his face. But the anger, the fury sizzled just beneath the surface. Fully alive. Fully deadly.

As a trained witch, one who had once been dangerous before becoming ill, she recognized a predator. Jase was all predator. Training whispered for her to keep the danger in sight. Even so, an odd, feminine instinct unfolded within her. The need to help—the need to heal. Could she help him? "I won't be used."

"We'll both be used, sweetheart." The endearment mocked them both. "But we'll get what we want."

She stood, no longer able to sit and discuss revenge and forever. "What is it I want, Jase?"

"You want to live." He unfolded his length, standing at least a foot and a half taller than she. Reaching out, he ran his finger down the side of her face. "You used to like me, Brenna Dunne."

The gentle touch slid right under her defenses and zinged around, warming her abdomen. Her breath quickened. Vulnerability and need battled through her at his obvious manipulation. "I don't know you anymore."

His upper lip twisted. "Nobody knows me anymore." The scar stood out, even on his bronze skin. "I won't hurt you."

So much for being over her childhood crush. Deep down, a base part of her awoke with the thought that he wanted to mate her. She didn't want to die, and she'd love to help him regain his gift. Hell, five minutes in his presence, and she wanted to jump him. But to mate out of necessity? "I don't know."

He gave a quick nod. "You have time to think about it." Calloused fingers slid the shirt off her left shoulder.

Cool air brushed her. Awareness flushed through her, but the chair kept her from stepping back. "What are you doing?" she breathed.

His gaze dropped to her neck. "I'm going to bite you, and then you're going to bite me."

Her lungs seized. She shook her head, dislodging his fingers. "Why?"

"To feel better." His thumb and forefinger grasped her chin, tilting her head back. "My blood will give you temporary strength, but I need to bite you first so your body can take it." The intensity of his gaze slammed awareness through her blood. "If you're going to consider my offer, I'd prefer you remembered how it felt to be at full strength."

Temptation smacked up against caution. Heat flushed through her from the firm hold on her chin. Commanding and strong, Jase tempted her in a frightening, primal way.

Taking his blood once wouldn't create any sort of bond, and the idea of having strength again, even temporarily, swelled her with hope. Curiosity stretched awake. Years ago, when they'd both been healthy and unharmed, she'd had more than one fantasy of his taking her blood. "All right."

His fangs dropped—low and wicked.

Intrigue hummed beneath her skin.

Releasing her chin, he slid his palm down her bicep and around her waist. With ease and deliberation, he lifted her with one muscled arm.

The intrigue shot into desire. His easy strength fluttered need around her body to thrum between her legs.

His free hand tangled in her hair and tugged her head to the side. Her fingers curled over his hard shoulders.

Lowering his head, he enclosed her neck with his mouth. The sharp points slid into her flesh.

Her breath caught. She opened her mouth, her mind swirling. Her nipples pebbled against his chest. Need ripped through her blood as his mouth pulled. Images of his mouth exploring her body in other ways flashed in picture-form through her brain, and she moaned.

Slowly, the deadly points retracted, and he licked the wound. His tongue was slightly abrasive. She shivered.

He set her down. She released his shoulders and glanced up at his face.

Lust shimmered in his eyes, and crimson spiraled across his high cheekbones. His fingers remained tangled in her hair. Keeping her gaze, he lifted his free wrist and slashed with his fangs. Securing her, he slid his bleeding wrist against her lips.

The moment held much more intimacy than she'd expected. Tingles jabbed her mouth. She opened, and the liquid slid in.

Fire.

She drank, and sparkles popped down her throat. Electricity shot inside her veins. It was almost too much. She turned away, and he removed his wrist. Tightening his grip, he tugged her back around to face him.

Her gaze wide on his, her veins flashing with power, she licked the remaining blood off her lips.

His eyes flared. His lids dropped to half-mast.

Then his mouth took hers.

Hot, desperate, he kissed her hard. She opened her mouth in reaction, and he dove in. Seeking, taking, he swept inside.

Lava bubbled through her veins, and her nerves fired. Desire crashed into her with an unnatural force. She'd thought she'd been kissed before. Not so. Or maybe this wasn't just a kiss.

It was a claiming. Her body ignited. Her heart rammed into full gallop.

Heat and hard male stepped into her.

He held her tight, the kiss fierce and deep—teeming with hurt, loneliness, and hope. All emotions he hadn't shown. With emotions that maybe he couldn't remember how to show. As he tethered her so she couldn't escape, as he gave everything he had, something inside her shifted.

She kissed him back, accepting all he was. All he could be. All they might be.

Finally, he broke the kiss and released her.

Stepping back, he ran a rough hand through his hair, his gaze shuttering closed.

Her lips tingled. Her scalp ached. Her sex pounded.

Going on instinct, she lifted her chin. She wanted to live, and life was full of dangerous risks. Always had been—for her, always would be. They both teetered on a precipice, trying not to fall over. Maybe they could save each other. She had to clear her throat to force out words. "I accept your offer, Jase Kayrs."

Chapter 2

Jase Kayrs stood in the swirling snow, his gaze on the row of windows lining the hospital's south side. "Why did you follow me?"

His brother shrugged and shuffled leather shoes in the powder. Kane apparently hadn't planned on venturing outside. "Why did you follow Brenna?"

"I wanted to see where she was going." Jase angled to the west in order to better look inside the building. Cedar blocks made up the walls, and it was at least eight stories. "I'm tired of people babysitting me."

Kane ran a rough hand through his dark hair. "I'm not babysitting you, but we do need to talk. If I have to follow you all over Dublin to make it happen, then I will."

Jase's older brothers were overbearing assholes, but at least Kane was the only one who'd flown to Ireland with Jase. "Talk about what?"

"Brenna," Kane said.

As if on cue, the woman swept into a small room where several children played with games, toy cars, and blocks while sitting on a plush rug. A stuffed Santa sat in the corner, and Christmas lights had been strung across the walls. At her entrance, the room brightened from pale to full sunshine. Several kids leapt up to receive hugs and kisses.

Jase narrowed his gaze. Brenna's dark hair brushed her slim

shoulders, while her unique gray eyes sparkled. Her seven older sisters were all redheads with green eyes. She was one of a kind, though just as petite as the other women. Then he focused on the kids. "The kids are all burned. She's visiting a burn unit." Kane peered closer. "That's sweet."

Yeah. It was. She sat on the rug and gave each injured kid some time. Even wounded, even scarred, they somehow glowed under her attention. An uncomfortable yearning filled his chest. What he wouldn't give to feel that warmth. "Brenna has always been sweet," Jase murmured.

"I know." Kane fidgeted.

Kane never fidgeted.

"What?" Jase asked, steeling his shoulders.

"This isn't a good idea." Kane buttoned his leather jacket. "And you know it."

"There's no alternative." Jase left his jacket open because he rarely felt the cold. In fact, he rarely felt anything. "If she doesn't mate, she'll die."

Kane shook his head. "Chances are she's going to die anyway. The last doctor report showed it might be too late to reverse the effects of the planekite."

A chill that had nothing to do with the Dublin winter slithered down Jase's spine. "Then why not give mating a shot?"

The snort from his older brother echoed around them. "Why you?" Kane asked. "We could've sent any soldier, even one of our cousins from Iceland, to mate with her. To give her a chance to live. If you mate her, and she dies—"

"She won't die." In that moment, Jase Kayrs knew two things with absolute certainty. One, Brenna would live. Two, he'd gain her skills and take out the demons. All of them.

Kane exhaled slowly, an old tell that showed he was trying to choose his words carefully.

Jase growled low. "Stop fucking handling me. If I mate her, and if she still dies, I'll deal with it." He ducked his chin for a better view as Brenna scooped a toddler, his face a blistered mess, onto her lap for a cuddle.

Kane pivoted to face him. "Right. Because you're so good at dealing."

"I'm dealing," Jase said. There was a time his brother would've slammed him against a tree to fight it out. Now none of his brothers came near him—it was almost comical how much they held themselves back from hitting him. They'd never see him as whole again. "I'm fine."

"Fine?" Kane's eyes swirled from a dangerous purple to black. "You disappeared until Talen tracked you down in the Andes."

Everything in Jase wanted to turn away and watch Brenna bring joy to the damaged. So he kept his focus on his brother. "The king needed me, and I came home to help. I'm *helping*."

"No. Dage wanted you home as a brother, and not as a soldier. As the king, he spends too much time worrying about you as it is. You *volunteered* for this duty. Volunteered to mate a witch you barely know." Kane slid to the side and blocked Jase's view of the room. On purpose, probably. "Why?"

"Why not?" Jase's shoulder lifted as he smoothed out his expression. "I'm not looking for a mate or kids, so why not save Moira's baby sister?"

"Why else?" Kane wasn't the smartest guy on the planet for nothing.

"I want her skills." Jase's feet itched with the need to move. "She's a witch, and if I can control molecules, maybe I can get my gifts back. But you already knew that."

Kane nodded, tucking his hands in his pockets. "There's more."

Jase gave up the fight and pivoted to the north so he could see. Brenna colored in a book next to a little girl with bandages down the right side of her body. The toddler smiled, so much happiness in the little girl's eyes that Jase's gut hurt. The girl handed her drawing to Brenna, who gasped and said something. The toddler nodded, her eyes lighting up. Then she lay down, her head on Brenna's knee, and Bren smoothed back the girl's blond curls.

"Jase?" Kane asked. "Why else?"

He couldn't look away. Didn't want to. The world was cold and shitty. Brenna was warm and kind. "She saved me," he said. "At my darkest point, Brenna Dunne saved my life."

"How?"

If Jase couldn't understand it, no way would he share it. "Doesn't matter. The fact is that she saved me, and I owe her. Period." Deep down, a dark voice he usually ignored rumbled up that maybe she could save him again. He shook his head. No.

There was no saving him this time.

A phone buzzed, and Kane read the face of his cell. "I have to go. We're not finished with this discussion." His footsteps echoed as he strode back toward his car and roared off.

Frozen molecules on the wind brushed Jase's face. Dark clouds spread to cover the waning sun. Yet he stood in the cold, legs braced, his gaze on the woman inside the hospital.

Five years ago, he'd been tortured until every nerve in his body screamed in agony. Yet standing in the snow, watching kindness without expectation, true pain sliced through his heart. Pure and absolute, the cut illustrated more than ever that he'd never be whole. Never be able to have the simple life, the life he had planned on before being taken. They'd killed a part of him, and whatever remained existed only for revenge. He'd get that . . . with Brenna's skills.

He turned away from the bright lights of the hospital to face the shadows.

Where he belonged.

Brenna tugged her gloves farther up her hands as she stepped into the billowing snow. As always, her visit with the kids served to lighten her mood, as well as remind her of her good fortune.

Late afternoon, the storm barreled full force. Tucking her head, she scurried toward her car. The second she reached the driver's side door, a van jerked to a stop on the opposite side of the street. She whirled around. Three men jumped out, the one in front holding a bouquet of fresh, red roses.

She sighed. "Henry? You have got to be kidding me."

Henry shoved his too-large hat off his forehead and extended the roses. "For you."

Jase Kayrs instantly stood next to her like a deadly apparition out of the storm. "Who's your friend, Brenna?"

Brenna's heart leapt into full gear. She clutched her chest. "What are you doing here?"

He shrugged, his sharp gaze on Henry and his buddies. "I thought you'd like an escort home."

Henry's thin Adam's apple bobbed. As a witch, he might be a century old, but he looked like a skinny thirty-year-old. "You're spending time with a *vampire*? No, Brenna. Please."

She shook her head, her fingers tightening on the keys. "Listen, Henry. Enough is enough. Please leave me be."

His muddy brown eyes widened. "Did you get my letters? My proposal?"

"Yes." In fact, she'd received more than twenty marriage proposals from him in the last two months alone. "I'm not going to marry you."

His thin shoulders hunched forward. "As our *chosen one*, you must mate, or you'll die. I've seen your medical records."

On all that was holy and pure. "Are my bloomin' records suddenly on the Internet?" An ache pounded behind her left eye.

"No. We broke into the hospital records." Henry slid forward and stopped when Jase growled. "You'll die if you don't mate. We only have five days until the solstice. Please meet your destiny."

Jase chortled. "This guy's your destiny?"

"Shut up." Brenna waved off the roses. "I'm not chosen. I'm not your destiny, and you're certainly not mine. I've told you before, the winter solstice has nothing to do with me."

The two guys behind Henry eyed each other, their mouths turning down. Way down.

Jase angled himself slightly in front of her in a clearly defensive move. "Who are you people?"

Henry cleared his throat. "I'm Henry Balcott, the head of Brenna's Warriors."

Jase cut his eyes to Brenna. "Brenna's Warriors?"

She sighed. No way did she want Jase to know how odd her life really was. "How about you head back to headquarters, and I'll meet you for an early dinner?"

Henry nodded, his thin hair flying around. "Yes. Good idea. Go away, vampire."

Jase stilled in that odd vampire way, and tension spiraled through the air. He stepped toward Henry.

Henry gasped and backed into his buddies. "No offense."

"Offense taken," Jase growled. "Explain yourself, peon."

Now that sounded like a full-blooded, pissed-off Kayrs male. Brenna's breath heated. She had opened her mouth to speak when a second van, this one white, jumped the curb. People waving signs of protest billowed out, apparently having been stacked end-to-end inside.

"Blast it," she muttered.

A woman with flashing blue eyes shook a sign. A muted orange cascaded off her skin as proof she was a powerful and irritated witch. "Get off the council now, Brenna Dunne."

Jase frowned and scratched his chin. "More friends of yours?"

Henry stomped over to the woman until they stood nose-to-nose. "You evil harbinger! Leave my intended alone."

Jase leaned closer to Brenna's ear. "Who are these people?"

Damn it. She licked snow off her lips. "The protesters are a group called Citizens Revolting Against Pagurus."

"CRAP?" he barked out. "You have a group called CRAP protesting in Dublin?"

The woman smacked Henry over the head with her sign. He yelped and backed away.

"We prefer *Citizens*, if you don't mind, Prince Kayrs," the woman said.

A harsh crease drew Jase's brows together. "How do you know me?"

She shrugged. "Your picture was plastered all over the immortal world when you were taken by demons. Everyone recognizes you by sight."

"I'm a damn milk-carton face," he muttered. "Brenna? What the hell is going on?"

The protesters shook their signs and surrounded the SUV. Henry and his buddies huddled close to their van. Embarrassment heated Brenna's cheeks. "I'll explain on the way home. Let's go."

A male protester jumped forward and shook his sign in Brenna's eyes. "Resign now, before the solstice, or you won't live to see the darkest day of the year."

Jase grabbed the protester under the chin and slammed him to the icy ground. His head impacted with the sound of a melon splitting. Dropping to one knee, his hand choking the male witch, Jase let his fangs drop low and sharp. "If any of you even thinks of threatening Brenna again, I promise you'll beg for a quick death when I'm finished discussing the matter with you."

The witch's eyes closed in unconsciousness.

Adrenaline ripped through Brenna's veins. If Jase tightened his hold, he'd decapitate the witch. She shuffled toward him and slid her hand over his shoulder. "Jase? Let's not kill the moron. This time."

He nodded, released the witch, and stood. Tension vibrated around the vampire in a more dangerous display than the swirling storm. His eyes morphed to a sizzling vampiric green as he flashed his fangs at the protesters. "I could kill you all before you thought to defend yourselves."

Absolute truth echoed in the soldier's tone. Brenna swallowed. She'd forgotten how dangerous he'd been even before being taken by demons. Now, she eyed him with a new awareness. The moments of his life had converged into making Jase one of the most deadly predators in existence . . . maybe the most deadly. He stood, his gaze steady, his biceps undulating with the threat of movement. "Leave now."

People scattered like cockroaches.

He turned toward Brenna. "Get in the car."

She swallowed and yanked open the door to climb inside.

Without looking at anybody, Jase stalked around and slid into the passenger side. "Drive."

Heated air blew out of Brenna's chest. She started the ignition and drove carefully over icy roads toward Nine headquarters.

Silence filled the car with a heaviness that made breathing difficult.

Finally, Jase stretched his legs out. "Why are you getting marriage proposals and death threats regarding the winter solstice?"

Nothing much got past the vampires. Brenna flipped on the windshield wipers. "You're aware half the world thinks I'm a freak, right?" She kept her tone even, as if the truth didn't still hurt just a little.

"You're not a freak."

"That's not what I asked you." She'd been coddled and protected by her family since birth and didn't need any more. "You know."

"Yes." He settled his bulk into the seat. "For your ridiculously superstitious people, a seventh sister of a seventh sister is always a powerful witch. Whenever in history there has been one born, that daughter is the last child born in the family."

"Exactly." Brenna took a deep breath. "Moira is the seventh, and man, is she powerful. I'm the eighth sister of a seventh sister. An unheard-of anomaly."

Jase shook his head. "That's all just so damn stupid."

"Maybe." Hell yes, it was stupid. Except, well, odd things had happened since her birth, including economic decline, new cults, and more powerful atomic reactions. Physics itself had changed with her birth. "My seven older sisters all have red hair and green eyes. I have plain brown hair and weird gray eyes." She shrugged. "It seems odd, even genetically."

"Genetics are genetics, and you know it. Do the protesters want you off the Council of the Coven Nine because you were appointed by Moira?"

"No." Brenna sighed. When Moira had beaten another witch for a council seat, she'd elected for Brenna to fill her spot so she could continue being a soldier. "There's a book about prophecies, one that doesn't exist as far as you know, that predicted my birth."

Jase glanced at her, eyebrows up. "Really?"

"Yes, and it predicted the convergence of my birth, a comet, and the solstice. The day I was born, on a winter solstice, the Pagurus Comet came too close to the earth and messed with our atmosphere and tides on a molecular level. Witches were all sorts of screwed up for a couple of months. My people were helpless."

Jase leaned forward. "This is news."

She shrugged. "Yeah. The comet wasn't close enough for anybody to spot, yet close enough to mess with us."

"So?"

"The comet is coming back the night of the winter solstice, and supposedly will somehow affect me, infusing me with some sort of power from the universe. In four days." She sighed. "I have a group that thinks I'm charmed and destined to be their queen of weirdoes. The other group wants me off the Nine and hopefully out of Ireland."

"So is it the comet or is it the winter solstice that's supposed to affect you?"

"It's the conjunction of the two." Brenna swept hair away from her face. "The winter solstice is always a time we gain power, but all witches gain it, and it's just a temporary enhancement. The comet messes with everyone's skills, and supposedly, I gain power somehow because I'm the only eighth sister born of a seventh witch sister ever, much less last time the comet was here. I'm such a wacko."

Jase snorted. "You're not a wacko. Do you know anything more than the comet will somehow give you power?"

"Nope. The legend is rather vague and unsettling."

"Okay. For now, maybe we should set the two groups up to duke it out," Jase said.

"The CRAP group will kill the Warriors." She bit her lip as she pulled into the parking lot outside the Nine's aboveground headquarters. "Though it would be funny."

Jase uncoiled from the vehicle and reached her door before she could open it. Helping her out, he tucked her hand at his arm. "How dangerous are these goofballs?"

A silly flutter spread through her abdomen from his touch. "I don't really know."

As they reached the wide glass doors, they opened, and Deb rushed out. She gasped for air. "Just had to warn you."

Jase frowned. "About what?"

Deb held up a hand as she regained her breath. "Everyone is waiting in the large conference room."

"Why?" Tingles of dread spread down Brenna's spine.

"To negotiate the terms." Deb tightened her coat and sidled toward her vehicle.

"What terms?" Brenna asked as Jase grabbed the door before it could close.

Deb gave a sympathetic grimace over her shoulder. "Your mating, of course."

Chapter 3

Brenna shook off the feeling of walking into a principal's office. Her aunt Viv, her sister Moira, and two witch lawyers sat on one side of a long conference table. Kane Kayrs and Conn Kayrs sat on the other side. Opposite ends of the table held empty chairs. Viv motioned Brenna toward one.

"No." Jase took her hand in his warm one, grabbed an extra chair lined by the door, and dragged it over to where he was apparently supposed to sit. "We sit together."

His palm warmed hers right along with her heart.

She sat, her gaze on her sister. "Moira? When did you get home?"

Moira's green eyes flashed. Her rioting red hair curled around her shoulders. "We jumped on a plane the second we heard about this crazy scheme. You are not mating for business reasons."

Conn, Moira's mate and Jase's brother, nodded. "I agree."

Even sitting on opposing sides of a table, the pair was united. A pang nicked Brenna's heart. She'd probably never have that sense of belonging. "I'm dying, Moira."

Moira paled. "You're not."

"She is," Kane said quietly. "I'm sorry, but I've examined her medical records. There's no cure to the internal poisoning from planekite, and she's declining quickly."

Brenna took a deep breath. "To be honest, I may have waited too long." She needed her sister to be prepared. "Even mating a vampire as powerful as Jase might not save me. I'm so sorry."

Blue mist smoldered along Moira's arms—proof the witch was agitated. "Why didn't you tell me?"

"I thought our doctors would find a cure, and I'm tired of everyone being worried about me." Damn, Brenna missed being able to make fire and plasma balls. She pushed her glasses up her nose. "There was nothing you could do."

"She's right," Kane said. "Her doctors have tried methods I've never heard of—probably because you witches are so secretive." Only fact existed in the brilliant vampire's tone. No judgment.

Moira shifted in her seat. "What's up with the eyeglasses?"

"I can't see," Brenna said. Just saying the words hurt. Even ancient witches retained perfect eyesight.

"Oh." Concern bracketed Moira's mouth. "Jase? Why are you agreeing to mate?"

His chin slowly lifted. "Besides the fact that Brenna is beautiful, smart, and sexy as hell?"

Heat slid through Brenna stronger than her uncle Paddy's homemade liquor. As the plain one in the family, nobody ever called her sexy.

"Yes." Moira's shoulders went back. "You've been avoiding all of us since you returned home, training constantly, all but consumed with the need to go and fight. Yet now you're willing to take a mate?"

"Yes," Jase said.

Silence pounded around the room. Apparently the vampire wasn't willing to expand on the subject.

"No," Moira finally said.

Brenna leaned forward. "My mind is made up, and I've agreed. So we're finished here." She moved to stand.

Viv waved her back into her seat. "I agree. But now we need to negotiate."

Brenna slowly regained her seat. "How so?"

"Well, our treaty with the vampires is tenuous at best. This will cement it." Viv nodded toward two male lawyers on her side of the table.

"Wait." Brenna eyed Moira, who sat with her arms crossed.

Their discussion was in no way over. "When Moira and Conn mated, we created a treaty, right?"

Kane cleared his throat. "Ah, kind of. Basically, after their, ah, accidental mating one night, that treaty prohibited Conn from contacting Moira for a century in order to prevent war. That's all. No future promises or obligations were created."

Conn flashed Moira a grin. "A whole lot of promises and obligations were created, if you ask me."

"Nobody asked you." Moira smiled back.

"I see." Brenna counted the distance from her chair to the door. They all knew that mating meant crazy, vampire monkey sex, right? How in the world did they plan to negotiate that one?

One of Viv's lawyers—Brenna could never remember the guy's name—shoved a stack of papers toward Kane. "This covers all contingencies," the lawyer said, yanking on his Burberry tie and flushing.

Interesting. The natural power vibrating around vampires often made witches uneasy. Brenna glanced at Jase. While he made her uneasy, it wasn't in exactly in a witch-type way. More like a female one.

Kane pressed his stack toward Viv. He then scanned the first page and reached for a marker to cross out several lines. "We agree to join our forces with yours to combat both demon and Kurjan attacks—but we will not follow your armies. We'll bring our own."

Viv nodded. "Fair enough." She took a pen from her lawyer and added words to Kane's document. "We'll agree to share all scientific knowledge gleaned regarding genetic diseases and/or viruses that affect witches and vampire mates, but we will not agree to share knowledge gained regarding quantum physics or string theory."

"Then neither will we," Kane said. He flipped his top page and frowned as he read out loud. "Any such mating will occur within the next week, and thus this document becomes final." He lifted an eyebrow and glanced at Brenna and Jase. "You two okay with that?"

Brenna's mind spun. They expected her to sit quietly during such a discussion? She lifted her chin. "My lady parts will be available for said mating during the next two weeks."

Jase barked out a laugh. "As will, ah, my gentlemanly parts."

Heat climbed into Brenna's face. "I believe we have an agreement."

"Wait. You should demand multiple orgasms," Jase said.

Brenna coughed. "Excellent point. I so demand." Her shoulders started shaking as she tried to hold in laughter.

Jase chuckled, sounding much more like the man she used to know.

Viv's eyebrows slanted down, and she pursed her lips. Conn looked at them like they were crazy.

Brenna bit her tongue to keep from laughing out loud.

Kane frowned. "Okay." He read further and then crossed out several lines. "Any child born will be a vampire, and we will train him."

"A vampire-witch," Viv said. "We want equal time with any children to train them in our ways."

Jase tapped his hand on the table and lost his smile. "My sons are not included in the document."

Brenna started. Wow. She hadn't thought about kids. If they had children, they'd be male. Vampires only made males with their mates, and the whole turning somebody into a vampire by biting them was just fiction. "There's a good chance I've sustained enough internal damage that I'll never have kids." The idea cut a path of pain through her body. But Jase needed to know the truth before signing.

He slid his hand over hers. "Don't worry about it."

Conn narrowed his gaze. "Jase is planning to fight demons and go out with a glorious fire. I don't think he's planning to be around long enough to procreate." Pure, pissed-off male echoed in Conn's tone. Along with concern.

Viv swallowed. "In that case, why don't we turn to the last page and discuss what happens if either party passes on?"

Brenna glanced toward Jase's hard profile. He hadn't denied his brother's statement.

Damn. She'd truly be alone again.

Well, if she didn't die first.

The rhythmic *clomp clomp* of Jase's boots kept time with his beating thoughts as he jogged. Was he making a mistake? By mating sweet Brenna, he was quite possibly keeping her from ever mating again. From ever finding love.

Love existed for some people.

Vampires and their mates only got one mating . . . for eternity. Shouldn't Brenna have a chance at the real thing?

He ran full-bore across the bridge, sending snow spraying. The storm continued to blast him with ice and snow. He ignored the pain and ran until his lungs compressed. Even then, he pushed on.

After sitting inside and listening to Kane negotiate his duties, Jase had all but leapt out the window for the outdoors. Even now, five years after being freed from an underground hell, the walls still closed in on him if he was inside for too long. He'd never again venture underground.

Brenna's humor during the negotiations had caught him off guard. His laugh had been genuine.

A real laugh.

He frowned and increased his pace. Tree boughs extended over the quiet street, dripping with icicles. Beautiful and deadly.

Brenna was beautiful and delicate. Her pretty gray eyes held both humor and kindness. While her illness had thinned her, very pleasing curves filled out her business suits. His groin tightened.

His gut ached.

He hadn't been with a woman since before he'd been taken. Before, he'd been with a lot of them. But now, damaged and so damn angry, he didn't trust himself.

How would he keep Brenna safe? He wanted her—more than he'd hoped. More than he could control.

A buzz alerted him, and he tapped his ear communicator. "What?"

"Brenna just headed home," Kane said. "You wanted me to inform you, right?"

"Right." Jase pivoted to head toward the Liffey.

Kane cleared his throat. "I know you both signed the contract, but I don't think that tonight, I mean—"

"Jesus, Kane. I just want to talk to her." When the hell would his brothers stop tiptoeing around him? Sometimes Jase felt like he was still lost, and they were all still searching for him.

"Oh. Okay," Kane said.

Jase closed his eyes and kept running, tuning in his other senses to guide him. Just in case the demons blinded him someday. "Why don't you go home to your mate?"

"I will. Soon," Kane muttered. "Amber staged a protest against some cosmetic company in Portland yesterday."

Jase snorted. "I bet she's running Dage ragged while you're out of town."

"Of that, I have no doubt. Be careful, Jase." Kane disconnected the call.

Careful with what? Brenna? Or his plans to destroy the demon nation? The scent of winter, salt, and spruce filled Jase's nose, and he opened his eyes. While he hadn't broadcasted his intent, his brothers knew him. Or at least they used to know him.

Now he didn't even know himself.

He reached the outside of Brenna's apartment building within a few minutes. Tall and elegant, the structure housed three penthouses on the top floor. One belonged to Brenna, one to Moira, and the third to their cousins, three male enforcers. Somehow Brenna had talked one of the enforcers into selling her his place for an excellent price when she'd taken the seat on the Nine. Or so Moira had informed Jase.

Ice crackled beneath his heavy boots when he slowed to a stop. Twisting his torso, he stretched aching muscles. The hour of inverted push-ups before the three-hour run had strained his biceps more than he'd liked.

The hair on the back of his neck rose. He lifted his head, searching the nearly empty street. Nothing moved. Narrowing his eyes, he loped across the road to reach the gaping mouth of the parking garage. The slope headed underground.

His heart seized and then bolted into a faster pace than when he'd run. Even the thought of being underground made his head spin. Besides, something was down there.

Sweat broke out on his brow to be instantly chilled by a freezing wind.

A rumble echoed in the distance. Brenna's red compact zoomed into view.

Vertigo caught Jase by surprise as the world began to swirl around him. Trees, falling snow, the top of the building, all seemed to roll like a drunken tornado. But he couldn't let Brenna drive into the structure. Every instinct he had bellowed for him to stop her. He stepped to the middle of the entryway.

Brenna's brakes engaged with a squeal, and her car skidded several feet to stop. The metal impacted his shins with pain, but not hard enough to knock him down.

She lurched forward, her eyes wide on his through the icy windshield. A crease formed between her brows, and she jumped out of the car. "What in the hell—"

Long strides propelled him around the vehicle to grab her arm. "I don't know. Something—"

A beaten-up black van rolled around the north end of the street. Seconds later, another van blocked the south.

Jase swallowed. Inside him, ever-present anger bubbled closer to the surface. He searched for an escape. An engine ignited inside the garage, and a box van cut across the entrance, blocking the entryway.

"We're surrounded," Brenna whispered, her body stiffening.

"Yes." Jase pressed her closer to the vehicle to better block her from all three waiting vehicles. "How strong are you?"

"Huh?" she asked.

"Since taking my blood. Can you fight?" How many people might be in the vans? If he locked Brenna in the car, would he have time to take them all out before somebody could get to her?

Her arm trembled. "I felt a little stronger for about an hour, but that's it. My strength is . . . subpar."

The angst in her voice cut through him. "Your own body has poisoned you from the inside for a decade, Bren. Anybody would have lost strength." Damn it. He'd probably scare the shit out of her if he went all psycho to defend her. He eyed the van blocking the garage. The front window had been tinted so darkly he couldn't see past it. A thought paused him. Were these witches or demons? Maybe they were there for him.

Fury lanced along his arms and tightened his legs, yet he kept his voice calm. "Do you recognize the vans?"

"No."

He opened his senses as wide as possible. While he'd lost many of his skills, he could still tell the difference between races. No demon vibrations filled the air. "I think they're witches."

As if on cue, the doors of all three vehicles slid open. Dressed in black, squads of five soldiers, men and women, stepped out of the vans. They carried green glowing guns—the guns of immortals. Damn it.

Jase kept his focus on the nearest group and stilled as he recognized the woman from the protest. The one who had told Brenna to resign.

The woman's lips turned down as she lifted her weapon to point at him. "I'm sorry, Prince Kayrs."

She fired.

Chapter 4

Panic slammed through Brenna, and she screamed in warning.

Then Jase moved quicker than she would've thought possible. He dropped and yanked her atop him. She landed on his hard body, air swooshing from her lungs. The laser bullet shot over the hood and downed a spruce. Wrenching the door open, he threw her inside the car.

Pain cascaded along her rib cage from striking the gearshift, and she grabbed the steering wheel for balance.

"Lock the door," he ordered, slamming it shut. Pivoting, he leaped the several yards to crash into the shooter. He impacted with such force that they barreled into three of the soldiers protecting the woman's back.

His hands and feet blurred they moved so quickly. Within a minute, all five soldiers lay on the ground, at least two of them with broken necks. Sure, they were immortal, but broken necks took a lot of recovery time. Brenna froze in the car, her heart galloping, her gaze on the deadly vampire.

He turned, his fangs low, his eyes a metallic vampire green.

The atmosphere leavened. Brenna gasped, her head whirling to see a male soldier from the north van throw a burning ball of plasma at Jase. She yelled in warning and shoved open the door.

Years ago, she could've used quantum physics to alter matter enough to create her own plasma and counter the attack. Now she could only scream.

The plasma hit Jase dead-center, lifting him several feet and throwing him into the stone above the garage. He impacted with the crash of a meteor hitting the earth. The stone splintered, sending shock waves to shake the building. Gravity took over, and he dropped to the ice.

Brenna shut the door and twisted the key in the ignition. The engine roared to life. While she didn't have fire, she did have a ton of metal. Yanking the wheel, she turned the car and aimed straight for the north.

The lead witch's hands gathered, and he created another plasma ball.

Blast it. Brenna punched the gas pedal. The car lurched forward and shot straight for the witch.

He threw.

Brenna swerved, and the plasma ripped off the passenger side mirror. She pummeled her foot down and aimed for the witch. He tried to duck out of the way, but the car clipped his hip and sent him flying. Pulling to the left, she hit another soldier. This one smashed into her windshield and then fell to the side. She yanked the wheel, sending the car into a slide. The rear careened into the van.

Reaching under her seat, she removed a weapon. Then she jumped from the car, already firing. Did they think she wasn't armed? Seriously?

Her first burst hit a soldier in the chest. He went down.

She continued spraying and shot the fourth soldier. A ball of plasma blasted into her wrist, and her weapon flew out of reach. Fiery pain ripped through her skin. Her eyes teared. Turning, she met the smiling face of the last standing person from this van. A woman she didn't recognize held another plasma ball in her hands.

The woman smiled with sharp teeth. "I'd like to take you alive, Councilwoman, but our destiny is to kill you and end your plague." She threw with impressive force.

Brenna dropped and slid across the ice, hitting the woman at the ankles. The woman fell and jabbed an elbow into Brenna's gut.

Pain exploded in her stomach. She sucked in air and punched the woman in the nose. Blood spurted.

The woman punched up with an uppercut, hitting Brenna beneath the chin. Her head smacked back against the ice. Shards of pain flashed behind her eyes with bright sparks. Nausea uncoiled in her stomach.

Nails dug into her neck as the woman straddled her and squeezed. Brenna's eyes flipped open, and she grabbed for the hands choking her. They struggled, the woman using her knees for leverage. Brenna flailed at strong biceps. Tears rolled from her eyes. Her lungs seized in agony.

She managed to maneuver her leg up and between them, but she couldn't dislodge her attacker.

The world turned gray and fuzzy.

She was so weak. Weaker than a human, even. God. Was this it?

Snow sprayed, and Jase grabbed Brenna's attacker with one arm. The woman catapulted through the snow-filled air, slamming into a sprawling spruce.

Brenna sucked in freezing air. Jase hauled her up. "Get behind me." He shoved her, not waiting for her to move.

Her lungs screamed as they filled again. She peered around him. The five remaining CRAP soldiers stalked forward in attack formation, brutal colors dancing on their skin as they formed deadly weapons of plasma. All were powerful witches. How could her own people hate her so much?

Jase's body vibrated, sending out waves of heat. Blood dripped from a wound in the back of his head, and shards of bone stuck out from his shoulder and one arm.

Brenna gulped. He couldn't beat all five of them with those wounds, and she wasn't much help. "Let's take the van," she whispered.

"No." His stance settled. "I want them. All of them." His voice dropped to a low, guttural tone that spiked adrenaline through her veins.

The squad advanced, determination in their eyes.

Brenna grasped Jase's uninjured arm. "Let's go, Jase. Now."

"Your CRAP group is well trained," he said.

No bloomin' shit. Using both her hands, she dug her fingers into his muscled arm and tugged. She might as well be trying to move the Liffey Bridge. Okay. Biting her lip, she released him. Shutting her eyes, she tried to alter oxygen molecules into plasma. A sputter erupted on her skin. Her eyes opened only to see the sputter snuff out. Her knees trembled, and she swayed.

Defeat hunched her shoulders. "We need to mate soon."

He stilled.

Oops. She'd said that out loud. Fighting the urge to kick the back of his knee, she cleared her throat. "I'm going for the van."

"Lock the doors."

She wouldn't leave him to fight alone. Shaking off fear, she angled to his side. "I guess we fight, then."

Jase's head jerked back. Good lord. Bravery, beauty, and kindness in such a small, delicate package. Unfortunately, in her current state, Brenna would only get hurt in a fight. He lowered his tone to the one he used when training the younger vampires. "Get your ass in the van, and lock the doors."

"No." Her thoughtful tone lacked heat.

What the hell? Most people jumped when he used that tone of voice. "Now, Brenna," he barked.

She turned her head, surprise filling her pretty eyes. "No."

His mouth dropped open. Irritation had him snapping it shut. He glared at her. She stood like an angel in the falling snow and stared back, a curious expression wandering across her smooth face. As if she truly didn't understand why he was quickly getting more pissed off at her than at the advancing soldiers.

"I'm not leaving you to fight alone." She patted his uninjured arm and turned back toward danger. "You've done enough of that. We're in this together."

Warmth flushed through him—so hard, so fast—he blinked. "Fine," he growled and grabbed her arm, fully intending to get in the van.

Suddenly, a black SUV smashed into the far van, sending it spinning. Three more SUVs halted. Coven Nine soldiers leaped out, guns cocked, headed for the CRAP squad. Conn, Moira, and Kane burst out of the second SUV.

Moira already held an oscillating fireball in her hands.

"The cavalry," Brenna murmured. "How?"

Jase pointed to the communicator still in his ear. "I called Kane."

"Oh." She waved at her sister, who immediately dropped her plasma ball and tackled one of the oncoming soldiers to the ground. A punch to the back of the neck, and the guy slumped unconscious. Brenna rubbed her chin. "Moira's having fun."

Jase frowned and mentally sent healing cells to his broken shoulder. "I need at least one of them able to talk."

"Why?" Brenna asked, shoving her hands in her coat pockets. "We know they're from CRAP and want to take me out."

"I want to know what the next plan was in case this one failed." He needed to get her out of the cold. His bones realigned with a loud *pop*.

"Oh." She stomped her feet, and her teeth started to chatter. "They're a pretty tough group. They won't talk."

He glanced down at the bluish tint of her lips. "They'll talk." Taking her arm, he led her toward the building. The gash in the back of his head mended with sharp stabs of pain. "I'll meet you upstairs in a few moments."

She nodded and slipped inside, quickly followed by her sister.

Jase stalked over to where the Coven Nine soldiers had the attackers facedown on the ground. He grabbed the biggest man and jerked him up by the hair. "I need a word with this guy." Without waiting for an answer, he threw the CRAP member ass-first at the van. The guy rolled up the hood and shattered the windshield. He sprang to his feet, blood pouring down his cheek, hands out. "I don't want any trouble."

"I do." Jase clasped the guy's belt and tossed him into a parking meter. The metal bent with a lonely shriek.

The guy dropped to his knees, more blood squirting from a split lip. Clapping his hands together, he began forming an orange ball.

Jase kicked him under the chin.

The guy flew back, his head thunking on concrete.

Conn cleared his throat. "If he's out, he can't talk."

True. Jase dropped to his haunches and slid his hand over the man's throat. "There are four more of you. Give me answers, or I'll kill you and move on to the next guy." He let death show in his eyes, which was easy, because he spoke the truth.

The man's dilating eyes widened. "Okay."

"What's the plan here?" Jase asked calmly.

The guy tried to swallow. "Ah, to take out Brenna Dunne."

Jase's hand tightened, and the guy started to flop like a beached fish. He loosened his grip. "What if you didn't kill her today?"

"We'd come up with a new plan. The solstice is just three days away." The guy blanched. "I'm sorry, but it's necessary. She's the plague—"

Jase crushed his larynx.

Standing up, he ignored the gasps around him and stalked toward the building.

"Jase?" Kane asked quietly.

Jase didn't turn around when he answered his brother. "I'm fine—just want to check on Brenna." He was already through the door when he heard Conn's muttered statement. "He is *not* fine. Not even close."

A quick shrug had Jase biting back an expletive. Damn shoulder. Sending more healing cells to the damaged tissue, he found the stairwell and jogged the many flights of stairs to reach Brenna's penthouse. He paused outside the wide double door. They weren't mated yet. He should probably knock.

He knocked, and Moira yanked open the door. "Everybody all right?"

"Yep." He breezed by her and stopped. Brenna stood in a cozy living room, a full wall of windows behind her showcasing the River Liffey. The gray of the day matched her stunning eyes. "How many times have they tried to take you?"

She blinked and quickly recovered, edging closer to the fire crackling in the stone fireplace. "Excuse me?"

Moira whirled on her sister. "This wasn't the first time? Are you kidding me?"

"This is the first time they've sent three squads of five," Brenna said. She clasped her hands together. "Would you care to stay for supper, Jase?"

So she wanted a moment to think of a good story, did she? Fine. He needed to get rid of the blood, anyway. "I'd love to stay for supper." He yanked off his destroyed sweatshirt. "May I use your shower first?"

She swallowed and pointed down a marble-lined hallway. "Of course. I'll have Moira fetch some of Conn's clothes from next door."

"Fetch?" Moira sputtered. "Did you just say *fetch*?"

Jase nodded. "This is what's going to happen, Brenna. I'm going to take a shower, and then we're going to talk about the CRAP group and the warrior group. You're going to tell me everything. Then, we'll decide what to do." He paused at the edge of the foyer, his mind finally settling. "We'll also discuss this mating business and negotiate our own terms. Regardless of our societies."

"Good plan," she murmured.

Glorious oil paintings created by Brenna lined the hallway. Her unique scent of vanilla and woman smacked him in the face when he entered her bedroom. Vivid jewel tones made up the bedclothes, and a sensual oil painting of two entwined silhouettes hung above the bed. Classy and sexy as hell.

His mind instantly spiraled back to his captivity and a similar painting. One of Brenna's paintings had been hung in the room of a female demoness determined to mate Jase. That painting had grounded him—maybe saved him.

He stood, bleeding and battered, in the feminine bedroom. Brenna Dunne had most certainly saved him.

Now he'd save her.

Chapter 5

Brenna finished stirring the Crock-Pot stew. Steam rose and warmed her cheeks. Jase Kayrs was in her shower. Naked. Jase. Naked. She swallowed. He'd left the bathroom door open, so she'd taken a quick peek when placing the clothes on the bed. Steam had blocked her view. Darn it.

Okay. She was a grown-up and could handle a dinner with Jase. They were old friends. He'd be dressed for dinner, certainly.

As the good daughter, the dutiful daughter, she'd predictably had a thing for bad boys. And Jase Kayrs was the baddest of them all.

Figured she'd be attracted to him. She nodded. Acknowledging that fact would help her navigate the next couple of weeks. Attraction was good, considering they'd need to have sex to mate. She could handle this logically and with maturity.

A rustle sounded by the door, and she turned as he strode into the kitchen.

On all that was holy and strong. She gulped.

The man wore all black. Cargo pants, long-sleeved shirt, a talisman on a leather cord around his neck. His short hair was spiked, and a shadow covered his cut jaw. "Smells good."

Since when did sex and danger go hand in hand? She needed to get a grip. "Thanks. Have a seat." Turning back to the Crock-Pot, she ladled two bowls.

A chair scraped. "Where's Moira?"

Brenna turned and delivered the dishes, sitting across from him at the round table. "I kicked her out."

His cheek creased. "I don't imagine that was easy."

Pouring two glasses of cabernet, Brenna shrugged. "What is?"

"Good point." Jase tasted the stew and both eyebrows rose. "You're a good cook."

Pleasure rippled through her. What a complete dork she'd become. "Thanks." Her stomach fluttered, suddenly not hungry. At least, not hungry for stew.

They ate in silence for a while. Not exactly comfortable, but not horrible, either. Finally, Brenna placed her napkin over her bowl. "What's the story of the talisman?" The iron-carved face showed a warrior with hard eyes.

Jase stilled and shifted his weight. "I traveled for a bit after I, ah, returned home. Met a shaman in Budapest who gave me the talisman, and I usually wear it under my shirt. It's supposed to guard and protect warriors heading into battle."

Now that was fitting. The man seemed so alone. "Are you heading into battle?"

His head rose along with his gaze. Dark, thoughtful, intense. "I never left it."

Awareness chilled her skin. "Are you talking about the demons out there . . . or the ones in your head?" she asked softly, fighting the urge to touch him. To soothe him.

His short nod was filled with self-acknowledgment, and those copper eyes darkened. "Brenna, you're a sweetheart, but don't waste your time trying to save me." He stood and took both empty bowls to the sink. "That last thing I want to do is hurt you—and I will." He whispered the last.

She rolled her eyes even though a flutter cascaded through her abdomen. Condescension from the vampire was unnecessary. "I'm not as fragile as everyone thinks."

He turned and leaned against the sink. Tall and broad, he dominated the small kitchen with the image of male. "You're a nurturer, and a tempting one at that. But I don't want to be saved."

She stood and handed him his wineglass before turning for the living room to sit on the leather sofa. "We all want to be saved."

His exhale sounded behind her before he followed and sat in the chair facing her. "Don't read anything into this mating other than I want your skills. Any other thoughts or hopes are going to end badly for you." He placed his wineglass on the sofa table and leaned forward. "I need to be honest with you, and you need to know what you're getting into."

Irritation heated her chest. "What I'm getting into? Don't tell me. I'll be mating an obsessed, wounded, scarred vampire who is damned determined to wipe out the demons and probably himself in the process."

Jase chuckled. "Well, maybe you do know."

She inhaled and then exhaled. "I understand your motivations."

"What about yours?" He frowned. "You could mate any vampire and certainly don't need to follow the Coven Nine's dictates that it be me."

"I need to mate to stay alive, and since it's not for love, it might as well be for the good of my people." She sipped her wine, allowing the taste of oak to soothe her nerves. "The treaty with your people will assure mine stay safe as the war continues." Plus, even damaged, the vampire was male and hot. Though she'd die before she told him that. A tiny voice in the back of her head whispered that maybe she could save him. She could be the one to help the wounded warrior and actually find love. Aye, she was a moron.

He nodded and focused on his hands. "I, ah, need to tell you that it's been awhile. I mean, for me."

Heat spiraled into her face. "Oh. Well, actually, me, too. Since I've been sick."

Whiskers rustled when he rubbed his chin. "I work out a lot, and I try to breathe deep, but sometimes . . ."

"The anger takes over?" she asked softly.

His gaze met hers. "Yeah. You empathic?"

"No." She set down her wineglass. "You're the angriest person I've ever seen. No empathic abilities needed." The fury was eating him up inside, and it hurt to watch. Why hadn't his brothers gotten him help?

"Yeah, well, I don't want to hurt you." His nostrils flared. "I've asked Kane to obtain dampening pills for the mating."

Her head jerked back. Oh no, he hadn't. She sat back and crossed her arms. "No way. No dampening pills."

"Yes." His jaw firmed. "I insist."

"Oh good, our first fight." Dampening pills had been used for centuries when a vampire mating was arranged. It took the edge off for the female and combined some sort of pain reliever with a relaxant. "I will not use dampening pills." Did he think she was some hapless human?

He hesitated. "Please."

A low laugh rolled from her stomach. "That had to hurt."

"You have no idea." His upper lip quirked. The man was dominant and used to giving orders. No doubt asking went against his every instinct.

"I'm not less than anybody else." For her entire life, she'd had to prove her worth and that she wasn't some anomaly. For her one mating, she intended to be strong enough to engage completely. "No dampening pills."

Watchful intelligence lived in his gaze. "When you bit me yesterday, my blood should've made you stronger for days. Yet it only lasted a couple of hours." He reached for her arm and tugged her off the sofa.

"I'm not weak." She landed on her knees between his legs. What was he doing? Heat uncoiled in her gut.

"I know." Threading both hands through her hair, he tilted her head back until she looked up at his angled face. "But you're not strong right now, either."

Her neck elongated. Vulnerability and need washed through her. She dug her nails into his hard legs. "I will be. After we mate."

A dark flush covered his high cheekbones. His eyes flashed into a sizzling green. Heat from his thighs pressed in on her. "Speaking of which, are you all right with the contract?"

Flattening her hands, she pushed away to stand.

But she didn't move. The vampire easily kept her in place.

She tilted her head, intrigue and warning swishing through her. Without question, she was out of her element with the formidable Kayrs brother. "I'd prefer not to be on my knees as we discuss this."

His eyes darkened.

Hers widened.

Lowering his head, his lips brushed her jugular. "You're so strong you don't need dampening pills? Then get off your knees." Low, rough, his voice rumbled right through her skin.

A long shiver wandered down her spine. She swallowed. Aye. Definitely out of her element. She pushed again, this time putting all her strength into it, and once again didn't move. "Stop playing games," she breathed.

"Who's playing?" His fangs slid into her flesh.

Pain. Dark pleasure. Need. Hurt edged with a sharp desire spiraled through her to pound between her legs. God. She arched her back, her mouth opening. He drank deeply, taking what he needed—taking what he wanted.

A low growl rumbled from his chest.

Rough, his tongue sealed the wound. The fingers on her head flexed, shooting erotic pain along her scalp. He lifted until his gaze met hers, his face an inch from hers. His lips within reach.

Lust and determination tightened the skin across his sharp bones.

Her chest panted out breath.

He slid to the edge of the chair and loomed over her, his thighs bracketing her. Trapping her. Then his mouth covered hers. The kiss the other day had been nothing. A mere meeting of mouths.

This one was Jase Kayrs in full force. Deep and hard, he took. Holding her where he wanted her, he did as he pleased. Dark pleasure cascaded from him and heated the air around them.

She opened to him, helpless beneath his onslaught. His tongue claimed her mouth, learning every curve. Firm lips, strong hold, devastating motions. All she could do was feel. So much pain, so much pleasure, so much damn demand. He tasted of red wine and determined male. The world narrowed to him.

The kiss went on forever. He didn't touch her anywhere else, yet her entire body burned for him. Desperate and primed. Slowly, he softened his assault and leaned back.

Clarity rushed into her brain. She'd never be able to match him. He watched her, his eyes hard, his sharp features wearing that male expression that said, *I warned you. Now you're on your own.*

Deep down, where reality and hope commingled, she understood without a doubt he'd break her heart. Even deeper, she knew it was too late to turn back.

He had warned her.

Jase stared at the little witch as his cock tried to punch through his pants. The woman was sexy as hell. The soft sound she'd made in the back of her throat as he'd kissed her had almost pushed him over the edge. Even now, with her soft gray eyes unfocused on him, temptation rode him to strip her bare.

What he wanted wasn't soft, and it sure as hell wasn't pure.

Her scent of night jasmine and vanilla filled his senses, while her dark hair curled around her shoulders, tangled from his hands. Those too-knowing eyes had taken on the hue of a lake during a storm, gray and mysterious. Her T-shirt outlined hard nipples. A primal being inside him reveled in having her on her knees before him. He hated himself for that as much as for everything else.

He wanted so badly to sample her bare skin. The woman probably tasted like candy. Her blood tasted like forever.

There was no forever for him.

Even so, as her nails dug into his legs like he was her lifeline to reality, no doubt whispered in his mind that *she* was *his* lifeline. Even temporarily, while in her presence, he was alive again. Finally.

An ache pounded through his wrist. He frowned and released her hair. Slowly, he drew back his arm and turned over his hand.

The Kayrs marking.

An intricate *K* circled with Celtic knots now pulsed with life on his right palm. The marking that transferred to a mate during the mating process. Shock filled him that he hadn't had to force it into existence.

Brenna gasped. "When?"

"Just now." His voice was more gravel than tone.

Her chin lifted, her eyelids dropping to half-mast. Female awareness shone through.

He nodded. "You have tonight to decide, and I'd spend some time with the decision."

"I've made up my mind, or I wouldn't have signed the contract." Her hands trembled on his legs.

He leaned forward until they were almost nose-to-nose, but he didn't touch her. "There's no turning back after tomorrow night. Make sure you want to be mine." The small part of humanity he still owned wanted her to refuse. To run fast and hard in the other direction.

At his order, her eyes dilated. Courage and strength lifted her chin. "Per the contract, after we mate, you go home and I stay here. I'm not worried about being *yours*."

The defiance in the gentle woman prodded the baser nature inside him. "Even so, I wouldn't push, baby. Ever." It was only fair to give her warning. Not that the woman seemed to heed it. "Besides, per the contract, I can demand your presence at my home any time during the first decade." A clause inserted by the vampires probably in reaction to Moira being kept from Conn for a century.

"We both know you won't be around for a decade, *baby*." Temper flashed across her classic face.

His temper pricked the back of his neck. "You're awfully brave, considering you're *still on your knees*."

The door burst open with a shattering of wood. A man stood there, dressed all in black, feet braced, fury on his face.

Jase leaped over Brenna, planting himself between her and danger. He stilled and shook his head. "Kell?"

Kellach Dunne dropped his leather duster to the floor. "You are not mating my cousin."

Anticipation flooded Jase's veins. At six and a half feet, they stood eye-to-eye. More important, Jase had been working out impossibly hard for the last five years. He could handle the witch enforcer. "Apparently, I am mating your cousin." He settled his own stance and flashed a grin. "Is there something you think you can do about it?"

Kell moved with the speed of a soldier and the fury of a witch. The first punch to Jase's jaw sent his head to the side. Jase slowly turned back, his smile even feeling dangerous. He pulled back his arm as a decoy and jumped up, slamming both feet into Kell's face.

The witch flew back against the damaged door. His long black hair escaped its band. Anger glowed deep in his odd black eyes.

With a roar, he shot forward, his fists punching too fast to see.

"Kell!" Brenna yelled and stumbled toward them. "Stop it."

Jase pivoted to keep her behind him and cracked his elbow up into Kell's nose. Cartilage broke with a resounding snap. Two bodies rushed through the doorway, and his brother tackled Jase into the wall.

Moira slid between them, her hands on Kell's chest. Green fire danced up her arms.

Jase struggled and nailed his brother in the cheek with a right cross.

Conn pinned his forearm against Jase's neck, shoving him harder against the wall. His eyes glowed with a mixture of anger and concern. "What the hell are you doing?" he growled.

Jase struggled, yet kept his legs still. He didn't want to hurt his brother—he wanted to hurt Kell. "Let go of me."

"No. Calm down, Jase." Desperation rode Conn's tone.

Jase turned his focus on his older brother. The brother who'd taught him to fight. Years ago, before he'd been taken, Conn would've cheerfully kicked his ass for that punch in the face. Now, not so much. He showed his teeth. "You want to go, big brother?"

Conn's eyes narrowed, and his forearm cut off more air. "No, and neither do you. Calm the fuck down."

"No. Let's go, asshole. You want a fight? You've got one." Even as the words spewed from Jase, nausea filled his gut. He couldn't stop the fury.

The desolation in Conn's expression cut deeper than any knife the demons had used. "I don't want a fight." He shoved away from Jase. "I want my brother back."

Jase straightened and tugged his shirt into place. "Your brother is long gone." He pivoted to face Kell, who had blood running down his face from the broken nose. "Mind your own business."

"No. This mating will not happen." Kell wiped blood off with the back of his hand. "Brenna, pack a bag. We're out of here."

Brenna stepped over shards of wood to stand next to Jase. "What in the world are you doing in Dublin? I thought you were fighting in the north."

"I heard you were attacked." Kell eyed Jase and clenched his hands into fists.

"She was. Great job protecting her, enforcer," Jase said.

Kell's left eyebrow rose. "You are not mating this self-destructive bastard."

Brenna sighed. "I love you, Kell. But my mind is made up, and you need to respect that."

"Over my dead body," the witch hissed.

"That can be arranged," Jase drawled.

Conn rubbed his head. "Shut the fuck up, Jase."

Brenna tangled her fingers with Jase's. "Everyone just calm down."

Jase kept his gaze on the witch and tried to ignore the sense of comfort he felt from Brenna taking his side. Her small hand felt fragile in his. "In fact, everyone get the hell out. Brenna and I weren't finished talking."

Moira held both hands out. Her wild red hair curled around her shoulders, and her eyes were pissed. "Enough testosterone, damn it. Kell, Brenna is a big girl who can make her own decisions. Besides, you should look at her medical records before being such a jackass."

Kell frowned. "What medical records?"

Brenna's hand trembled in Jase's.

Jase growled. "Get out, and go look at them."

Kell scratched his chin. "Fine. But nothing is happening before the cultural event tomorrow, right?"

"Right," Brenna said.

"Good." The enforcer smiled, his gaze on Jase. "Then we'll discuss this further tomorrow."

Jase's shoulders went back. "I look forward to it." He glanced down at the small woman so bravely facing one of the most dangerous predators on earth. What in the world was he going to do with her? Then he frowned. "What cultural event?"

Chapter 6

Brenna stood in the foyer and patted her pinned-up hair. "I'm not sure 'bout this dress."

" 'Tis perfect." Moira shimmied her blue dress down over the gun strapped to her inner thigh. "You look gorgeous."

"Hmm." Brenna glanced down at the beaded mesh halter gown. The sparkly material revealed the tops of her breasts and cut in severely at the waist. It was backless, yet the skirt allowed enough room for her weapon. "Thanks for the new gun."

"I thought you'd like it." Her sister smiled, but humor failed to reach her stunning green eyes. "The vampires created the stub-version a couple of months ago. It's as deadly as a normal laser but fits much better in a smaller hand."

Brenna sighed. "Stop worrying so. Everything is going to be fine."

"I'm not worrying." Moira slipped a knife into her evening bag. "It's just, well, the Jase who came back from captivity isn't the same Jase we all knew and loved. We still love him, but I'm not sure he's safe."

Of course he wasn't safe. The guy was dynamite with an already lit fuse. "I need his strength and bloodline. Even with that power, there's a chance I still won't recover from the poisoning."

"Don't say that." Panic swept the color from Moira's face. She clutched her bag. "Why did you wait so long?"

"I don't know. I guess I figured the doctors would find a cure."
Plus, she hadn't really had someone in mind to mate. Until now.

Moira nodded. "I get that."

"Why hasn't the king gotten Jase some help?" Brenna asked.

Moira snorted. "Have you met Jase? You can't help someone
who doesn't want it."

Dread slid through Brenna's veins. "There's only one thing he
wants. Revenge against the demons."

"I know." Moira reached for the damaged front door to tug open.
"Just make sure you don't get caught in that crossfire, little sister.
He'll go through anybody to reach that goal."

Yeah, he would. "I understand."

"Oh." Moira paused halfway into the hallway. "I forgot to tell
you. We rounded up all the members of CRAP and will hold them
until after the winter solstice. You're safe."

"Good." Frankly, she hadn't felt much fear after Jase demolished
most of their soldiers. But it was a relief to know the group wouldn't
be protesting at the cultural event. Sometimes the protests took a toll
on her, although she never let the strain show. "I guess there's no reason for Jase to attend tonight." A surprising disappointment slid
through her at the thought.

"Yet, here I am." Jase suddenly loomed in the hallway.

Moira hurried over to the other doorway, where Conn had just
emerged.

Brenna smiled at the vampire to mask her racing heart. The
black tuxedo emphasized Jase's long and lean body in a way that totally failed to hide the predator beneath the suit. In fact, the civi-
lized style only enhanced his wildness. His gaze ran over her dress,
and her body reacted as if he'd used his hands.

"You look stunning," he said.

Pleasure bloomed in her chest. "Thank you. You clean up really
nice, Kayrs."

A rare dimple flashed in his right cheek. "Using my last name
won't work to distance yourself from me, baby." He held out an
arm. "Now tell me what exactly this shindig is, will you?"

She slid her hand through his arm, marveling at the hardness.
"It's the Coven Nine's winter ball. We invite dignitaries from many
witch organizations as well as some fairies, vampires, and shifters.
Truth be told, it's our Nine Christmas party, too." Speaking of

which, she had to finish her shopping before all of this mating stuff took place.

He nodded. "I am not sitting on Santa's lap."

"Did you just make a joke . . . *Kayrs?*" She pushed her ever-present glasses up her nose.

"I'm a funny guy . . . *Dunne.*" He escorted her to the elevator, and once inside, leaned out to where Moira was assisting Conn with cuff links. "We'll meet you at the car." Pressing a button, he waited until the door shut.

Brenna frowned. "We could've waited."

"No. We didn't finish earlier."

She stepped back. "Finish what?"

One eyebrow rose. Slowly, his fangs dropped low.

Her rear hit the side wall too quickly. There was no escape. "What are you doing?"

He slashed his wrist. "Drink."

Heated breath rushed out of her lungs. "Oh."

"Yeah. I bit you, now you bite me. We'll get your strength up in no time." He waited, dripping blood onto the floor. "Come here, Brenna."

One step and he could be in her space. But no. He wanted her to move. She steeled her shoulders. "No."

His chin lowered while his gaze kept hers. The slightest of curves tightened his lips. "I find I don't like hearing that word from you."

She raised an eyebrow. "Watch yourself, Kayrs. You're sounding like a vampire mate."

"You'd better hope I'm not feeling like one." The elevator stopped, and the doors slid open. Smooth as silk, Jase moved in front of the exit, easily blocking any escape. "Now come here and take my blood."

Fire swept through her. Some anger and a whole lot of desire. The calm, clearly demanding tone of voice he used slid right under her skin to soften her sex. What in the world was wrong with her? One time was safe, but taking more of the vampire's blood would give him a bigger hold on her. Of course, mating him would pretty much clinch the deal. "I don't take orders well. Ever."

"That's unfortunate." All of his formidable concentration focused right on her. "We're not leaving this space until you take some blood."

The elevator doors tried to close, and he blocked them with his body. An alarm began to buzz. Bollocks.

"Fine." She moved toward him, grabbed his wrist, and bit. Hard.

"I was already bleeding," he murmured.

She sucked in the life-giving liquid and stepped back, dropping his hand. Energy rippled down her throat, igniting her blood. "My bad."

He lifted his arm to lick the wound closed. Lucky vampire spit. "As the youngest, I have a feeling you've gotten away with quite the bit in the Dunne family."

True. Since a good part of the world was against her, the entire family had banded around her for protection. Yet sometimes, they'd stifled her. "Your point?"

"I'm not part of your family. You push me, and I'll pull you exactly where I want you."

The damn man couldn't even deliver a predictable cliché. Even so, a shiver of awareness tickled down her spine. "I will keep that in mind." She'd been raised by volatile, plasma-throwing, stubborn witches. Did he really think a vampire scared her? "Though you should probably remember that the second I regain my strength, I could blow up your entire world."

He pivoted and held out an arm. "I look forward to your attempt."

Sliding her hand along his arm, she moved from the elevator and tried to ignore the voice in her head laughing hysterically. Of course Jase Kayrs was a man to be feared. But showing that fear? No bloomin' way.

The stairwell door opened, and Conn rushed out with an irritated Moira right behind him. "What the hell's wrong with the elevator?" he asked.

Jase shrugged and headed for the car. "How the hell should I know?"

The McMannis Hotel ballroom glowed with Christmas lights, sparkling trees, and shimmering dresses. Jase tugged on his collar and willed his heart to stop beating so hard. He'd nearly had a panic attack in the damn elevator once the doors had closed. Only messing around with Brenna had kept him from going berserk.

Damn claustrophobia.

But he'd hidden it well. Once again.

He leaned against a pillar by the bar and out of the way of the festivities. Conn and Moira were completing perimeter checks, and Brenna had launched into dignitary mode in a meet-and-greet frenzy that had instantly set his fangs alive. So he'd headed for the bar.

Once again.

His metabolism was such that the five shots of tequila he'd downed would be absorbed and gone within an hour. But for now, he allowed the alcohol to calm him. The room held seven exits, not including the long row of windows showing the river. He could easily jump through the double-paned glass if necessary. Ever since being freed, he sought exits to any habitat.

Though his gaze kept returning to the elegant woman working the room. Her dress hugged her figure and highlighted creamy breasts. In fact, her skin was perfect. Pale and smooth, it tempted his mouth more than he'd like. When she'd turned to reveal a bare back, he'd almost groaned out loud. His hand itched with the need to trace her spine.

The woman was calm in a tumultuous storm. A sense of peace surrounded her, and he found himself oddly put out with the group of Scottish businessmen she was currently conversing with. Damn lucky Scots. Her friend Deb chatted, as well, every once in a while sending him a hard glance. Apparently the witch didn't like him much. Couldn't blame her.

Though he also couldn't help watching pretty Brenna.

As if sensing his perusal, she glanced up.

Her smile hit him hard in the gut. Sweet and genuine, the woman's expression warmed him in places he'd thought would always remain frozen. So he frowned.

Her smile widened. Saying something to the men, she turned and glided his way. Reaching his side, she slid her hand along his forearm. "You remind me of an arctic wolf that got caught in our barn one year. Caged and ready to rumble."

He lifted an eyebrow. Her gentle touch settled him. "Is that an invitation?"

She leaned in, and the scent of jasmine washed over him. "You wanna rumble?"

Oh yeah. He wanted to rumble. The orchestra changed to a slow tune, so he held out a hand. "How about we dance?"

She blinked. Hadn't expected an invite, now had she? Almost

warily, she slipped her hand in his. "Didn't think you were a dancer."

He swept her onto the floor and flattened his palm against her lower back. Her bare, lower back. "I'm three centuries old, baby. I can spin you around a bit." Then he pulled her close.

Her breath hitched.

His blood heated.

Brenna Dunne was an honest, beautiful, delicate woman in a completely shitty world. He shouldn't be touching her, and he sure shouldn't be having thoughts of stripping her naked and making her scream his name. He stiffened.

She stepped even closer and ran her hand down his arm again. Offering comfort. "Relax, Jase. I won't step on your feet."

His instant smile shocked the hell out of him. So he closed his eyes and lowered his head until his jaw rested on her forehead. The music wound around them as he led her gently around the floor. Although small, she fit nicely against him. His hand spanned her entire lower back. A protective urge rippled through him with a force that would've staggered him if he hadn't been moving. Nobody would hurt this woman. Ever.

He'd die for any one of his brothers. Hell, he'd killed for them often enough. Yet for the first time, a possessive edge sharpened his every protective need to keep the limited people in his life safe. An edge just for Brenna.

He didn't like it. Yet he couldn't help but brush a soft kiss across her forehead.

The hair on the back of his neck prickled. Turning them, he opened his eyes to see Conn watching him from the far side of the ballroom. Thoughtful calculation narrowed Conn's gaze, but for once, no concern lived in the metallic depths.

The ever-present guilt inside Jase flared to life. Because of his weaknesses, the Realm's ultimate soldier had been reduced to a matchmaking babysitter. Conn should be out fighting enemies, not trying to hold Jase's hand. No matter how hard he tried, he couldn't be who they needed him to be. But no, now Conn watched him with hope in his eyes, hope that Brenna Dunne would save him.

She couldn't.

He had to save himself.

For the first time in five years, he wondered if maybe he could. If maybe he should.

Brenna sighed and snuggled closer to him. The bittersweet moment cut through him with the sharpness of a blade.

Even so, he closed his eyes again and held her tight. He'd figure out the rest later. For now, in this moment, he just wanted to feel this woman against him.

Brenna maneuvered through tables and bodies, acutely aware of the vampire's gaze on her backside. Her butt actually heated. She hadn't expected him to ask her to dance, and she sure as heck hadn't expected to be a puddle of hormonal randiness afterward. So she'd excused herself and headed to the restroom. Although tight, her dress brushed her aching nipples in a way that made her want to whimper as she moved.

The idea of mating Jase Kayrs was exciting and intriguing. The reality was frightening and overwhelming. Vampires exuded dominance, maleness, and strength as a species. And after what he'd gone through, Jase was in a class all his own.

She closed the restroom door with a sigh of relief.

A plush lounge area held a long sofa across from a makeup table. She took a moment to straighten her hair and apply lipstick. Her eyes were flushed, her cheeks rosy. Signs of the fire roaring through her blood. All from one dance with Jase.

The door swished open, and two men stepped inside. The lock engaged with a loud click.

Sighing, she turned around. "This is the ladies' room."

Henry's Adam's apple bobbed as he nodded. "I know, but the solstice is in three days, and we need to get moving." He motioned for his hulking friend to sit on the sofa. "This is Albert McGillicutty, and he's one of Brenna's Warriors."

Albert sprawled, overwhelming the feminine divine. At least six feet tall, the guy was all muscle. Even his neck. He was definitely an Irish farm boy. "Hi." Dull blue eyes took her measure.

What in the world? "Hello? You're in the ladies' room." Brenna inched toward the door.

Henry blocked her way with his skinny body. "Albert is here to mate you."

Brenna snorted a laugh and then covered her nose. "Excuse me?" Henry cleared his throat. "You apparently like them brawny, so I'm willing to sacrifice my love in order to save you. To save our people." He nodded toward a window in the far wall. "We have a vehicle waiting to take you to Albert's place."

"So we can mate." Albert was missing one of his front teeth.

She shook her head, the bizarreness of the situation fuzzing her brain as she turned to Albert. "Forgetting for a moment that there's no way I'm mating you, you're a witch. Even if I wanted to mate you, my illness would kill us both."

Albert straightened. "Henry? You said mating would cure her."

"It would," Henry assured him. "Don't worry. Brenna's a sweet girl, but she's not scientific. She doesn't understand the illness."

"Oh. Okay." Genius Albert sat back again.

Brenna dug deep for patience. She had to get the men out of there before Jase found them. He couldn't discover how ridiculous her life sometimes became. "If you blokes leave right now, I won't press charges or let the enforcers know you harassed me." God, she longed for the days when she could just burn people with plasma balls.

Henry sighed and dug out a glowing green gun. "You're not thinking clearly, and that's okay. But you're coming with us."

Heat filled Brenna's lungs. "Henry? If you shoot me, then you can't save me. Got it?"

His eyes drooped. "I'll just shoot you in the leg. Then, after you mate Albert, you'll get your healing abilities back."

The first tendril of panic stilled Brenna's movements. Maybe the dumbass *would* shoot her. "Let's talk about this."

"Nope. Done talking." Albert stood, hulking and strong.

Brenna settled her stance. A groin shot would take him down, but then she'd have to worry about Henry's gun.

A knock sounded on the door. "Brenna? What's taking so long?" Jase asked.

Blast it. Figured he'd come looking for her. Vampires never knew when to stay the heck out of the way.

Henry turned and aimed for the door.

Brenna instantly kicked up as hard as she could into Albert's groin. He shifted at the last moment, and she caught his thigh. Rage filled his eyes. He lunged for her.

"Help," she yelled.

The door shattered with the force of a battering ram. The pieces plowed into Henry, and he went down.

Jase stepped over him, his gaze on Albert. "Problem?"

Albert nodded to Brenna. "Mine."

Jase's eyebrows rose. "I don't think so."

Albert's smile widened to reveal another missing tooth. He clenched his hands into fists.

Real panic ripped through Brenna. "No, no, no. We're not doing this. Everyone out of the restroom."

Jase brushed her to the side, his gaze steady on Albert. Wood crumpled under his shoes. "Apparently, we are doing this. Anyone care to explain first?"

She gulped in air and grabbed his jacket, not sure where to look. "Albert is a Brenna's Warrior who wants to matc. To save me."

Jase pursed his lips in anticipation, his eyes lighting up. "I see. Why don't you go find your sister? I'll just be a moment here."

Albert swung one beefy arm, and Jase shoved her out of the way, taking the hit. He staggered back, shaking his head. "Guy hits like a brick building." Twisting, he jabbed Albert in the nose before following with an uppercut. Albert smashed into the wall, and shot back, arms swinging.

Brenna yelped and sidled out of the way. Conn had appeared to block spectators from the doorway.

The fight was brutal.

Albert had size and a bit of strength; Jase had speed, training, and pure fury. In the end, there was really no contest.

Jase shoved Albert back into the wall, stepping into his space. Albert's eyes glazed, and he tried to bring up his left arm for a weak hit. Jase trapped it with his, took a second, and nailed Albert with his elbow. Albert dropped to the ground, out cold.

Jase turned toward her. Blood flowed from a cut in his forehead, danger etched in every line on his face.

She swallowed at the devastation in the bathroom and shook her head. "You're always fighting."

His eyes narrowed. "Every fight I've been in lately has been because of you."

Her spine steeled. Well, hmmm. That was true. "Whatever."

He stalked toward her and tilted her chin up with one knuckle. "There's only one way to solve this. Tonight, we mate."

Chapter 7

Brenna ditched her heels and padded from the kitchen, two tumblers in her hands. She gave one to Jase before sitting next to him on the sofa. "Kilbeggan whiskey."

Jase nodded and sniffed the glass. "One of many Irish treats." He swallowed, his throat moving. "Fifteen years old?"

"Yes." Brenna sipped, allowing the smooth heat to slide down to her stomach. "I'm sorry I got you into another fight."

He lifted a shoulder. "I like fighting." The vampire had built a crackling fire while she'd been in the kitchen. He'd also removed his coat and tie, leaving his white dress shirt unbuttoned at the top. Very nice muscles filled out the sleeves and chest. "Though I've never brawled in a women's restroom."

"Me, either."

He kept his gaze on the fire. The soft sounds of Celtic music enhanced the night. "Did taking my blood earlier today give you any extra strength?"

"No." In fact, she'd already forgotten about taking his blood.

"I see." He reached in his pocket and handed her a small box. "Take the pills."

She flipped open the lid. Three pink pills sat on cotton. Flutters washed through her abdomen. "Three, huh? You must be a dynamo in bed."

He didn't smile. "I don't want to hurt you."

"Then stop treating me like fragile glass."

"You're more fragile than glass."

Irritation snapped her chin up. "Perhaps. But I won't shatter."

He finally focused on her. "No. You'll bruise and break."

She frowned. "Vampires have mated with humans for centuries, and the pills aren't used all the time."

He rubbed his chin. "I know. But those matings are destined, and those vampires are in control. I'm not."

She sat back and crossed her legs, the sparkly fabric stretching. "You need to get over yourself."

Humor rode his exhale. "You're not the first to say that."

She eyed the door. "I'm surprised Moira isn't here trying to interfere."

"Conn won't let her. We had a discussion earlier." Jase downed the rest of his glass. "If this wasn't necessary to save your life, I'm sure your family would stop it."

"They'd *try* to stop it." She shook her head. "I make my own decisions. Don't ever forget that."

"All right." His voice lowered to a timbre that licked along her skin. "If you won't take the pills, drink your whiskey, Brenna."

The way he said her name. As if she was the only person in existence, and as if he owned each letter. She took a deep breath to relax. There was no helping the thrumming through her veins or the softening of her thighs. Her mind was made up, and she wanted this to happen. So she tilted back her head and swallowed the potent malt.

A blast of heat flared in her stomach as the drink landed. Her body melted.

Jase's powerful shoulders shifted, and he grasped her around the waist. Another smooth movement, and she sat on his lap, straddling him. Her dress rode up her legs, and an impressive erection rubbed against her.

She swallowed.

He reached up and removed the pins holding her hair. The mass fell down around her shoulders, and he brushed it away from her face.

"Are you sure?" he asked, his voice a low rumble.

Her lids dropped to half-mast. "I'm sure."

His eyes flared. Gently, he removed her glasses, folded them, and set them on an end table. With a finger, he drew down one side of her dress before doing the same with the other side. Her breasts sprang free. The material stopped at her elbows, effectively pinning her. Intrigue caught on her breath.

He made a low noise in his gut and smoothed both hands over her breasts.

Electricity ripped down to her clit. She bit her lip to keep from groaning.

"You're gorgeous, baby," he whispered, brushing his thumbs across her nipples.

She breathed out, her mind spinning. Shrugging her shoulders, she lifted her arms free of the material, and the dress dropped to her waist.

Her hands trembled as she reached for his shirt buttons, and it took a minute to finish releasing the last one. She pushed the sides apart. Hard, defined muscle enhanced his broad chest—along with several scars. Deep, vicious, shattering, the knife and whip wounds showed his time of captivity.

It was too easy to say the wrong thing about his pain, so she kept silent. Unable to help herself, she leaned forward and kissed a long gash above his heart.

His breath hitched, and his hands tightened on her breasts. Then he tangled one hand in her hair and tugged. She lifted, her gaze meeting his.

Strength, anger, and vulnerability commingled in the vampire's eyes. A dangerous cauldron of emotion. One she wasn't powerful enough to protect against. So she did the only thing she could—she opened herself completely to him.

She ran her hand along the side of his face, her heart breaking when he turned into her palm. As if a gentle touch was too much for him to resist. Tears pricked the back of her eyes. "I won't hurt you," she whispered from somewhere deeper than the moment.

"Don't let me hurt you." The gentle plea matched his devastated tone.

Grasping his chin, she leaned in and wandered her lips over his. Memorizing the firmness. The strength. The very maleness of his mouth. She'd worry about her heart later. It was much too late now.

His fingers spread through her hair, cupping her head, subtly taking over the kiss as if he couldn't help it. Gentle and seeking, he explored her, conveying more than a kiss. The need for touch, the need for connection lived in every stroke of his tongue, every slant of his lips.

She lost herself in the maelstrom, her mouth opening, accepting all he could give.

Whether he liked it or not, he was giving. To her. The Dunnes' youngest, freakiest, almost plain daughter. In this moment and in this vampire's arms, she was invincible. Stronger even than he.

The truth of that sparked shards of demanding need through every nerve. Sighing deep in her throat, she rubbed against his erection. Hard and full, he pulsed beneath his slacks. Through her flimsy thong, his heat all but demanded entrance.

He broke the kiss, and they both breathed heavily.

She yanked his shirt down his arms. More scars and more muscle. Her hands caressed him, and she marveled at his strength. Vampires were naturally cut and hard. This one had worked beyond a gifted biology to create a body of pure steel. Her sex quivered with the knowledge, while her heart ached. This was a body ready for battle.

"Jase," she whispered.

"Shhh." He stood and waited until she'd wrapped her legs around his hips before carrying her to the bedroom. He laid her on the bed and removed her dangling dress. His eyelids dropping, he reached down and slid her panties free. "You're beautiful, Brenna." His gaze ran over her, softness lighting his eyes.

For the first time, she felt beautiful. She'd carry the look on his face into forever, no matter what happened. She forced a smile. "You're still dressed."

His nostrils flared. Sure fingers unbuckled his belt, unbuttoned his slacks, and shoved them to the ground. He stepped out of them and out of his shoes, resting one knee on the bed.

God, he was huge. Huge-huge. Not just kinda huge. She licked her suddenly dry lips, and he groaned low.

Feminine panic swept through her. Okay. They were meant to fit. Somehow, they'd fit.

His half smirk proved he'd seen the panic. Flattening his hand on her abdomen, he watched his hand trace up between her breasts. She reached for him.

"No. Let me play." He leaned down and flicked a nipple with his tongue.

"I want to play, too," she gasped, her fingers curling over his shoulders.

"Wait your turn," he rumbled as he stretched over her, settled between her legs, and drew a nipple into his mouth.

Lava surrounded her. Good God, his mouth was on fire. She shifted restlessly against him, her mind swirling, her body aching. He paid attention to both breasts, nipping, licking, and sucking. Finally, he lifted his head. "I thought you'd taste like candy. You don't. Sweet raspberries—all the way." He reached down and slid a finger inside her.

She gasped and arched her back. Mini explosions ripped through her sex.

Pleasure curved his smile. "You're wet."

"Of course." She flashed him a challenging smile.

His eyebrow lifted, and he scraped his thumbnail along her clit.

She stopped breathing and her eyes slammed shut.

Warm lips wandered across her stomach, his breath heating her skin. Her abdominal muscles shifted, and her internal walls clenched. His broad hands curled around her thighs, and he dipped lower.

Instinct pushed her to struggle, but his hold was absolute. She couldn't get away.

His tongue licked into her, and she forgot all about getting away. But still, this was an arranged mating. He didn't need to—

"Ahh," she moaned when his mouth found her clitoris. His tongue took over, moving and teasing with tiny flicks, so that her breath stopped.

The need to arch into him made her back tremble, but he kept her immobile. Open to him—open to whatever he wanted to do to her. The thought sent a rush of fire beneath her skin.

She swallowed and sucked in air. "Jase, this isn't really necessary." The words came out in pants.

He lifted his head. "We're mating, Bren. I plan to taste every single inch of you." One finger slid between her swollen folds. His teeth scraped her thigh, and she had a second to clench before his deadly fangs plunged deep.

She cried out, her body firing, her back arching.

Dark pleasure coursed in her veins. Pleasure from him as he drank. He sealed the wound, and his short hair tickled her skin as he turned his head to kiss her mound. "You taste like honey and spice." Then, rotating his finger, he sucked her clit into his mouth.

She exploded.

The orgasm flared through her with a burst of wild energy, cresting, and then rippling in waves. Sparks flashed behind her eyes. She rode the waves, her body jerking, her legs held open by his wide shoulders.

Finally, with almost a sob, she came down. Her body relaxed into the bedspread.

He released her, slowly moving up her torso. A rogue's smile curved his lips. "We're gonna have to do that again."

She shoved hair off her face and widened her knees. "My turn to play." Grabbing his flanks, she caressed down to his butt. Firm and hard, his warm flesh filled her palms.

He rested on his elbows and slowly slid the head of his cock inside her. She bit her lip as her body resisted his size. Pain and pleasure melded together. "I don't know."

His lips brushed hers. "I do. You'll take all of me."

The order loosened something inside her, and she willed her muscles to relax. Her nails bit into his biceps, and her thighs pressed against his hips.

He slid out and then back in several times, finally filling her completely. Oh God. She couldn't take it.

Her whimper brought his focus to her eyes. Then his mouth took hers. Firm and absolute, he swept his tongue inside. Tingles of need filled her. The time for gentleness had passed, and he took what he wanted.

Her body softened around him—accepted him. He tweaked her nipple, and she groaned. Pleasure and pain combined into an irresistible need to move. Her feet pressed onto his butt.

He eased out and slammed back in. His groan coincided with her sigh. "Hold on, baby." Manacling her hip, he began to plunge. He thrust hard and deep, holding her tight, controlling them both.

She caressed the ridges and scars along his back, meeting his thrusts as much as possible.

With a growl of her name, he pounded harder. Her internal walls flared with fire, and she gasped. Oh God.

Scraping his teeth along her jugular, he sank his fangs deep. She cried out, her body instantly spasming in something too intense to be an orgasm. A flash of fire lit her butt, and she sucked in air. The waves rode her instead of the other way around, so she held on and just felt. Her body was plucked tight as a string as the sensation rippled through her. Finally, with a sob of his name, she went limp.

His fangs retracted, and he ground against her as he came.

He stopped moving. Still embedded in her balls-deep, he smoothed the hair from her face, his gaze a dark green and on hers. "Mine."

Chapter 8

Jase punched the bag with a hard rhythm, his feet dancing, his thoughts swirling. Skin split on his knuckles, so he hit harder. Heavy metal music blasted from a stereo in the corner, and he was the only person in the basement gym. Three downed punching bags flopped over near the door, their leather mangled, their stuffing out. He'd have to buy Kell new equipment if he stayed any longer.

He'd left sweet Brenna in bed at dawn so he could run for a couple of hours before lifting weights and punching the bags. What in the hell had he been thinking to mate her? He'd stupidly thought he'd be able to do her a favor and leave town. Even now, hours later, his blood hummed for her. His fucking cock was ready to play. And something in the center of his chest hurt. Bad.

Blood sprayed as he slammed his hand into the leather.

The music cut off.

He stilled, turning only his head to see Conn leaning against the wall, arms crossed. The expression on his brother's face reminded him of when Conn had tried to tame wild horses for a brief time. Turned out horses and vampires didn't belong in the same vicinity.

But now, Conn was measuring how to talk to him.

That pissed him off beyond belief. "Turn the fucking music back on." He began punching the bag again.

"No. You're bleeding all over Kell's gym."

He stopped and turned. "What do you want?"

"I want to make sure you're all right." Conn rubbed his prominent chin. "I mean, after last night."

Jase blinked. "What do you know about it?"

Conn rolled his eyes. "I can smell her all over you. Don't be
daft."

"What is this, a slumber party?" Jase snorted, his shoulders
tightening. "I don't need to share, Conn. You're going soft."

Temper flashed through Conn's eyes. Anticipation lit Jase's
spine. Then Conn snuffed out the fire. "I'm not soft, but you need to
talk."

Disappointment tasted like ashes. "I'm fine. We mated, she'll be
cured, I'll get her skills, and now we have a good treaty with the
witches. Simple as that."

"Mating is never simple." Conn kicked a barbell. A crease lined
between his eyebrows. "Are you really going to leave her?"

The thought was a fist to the gut. His mind rebelled against leaving Brenna. "Of course. That was the plan, wasn't it?"

"I thought that maybe after last night, you'd—"

"What? Fall in love and be cured? Be able to have a normal life
so all of you could relax and stop feeling so fucking guilty?" The
words spilled out of him, the venom burning his tongue.

"Yes."

He curled his lip. "Sorry. We fucked, I branded her, and it's over.
Deal with it, brother."

Conn fixed him with a look that at one time would've made him
think twice. "Don't talk about Brenna like that."

"She's mine." Jase lifted his chin, hating himself more than
Conn probably did. "I can talk about her any damn way I want."
Even so, he glanced at the doorway, his breath heating. Nobody
stood there, so he relaxed and focused back on his brother.

Amusement lifted Conn's lip. "Who are you looking for?"

Heat filled Jase's face. "Nobody."

"Right." The amusement slid into a full smile. "Keep telling yourself that." Whistling an Irish tune, Conn sauntered out of the gym.

Asshole. Jase took a deep breath. He should probably check on
Brenna. Jogging toward the doorway, he rushed past the elevator to
the stairs. Climbing the many stories would be a good way to end
his workout.

He arrived at the penthouse sooner than he'd expected. It was quiet, so he strode silently through to peek in the bedroom. The bed was made, and Brenna was nowhere to be seen. Okay. Turning on his heel, he wandered the penthouse, finally coming to a locked door behind the kitchen. He knocked, but there was no answer.

A locked door. Why would Brenna have a locked door? Well, they were mated now, and there would be no locks. Yeah, he was a bastard. A shoulder to the edge shoved open the heavy oak.

The smell of oil paint hit him first. Ah. Her studio. Curiosity propelled him inside. Bright light cascaded in from a wide wall of windows as well as skylights. Several half-finished paintings stood on easels. Rich, full colors exploded on the canvases. Sensual and erotic paintings of silhouettes caught in passion.

The woman was incredibly talented.

He reached for a sketchbook on a battered table and flipped open the first page. His face stared back at him, so much pain in his eyes he stepped back. When had she sketched him? Considering his face bore the ever-present scar, it had been within the last couple of days. His hands shook when he flipped the top closed. She'd seen him. The real him.

God. He had to get out of there.

His phone buzzed, and he absently pressed it to his ear. "What?"

"It's Conn. We have a report of demons being in Dublin. Somehow they got word of the contractual mating."

The world stopped. Jase's head snapped up and his heart clutched. "They're after me?"

"No. Our contacts confirm they're after Brenna."

Terror rippled through him so quickly he swayed. Where the hell was Brenna?

Brenna tucked her packages under one arm and skirted a mom with three toddlers. "Thanks for coming shopping today."

Deb nodded, her gaze on the huge Christmas tree set in the middle of a mall. "Are you kidding? I wanted to hear all about the crazy, fanged sex you had last night."

Brenna forced a laugh. The sex had been more emotional than crazy, but it had been wild. "I have to admit, my ass really hurts."

"The branding?" Deb asked.

"It's a marking." And yes, her butt burned like she'd been

branded with a cattle prod. Though the *K* marking was truly stunning—and perfectly placed on her left buttock.

"Same thing." Deb set down her many shopping bags and stretched her neck. "Are you thinking forever now with the vampire?"

Brenna shrugged. Well, maybe. It could work out, right? "No. I'm not thinking forever."

"Liar. I know you. No way would you have slept with him without some emotion, and now, you're probably thinking you're in love with him." Deb shook her head.

"I'm not in love. But he's got a sweet side. Deep down, he's so hurt—"

"Stop." Deb held out a hand. "Please don't tell me you're going to save him. That you're going to be the one woman to get through his hard shell and make him whole." The words were snarky, but the concern in her eyes was genuine.

Brenna swallowed. "I don't know."

Deb groaned. "I knew this would happen. Didn't I say this would happen?"

"Yes." Brenna wrinkled her nose. "You warned me."

"Okay." Deb frowned and glanced around. "By the way, how did you get loose without Coven Nine security all over you?"

Now that was a good friend. One who made her point and then changed the subject so Brenna didn't cry. "Well, the CRAP group has been taken out of the picture, and Brenna's Warriors are no longer a threat since I've mated. I'm free."

Deb hopped once. "That's wonderful. Those stodgy bodyguards were no fun." She glanced at her watch and frowned. "But I have to go pick up the boys at practice. Do you want to come?"

"Nope." Freedom rushed through Brenna like a warm breeze. No more bodyguards. At least for a while. "I need to finish shopping today."

"Okay." After giving her a quick hug, Deb sprinted out of the mall.

There was a time when Brenna had energy. Maybe now that she'd mated Jase, she'd get her spunk back. With a sigh, she turned to finish her shopping. Store after store, she added to her purchases.

Finally, she headed to the center of the mall.

She felt him before she saw him. Slowly turning, she faced Jase, who stood looking at her with pure relief. Heat slammed into her face. "Hi. What are you doing here?"

He took her arm, his gaze sweeping the area. The relief turned to absolute concentration. "You left without bodyguards."

Well, that was romantic. "So?" She tried to tug free, and his hold tightened.

"So?" He lowered his face, his focus suddenly on her. "You don't go *anywhere* without protection. Got it?"

Her breath caught at the fury in his words. Then her temper sprang to life. "I believe I explained I don't take orders from anybody. Got it?"

He stilled, though tension all but vibrated around him. "Let's go. We'll discuss this at your penthouse."

"No." She yanked free. Who the blazes did he think he was? "I'm not done shopping."

The hard smack to her ass shocked the hell out of her. Her mouth dropped open.

A couple of women passed, and one giggled to the other, "Somebody's been reading *Fifty Shades.*"

Brenna closed her mouth, rage shaking her arms. A blue tinge of fire cascaded on her skin to be quickly snuffed out. They were in public. But had she almost created fire?

Jase jerked his head toward a bench. "Choose. Either we go now, or I flip you over my knee and beat your ass. Then we'll go."

Oh. He. Did. Not. More blue cascaded along her wrists, but she couldn't hold the plasma. "I'd blow you up if I could."

He grabbed her arm and tugged. "The bench it is."

"No." She dug in her heels. Panic constricted her airway. "I'll go." Then she'd teach him a lesson about bossing her around. Somehow.

"Good." He changed directions and headed for the main exit.

She could either step in line or fall on her head. "How did you find me?"

"You left word at headquarters you'd be shopping, but you didn't say at which mall." Jase scanned the area, keeping her close. "We have squads heading to each one. I arrived here first."

"I didn't think I needed to leave my location." The danger had been eliminated for her. A blast of energy smacked her between the eyes. She faltered. "What was that?"

Jase swore and stopped cold. "Demons."

Fear blasted into her solar plexus. "There are no demons in Ireland. We keep them out."

"They got in." His jaw clenched, and he tapped an ear communicator. "Conn? I'm at the west end of the Farside Mall. They're here." He propelled them both into motion and toward the stairwell. "An exit to the north leads to outside parking. Backup is five minutes away."

She tucked her packages against her ribs, fighting to keep up. "You studied the mall schematics?"

"On the way here."

They reached the top of the stairs, and he stopped. His head lifted, his eyes going flat. "They're up here, too."

She yanked a gun from her handbag and tossed her packages toward the wall. Normal witches had a decent defense against the demons' mind attacks because of the plasma balls, but she was useless in a fight right now. "I can't create fire."

"I know," he said grimly, surveying the area. "What's over there?" He pointed to a construction area blocked off by signs and strung tape.

"New stores moving in—they're remodeling the area."

"Good." Taking her hand, he pulled her past the signs and under the tape. "We'll lead them away from humans at least." Then he tapped his ear. "Conn? We're on the second level in the east wing. I sense three of them—maybe four."

The oxygen in the air swelled, adding weight. Brenna struggled forward, her mind fuzzy. "They're not attacking yet, but my head is beginning to hurt."

He edged them along the roughly plastered wall. "Have you ever felt a demon attack?"

"No." Her lungs heated, while the plaster scratched her hand.

"They'll shoot horrific images into your mind, and then it'll feel like a scalding blade is cutting your brain. The wound is not real, and you can push through the pain." He drew a gun from his waistband and dodged into one of the empty stores.

She followed, sweeping her gun behind them. "Can you push through the attack?"

"Yes. After five years of torture, I can shield. Somewhat."

Her ears rang. Adrenaline flooded her system. Rough walls and subfloor made up the octagonal room. Construction plastic hung from the ceiling, while toolboxes and flooring materials were scattered throughout. The smell of plaster dust tickled her nose, and she bit back a sneeze.

Jase pointed to a framed hole in the wall that would probably lead to dressing rooms. "Go in there and don't come out until I get you."

She shook her head. "You can't fight three of them alone. I have a gun, and I know how to shoot."

He whirled on her so quickly she stepped back, her ankle colliding with a stack of tiles. She would've fallen had he not grabbed her arm. His jaw firmed, his muscles undulated, and his eyes flattened to death. "Obey me."

Her entire body tightened with awareness. With real fear. The vampire had morphed from man to killer within seconds. The hard face, she could handle. But the dead eyes? They broke her heart— while every instinct in her body screamed for her to run. Away. From. Him. So she nodded, and the second he released her, she scrambled toward the dressing rooms. But she stopped at the doorway, turned, and settled her stance.

The look he gave her chilled her bones.

Then the demons entered the room.

Chapter 9

Two males entered first, followed by a female demon. Brenna steadied her grip on the gun. A real female demon. They were almost a legend, they were so rare. This one had the white-blond hair and black eyes of a purebred. She was tiny, but power shimmered around her until sparks popped in the air.

The two hulking men also showed their heritage with fathomless eyes and white hair. Dressed in all black, with silver emblems covering their right breasts. High-up soldiers.

The woman flashed sharp teeth. "Miss me, Jase?"

He growled low and shifted to the right, his position allowing him to scan the entire room. "No. In fact, I hoped you died when my brothers demolished the Scotland headquarters, Willa."

The woman pouted red lips, eyes sparkling. "Such mean language after such wonderful times in my bedroom." She flicked her glance at Brenna. "There was no way we could work out. You always did like them helpless."

Brenna cocked the gun. What times in her bedroom? Had Jase been with this bitch?

Willa's smile widened. "A gun won't stop me, witch, and considering you're at death's door, neither will you." She sighed. "I had hoped for more of a fight when I killed your mate. 'Tis a pity."

Jase flashed the grin of a killer. "Jealous?"

Willa hissed out a breath. "Of what?"

Cold calculation quirked Jase's upper lip. "Of the pretty witch I decided to mate. You know, after you all but begged for my cock."

"I wanted your marking." Fire lanced through the woman's eyes. She lifted a shoulder. "Besides, I've had your tongue in my mouth, vampire. We both know you wanted it."

Bile rose up Brenna's throat, and she shoved the acid down. "The Coven Nine isn't going to allow this trespass on our land. Get out now."

"Do you honestly think we're afraid of the Coven Nine?" Willa swept her hand out, and the air chilled. "We've never taken your land because we don't want it."

Fury and fear steadied Brenna's aim. "We both know you're afraid of the Nine. Witches can handle demons, and you know it. Get. Out. Now."

Icicles of pain instantly ripped into her brain. She fell back against the wall, crying out. Images of tortured children flashed behind her mind's eye. She shook her head, aimed, and fired.

The bullet glanced off Willa's shoulder, but the mental attack stopped.

Jase jumped for the nearest guard, his knife flashing. The soldier countered, slamming Jase into plastic sheeting. Shaking off the cover, Jase dodged forward and punched the soldier in the face, kicking back to stop the other guy's advance.

Brenna gulped down fear and fired again. This round hit Willa in the chest. The demon snarled and attacked with brutal accuracy to Brenna's frontal lobe. The explosion in her head weakened her knees. She kept firing as she went down.

Jase bellowed and grabbed his temples. Then, straightening, he shook his head and lunged into the soldier, knife out. Quick twists had the demon on the ground with a blade sticking out of his neck. The other demon tackled Jase and sent them rolling across the floor.

The doorway filled with Kell, Conn, and Moira.

Brenna gasped in relief even as her limbs went numb. The gun clattered against the wood. She turned her head, helpless, to watch.

Willa took in the situation, pivoted, and ran full-bore for the boarded windows. Wood and glass shattered as she flew through.

Moira skidded across the room, landing on her knees to cradle Brenna's head. "Bren?"

"I'm fine." Brenna pushed herself to sit, heated blood sliding from her nose and eyes. "Damn demons."

Moira slid an arm around her shoulders, offering support.

Across the room, Jase and the third demon grappled. Jase flipped the guy onto his back and straddled him, fists swinging. The demon's cheek caved. Yet Jase continued to punch. Hard, crazy, out of control, he broke every bone in the demon's face.

A wave of pain cascaded out, attacking, from the guy with a knife in his throat. Conn instantly dropped to one knee and shot a fierce punch to the demon's jaw. The guy slumped unconscious.

Jase beat the downed demon, who was out cold. Blood sprayed. Brain matter oozed from the guy's ear. With a hard look at Moira, Conn shot forward and captured Jase in a hold from behind. Jase kept swinging, struggling against his brother's grasp.

Conn yanked him to the side and off the demon. "He's had enough."

"He's still alive," Jase growled, fighting to get back to the ground.

Conn twisted and tossed Jase into the wall. "Enough. We need to question him."

Jase shoved off the wall, his face a brutal mask. Cuts lined his cheek and jaw, while blood flowed from a gash above his right eyebrow. No recognition lived in his eyes. Slowly, he straightened, and his eyes focused. His chin lowered. A warrior after a battle—a warrior still in the battle. His fists clenched. His body vibrated. Then, he went cold. No emotion . . . nothing.

Brenna trembled against her sister. Good God. What had she done?

Brenna danced on the mats in the training room, waiting for the right opening. Her sister moved to the side, so she shot in and tossed Moira to the ground.

Moira flipped to her feet. "Nice move."

"Thanks." Brenna stretched her neck. "You're taking it easy on me."

Moira shrugged. "You're not at full strength yet." She reached for a towel to wipe her forehead. "Do you feel any difference since the, ah, the mating?"

"Not really." Brenna unwound the tape protecting her wrists.

"Though it hasn't even been twenty-four hours." She glanced at the clock. "I wanted to sit in on the interview with the captured demons."

"No, you didn't," Moira murmured. "Believe me, Jase had blood in his eye. Conn went only to make sure Jase didn't kill them. Well, before we got answers."

Brenna reached for a bottle of water. "Jase was out of control in the mall. I mean, I understand it, but—"

"Anger issues, much?" Moira tossed the towel into a bin. "He's definitely over the edge."

"I know." Brenna sighed. "I feel like he's my responsibility now. Since we mated."

"He's not. Your mating was arranged, and you're protected by contract." Moira slid into the splits, leaning her head back to her knees. She straightened up, her brow furrowing. "You're not thinking you're in love with the guy, are you?"

Well, she definitely had feelings for him, but they ran the gamut from desire to wariness. "I have no bloomin' clue."

Moira chuckled. "Welcome to matehood with a Kayrs. If we're not confused, the earth isn't spinning."

Brenna paused. "Problems?"

Moira cracked her neck. "We're all on eggshells. Rage is eating Jase, and guilt is eating the rest of the brothers. They all need an emotional exorcism, if you ask me."

"How so?"

"Well, as king, Dage is furious the demons dared take and torture his younger brother. Dage has to retaliate, and I think he's afraid of how far he'll go." Moira stretched her neck.

The king had always seemed to carry the world with ease. But when family was involved, things always got dicey. "How is Emma holding up?" The king's mate was a kick in the pants as far as Brenna was concerned.

Moira shoved curls off her forehead. "Emma is obsessed with curing Virus-27. I've never seen anybody work so hard and with such single-minded dedication."

"Well, her younger sister has contracted the virus. That would motivate any of us." Brenna twisted her torso to release tension. "Plus, if the damn bug goes airborne, as we're all predicting it will, then every vampire mate and witch is susceptible."

"I know. It's too bad we haven't wiped the Kurjans off the map." Fire danced on Moira's skin.

The Kurjans were an evil vampire race, who were allergic to the sun. They had created Virus-27 to destroy vampire mates and witches by unraveling their chromosomal pairs. Vampire mates had twenty-seven pairs, while witches had twenty-eight; decrease those . . . and they could end up dead. "Good thing the virus is so slow-moving," Brenna mused.

"Slow-moving for immortals is fast-moving for humans. The bug will kill, I'm afraid. Eventually." Moira scrubbed both hands down her face. "It's difficult watching Talen try to handle Cara's illness."

Cara was Emma's younger sister, and she'd mated Talen right before contracting the virus. "I'm sure Emma will find a cure." Brenna hoped. "Or Kane will." Kane was the middle Kayrs brother, the voice of reason, and the smartest person on the planet.

"Aye, Kane will find a cure just to make sure his mate never gets infected. For a logical vampire, he has fallen so hard, it's adorable." Moira grinned.

"Look who's talking."

Moira shrugged. "Connlan Kayrs is everything I ever wanted in a mate. How could I not fall for the sexiest soldier alive?"

Now that was sweet. "So he's doing all right?"

"No. I'm worried about him." Moira took a deep breath. "But we'll figure it out- -we always do."

Brenna nodded. "I'm glad you're happy."

"You will be, too. Just as soon as we get through this difficult time with Jase. All of the brothers will relax." Moira sighed.

"Vampires aren't very good with the feelings stuff. If it's something they can't fight or kill, then it just pisses them off." Brenna smiled. "Look at me. I've been a vampire mate for less than a day, and I'm full of wisdom."

Moira nodded. "Unfortunately, I think you've nailed the situation. There's a Kayrs-sized explosion coming, and I can't tell which direction it'll come from. I'm afraid there's no way to stop it."

"Well, maybe we should get out of the way." Though every instinct in Brenna's arsenal urged her to help Jase.

"That would be wise." Moira stood. "But that's not who we are, now is it?"

Unfortunately . . . no. "I have a terrible feeling I'm going to get burned."

"Burn 'em back." Moira's tone was light, her eyes dark.

Not good. Not good at all.

Brenna opened her mouth to argue when Conn Kayrs filled the doorway. Tall and strong, the Realm's ultimate soldier held presence in spades. Add in dark green eyes and a hard jaw, and he was something to look at.

His focus was entirely on his mate, amusement filling his eyes. "Did I just hear you threaten to burn me, *Daitlín?*"

Moira batted her eyelashes and flashed him a saucy grin. "If necessary, I'll turn you crispy."

He cocked his head to the side. "Hmmm."

Brenna cleared her throat, well used to Conn's pet name for Moira. *Brat.* "Is the torture over?"

Conn nodded. "Yes."

"And?" Brenna asked.

Conn took her measure. "There's a ten-billion-dollar contract out on Jase—to take him alive."

Good lord. "Billion?" The demons had some serious cash.

"Yes." Conn eyed Moira.

Awareness prickled down Brenna's spine. "What else?"

At Moira's nod, he sighed. "There's a fifteen-billion-dollar contract out on you—if you're taken before the winter solstice. Afterward, it's ten billion."

Brenna coughed. "The demons believe in the damn solstice nonsense?"

" 'Tis not nonsense," Moira said slowly. "The Coven Nine has ignored the issue since you've been so ill, but now that you're mending, we should investigate."

Aye. Good idea. "At least they want me alive," Brenna said.

"Sort of. Alive before the solstice, dead after." Conn rubbed a hand through his thick hair. "Apparently Willa is rather pissed Jase mated a witch."

"Who the hell is Willa, anyway?" Brenna asked.

"Sister to Suri, the leader of the demons." Conn strode toward Moira. "Willa messed with Jase's head while Suri and one of his lieutenants spent time destroying his body." Barely contained anger rode Conn's hard tone.

Dread slid through Brenna. "How did Willa mess with Jase's mind?"

Conn turned his head. "You'll have to ask him that."

Yeah. Because Jase was so darn forthcoming. "Right."

Conn grabbed a pair of grappling gloves from a rack and handed them to Moira. "Let's discuss your threat to burn me to a crisp, shall we?"

Moira grinned, blue dancing along her skin. "I'd love to roll around with you, handsome."

"Get a room," Brenna muttered, grabbing her glasses and heading for the doorway. Now the demons had a bounty on her head, and Jase needed to come clean with all the information. She hustled out to track down her mate.

Chapter 10

She found him in her penthouse living room gazing out the windows at the tumultuous water as the sun set. Closing the door, she hesitated. He looked so alone . . . and so dangerous. Large and formidable.

"I'm sorry I scared you at the mall," he said without turning around, hands in jeans pockets.

She blinked, her mind spinning. The distance between them seemed much farther than a few yards. "I'm fine. But I think you should get help when you return home."

His head lifted, and his shoulders went back. Muscles shifted under his dark T-shirt. Slowly, as if not to frighten her, he turned, a guarded expression on his hard face. "I don't need help."

A pang dinged her heart. "Your choice." Her sister was correct. The wounded needed to want help. "I'd like it if you stayed in touch, anyway."

He exhaled, his gaze reaching across the room and tethering her in place. "You're coming with me."

She stiffened. "No, I'm not."

"I'm invoking clause eight of the contract." His tone remained so level, they might have been talking about the oncoming storm.

Shock froze her. "No. We have an understanding. I'm not going anywhere."

"You signed the contract."

"I know." She exhaled, struggling for patience. What the heck was wrong with him? "We always intended to keep our own residences."

"Things have changed." No give showed on his face.

Her feet tightened with the need to run. She didn't know this man. At full power, she'd face him and burn the hell out of him. Now? Vulnerability caught on her breath. She didn't stand a chance against him. If she protested publicly, her people would support her, but she'd be breaching the contract.

"If you breach"—he clearly read the panic she could feel in her expression—"then your people will bow to mine in all military matters."

Oh God. A terrible liquidated damages clause inserted so nobody would breach. Damn the lawyers.

"You wouldn't," she gasped.

His eyes took on a dangerous edge. "You're right. I won't claim breach of contract or hinder our treaty."

She stilled. Relief relaxed her stance. "That's good."

"I will, however, drag your ass all the way to Oregon if need be."

Such an overt action would cause war. Real war. One that would put Conn and Moira on opposite sides of the line. Brenna shook her head. "Why? Why are you doing this?"

"You're my mate."

"Oh no, you don't." Finally, anger leapt over the surprise. "You don't want a mate, and you sure as hell don't care."

For the first time, his gaze wavered. A softness spiraled into his eyes. "I do care. Much more than I'd like."

Her head shook in jerky motions this time. No. He wasn't going to manipulate her like that. This hurt enough as it was. "Too bad. Stick to our original understanding, the one we didn't really say, and leave me the hell alone."

"I can't," he whispered. Sliding his hands free, he stalked across the room like a jaguar tracking prey. Like prey, she stood frozen. Reaching her, he ran a gentle knuckle down the side of her face.

Her stomach quivered, and not only from anger. "Jase—"

"The demons want you, Brenna. Because of me." He speared his fingers through her hair and forced her head back. As he leaned in, his breath brushed her lips. "They. Won't. Get. You."

So much murderous promise lived in his words, her knees went weak. "I can take care of myself. Plus, I have Coven Nine body-guards."

"Sorry." Not by one inch did he look sorry. "Not good enough. You're with me where I can keep you safe until I end this."

A slow ball of lava rolled through her at his nearness, at the intensity of his hold. She tried to ignore it. "No. I make my own choices."

His upper lip quirked, and his gaze dropped to her mouth. "When it comes to safety, I make your choices. You should've known that before you mated me."

Aye, vampires were over-the-top protective and possessive. Those were vampires who mated for love. This one had mated for other reasons. "I won't always be so weak. You don't want me for an enemy." She kept her voice clear and tried to stifle the desire flaring awake inside her.

His hold tightened, and his other hand flattened against her lower back, bending her. A slow blink revealed a new light in his eyes. "Threatening me is not a good idea, little one."

"Heed the threat. You have no idea who you mated."

"Neither do you." His nostrils flared, apparently catching a scent.

Blast it. He could smell her arousal. This was beyond twisted. She shoved both hands against his chest.

His instant smile was carnal. Dangerous. Knowing. "Maybe it's time I showed you."

Icy-hot whispers tingled along her skin. "I don't think so."

Deadly fangs dropped low.

Waves of heat cascaded up her chest, lifting her chin, burning with need. Just from a look at those fangs.

Enough. Releasing his chest, she dropped down, used his hand as a base, and flipped backward. She landed on her feet, her hair swirling around.

She had a half a second to appreciate the surprise on his face before he moved. His hand fisted in the center of her shirt, and he yanked her against him. Hard. She opened her mouth to protest, but it was too late.

His fangs retracted as his mouth crushed hers. Anger rode his kiss, and he plundered deep, showing her in no uncertain terms who was stronger. Not only physically, but as he softened his assault, as he shot fire through her until her ears rang, he showed her true strength. After one night with him, he controlled her responses. He could make her want on demand. Possibly from the mating, from the marking . . . but more likely from Jase himself. The man was sex, danger, and fire combined.

She whimpered in her throat, her eyes fluttering shut. Desire slashed with jagged edges as it ripped into her.

His kiss held nothing back. No smoothness—no persuasion. He took everything she had and then demanded more. Demanded everything. The male wasn't taking no for an answer.

Furious hunger moved his mouth across hers, a hunger that dug down deep in her belly and clawed.

Yanking back, he whipped her shirt over her head. A second later her yoga pants hit the floor. He bent her forward over the back of the couch. "Tell me it's okay," he rumbled, his voice beyond gravel to asphalted spikes.

Her stomach rubbed against the leather, while cool air brushed her bare backside. Need and want had her vision blurring. "It's okay. Hurry." Was that her voice? Husky and needy?

His zipper rasped. She shivered. Both hands grabbed her hips and he plunged inside her with one strong stroke. Crying out, she lifted up on her tiptoes.

He stilled, his breath heated on the nape of her neck. "Breathe, baby," he whispered.

Breathe? She forced out air, her entire body short-circuiting from too many sensations. Hunger—pain—pleasure. Slowly, she dropped down.

Reaching around, he palmed her breast, tugging the nipple. Shards of electricity shot straight to her sex. "What are you doing?" she panted.

"Whatever I want to do."

The dominant tone, edged with dark amusement, almost threw her into an orgasm. Panic inched for a foothold, and she tried to rise.

His hand flattened on her bottom, right across the still burning marking. A quiver shook her. She swallowed, fighting to remain sane while her body went crazy. She felt taken, all control stolen from her, and somehow, she wanted nothing more than to beg him to continue. To start moving. To take her over that pinnacle where the need wouldn't hurt so badly. "Jase—start moving. Now."

His low rumble of a laugh brushed her ear. "I'll accept begging or whimpering from you, darlin'. But your time for commanding has passed." With a sharp tug on her nipple, his hand slid down and pressed on her clit.

"Oh God," she moaned.

"Praying will do." He touched where she was stretched around his cock. One wet finger ran up to circle her clit. She hissed at the blast of sensation. He played, making circles, torturing until her internal walls clenched him hard enough that she gasped. She tried to rub against him, to get relief, but he held her tight.

Then that dangerous hand ran up her torso to grip her neck, his thumb under her chin. Pressing up, he tilted her head. She couldn't move. Controlled by one thumb.

Warmth brushed her spine as he covered her.

She tensed, expecting fangs. Instead, he licked the vulnerable area where neck met shoulder. The gentle touch pounded fire through her. Then his fangs dropped low.

Her head jerked, but he held fast. He drank, a groan of pleasure rumbling from him. The groan slid under her skin and into her heart. She could already feel his reactions. Opening herself, she tried for a connection.

A hard slap against her marking caught her unaware. She opened her mouth in shock as vibrations shot straight to her core.

His fangs retracted and a rough tongue laved her wound. "Stay out of my head." The order held bite and a hint of fury. He grabbed her hips and slid out only to thrust back in.

Nerves flared inside her. God. Too much. Way too much. She pressed her face against the sofa.

Pleasure coiled tight inside her, climbing higher. His grip bruised as he yanked her bottom higher, driving his shaft deep. Harder and faster, he pounded until she forgot all thought. She forgot the world. The only thing that mattered was that edge she needed to scale.

His fingers tangled in her hair, drawing up her head. Arching her back. Controlling her so easily.

Muscled thighs pushed hers even farther apart. He thrust hard, his balls slapping against her butt. The hold on her hair tightened. "Now, Brenna."

A rush of energy gathered in one place inside her and detonated. Shock caught her at how quickly her body obeyed his order. She screamed his name as white-hot lava sprayed through her in cresting waves. Riding them, she could only shut her eyes and be swept along.

With a clenching of his hand and a growl of her name, he ground against her as he came.

They came down together, both panting.

His fingers spread along her scalp, rubbing gently. Slowly, he withdrew from her. She moaned as her internal walls protested.

He lifted her, tucking her head under his chin. Striding toward the bedroom, he crossed the darkness and slid her gently into bed. Turning, he headed for the doorway and stopped. The living room light illuminated him, a strong silhouette of maleness.

His shoulders straightened, his back to her. "Are you all right?"

The sheer number of emotions shooting from him nearly stole her breath. She could read him now, whether he liked it or not. "Yes," she whispered. "I'm fine."

He gave a short nod. "Sleep now. I'll be back later."

Then he was gone.

Brenna worked all morning in her Dublin office, fingers tapping the computer keys, finishing the reports on Coven Nine grants. Several Dublin businesses would be able to climb out of debt now. The computer light spread softly across her pristine desk, while a snowstorm bombarded the windows.

Deb reached inside the office and flipped on the light. "Why in the world do you work in the dark?"

Brenna shrugged and shut down the computer. "It's peaceful." She'd placed rich oil paintings on the two side walls, and in the dusky light, the fighting figures came alive.

Deb followed her gaze. "I've always wondered why you chose battle scenes for your Coven Nine office."

"Because we're always at war." Sad, but true. Even before the current war, the witch world was tumultuous. "Take a species that can manipulate space and matter . . ."

Deb loped inside to drop into one of two plush guest chairs. "So."

"So." Brenna studied her best friend. They'd become inseparable in kindergarten when Tommy McMannis had thrown a frog at Brenna's head. Deb had instantly tackled him into a rosebush. "What have you heard?"

"I've heard you're heading to America." Deb's brown eyes softened.

"So you're here to talk me out of it?"

"Um, no." Deb tangled her fingers together over her dress pants. "Here's the thing. Mating is hard. I mean, marriage or mating or both . . . either way, combining lives isn't easy. No matter what."

Brenna frowned. "All right."

"So, ah, well. I'm thinking you should go and maybe give it a try." Deb flushed.

Surprise jerked up Brenna's head. "You want me to go?"

"Of course not. I want you to stay here and have everything stay the same. But I don't want you to ever wonder."

"Wonder about what?"

"If you could've had something great. I know you. Already, you're half in love with the guy . . . maybe all the way in love." Deb leaned forward, her gaze earnest. "So give it a shot. You'll never wonder if you should've gone."

Brenna exhaled slowly. "If I get my heart demolished?"

Deb smiled. "Then come home. We'll plot revenge of the quantum physics kind." She eyed the storm outside. "Besides, now you have more bodyguards than ever before, and I practically got frisked just trying to get to your office. If you leave town, you might be safer."

A shadow filled the doorway. Brenna's breath caught. Jase stood, hands in faded jean pockets, strong face expressionless.

Deb turned her head. "Vampires know how to make an entrance, now don't they?" She stood and sashayed her way to the door. She paused as Jase stepped to the side. "You hurt her—I'll cut off your head myself." Then she disappeared.

Jase raised both eyebrows, his gaze on Brenna. "I think I'm growing on her."

Aye, like a fungus. "You're a charming guy." Brenna stacked files together in order to keep her hands busy.

"I used to be." He glanced around the office, gaze lingering on the oil paintings. "Did I hurt you last night?"

Heat washed through her. "Of course not."

"I was rough." His shoulders hunched, and suddenly, she could see the boy he'd once been.

"I'm fine, Jase." She pushed away from the desk. "Where did you stay last night?" After tucking her in, he hadn't returned. She'd wanted to kick herself when she'd awakened at dawn and reached for him.

"Nowhere. I went running—got back an hour ago."

The guy had run until dawn? "You do that a lot. Run, I mean." Did he think he could outrun his own memories? She fought to keep sympathy from her face. That would just piss him off.

"Yes, I like to run. Have you packed?"

She stood. "No."

"We leave today." His jaw firmed.

"I haven't decided to accompany you to America. If I do, I'll fly over after the holidays." Confrontation always dropped a rock in her stomach. The man would have to be reasonable.

"We leave today, Brenna," he repeated very softly.

Why was it the deadlier the guy, the scarier he sounded when he quieted? Softness should offer comfort, not warning. The marking on her butt began to burn. Damn vampires.

She shook her head. "After Christmas."

His chin lowered, while his gaze hardened. "The plane leaves at four this afternoon. You will be on it, packed or not."

She'd already been lectured by her aunt Viv as well as her sister, Moira. Of course, Moira just wanted Brenna close enough to keep an eye on in case the demons attacked again. Aye, she needed to go. But why make it easy on him? "I'm surprised you fly since being inside makes you edgy."

"You've noticed the claustrophobia?"

"It's hard to miss." Sure, she was sympathetic, but getting caught in a private jet with the guy if he had an attack would be suicide.

"Well, it's all right in the jet because I pilot it."

She stilled. Why didn't that make her feel better?

Chapter 11

Realm headquarters looked like a subdivision where doctors and soccer moms lived. People like those housewife ladies on reality television. Well, except for the innocuous armed guards, patrolling Dobermans, and over-the-top security.

Brenna stretched her neck. She'd fallen asleep on the plane with her neck at an odd angle. Conn, Kane, and Moira had worked the entire trip, and Jase had piloted the plane.

She glanced at Jase when he pulled into the driveway of a single-story rancher with intricate stone detail. "Where's the tennis court?"

He grinned. "East of the main lodge."

"Ah." She stepped out of the SUV, wondering if there was a way out of this rabbit hole. Skirting the sensors planted in the ground, she headed up the brick walkway. The air swished, and she found herself cradled in a pair of hard arms. "What in the world—"

"Carrying you over the threshold." Jase climbed the several steps and pushed open the door.

"Oh." Her cheeks heated, while her heart thumped.

He set her down inside the foyer. Across the spacious living room, wall-to-wall windows showcased the Pacific during winter. Gray and dark. "You don't have any furniture," she murmured, her voice echoing.

"We should probably get some." He slipped his fingers through hers and led her around the sparsely furnished house—grand kitchen, guest room, office, bonus room she might use as an art studio, and finally, the master bedroom.

She swallowed. At least he had a bed.

He cleared his throat, passed the bed, and opened the walk-in closet. His fingers danced across a keypad by the door, and the side wall slid open to reveal steps leading down. "The tunnel leads to the underground headquarters. If we're attacked, if we're in danger, punch in 4425, and run."

Ah. Figured the headquarters would be in the mountains.

Jase shut the passageway. "Why don't you freshen up and then spend time on the office computer buying whatever furniture and art supplies you'd like. I'm going to go work out." With a soft kiss to her forehead, he turned and strode from the room.

She'd wondered how long he'd last after being cooped up in the plane for so long. With a last glance at the keypad, she wandered back through the lonely house. No personal touches had been added—besides the big bed. The refrigerator was empty, as was the pantry. A big walk-in pantry shouldn't be empty. She paused. Neither should the room have a long wall in the back without shelves.

Curiosity prodded her forward. She stepped into the small room, spreading her palms along the wall. Then she felt until her finger hit a groove. She tugged.

A door opened.

Sliding her hand inside, she tapped until finding a switch. Light instantly sparked off a myriad of weapons along two walls. Guns, knives, stars . . . some that had been banned by treaty centuries ago. The final wall held a series of photographs. Pictures of several demons, including Willa, had been tacked up in logical order.

His kill wall.

A chill swept down Brenna's spine. While she understood Jase's need for revenge, this was just creepy. How obsessed was the guy?

The doorbell rang, and she jumped about a foot. Hurriedly shutting the wall, she rushed to open the front door.

"Welcome to Oregon." The queen pushed a bushel of white tulips into Brenna's hand. "My sister cross-bred them in the lab. Smell."

"Thanks, Emma." Brenna buried her nose in the sweet scent of flowers. How odd to see Emma outside a lab. A former human, she'd worked as a geneticist until discovering the existence of the

Kurjans and going on the run. Dage had rescued her, and they'd fallen in love and mated. The queen often joked that she'd mated a vampire just to get access to their amazing laboratories and machinery.

Though she glowed whenever the king smiled at her.

Brenna glanced behind her at the empty room. "I'd bet anything I don't have a vase."

Emma laughed and tugged Brenna outside. "That's okay. Bring them to the lab, and I'll find a beaker."

Brenna sighed. "Don't tell me. You want to run tests." The queen usually wore a lab coat and had syringes in her hand.

"I do." Emma's deep blue eyes sparkled. "I'm supposed to share your results with the doctors in Ireland, but I'll keep them private if you wish." She shoved her black hair off her forehead and glanced at Brenna's sweater. "Oops. We should've grabbed you a coat. Oregon winters aren't freezing, but they do get chilly."

Brenna glanced at Emma's thin shirt. "You're not wearing a coat."

Emma eyed her shirt. "I guess I forgot." She shrugged.

They walked by manicured lawns until they reached a massive log building. Emma led her inside. "We have a rec room, conference rooms, offices, a huge gym, and several laboratories in this building. When we're not underground in the mountain, which has more of the same, then we're here." She wound past a room holding several pool tables to a pristine lab. "Have a seat on the exam table, and I'll draw blood."

Brenna followed the command.

The air shifted, becoming heavy. Dage Kayrs filled the doorway.

As kings went, Dage had presence . . . and power. Sizzling silver eyes and dark hair, the king was something to look at. He smiled and stepped inside to reach for the flowers to shove in a beaker. "Welcome to the family, Brenna."

Brenna forced a smile. Truth be told, the king had always seemed a bit scary to her. Anybody with so much power should be watched. Of course, Jase had gathered quite a bit of power, too. "Thank you."

He tugged on Emma's hair. "I told you to put a coat on before heading outside. There's a storm coming."

Emma rolled her eyes and approached Brenna, syringe in hand. "There's always a storm coming."

"Good point." The king leaned back against a granite counter as Emma took blood. "How soon will we know if the mating has improved Brenna's health?"

"A couple of hours." Emma finished drawing blood and pressed a cotton ball to the wound. "So, Brenna, the Coven Nine has been rather secretive about any witches infected with Virus-27. Do you suppose you could get me data?"

Brenna's lungs heated, and she glanced at the king. He lifted an eyebrow in a "you're on your own" expression. She sighed. "To be honest, I've been more concerned with the poisoning from the planekite than with Virus-27, since planekite is dangerous only to witches. Anybody could use the damn stuff against us if the truth got out that it's like poison to us. A weird little mineral found in Russia, and it can kill us. In comparison, while all witches are susceptible to Virus-27, we've managed to avoid exposure for the most part."

"I know, but if the virus goes airborne, there is no avoiding it." Emma focused on Brenna.

"The Nine has chosen to keep our data private, as you know." A choice Brenna disagreed with. The virus was created by an evil vampire race to infect the chromosomal pairs of vampire mates in such a way that the mate became human again . . . maybe. The chromosomes unraveled and might keep going. Any formerly human vampire mate—or any witch—was susceptible to the virus because the bug attacked the twenty-seventh chromosomal pair. Vampires, Kurjans, and demons were all safe from the virus because they had more than thirty chromosomal pairs. Kurjan mates were susceptible to the illness, too, but the Kurjans didn't seem to care. "I'm sorry about the secrecy."

Emma huffed. "Can you tell me anything?"

"The virus progresses in witches the same as in vampire mates, and we're no closer to a cure than you are." Which was pretty much all the information there was, frankly. Brenna hopped off the table.

Dage stepped to the side. "Where's Jase?"

"Working out." Brenna edged toward the door.

"That's a new one," the king muttered. He sighed. "The demons have increased the bounty on your head by another five billion—if you're taken by the winter solstice. Apparently they believe the Pagurus myth."

Brenna stopped. "You know about the comet?"

"Sure. There may be something to it, maybe not." He shrugged and focused on Emma. "Why does everyone always forget I'm the king?"

Emma snorted. "You wish."

Their easy banter made Brenna's chest hurt. Did she have a chance of finding such closeness with Jase? The image of his kill wall wavered through her mind.

Probably not.

Jase's shoulders strained as he lifted himself arm-over-arm up the thin rope. It was good to be home in his own gym. Well, if one could call the revamped metal shop a gym. Rough and dirty, the area suited him well.

Weapons lined one wall, and fighting dummies perched in front of them.

Swinging his legs up, he used his ankles to grab the rope, hanging upside down. With a quick twist of his torso, he threw the metal disk across the room and decapitated two of the dummies.

"Now, that's illegal," a low voice rumbled from the doorway.

Jase turned his head to find two of his brothers inside his gym. "So turn me in." He crawled down the rope headfirst until reaching the dirt floor. A quick flip and he faced his brothers. "What?"

Conn and Talen stood shoulder to shoulder in leather jackets—both soldiers, both deadly.

"The Degoller Star has been banned for three centuries. Any particular reason you're training with forbidden weaponry?" Talen asked calmly, his golden gaze on the headless mannequins. He held another jacket by the collar.

Jase shrugged. "The very reason the Degoller has been banned is why I want to use it." Beheading killed all immortals, which was why they'd agreed years ago to ban the disk that so easily cut off their heads if thrown correctly. "Are you going to rat me out to Dage?"

Conn snorted. "Talen is the strategic leader of the Realm, and I'm the highest ranked soldier. What makes you think we need

Dage to arrest your ass?" The tone remained congenial, but irritation shone through his green eyes.

Interesting. Had two of his older brothers decided to stop tiptoeing around him? "So try it."

Conn stepped forward, and Talen grabbed his shoulder.

Talen shook his head. "We want to go for a drink and celebrate your mating."

Jase paused. "Where?"

"Biker bar—a couple of counties over. We could take the new motorcycles." A dimple flashed in Talen's cheek. "That is, if you think you can keep up." He threw the leather jacket at Jase. "Dage, Kane, and Max are all tied up with business. The three of us are the fun ones, anyway."

Part of him wanted to refuse. Hanging with his brothers, acting like everything was all right, was the second-to-the-last thing he wanted to do. The first thing was hurting them. If he refused, he would. Sure, they'd be pissed. That he could handle, but disappointing everyone all the time churned his gut. He caught the jacket midair. "All right. Let's see the new bikes."

The two-hour ride took approximately forty minutes at the speed they traveled. The wind, the air, the speed all rushed through Jase, making him feel alive. He'd forgotten how that felt. Finally arriving at the hole-in-the-wall bar, they stomped inside and commandeered a table in the back. Conn ordered four bottles of silver tequila, which the waitress delivered before pouring shot glasses of the shimmering liquid.

Jase lifted an eyebrow. "I take it we're getting drunk."

Talen held up his glass. "You take it right."

They all followed suit. Conn cleared his throat. "To pretty Brenna Dunne. We'll kill all the demons before we let them take her."

Jase took his shot. The liquor burned down his throat to slam into his gut, and a tight knot inside him started to unravel. His brothers would protect Brenna. He slapped his glass down. "Ready for round two?"

"I'm on round three," Talen said, sputtering.

Several bottles later, the room started to tilt. Jase downed another shot. "We *are* the fun ones."

"I know, right?" Conn wove on his seat. "Dage is all serious with the king-shit, and Kane, well . . . he's Kane."

Talen nodded in slow motion. "Yeah. Kane is Kane."

"Aptly put." Conn leaned forward and knocked his glass on the wooden floor. "Oops. But I gotta say, I like his mate."

Talen snorted. "Amber's a pistol. Exactly what Kane needed."

"Yeah. A vegan." Conn started laughing. "A vegan."

Jase snorted. "I mated a witch."

"Me, too." Conn laughed harder.

"Mine was human," Talen said softly, losing his smile.

Jase caught his breath. Talen's mate had been infected with Virus-27 nearly twenty years ago. "How is Cara?"

Talen shrugged. "The virus is slow-moving, but it's still moving. It could take decades to finally run its course, whatever that may be. She's weaker lately and hides it, but not well."

"She's a strong woman. She'd have to be . . . to give birth to Garrett." Jase forced a grin. Garrett Kayrs was everything Jase used to be. Tough, fun, charismatic. At nineteen years old, the kid had the world at his fingertips.

"I know. We just need to cure the damn bug." Talen exhaled slowly.

"Witches are susceptible to the virus, too," Conn said, his gaze on his shot glass.

"Yes." Jase motioned for the waitress to bring another bottle. "Yet very few witches have been infected."

"For now." Talen tipped his glass, gaze on the swirling liquid. "Kane thinks the damn virus will go airborne at some point. Maybe."

"No. Kane will find a cure before that happens." Jase ignored a tendril of doubt. His brother was a genius, but not all bugs could be killed.

Conn wove to his feet. "I'm headed to the can, and then I want to go home and check on my witch." He stumbled around several tables toward the restroom.

Talen coughed. "We should be sober in about fifteen minutes."

Make that an hour. They'd drunk more bottles than Jase could count. His brother's face blurred. "Maybe we should walk a bit before riding."

"Good plan." Talen nodded and shoved away from the table, sending it spiraling.

Jase grabbed the bottle before it could fly. "Hmph."

"Keep it the fuck down over there," someone bellowed.

Jase tilted his head toward his brother, as Talen narrowed his gaze. "We didn't just hear that, did we?" Talen asked.

"Sure did, asshole. Now keep it down before I kick your ass," the guy yelled.

Jase turned to spot four guys at the bar. Hulking and drunk, they stared. "I think they wanna fight," Jase murmured.

Talen stood, swaying slightly. "Humans?"

Jase tried to focus. "Shifters. Wolf would be my bet."

"Even better," Talen muttered. "Hey, asshole. My five-foot-nuthin' wife could kick your ass." He snorted and mock-whispered to Jase, "She probably could, too. I've been training her."

The wolf lunged across two tables and tackled Talen into the wall.

Jase saw red. Fists swinging, he met two of the charging shifters more than halfway. He kicked one guy in the throat, throwing him across the bar. Glass shattered, and tables broke. Two sidesteps and he had the other guy in a headlock. He tightened just enough to cut off the guy's air.

The final wolf tried to shake him off his friend.

Jase held tight, waiting until the guy dropped unconscious to the floor before facing the remaining wolf. A quick glance toward the corner showed Talen knocking his attacker to the floor, waiting patiently for the guy to stand, and then beating him down again. A moronic smile lit Talen's face.

A right cross to Jase's jaw jerked his attention to the last shifter. He hissed, his fangs dropping.

The shifter's eyes widened. "Vampire." Dodging left and then right, he ran behind the bar.

Jase frowned. "You can't run." Damn it. He hurdled the bar and followed the guy down a narrow hallway to a flight of stairs leading down. He made it three steps down and into darkness.

Heat and panic rushed through him. His ears rang. A low growl rumbled up from his gut. Slowly, his hands shaking, he backed up the steps. Reaching the hallway, he took a deep breath and slammed the door. Sweat rolled down his back.

Smoothing his face, he turned and ran into his brother. The sympathy on Talen's face almost broke him.

Talen smacked him on the shoulder. "Let's go before they call the cops."

Swallowing, Jase nodded and followed him back into the bar.

Conn emerged from the restroom and glanced around the demolished room. "What'd I miss?"

Chapter 12

Alone in the big bed, Brenna pushed her glasses up her nose as she read the latest report from the Coven Nine regarding witches misusing magic. The problem seemed to be getting worse. She sighed and glanced around the empty bedroom as dawn slipped under the shades. While she'd never really thought about mating, if she had, this wouldn't have been her dream.

For several hours, she'd tried to sleep. Finally, she'd given up and decided to get some work done.

The front door swished, and something fell inside.

She stiffened.

A low, male curse echoed before lumbering steps came down the hallway. Jase staggered into the bedroom.

"Good lord," she murmured.

His clothes were ripped, and blood dotted his shirt. A purple bruise spread under his right eye. "Hi."

"Hi." She frowned. "Who hit you?"

"Got in a bar fight with a bunch of shifters." He flashed rare dimples and awkwardly kicked off his boots. Then he swayed. "Don't worry—nobody died."

"Good to know." She set down the reports. "Do you need help?"

He sagged against the wall. "I need more help than is possible." His lips turned down. "We stopped at several bars on the way home, or I'd be sober by now." Inching forward, he fell to his knees by the bed. "You're so pretty, Bren."

"You're drunk." She slid from the bed and grasped under his arms. "Let's get you cleaned up."

He stood, throwing an arm around her shoulders. "Sometimes I feel like I'll never be clean." Stumbling into the bathroom, he allowed her to pull his shirt off. "You're pretty."

"So you said." Jase was an affectionate drunk. Brenna smiled, warmth spreading through her. What in the world was she going to do with him? "Um, take off your jeans."

His eyes darkened. "We're mated. You take them off." A hiccup took the edge off the order.

Aye, they were mated, and he needed help. She'd always been a nurturer, and being able to assist him filled her with pleasure. Even so, her hands shook as she unsnapped his jeans and shoved off his clothes. A dark purple bruise cut into his muscular thigh. "What happened?" she asked, running her fingers along the wound.

"Training yesterday. I fell." He closed his eyes and hummed. "You have great hands."

"Thank you." She reached in and flipped on the shower faucet. Steam quickly rose. "Get in." She nudged him in the back.

He slipped inside, groaning as steam swallowed him.

The doorbell rang. What in the world? She turned and padded through the house to open the door. Moira and Emma stood on the front porch, Moira in training gear and Emma in sweats. "It's a little early." Brenna motioned them toward the empty living room.

Moira swept inside. "I know. We don't sleep much around here, especially when drunk vampires pass out on our floors."

Emma tapped a manila file. "I was in the lab."

As usual, apparently. Dread filled Brenna. She already knew the lab results. "Did Dage get drunk, too?"

"No. He spent all night negotiating a treaty between two shifter clans out of Iceland." Emma pursed her lips. "There's nowhere to sit."

"Just tell me." Brenna sighed, her gaze on Moira as her big sister tried to look stoic.

"There's no change in your blood." Emma handed the file to Brenna. "Your results are the same as the ones sent over from your doctors. The mating hasn't slowed down the poison in your system."

Moira grabbed her arm. "You just mated and need to give the cure time."

"I agree," Brenna lied and forced a smile for her sister. "I'm feeling better even if the blood results don't show that."

"Bollocks." Moira pushed her. "Don't placate me, you brat."

"You're the brat, *Dailtín.*" Brenna pushed back.

"Ladies"—Emma rolled her eyes—"knock it off and grow up."

Moira snorted. "Look who's talking. You called your sister a jackass the other night."

The queen sniffed. "Cara was cheating at poker. She was being a jackass."

"Using empathic abilities isn't cheating," Moira countered.

"You're always on her side," Emma huffed.

Brenna grinned. "You two sound just like sisters."

Emma slipped an arm through Brenna's. "We mated Kayrs men. We need a sisterhood—blood or not."

Jase loped into the room, a towel loosely tied at his waist. He stopped cold at the gathering.

Brenna shoved down desire. A chest like that should never be hidden behind cotton. "Feel better?"

"I'm fine." A shadow lined his jaw. Combined with the purple bruise, he looked like a rogue searching for a rumble.

A firm knock echoed on the door. Emma glanced at Moira. "Yours or mine?"

"Mine's passed out on the floor," Moira said, yanking open the door to reveal Dage. "Told you."

The king appeared . . . ruffled. His eyes shone a dark silver, and his dark hair had escaped the band he always tied it in. Tension emanated from him so heavily the oxygen in the room diminished. His gaze met Jase's.

Jase took a step back. His face hardened to blank granite. "What?"

The king didn't move. "The Kurjans have our nephew."

After being briefed by Dage, Jase stood in the armory and slammed a clip into his gun, his mind swirling. Not the Kurjans. An evil vampire race, they had white faces and a serious aversion to the sun. They'd also created Virus-27, a strong entry into germ warfare.

Now they had Garrett, the fun-loving kid he'd helped to raise. While he understood the plan, he couldn't figure out why they needed a damn plan. "What the fuck happened?"

Talen shook his head, tightening his bulletproof vest. "He and two of his buddies snuck out and partied in town all night. I don't know if the Kurjans happened upon them, or if it was a calculated move."

"It was a calculated move." Jase grabbed two more knives. "Makes sense. Everyone knows our headquarters is here . . . figures the kids would head to town at some point."

Talen staggered and slapped a palm against the wall. "I knew," he whispered. "I knew they were sneaking out and having fun, but they're nineteen and smart." Guilt washed down his face. "I've trained my son since he was old enough to walk, but he's not ready for this."

Nausea shot through Jase's gut. He grabbed his brother's arm. The other two kids had been found beaten and unconscious in an alley. Only Garrett had been taken. "We'll get him back. Tonight." If they didn't, Garrett would never be the same. "I swear to God. We'll get him."

"You understand what the Kurjans want, right?" Talen asked.

"Yeah." Jase steeled his shoulders. "They want Janie." Janie was Talen's adopted daughter, the key to the future for all immortal species. In fact, the current war had begun as the Kurjans and vampires fought to get to her first. As Garrett's older sister, she'd probably give up her life in an instant to save him.

"Janie isn't the prize—this time." Kane charged into the room, already suited up. "They want Brenna."

Jase paused. "Excuse me?"

Kane grabbed another gun to add to his impressive arsenal. "The Kurjans want your mate before the damn winter solstice."

What the hell was it with Brenna and the solstice? Jase growled. "The demons and the Kurjans seriously believe that nonsense?"

"Isn't nonsense." Kane shook his head. "It's quantum physics, string theory, and one incredibly powerful witch."

"But she's not." Jase ran a rough hand through his hair. "Not yet. She's barely strong enough to pass for human right now."

"I know. But now that she has mated, when the comet gets

closer, I'm hoping she'll be able to harness incredible power." Kane rubbed his chin. "If your mating finally takes hold."

Jase lifted his head, focusing on his brother. "What exactly do you want from her?"

Kane's eyes swirled black through the maroon. "I'm hoping she can cure the virus. Somehow untangle it from the chromosomes of the victims."

Jase shook his head like a dog with a face full of water. "You're telling me that this solstice crap is real? Not just another stupid witch myth?"

"It's real." The smartest, most scientific man on the planet nodded. "Very real."

Well, shit. "Does she know the full truth?"

Kane shrugged. "I doubt it. Her family and the Coven Nine have done nothing but protect her from being different. I'm sure they would've started preparing her if she hadn't gotten so ill."

"So they don't think she'll be able to harness the power?" When had things gotten so damn unsteady?

"No." Kane eyed his watch. "I spoke with Viv earlier, and they think Brenna's pretty much done for. No power, no hope of recovery." He glanced up, his gaze sympathetic. "I'd like to keep that from you, but that's not what we do."

"So why let me take her?" Jase frowned. Not that they could've stopped him. "If they think she's dying, why let me bring her here?" Reality slapped him in the face. The fucking bastards. "It's temporary. They only let me take her until after the solstice."

Kane nodded. "That's my guess. She's in too much danger in Ireland—not only from her people, but from demons. This way, we keep her safe, and then they'll demand she come home after the holidays."

So she could die among her own people. Fury rippled through Jase. "She's not dying, damn it."

"Nobody is dying," Talen said grimly, heading for the door. "Enough talk. Let's go."

Jase nodded, tucking one more knife in his vest. He followed his brother into the hallway, his breath catching at the agony on Cara's face. The tiny blond woman stood next to Moira and Brenna in the hallway, looking even more pale and fragile than usual. Next to the hulking Talen, she looked downright miniature.

Talen placed his hand on her shoulder and lowered his face to within an inch of hers. "I'll bring him back, mate. You have my word."

She lifted her chin, blue eyes flashing. "Just don't get shot."

Talen grinned. "I promise."

Brenna hurried forward, her gaze wary. "Apparently I'm in great demand."

Jase steeled himself for the request.

It came in the form of a statement. "They want me . . . so I go." She pushed her glasses up her nose. "I can still shoot a gun damn well."

"I know." His heart warmed at her bravery and then chilled at the thought of losing her. "You're part of Plan B, little witch."

She lifted both eyebrows. "Plan B?"

"Yes. The meet and exchange is in three hours. We're storming their location first." Jase fought the urge to hug her, considering the hardware he'd tucked into his combat gear. "If that fails, we'll try a bait and switch." But Plan A wouldn't fail, because no way in hell would he allow Brenna to put herself in danger.

She frowned. "How do you know where Garrett is?"

Talen turned around. "After Jase was taken, we plugged every-one with trackers. We've tracked him."

The Kurjans weren't stupid. Jase nodded. "The trackers are still live, so the Kurjans haven't figured it out. They will."

Moira cocked a laser gun to tuck in a pants pocket. "Let's go." She turned and headed outside to the waiting helicopters.

Brenna frowned. "Moira gets to go."

Jase gave in to temptation and dropped a kiss on the witch's nose. "Moira's trained for combat . . . and is at full strength. You get your strength back? You can come." Maybe. Well, probably not. His time as a POW would more than likely keep him from allowing her to fight, but she didn't need to know that right now.

"Hmmm." She grabbed his face and tugged him down for a soft kiss on the lips. "Be safe, Jase."

His heart lurched. He gave a short nod, his voice gone. When she released him, he turned and ran into the early morning.

Time to fight.

Chapter 13

Garrett Kayrs stretched his neck and tried to focus his eyes. What-ever they'd shot into his veins had taken hold hard. His dad was going to kick his ass to hell and back for this one. He'd fought as hard as he could, only surrendering when the Kurjans offered to let his friends live if he allowed them to take him. Considering the vampires had been seriously outmanned, he hadn't had a choice.

A guy had to save his friends.

As the world swam into clarity, he sat up on a cell floor. It was carpeted?

An outside door opened, and a figure stalked closer to the bars. A Kurjan stood, white-faced, green-eyed. Weird. Didn't Kurjans have purple or red eyes? Shoving to his feet, Garrett allowed the room to settle. "So you're a green-eyed bastard, huh? There proba-bly aren't many of you."

The Kurjan lifted one dark eyebrow, amusement curving his red lips. He had to be in his early thirties. "You don't know who I am?"

Sure. Garrett knew exactly who the asshole was. "Nope. Let me guess. Kermit the Kurjan?"

"Funny. Your sister has a similar sense of humor."

Thought so. Kalin, the Kurjan butcher, stood close enough to touch. The guy had been communicating with his sister, Janie, in a dreamworld most of her life. If he'd just get closer to the bars, Garrett could reach through and grab his neck. He smiled. "Now that's weird. I don't have a sister."

Kalin rubbed his chin. "You look like your father."

"I can't make a similar comparison—considering my father wasted yours." Decades ago, Talen and the Kurjan had fought over Garrett's mother. Cara. The Kurjan lost.

"I plan to even that score." Kalin flashed sharp fangs. "Now that we've admitted we know each other, tell me, have you forgotten I saved your sister's life?"

Garrett stepped closer to the bars. The world kept tilting. "My sister wouldn't have been in danger had you not attacked our headquarters with a band of werewolves."

"True." Color washed through Kalin's face. For a moment, he looked human. "Ah. Speaking of Janie."

Everything inside Garrett stilled. "Excuse me?"

"Your sister is calling me."

Was the guy a nut-job or what? "As far as I can tell, you're not asleep, asshole."

Kalin chuckled, an odd purple swirling within the green of his eyes. "Don't need to be. Your sister has gained considerable power through the years and no longer needs to be asleep to communicate. I believe she, ah, meditates."

"Bullshit." Damn Kurjans always lied.

Kalin tipped his head. "Oh my. She hasn't told you. Not only can we meet in her odd little dreamworld while fully awake, she can no longer keep me out. If she's open and not shielding, I'm invited."

The fucking asshole was trying to mess with his head. Garrett forced a laugh and tried to ignore the fact that the room was still wavering. "Nice little fantasy world you've got there."

"Boy, she's in every fantasy I have." Kalin grabbed the bars. "Her blood tastes like honeyed sunshine, and since I've tasted, I can visit any time I wish. Mentally, of course."

Bile rose in Garrett's throat. No way had this guy bitten his sister. No way. "I'm going to kill you slowly."

"Sounds like a date." Kalin leaned in. "But I'm busy right now. We're supposed to exchange you for the witch in three hours."

"Witch? You want Moira?"

"No. The other one."

Drawing a bored expression, Garrett slid back his right foot. "Why?"

"She's powerful, and we want her," Kalin said, an odd light entering his eyes.

Garrett lunged, reaching through the bars to grab the Kurjan's neck. Kalin kicked between the bars, nailing him in the knee. Garrett went down and just as quickly flew back up.

Kalin stepped back, smiling. "You're quick."

His knee pounded with pain, echoing up his thigh. Garrett snarled. "Quick enough. How about you let me out of here, and we see how quick you are?"

Kalin clicked his tongue. "As tempting as that is, I'm not ready to kill you. Yet."

Garrett studied the soldier. He was almost seven feet tall, and broad. The medals on his chest showed a life of combat. He'd be tough to kill. "There's no way my people will hand over a mate to you—not even for me."

"I'm aware of that fact." Kalin clasped his hands at his back.

Garrett mentally shoved the drugs through his blood faster, speeding up his heart rate. He needed balance. "So, what's your plan? Big trap?"

The purple disappeared from the shimmering green. "Oh, this was all about you, Garrett. The big trap is just a bonus."

"Me?" Garrett lifted his chin.

"Sure. You're a means to an end, boy."

Ah. The Kurjan didn't want a witch—he wanted Janie. Garrett's smile came naturally as he shook his head. "You're a moron. No way will my father let Janie sacrifice herself for me."

"Considering Janie is of age—twenty-four, I believe—that decision is up to her, now isn't it?"

"No." The guy really didn't understand family, did he? Garrett stepped up to the bars again. "The second I was taken, I guarantee an entire squad of guards was assigned to my sister. She won't be able to take one step in your direction."

Kalin drew a wicked knife from his back pocket. "You willing to die for your sister, young Kayrs?"

Garrett lowered his chin and allowed his fangs to drop. "In a heartbeat."

"How about kill for her?"

"Gladly. Unlock the bars, and I'll prove it to you."

Kalin ran the blade along his hand. "Have you killed before?"

Garret eyed the weapon. An inch or two closer, and he could grab it. "Yes."

"Liar," Kalin said softly. "At your age, I'd killed more men than you know."

"Women," Garrett countered just as softly. "You hunt and kill women just like a waste-of-human serial killer." At Kalin's startled look, he flashed a knowing smile. "We know all about you, and so does Janie."

Kalin's upper lip twisted.

Ah. That hurt, huh? Garrett grinned. "You're a dead man, Kurjan."

"Maybe." Kalin headed for the door. "But at least I'm not bait." He disappeared from sight.

Why hadn't the world exploded? If the trade was in three hours, surely they'd tracked him. Garrett settled his stance, ready to fight when they arrived. Any moment now.

The two helicopters flew low enough to avoid radar and dropped into a vacant field three blocks from the metal building set into the industrial park.

Jase jumped to the ground, shoving his earpiece more securely into his ear.

Talen's voice came through loud and clear. "Three teams. One— take the front entrance. Two—take the back. Three—scale the fishing headquarters to the east, approach the target via rooftops. It's a two-story building—set up for offices on level two and an old iron business on level one. Has been vacant for over a decade. Everyone wait for the go order."

Jase tucked his rifle along his back and followed Conn toward the east building. Moira and a squad waited to protect the helicopter. Talen had stuck Conn and Kane on Jase duty, while he took a team, and Max, Dage's bodyguard, flanked the king. There was a time Jase would've taken and led the third team. Not today, apparently.

He easily climbed up the rickety fire escape and reached the roof. Bending low, he ran along rooftops, jumping several yards from building to building, finally reaching the one adjacent to the

Kurjan encampment. A quick study showed an innocuous metal building with darkened windows. He gulped air. It would be seriously dark inside if the lights went out. So he tapped his ear communicator as Conn and Kane took position. "Team three in position."

The other teams checked in.

"Go," Talen ordered.

Jase jumped the distance to the metal building, hitting and rolling to his feet. Staying low, he ran across the slippery metal to the locked door. "Fire in the hole." He fired several shots into the lock and kicked the door open.

Conn dashed inside, weapon out. Jase followed, with Kane protecting his back as they ran down a series of metal stairs. He breathed in relief when Conn kicked the door to the second floor. The stairwell was too tight.

Conn swept left, Jase right, and Kane stayed low through a hallway littered with garbage, crumbled drywall, and exposed rebar.

Windows cut into the walls up high, while closed doors lined the hallway. One by one, they swept the abandoned rooms. Gunfire echoed from the first floor in short bursts. They'd cleared the fifth room when a glint caught Jase's eye.

He held up his hand for all to stop. As he dropped to his haunches, his gaze traveled the tripwire to the explosive hidden by some boards. His breath caught, and he slowed his heartbeat. Drawing wire cutters from his boot, he leaned forward and cut the wire. A second wire had been strung a foot away. He tilted his head so his brothers saw and then inched forward to dismantle that wire, as well.

They needed to step lightly.

His earpiece buzzed. "Any sighting?" Talen asked, gunfire peppering in the background.

"Negative for team three," Conn said.

"Negative for team one, but we found a stairwell," Dage said. "We're heading down now."

Jase stretched to his full height, turning a doorknob to enter a room. A battered desk sat in the middle, and a closed door was in the wall. The hair on the back of his neck rose. The first closet they'd seen—if it was a closet. He and Talen settled into position, guns trained on the door as Conn inched along the wall and yanked it open. A long, dark stairwell led down. A hidden stairwell?

Panic heated Jase's breath.

"Cover me," Conn whispered as he produced a flashlight and headed down. Talen stepped into the stairwell, gun pointing down. Jase turned to cover the hallway. His mind spun, and his gut clenched. His brother was walking down into hell. Sweat rolled down Jase's back.

Damn panic attacks.

A tortured moan filtered across the hallway from a closed room. Garrett! Jase's head jerked up. His legs leapt into motion before his brain could bellow a caution.

"Wait—" Talen yelled, leaping for him.

Jase's foot hit a tripwire, and a loud *click* echoed. Talen caught his shoulders and threw him just as the device detonated.

Then the world slowed.

Jase flew through the air, all sound disappearing until he smashed into the block wall. With the rush of a sonic shriek, sound pierced his ears. Pain crumpled his bones. He slid to the floor, his vision going black. The gun clunked next to him. A body landed solidly on his legs.

God. Talen. Jase shook his head, his body screaming. His vision returned, tinged with red. Smoke filled the air along with an odd buzzing. Or maybe that was in his head. He tried to focus, but the hallway took on a surreal tint. Using his good hand, he rolled his brother over.

Talen coughed, blood dribbling out of his mouth.

Thank God. He was alive. This was Jase's fault. He'd forgotten all his training and had almost gotten his brother killed. Jase shook him and grabbed his vest. "Get up."

Three Kurjans ran out of the room at the end, hissing through yellow fangs. Shit. Jase dropped his brother and crawled over him as a shield. The closest Kurjan pointed a green gun and fired.

Pain ripped into Jase's chest, and he flew back into the center of the hallway. At least a couple of the bullets had missed the vest, damn it. Blood bubbled up from his chest, and he coughed it out. Blades of damage ripped into his lungs.

Conn stormed out of the room, bullets spraying.

Talen shoved up, gun out and firing.

Jase grabbed his pistol, aimed in the general direction of the Kurjans, and fired.

Dizziness caught him. He swayed and fell back, sparks detonating behind his eyes as his head hit the floor. Then, he was out.

Jase awoke to find himself sandwiched between Talen and Conn in the back of the helicopter as it descended through a blowing rainstorm. Dusk had fallen. Man, they'd been at the warehouse all day. He hoped they'd found Garrett.

Jase shook his head. "Status?" he croaked.

Talen didn't open his eyes, and a sense of healing came from him. Good. He was repairing the damage Jase had caused.

Conn kept his gaze out the window. "Garrett wasn't there. His tracker led to the basement, but it was hidden in some rock. We have four injured, two dead."

Damn it. Two bullets were still burrowed deep in Jase's upper chest. He'd lost the ability to push them out mentally, the same way he'd lost the ability to alter the elements. Those gifts took mental concentration, and for some reason, he couldn't focus long enough to make it happen. "It was a trap."

"A good one," Conn muttered.

Guilt pierced sharper than the bullets. Jase nodded. "I know."

The helicopter set down.

Dage looked over his shoulder. "Report to the infirmary."

Jase slid from the helicopter. "I'm fine. Going home." Without a backward glance, he fought the pain and jogged through the storm. Lightning flashed, not nearly as hot as the piercing gazes from his brothers.

They should've yelled at him. Shit. They should've beat the hell out of him. His actions had almost killed Talen.

He didn't belong there anymore. It was time to find the demons and end this.

First he had to get the bullets out of his flesh.

Chapter 14

Brenna stirred the stew on the stove. She'd ordered groceries, and a very nice vampire had delivered them. Moira had called to say they hadn't found Garrett. She'd also mentioned Jase had been injured.

As a vampire, he'd probably be healed before he arrived home. So, Brenna had made dinner. By the time he showed up, they'd have a late meal. Though she'd reached out to every contact she had in the immortal world, nobody had a line on Garrett. Yet. But she was still waiting to hear from a couple, so maybe she'd have good news for him.

A thump echoed on the front porch. Brenna tilted her head. Another thump. Setting down the spoon, she hurried to open the door.

Jase fell inside.

Brenna gasped and reached for him, almost hitting her knees as she took his weight. He grabbed the wall for support and left a bloody handprint. Bruises and burns marred his face and exposed skin.

Panic shoved Brenna into motion. "You need a doctor."

"No." Half-leaning and half-tugging her along, he maneuvered them into the kitchen, where he dropped into a chair. "There's a medical kit in the cupboard by the fridge."

A medical kit? Was he freakin' crazy? Her heart pounding so

hard her ribs hurt, she stumbled to the counter and yanked out the metal box. "I'm not a doctor."

"I know." Groaning, he tried to unhinge his vest.

She placed the box on the table and slapped his hands. "Let me." Ignoring his wince of pain, she pulled the Velcro free.

He exhaled sharply when she slid the vest over his head. Wounds dotted his upper chest—two bullet holes.

She leaned closer, and the scent of smoke and gunpowder assaulted her nose. "The bullets are still in?" That wasn't possible.

"Yes." Closing his eyes, he reached for the bottom of his tattered shirt and gasped in pain. "My healing abilities haven't returned completely."

Her breath caught. "Oh." After years of being free? What the damn demons must've done to him. Then she grabbed his hands and stopped him. "Hold on." Reaching for a junk drawer, she retrieved scissors and cut his shirt free. Stepping back, she stared.

Purple, red, and yellow bruises covered his torso along with plenty of blood still sliding from the bullet wounds. "What in the world?"

"Explosive." Jase tipped back his head. "I don't suppose you'd mind taking out the bullets?"

Bile surged from her stomach. "Why didn't you go to the infirmary?"

"Why didn't you tell your family you were dying?"

Good point. "I can get the bullets." Probably. She eyed the sink in case she needed to puke. Her hands trembled, so she shook them out. Grabbing a scalpel, she peered closer at his injury. "Take a deep breath and hold it."

He sucked in air, his eyes remaining closed.

She sliced a bigger opening in his wound.

He didn't even twitch.

Okay. That had to have hurt. She clasped tweezers and slipped them into the hole. Blood spurted. Searching, she caught on something. Angling the metal closer, she pinched and tugged out a green bullet. His flesh made a squishy sound as the projectile was removed.

She swallowed several times and released the bullet onto the table. Then she went for the second wound. "Did you know that my people invented the lasers that turn into metal bullets upon hitting flesh?"

"Yes. Anything that includes altering matter to another state is usually from you crazy witches." His lower lip tipped on the last.

She found the other bullet and removed it. "You're just jealous."

"Very." He grimaced.

"Do I, ah, need to stitch you up?"

"No." He lifted his head, desperation and anger sizzling in his eyes. "I can heal the holes now that the bullets are out."

Brenna nodded and cleaned up the mess, turning to face him.

He sprawled in the chair, wounded and hurt. She shook her head. "What happened?"

"I forgot all my training and almost got my brother killed," Jase whispered.

"Is he all right?" It didn't really matter which brother, so she didn't ask.

"Yes."

"Then it's over." She reached for him. "Let's get you cleaned up so you stop bleeding all over this too-perfect house."

He staggered up, and she helped him to the shower, removing his boots and pants.

He leaned against the wall. "Weren't we just here?"

She turned on the steam. They had been, and she was in danger of getting her heart demolished by the need to save him. The silly, feminine urge to rescue. The fact that she recognized the problem didn't mean her heart would protect itself. "Get in the shower."

He slipped into the steam. Almost instantly, two broad hands yanked her under the spray.

"Hey—"

"You're bloody." Jase angled his body to protect her face from the hot water.

She glanced down at her hands. Blood had already crusted in her nails. His blood.

" 'Twas my first surgery." The smile she tried to force trembled on her lips. Her stomach lurched.

"Easy now," Jase murmured, turning and holding her hands under the stream. "You did a good job, Brenna Dunne."

"Another skill for my résumé." The fatal lilt of her voice echoed through the steam.

Jase cupped her chin, lifting her face and removing her fogging glasses. "I'm not going to let you die."

The world blurred to heated steam and wet male.

"You should save yourself first." She allowed him to turn her hands palms-up to wash away his blood. "Please." The plea made her wince.

He stilled, and tugged her hands to his chest. "Why?"

Her gaze met his. Tears pricked the back of her eyes. "I want a chance. I deserve one."

His eyes filled. "I know."

"So give me one." Maybe, just maybe, they could save each other and not be so alone in this damn world.

He studied her until she'd figured all her secrets had been delved into. Even so, turmoil chased across his face. Giving a short nod, he brushed wet hair away from her forehead. "All right."

Her heart leapt. "All right?"

He shrugged. "All I can do is try. Whatever the hell that means." For her. He was going to try for her. "I'll help."

"I know." A thumb under her chin angled her face for his kiss. A soft brush of his lips against hers.

Hope and desire spiraled through her abdomen. She ran her finger over a bruise lining his jaw and opened her mouth.

He slid inside, drugging her with his taste. Male and spice. Pleasure and ache whispered through her—from him. They'd mated, and his feelings poured into her.

The vampire held back— and always had. The tight rein he kept on his emotions, on his passion, gave her pause. Temptation to unlock him, to free him, warred with self-preservation. For now, she kissed him back, dropping her emotional shields.

He groaned low and took the kiss deeper.

Heat and steam surrounded her. She flattened her hands against the bruised ridges on his abdomen, keeping her hold light. Even wounded, Jase lit her on fire. With a slow stretch, she coasted right into the flames.

His hands manacled her hips. Before she could protest, he lifted her.

She stiffened, breaking her mouth loose. "You're hurt."

"I'm not that hurt." With a powerful thrust, he embedded himself balls-deep in her.

Pain and pleasure ripped through her. She arched her back, her mouth opening. His weight pressed her into the stone tiles, his body as hard as the wall.

The billowing steam wrapped her in safety, stealing her thoughts. For the moment, she could only feel.

Hot male, chilled tiles, throbbing cock.

She rested her head back, sliding her palms up to his shoulders. The bullet holes had closed, and relief fluttered her eyelids. The man could still heal himself. 'Twas a promising start.

His head dropped to her neck, where he nipped and sucked. The pull zinged right down to her sex. She secured her ankles at the small of his back, holding tight.

His hands flexed, then slid around to where he penetrated her. One thumb brushed her clit.

It was too much. She stiffened. "No—"

"Yes." He did it again. Then he tugged.

She reared back, shocks of pleasure bombarding her, seeking his darkened gaze. Needing to see him. Reality and fantasy all whirled away, narrowing the moment to this man and this time. Nothing else mattered except the way he held her, the way he took her. All-encompassing until she was complete.

His muscles undulated as he kept them both still. Green darkened the copper in his eyes to midnight. "Brenna."

Flutters of heat coursed through her skin. The way he said her name—as if it was his alone. As if she were his.

Slowly, he slid out and then back in, torturing them both. Then again. She clenched around him, her thighs trembling.

Sharp fangs dropped low. She groaned in response and tilted her head, exposing her neck.

The sharp points cut deep before she could blink. A climax tried to take hold, tried to bear down on her. She fought it, wanting the closeness to remain. Biting her lip, she tried to hold back, but the flames kept building higher. Higher, hotter, and faster.

Jase pounded harder, holding her in place, drinking her blood.

His tongue lashed the wound, closing it. "Now, Brenna."

The shower sheeted white through the fog. She cried out, the orgasm rippling through her. Riding the waves, she dropped to his chest, biting his pec.

He growled and ground against her.

They came back to reality together. He set her on her feet, tipping back her head. "I'd do anything for you, Bren." Softly, gently, he kissed her with so much hope, tears pricked her eyes.

Jase kept his body perfectly still in defense against the need to fidget. His bulk dwarfed the flowered chair, and he felt like an overgrown dumbass in the feminine office. He'd never ventured into any of the private offices in the main lodge that weren't commandeered by his family. This was not what he meant when he'd told Brenna he'd try.

Lily Sotheby smiled and settled her skirts around her petite body. Well over three centuries old, the blond prophet had sparkling blue eyes, frighteningly delicate features, and a wicked sense of humor. As one of the three Realm prophets, she was tasked with bringing hope and faith to their people.

Who the fuck knew she was also a shrink?

She took a sip of something raspberry-smelling from a dainty teacup. "So, you're going crazy?"

Jase frowned. "Um, no?"

"Then why are you here?"

His meddling mate had made him an appointment. "Apparently I need help of the psychological type."

"Why?" Lily lifted a delicate eyebrow.

"I'm angry."

"Well, of course you are. The demons kidnapped you, tortured you, and nearly killed you." She smiled, a dimple flashing in her smooth cheek. "I'd be angry, too."

Um, okay. "Everyone thinks I need help."

"Do you?" She tilted her coiffed head to the side.

"Shit if I know." He coughed, heat rising in his face. "Pardon the language, prophet."

"I know what shit is, Jase." She took another sip. "So, you're angry. Any plans for revenge?"

"Yes."

"Are they reckless, stupid, or desperate plans?"

"I'm not sure."

"Then what's the problem? Of course you want revenge. Who

wouldn't?" Her tiny feet kicked out from under the skirts. The dress was somewhat reminiscent of the last century, yet on Lily, it worked.

"Okay." He shook his head. "I'm confused."

Her eyebrows rose. "Good. Let's talk about that."

Irritation and an odd panic shot down his spine. "Aren't you sup- posed to help me get rid of the anger?"

"Why would I?"

"Because anger is bad."

"Says who?"

"Everyone." The word exploded from his gut.

"Ah." She leaned back. "So, you're not responding like you think everyone else wants you to?"

"I can't be who they want." The words hurt as they spilled from him.

She pursed her lips. "I assume you know your brothers fairly well."

"Yes."

"Well, let's take a look at this. Knowing the king, what do you think Dage wants to do with the demons who hurt you?" Lily's voice softened even more.

Jase exhaled, his fists clenching. "Knowing Dage? He's torn be- tween wanting to rip their world apart and fulfilling his duties as king to find peace."

"Talen?"

"Talen wants to kill them all." Jase fought a rueful grin.

"Conn?"

"Same as Talen, but probably with more finesse."

Lily nodded. "And Kane?"

"Kane wants to take them out cleanly but with great precision." Jase sat back, his mind spinning. "I hadn't thought about it like that."

"Like what?" Lily asked.

"Like they're all feeling pretty much what I am." He shook his head. Since when had he only thought about himself? His hands shook, so he tucked them in his pockets.

"What does that tell you?"

"I have no clue." But it made him feel both relieved and guilty as hell. "I'm afraid I'll never be the same."

"You won't." Her blue eyes darkened.

His chin jerked up. "Aren't you supposed to reassure me?"

"Why the heck would I reassure you?" She smoothed down her long skirt.

"Um, that's your job?"

"Nope." She smiled. "I'm here to help you heal, and the truth heals. You went through hell, and you'll never be the person you were. Doesn't mean you can't be an incredible person, a happy person. But if you expect to be able to forget . . ."

"I want to forget."

"Why?"

"Because . . ." He stilled and drew in a deep breath. "I didn't like who I became underground."

"Who would?" She tilted her delicate head to the side. "But you survived, and whoever you became during that short time helped you to live, Jase."

He shrugged, his gut churning. "Okay."

"You know what?" she asked.

"What?"

"Who you became underground isn't who you are now. You're different already, and you can become whomever you wish."

He studied her and let the words sink in. Was she correct?

Lily stood, and his manners instantly shot him to his feet.

She smiled and took his arm to escort him to the door. "That's enough for today."

He stumbled. "That's it?"

"Yes. Next time we'll talk about the anger." She opened the door.

He paused. "You said anger was good."

"It's good if you use it—not so good if it eats you up." She patted his arm and all but shoved him into the hallway. "See you in a few days." The door closed.

He rubbed his chin, the world settling. How odd.

A feminine laugh bubbled from behind him. He turned to find his niece sitting on a bench. "Jane?"

"Yeah. The prophet is a kick in the pants, isn't she?" Janie stood, barely reaching his chest. In her twenties, the young woman held the world on her shoulders. "I'm usually confused, yet somehow feel better when I finish talking to her."

Jase nodded, his head cloudy. "All right. What are you doing here?"

"Sometimes Lily helps me to focus a vision. I'm hoping to see Garrett and find him." The young psychic pushed open the door, her shoulders slumped as if the air pressed down on her.

"You're not responsible for your brother, Jane."

She sighed, glancing back at him. "Sure I am. He's my little brother—vampire or not." Agony and fear flashed in her eyes to be quickly quashed.

"How often do you see Lily?"

"Often. When I'm not in immediate crisis, we try to figure out how to end the war. The usual." Slipping inside, she disappeared.

Jase spent a minute staring at the closed door. Shaking his head, he turned down the hallway.

Brenna tapped her foot beneath the conference table, trying to concentrate on Kane's words. The brilliant scientist sat across the table, while Jase sprawled next to her in the small room to the south of the main lodge. He'd actually gone to counseling. For her.

Maybe they had a chance to make it. Heck. She was as stubborn as they came, and Jase topped that. If they worked together and decided to make it, they would.

Kane pulled out another pie chart.

Jase groaned. "Quit with the charts. She understands."

Actually, she'd been daydreaming for most of the meeting. But she nodded, having been briefed on the virus years ago. "I get it. Virus-27 binds to the twenty-seventh chromosomal pair of vampire mates and witches. Then it goes to work unraveling the pairs, taking the infected down to human genetics, if not below that. But the virus is slow and may take decades." As immortals, they had decades.

"Yes." Kane leaned forward, his maroon eyes focusing. "So, when the comet draws closer to earth, I'm hoping you can unbind the damn bug."

Great goal. "How?" How in the world could she unbind anything?

He reached in his pocket and slid a necklace across the table.

Jase reached for it, twirling a milky pendant. "What is this?"

"The virus is inside the glass—just like a miniature petri dish." Kane sat back. "When the comet is near on the solstice, I want Brenna to focus energy inside to mutate the bug."

"Why in the world do you think I could do this?" Brenna asked.

"As a witch, you can create plasma fire out of air. You can alter any matter into another form when you're at full power." Kane leaned back.

That was true. "But nobody has been able to alter the virus. Why me?" she asked.

Kane lifted a shoulder. "It's a logical progression from your natural talent. If you can alter matter normally, then why not alter the virus? And it's *you* because the confluence of the comet's power and the energy of the winter solstice will create incredible power for you and you alone."

Brenna coughed out air. "That makes no sense. Please tell me you don't believe in myth and legend."

Kane's eyebrows rose. "Of course I do. Just because we can't explain it doesn't mean it doesn't have an explanation. I'm sure there's one, and I'm sure I'll figure it out someday."

Her head started to pound. "I'm not special. There had to have been other witches born on my birthday."

"Sure, there were. But you're the only eighth sister born to a seventh sister in the history of the witch species." Kane nodded toward the pendant. "You are special—whether you like it or not. All I'm asking is that you try. If it works, wonderful. If not, then we'll move on to another line of research."

Jase frowned. "Can she be infected?"

"Not unless she swallows it." Kane steepled his fingers under his prominent chin. "Right now, the virus isn't airborne."

Brenna took the necklace and slid it over her head. "This is incredibly far-fetched, you know."

"Yes. But it's all I've got." Kane shook his head. "The time to deal with this virus is coming, and it's coming fast."

Brenna swallowed. The pendant lay heavy between her breasts. An ominous weight of the future to come? She exhaled. "I'll do my best." For now, she needed to find out more about her strengths and how they related to the solstice.

Chapter 15

Janie Kayrs settled into a pose on her yoga mat, her mind clearing. Her time with Lily hadn't provided answers, so she'd decided to seek her own. Alone in an underground office, she'd set up a fountain in the corner, and the bubbling water offered solace. Humming along, she slid into a world that used to belong to dreams only. Dreams that had been filled with her best friend, half-vampire Zane Kyllwood, as well as with Kalin, the Kurjan. They'd met as children before the war broke out.

Then war began, and lines were drawn. Unfortunately, she couldn't get a handle on where Zane stood. Or even who Zane was, considering he wouldn't tell her. The last few times they'd met, he'd been angry and focused. In fact, he'd all but admitted they weren't on the same side any longer. But today, she had to deal with Kalin.

With her imagination, she created an outcropping of rock, smooth grass, and a forest with shimmering trees. She chose a flat rock to sit on and wait.

He didn't keep her waiting long.

Kalin strode out of the forest, his gaze on the pretend sun providing such warmth. For as long as she'd known him, he'd always taken a moment to appreciate the sun. The sun fried the Kurjans, making them similar to horror vampires from fiction. How sad it would be to live only in darkness.

Maybe that's where he belonged.

A tall figure, he'd only broadened in the last few years. The boy she'd known was gone. In his place stood a soldier—an enemy soldier. The pale face and green eyes might almost pass for human, but he'd chosen his path, and it was evil.

Even so, she'd been his only friend so long ago. "Let my brother go free."

Kalin towered over her, throwing her into shadow. The sun glinted off the red tips of his black hair. "It's nice to see you, too." Low and cultured, his tone lacked warmth.

But heat lived in his odd green eyes.

"You want niceties?" She smoothed down her jeans. "Then let my brother go."

"Sure." Kalin dropped to his haunches to meet her gaze. "You know what I want."

She grimaced. "Is he alive?"

"Of course." Kalin frowned. "The second you're mine, he goes free with the guarantee no Kurjan will ever touch him."

Relief flushed through her. Garrett was alive. Now she needed to keep him that way. No easy task. Even if she agreed to meet Kalin in person, she couldn't get free of the vampires. "I'm not destined to mate a Kurjan."

He chuckled. "You have no clue of your destiny. It isn't set until you mate."

Sometimes she forgot other people had visions. But visions changed, and he was probably correct. Speaking of which—"I've seen your death. Well, one of your deaths."

Kalin drew back. "Those psychic visions must come in handy. Tell me. How do I die?"

Janie opened her eyes wider. "Actually, it's up to you. If you let go of the war, find your own mate, and rule your people, you'll live to see a thousand years."

"And if I don't?"

"You'll die young. Very young." Janie leaned forward, lying with everything she had. "As you are now, as the war stands now. Let my brother go and give up this fight."

"You're lying." Kalin sighed.

"Am I?" Janie had learned to play poker from her aunt Emma, who was a master at bluffing. "We were friends once, and I'd rather see you redeem yourself than go out like this. As a killer."

Kalin leaned forward, his minty breath brushing her face. "But I am a killer. You know that, Janie."

"Get your face away from hers before I rip it off." Zane Kyllwood strode out of the forest, irritation shining bright in his eyes.

Fire lanced through Janie so quickly, she had to grip the rock to keep from falling. She'd been raised by deadly vampires, yet danger surrounded Zane in a way that sped up her heart rate.

"The gang is all here." Kalin sighed and stood. "I'd heard you were dead."

"You heard wrong." Zane's gaze raked her. "I believe I said no more meeting in dreamworlds since you can't keep either of us out."

His look left tingles where it roamed. There was a time she'd controlled who could enter her odd world. That was before she'd given both men blood. Of course, she'd taken theirs, too. Now she could yank them into her world if they were weak or sleeping.

Janie saw no reason to stand and show how much shorter she was than the hulking men. "Something came up."

"Something personal . . . vampire." Kalin flashed his teeth. "Go away."

Janie frowned. "Why did Kalin think you were dead?"

"Battle in Iceland with some shifters. The entire region is unsettled. Rogue vampires, demons, shifters, and even a few witches are all fighting over limited territory." Zane edged closer. "What came up?"

Even though they might not be on the same side any longer, she trusted him. Always had—always would. "Kalin kidnapped my brother."

"Unbelievable." Zane reached for a knife to twirl. "The Kurjans are weak enough to need leverage with a human woman?"

"You're just pissed I thought of it first," Kalin countered. "Or maybe not. You make your move to rule yet, Kyllwood?"

Zane stilled, and his eyes swirled the color of an angry river. Deep and green. "What do you know about it?"

"More than you'd like. In fact, I expect you to be dead soon." Kalin shoved his hands in his pockets. He gave a short bow. "Janie, as always, it was a pleasure. I'll call for you soon with a plan so you can save your brother." Whistling a jaunty tune, he sauntered into the forest.

Zane exhaled, looking every one of his nearly thirty years. "When was your brother taken and from where?"

"The night before last and outside of Portland." Janie stood and studied her old friend. Tall, broad, and deadly . . . he looked like the soldier he'd become. A long scar ran from his temple to his jaw, while another scar cut across his exposed clavicle. "The scar on your collarbone is new."

He shrugged.

"You'd only be scarring if you're so wounded you can't heal. Where are you fighting, Zane?"

He rubbed his chin, regret twisting his lips. "There isn't a place I haven't fought, I don't think."

A short time ago, he'd threatened to come and get her. She was ready. It was time the war ended . . . no matter the cost. "I thought you said we'd meet soon."

"We will." He flipped the knife around. "Something has come up to delay my time line."

"A move to rule somebody?" she asked softly.

His lids dropped to half-mast. "There's no move—I don't know where Kalin is getting his information."

As an immortal, Zane sucked at lying. "We should play poker sometime."

"I'm telling the truth." He tucked the knife away and stepped toward her. "We have some sources in the Kurjan organization. I'll contact them and see if I can find your brother."

Her heart leapt. "I'd appreciate the help." Then she cleared her throat and stood. "Who are your people?"

Regret rode his exhale. "Damn good question, Belle." He'd given her the nickname Janie Belle as children, upon learning her name was Janet Isabella. "The day I figure that out, I'll let you know."

She stepped into his space, lifting her head to keep his gaze. So many times she'd wondered what he smelled like—the dreamworld had always masked his scent. "Have you decided if we're on the same side or not?"

He held his ground. "Have you decided to stay out of the war?"

An old argument. "The war has always been about me—about some grand destiny to do with my psychic powers. You know that."

"Doesn't mean you need to participate."

Yet, she did. She'd always known the end would come down to Zane, Kalin, and her. But the actual ending? That she couldn't see.

There was a time she'd imagined a happy ending with her and Zane conquering the world. Now she wondered. Would the sacrifice come from her? If she had to choose between Zane and her family, she would. But how would she survive betraying him?

Maybe that was the key. Nobody said her survival was part of the end-game.

She forced a smile. "Remember when we used to meet as kids? Thought we could save everyone?" The time had been too short.

"I remember." He clasped her shoulders and slid his palms down her arms. "After my father died, my childhood became almost unbearable. You kept me going."

Heat washed through her from his touch, but his words chilled. While she'd known his moving to live with his mother's people, whoever they were, had been difficult, apparently he'd hidden just how difficult. "You've always been my best friend." If he betrayed her, she'd never recover. Sometimes dreams had to live.

"You, too, Belle." Sadness tinged his smile. "Sometimes duty asks more of us than we'd ever imagine."

"As does family," she said softly. There was no question family ties bound them both.

"You got that right."

She studied his darkened eyes. "Half of the immortal world wants me to mate and pass on my gifts. The other half wants me dead and unable to do so." Gathering her courage, she flattened her palms across his broad chest. "Which are you?"

"I want you to live." Sliding a knuckle under her chin, he lifted her face to his.

Heat engulfed her mouth as his lips met hers. He kissed her slowly and with a soft hum of appreciation. Then he released her.

She licked her tingling lips. While she'd been kissed before, nobody came close to Zane and what he could do with the softest of touches. What would he be like in bed for an entire night? Her face heated and she tried to concentrate. "What about your people? They want me alive?"

His gaze dropped to her mouth and then back up. "No." He turned and stalked back toward the forest. "I'll be in touch about your brother." Seconds later, the trees swallowed him.

Janie took a deep breath and returned to her meditative pose.

No? Well, that sucked. Zane was a warrior, and if she didn't miss her guess, an enforcer. That meant he took care of all problems facing his people.

If his people wanted her dead . . . they'd send him.

Brenna nudged open the metal door to Jase's workout space. AC/DC's *Back in Black* blasted through the space. Bare to the waist, he hung upside down from a ceiling beam, throwing stars at mannequins. One by one, the heads flew off.

Squinting to accommodate the dim light, she stepped inside. "Those are banned by treaty."

He threw himself back, flipped twice, and landed on his feet. Dust billowed from worn planks. "You gonna turn me in, darlin'?"

Probably not. "I came to see if you've heard anything about Garrett."

"Not yet." Jase's jaw firmed.

"Do you really think the Kurjans want me?" Brenna kicked a battered mat.

"I think the Kurjans would like to have you, but they really want Janie." He tugged off leather gloves. "The request for you, as well as the booby-trapped industrial building, were just to throw us off the scent."

She picked her words carefully. "How are you doing? I mean, with Garrett being taken?"

Jase frowned. "Not good at all. But since the Kurjans want to trade, they won't hurt him. Plus, his mother is an empath, and she believes he's unharmed. So I believe it."

Hopefully. "Well, that's good. Um, how was your visit with Lily?"

Jase lifted an eyebrow and reached for a set of boxing gloves. "She's nuttier than I am."

Brenna grinned. "I've heard that before." Jase strode toward her, and she fought the urge to step back. So she lifted her chin.

He grasped her hand and shoved on a glove.

"What are you doing?" she asked.

"It's time to train." He tied both gloves around her wrists. "How's your strength?"

She sighed. "No better. How about you?"

"The same. Can't control the elements yet." No expression sat on his face.

"Does that bother you?"

"Not yet. We have time." He danced back on the mats. "Let's see what you've got."

For some reason, she felt silly. "I'm not into training."

"I'm sure. As a Nine member, you always have bodyguards." He slid to the right, fists up. "As my mate, you'll learn to fight."

Was that a fact? She lifted her arms. "What now?"

"Bend your knees."

"Fine." She bent, sliding one foot back. "Now?"

"I'm going to come in with a right cross. You block with your left arm."

She nodded.

He came in, slowly for a vampire, his fist going for her head.

She ducked, punched him in the gut, and swept his legs out from under him.

He hit the mat, his shoulders slamming hard. Sliding to his elbows, he raised an eyebrow. "I thought you said you didn't train?"

She smiled. "I said I didn't like to train. There's a big difference."

"There is, huh?" He kicked out, aiming for her knee.

She flipped back and out of the way. The world spun. Darn it. Her strength was truly deserting her.

He tried again, and this time knocked her down. A quick roll, and he flattened her to the mat. "I bet at full strength, you'd be fun to grapple with."

The man knew how to deliver a compliment. "I'd kick your arse."

"There's that pretty Irish brogue." He settled more comfortably between her legs. "There are other ways we could train."

She pressed up against him. "You're insatiable."

"Maybe."

Taking advantage of his preoccupation, she slammed her heels into his hips and tossed him off, following to straddle him. "You know, there is something I'd like to try." She untied her gloves with her teeth and yanked them off.

"What's that?" he asked.

She slid her thumbs inside his waistband. Since the first time she'd seen him naked, she'd been curious. "I've wondered how much of you I can take in my mouth."

His sweats instantly tented. He kicked off his shoes.

Power flushed through her as she slid his pants off his legs. His cock sprang free—large and ready to go.

She reached for her glasses.

"Leave the glasses on." His voice thickened.

She smiled, taking him in her hand. One lick, and his body stiffened.

Power of a new sort sang in her blood. She stilled. Green danced on her arms. Oh God. Joy ripped through her. Her strength and powers were returning.

Fire lanced down her arms.

Jase yelped. His hands slapped the mat, and his legs kicked.

She frowned, tightening her hold. "What?"

"Fire. Fucking fire," he bellowed, trying to twist away from her.

Shit. She was burning him. She dropped his cock.

He yowled like a burning cat and twisted. His knee smacked into her ribs, and she fell onto his thighs. He yelled. The smell of burnt flesh filled the room. With a growl, Jase grabbed her armpits and tossed her across the mat. Jumping to his feet, he hopped toward a water cooler set into the corner. Ripping off the huge container, he dumped it on his groin. Steam rose.

She scrambled to her feet. "Oh God. I'm so sorry—" Her arm swept out, and plasma balls shot for his head.

His eyes widened, and he dropped to the ground. The balls split the metal, raining shards down on him. They impacted his flesh with a sizzling echo. She gasped and started for him.

He held out a hand to stop her. "Jesus. Stay there."

She stopped moving, her arms windmilling for balance. Green plasma balls flew in every direction, burning holes through the metal. One hit a dummy, and it erupted in flames. The fire spread from dummy to dummy. Wafting, flame-filled cotton hovered in the air.

Brenna stomped out a spark on the mat, only to drop another plasma ball. It popped on the mat, spreading fingers of fire.

Smoke billowed from every direction.

The outside door opened, and Moira leapt inside.

Brenna turned, shooting balls of fire.

Moira frowned, formed a blue ball, and threw it to waver around Brenna.

Brenna sighed, slowly relaxing. The flames on her skin died out. She grinned.

Moira glanced at Jase in the corner, the burning building, and then at her sister. "So. Guess you got your powers back, huh?"

Chapter 16

Jase shifted on the leather chair, his testicles still on fire. The king's battle room held a screen on one wall, a myriad of maps on another, and a full wall of windows on the third. The battle room underground was better equipped, but today they strategized in the lodge's main conference room. So he didn't have to go into the earth again.

Talen punched in keys on a laptop, and a region of the Pacific Northwest came into view. "We've been watching a Kurjan encampment located east of Seattle. There's been additional activity in and out the last two weeks."

"Any proof Garrett is on site?" Dage asked, shifting papers aside on the onyx table.

"No," Talen said. Harsh lines cut into the sides of his mouth as he discussed his son like any other mission. "Another message came earlier today about the exchange for Brenna before the solstice."

"That's a smokescreen. They want Janie," Jase said. He glanced at the wall and fought the urge to massage his healing balls. "Why don't we take the Kurjans' main headquarters in Canada and take the Kurjan leader? It's time Franco came out of hiding. If Kalin has Garrett, and we think he does, then let's exchange Franco, his— what the hell is he, anyway?"

"Cousin, I think. Maybe nephew?" Dage muttered. "I can never keep them straight."

"The problem is, Kalin might let us keep Franco. Word has it Kalin is stepping up his game to rule the Kurjans." Kane spoke up even as he kept reading a report.

"So he'd kill family to rule?" Jase frowned. "Are you sure?"

"Yes." Dage nodded. "So the Kurjans think we'll focus on Brenna and not notice Janie sneaking off to save her brother. We might be able to use that." He focused on Talen. "Has Kalin contacted Janie with demands?"

"She says he hasn't," Talen said.

"Is she lying?" Dage asked.

"Yes." Talen spread papers out on the table. "I have Max and another guard on her as well as five men she doesn't know about. She's not going anywhere."

Dage nodded. "Good. Give me your three best plans."

Talen grabbed a notebook. "One—we take Seattle and search for intel on Garrett. Two—we take Franco out of Canada and try for an exchange for Garrett. Three—we agree to the exchange, dress Moira up as Brenna, and set a trap for them here when they come for Janie."

"I dislike the third option," Conn said from where he leaned against the wall, arms crossed. "However, my witch is a badass, and it's a good plan."

Dage rubbed his chin. "Do we have the manpower to implement all three strikes at once?"

Kane leaned forward. "We do if we use our shifter allies near Seattle. Then we hit Canada and set the trap here."

"Okay." Dage pushed away from the table. "Talen? You have three hours to come up with complete battle plans. We'll meet back here then."

The men stood and headed for the door.

"Jase? Stay, please," Dage said.

Jase's gut lurched. He waited until his brothers had left and then shut the door. Turning around, he dropped back into a chair and winced.

Dage frowned. "You all right?"

Apparently Moira hadn't reported back about his flaming balls yet. "Fine."

"Good. I'm benching you for this one."

"No."

Dage lifted one dark eyebrow. "That was a directive from the king, not your older brother."

"No. That was from my older brother," Jase said softly. "You need everybody you have for this strike. I'm strong, and I'm ready."

"No—"

"I screwed up, and I know it." Jase leaned his elbows on the table. "It won't happen again."

Dage blew out air. "You don't talk about it."

Everything in Jase stilled. "About what?"

"You know what. Your time with the demons." Dage shook his head. "I've given you years to deal . . . yet you never talk about the captivity."

"There's nothing to say."

"Why didn't they kill you?" Dage asked.

Jase blinked. Now that was the question that kept him up at night. "Honestly? I think they hoped I was so fucked up after five years of torture, I'd come back here and be a distraction." Upon his rescue, his own doctors had probed him head to toe. There were no weapons, capsules, anything in his body that would harm his family. "I passed every psychological test Kane could come up with to make sure my brain wasn't changed."

But he'd been changed, and he had returned seriously fucked up. As a plan, it didn't suck. "I've already screwed up—nearly getting Talen killed." Jase leaned forward. "But I can beat this. You just need to trust me." Yeah, it was a manipulative move that played on an older brother's emotions. But Jase needed to be in the action. He needed to help save Garrett.

Dage eyed him. "Talen's the strategic leader for the Realm and is creating this plan. It's up to him if you go."

Excellent. Talen was a much easier sell than Dage. Of course, Jase had almost gotten him blown up a couple of days ago. "Great."

Dage stood. "When this is over and we have Garrett back, you and I are talking about your time in captivity. I want to know all of it."

Jase lifted his chin and eyed his older brother. "You really don't." Without waiting for a reply, he pivoted and strode out of the room. He'd worked hard to bury the pain, and no matter how well-meaning Dage was, opening that wound would cause more damage than he could repair. He glanced at his watch. Crap. He was late.

Several corridors later, he knocked on the prophet's door. Lily opened it and gestured him inside. The woman always smelled like strawberries.

He tried to step lightly over her Persian rug, but his boots left huge prints. The chair creaked when he lowered his bulk. He winced when his ass hit the cushion.

Lily frowned. "Are you all right?"

Heat climbed into his face. "Fine. Thanks."

She sat on a tiny chair and leaned forward. "Did you harm yourself training?"

"No." There was no way to explain.

Lily nodded. "All right. Tell me about the anger."

Brenna took a deep breath and tried to control the power. Fire danced down her arms again.

"Shit." Moira tossed a ball around her. Again. "Concentrate, Bren."

"I am." It was like being a teenager again and just coming in to power. "I can't believe I'm failing to control plasma."

Moira wrinkled her nose. "You have ten times the power of a newbie, and yet, no control." She coughed back a laugh. "Did you see Jase's face?"

Brenna snorted before she could stop herself. "His face? I don't think his face was the problem."

Moira erupted into laugher until tears glimmered in her eyes. She dropped to the mat in the quiet gym. "I'll never get that sight out of my head."

Brenna sobered. "So you felt my power return from across the subdivision?"

"Aye. I always feel when another witch is altering matter." Moira sat up, losing her smile. "But, well, yours felt different."

Brenna batted Moira's plasma out of the way. "Different how?"

"Dunno." Moira back-flipped to stand. "Here's the deal. We're the closest in age, and we've always shot straight with each other, right?"

Even though there was still a century of age between them,

Moira had always been Brenna's closest confidant. Brenna steeled her shoulders. "Aye."

"You know about the Pagurus Comet, right?"

Brenna stilled. "Yes. Why?"

"Well, it's real. Maybe." Moira scratched her elbow. "I remember when you were born. The very air felt different."

A shiver racked Brenna. "Are you serious?" This was crazy. Even though Kane seemed to give credence to the legend, Brenna still hadn't really believed it. She peered closer at her sister. Was Moira playing a joke?

Moira nodded. "I'm deadly serious. There's something to the legend, and the fact that your power is back so suddenly makes me wonder."

Brenna's mind spun. "My power is coming back because I mated one of the strongest vampires on earth."

"Maybe." Moira slid a few feet away. "Maybe it's a combination of the two."

"So? What does that mean?"

"Dunno. Just that if the legends are true, or if the seers really know diddly, you'll be one seriously strong badass on the solstice."

The door opened, and Janie Kayrs eased inside, a longneck in her hand. "Hello, Auntie Witches."

Moira flashed a grin. "Funny. Shouldn't you be communing with the gods or something?"

Brenna frowned at her sister. "Leave her alone." While Janie might be in her mid-twenties, an air of ancientness surrounded her. Most psychics seemed like old souls.

Janie took a sip of the beer. "That's actually why I'm here."

Moira stepped closer to their niece. "Did you have a vision?"

"Yes."

"About Garrett?" Brenna asked.

"No." Janie twirled the beer bottle. "About you, Bren."

Lovely. Brenna searched for calm. "Don't tell me. I blow up the world on the winter solstice."

Janie shifted her feet, her pretty blue eyes clouding. "Maybe."

Moira's smile stopped halfway across her lips. "Wait a minute. Are you serious?"

Janie rubbed her mouth. "Yes."

Moira cut a look at Brenna, instantly turning into the deadly enforcer she was. "Tell me what you saw."

Janie leaned against the wall, fatigue darkening into circles under her eyes. "I saw Brenna and waves of liquid oxygen. Vibrating with power, unstable, and on the brink of exploding."

Brenna swallowed, chills rippling through her spine. "Where was I?"

"Don't know. But it felt hot—and scary. You were totally out of control." Janie took another deep gulp of the beer, concern etched into her face. "I thought I should warn you."

"Have your visions ever been wrong?" Brenna whispered, her mind searching for reason.

"No. But there are always many paths to the future, and this is just one. It may not happen." Janie's face lost all color and she swayed.

Moira instantly shot forward and helped her to the mat. "What in the world?"

Janie's head dropped forward as she gave a low moan. "Oh God. I should never have let them take my blood."

Moira shook her shoulder. "Who? Who did you give blood?"

Janie swallowed and lifted her head. "Nobody." Using the wall for leverage, she pushed herself to stand. "I need to go." Her gait hitched as she headed out the door.

Brenna frowned. "I sometimes forget the burden that woman carries."

"Not me," Moira murmured, her gaze on the empty doorway. She turned her full attention to Brenna. "If there's a chance your powers will really increase, we need to get them under control. Now settle into a fighting stance and concentrate."

Brenna flashed back to her thirteenth year when Moira had first trained her to alter matter into weapons. "Fine. But no burning my feet this time if I don't catch on quick enough."

Moira rolled her eyes. "You're such a baby."

"Oh yeah?" Drawing on her center, Brenna re-formed the air into a pulsing ball of fire. She drew back her arm to throw it, and the fire ripped right up to the ceiling. A light exploded, shooting sparks. She yelped and jumped out of the way.

Moira tossed up three lasers to instantly snuff out the fire. "You are out of control."

Yeah, but it felt damn good. To go without a part of her for so long had hurt. Her heart whispered that Jase faced a similar lack every day. Maybe his powers would return, too.

Moira slammed a ball of energy at her foot.

Brenna hopped back.

"Concentrate. If we have a big problem coming, we need you at full speed. Block me. Now." Her big sister, the one person she had always trusted unconditionally, threw a devastating ball of fire at her face.

Chapter 17

Jase found Brenna in the kitchen using a fire extinguisher on the microwave. His counter smoldered, his fridge showed long burn marks down the front, and most of his tile lay in burnt pieces. "How are the lessons in control coming?"

She settled the extinguisher on the ground, glancing around the damaged kitchen. "Not so well."

A smudge marred her cheek, and he had the oddest urge to brush it away. "How about your energy?"

She shrugged. "Better but not full strength yet. How about you?" Those pretty gray eyes focused on him.

"No additional power. Yet." He rubbed his head, gaze on the waning sun outside. Several times during the day, he'd tried to alter water into steam. He'd failed repeatedly. His gut clenched—it was almost time to go. "Did Moira get a chance to explain the plan to you?"

"Yes." Brenna blew out a breath. "I'm to be contained in the underground bunker while my big sister dons a wig, looks like me, and goes to fight the bad guys." She kicked a burned piece of metal out of the way.

"Exactly." If she was looking for sympathy or for somebody to send her into battle, she'd mated the wrong guy.

"I'd argue if there was a chance I wouldn't accidentally blow up the helicopter on the way."

Jase leaned against a safe area on the wall. Sometimes he was so damn tired; it was all he could do to stand. "We think the Kurjans will attack headquarters from the north while we're off chasing Garrett. I don't believe there's any way they'll get past our forces, but worst-case scenario, there are several escape routes out of the mountain."

"Already been briefed and tested." Brenna rolled her eyes. "Several times, actually."

"Good." He hated the thought of putting her in the mountain where he couldn't get to her. "I've talked to Max, and the bunker you'll be in is safe from, ah, fires."

"Funny."

He wasn't trying to be funny. "Just stay safe, okay?"

She eyed him. "How are things going with Lily?"

Heat pricked his neck. "I don't know. There are some things that should stay buried."

Brenna studied him, indecision filtering across her face. Maneuvering around crumbling tiles, she slid her arms around his waist. "Like what?"

He closed his eyes against a rush of emotion that took him by surprise. "Things I saw, things I did," he murmured. No way would he allow her to shoulder that burden with him.

"Tell me." She snuggled into his chest.

He'd known from day one she'd be a cuddler. "No."

She tilted back her head. "Yes. Just one thing you don't want to admit. Tell me."

Temptation expanded his diaphragm. "You tell me something first."

She paled, yet bravely kept his gaze. "Okay. I, ah, remember being forced to drink the planekite. When it happened, I couldn't fight back."

Surprise filtered through him. "You knew you'd been poisoned?" She'd lied to everyone?

"Yes. I knew and didn't want everyone to worry, but I did visit the doctors immediately." A sliver of pink wandered over her high cheekbones. "With the war and everything, we've had enough to worry about."

If she got any sweeter, his heart would just stop. "I'm glad your powers are returning."

"Me, too." She grinned. "Though we don't know yet if they're back because of the mating, or if I'm totally on the mend. Now it's your turn."

Dread tasted like battery acid. He took a deep breath. If she could be brave, so could he. "When I was underground for so long, I saw faces in the rock."

"I'm sure."

"No. I mean I really saw them—talked to them." Different faces, as real to him as she was right now. "One of the reasons I can't go underground . . ."

"You think you'll see them again?"

Feared he would. In fact, it scared him shitless. "Yes."

"I can understand that." She brushed her fingers across his jaw. "Our brains do the impossible to keep us alive. Thank yours instead of trying to forget." Releasing him, she stepped away.

Coldness instantly surrounded him. So he grabbed her arms and yanked her back, his arms circling her waist. Warmth returned. "I'll think about it."

She pushed him and laughed as he kept her close. "Will you be guarding headquarters?"

"No." Maybe he should be, considering his mate would be underground. Although, she'd be perfectly safe. No way could the Kurjans breach Realm security. Besides, Talen wanted him in the rocks of Nevada. "The Kurjans have agreed to the trade in two hours at a location somewhere in the Nevada—lots of red rock to hide in. They'll send the coordinates once we're in the air—we can have a maximum of three soldiers on the ground, or they kill Garrett."

Brenna frowned. "What about backup?"

"Three armed and fully manned Blackhawks just out of range."

"Do you think the Kurjans will be there?"

"Oh, they'll send a squad to Nevada. Garrett may even be there—we'll see. But they want our forces divided so they can attack here and take Janie, if you ask me."

Brenna nodded. "Our allies in the north are going to take Franco? So we're pretending to fall into their trap in order to set our own."

"Exactly. Talen is a genius . . . sometimes." Jase released her.

"Come help me suit up, and then I'll take you over to headquarters." Nausea tried to swirl in his gut at the thought of her under tons of rock. "You'll be safe."

She tangled her fingers with his, following him through the pantry to the weapons room. Then she wandered toward the pictures on his wall. "I figure this is your kill wall."

"Yeah." He bit back hatred as he stared at the three photographs. "You know the demon leader, Suri, and now you've met crazy Willa. The third man is Melco, one of Suri's top lieutenants. The guy likes to use knives."

Brenna sucked in air. "Sounds like a charmer."

A charmer who was going to die slowly while choking on his own blood. "Yeah. I promised him once that if I survived, I'd hunt him down with my last breath. And I will."

Brenna turned, sadness in her stunning eyes. "Just be careful."

His head jerked. He focused solely on her. "You're not going to tell me to deal with it, just be glad I'm alive? To let go?"

She lifted a delicate shoulder. "I wouldn't." Green danced on her arms for a second to wisp into nothingness. "I'd make the bastard fry."

She'd make the bastard fry? Jase settled into the backseat of the Blackhawk, his mind spinning. How could she be so damn sweet one moment and so homicidal the next? Were the words just talk?

And why in the hell did her bloodthirstiness turn him on so much? Man, he was a deviant.

There were layers upon layers to Brenna Dunne, and he wanted to savor each one as he unpeeled them.

Moira sat next to him, eyes closed, probably planning. Conn flanked her other side, his fingers tapping a tune on his cargo pants. Lines of stress cut into the sides of his mouth—worry about Garrett and concern for his mate stamped in his hard eyes.

How difficult it must be to allow his mate to go to battle. Jase felt a renewed respect for his older brother.

Talen sat in the passenger seat next to the pilot. As usual, he'd shut down once the mission had been planned. No emotion had emerged from him as he'd detailed the three attacks—no sign that his gut had to be churning at the thought of what the Kurjans were doing to young Garrett.

A familiar rage welled up in Jase. If the Kurjans had harmed one inch of Garrett, he'd take them all out.

He had to believe that they wanted Garrett safe for now in order to trade, or he'd go crazy. Well, crazier than usual.

"We have the coordinates," Talen said through the earphones as the pilot banked hard left. "Touchdown in fifteen minutes." He leaned closer to a monitor set in the dash. "There are tons of rock outcroppings to hide in—they probably also have an underground bunker. Satellite in position in ten minutes."

Heat exploded in Jase's chest. Underground? Shit.

The minutes slid by in slow motion. Finally, they neared the site.

Talen punched in buttons on the dash. "No sign of an underground bunker or any activity. Once we set down, everyone scatter and take cover in the rocks. The meet is in a gully between rock outcroppings. Stay out of the fucking gully."

Seconds later, the helicopter thumped to the earth. Jase threw open the door and ran out, bending low, eyes fighting against the swirling sand. He climbed through rocks to the north, waiting until the helicopter lifted back into the sky before stopping.

Silence descended. Moonlight and twinkling stars illuminated the wind pushing scrub brush end-over-end.

Jase kept his weapon pointed low, his stance set, his back to a rock still heated from the desert sun. The irony wasn't lost on him. The Kurjans who'd taken his nephew would be strung to the desert floor in the full sun, and then they'd see irony.

A rattler hissed in the distance, sending a slow chill down his spine. He hated snakes. Damn reptiles.

The humming of a helicopter echoed through the air. He straightened. Lights came into view, and an attack copter set down. A door opened. Two Kurjan soldiers emerged, a prisoner between them. They'd bound the prisoner's hands as well as stuck a sack over his head.

The guy was big—big enough to be Garrett.

One of the soldiers stepped in front of him. "Where's the witch?" he called out.

Moira moved into the gully. "Right here, dickhead."

"Hands up—no weapons," the soldier yelled.

Moira slowly lifted her hands. Jase slid closer, his rifle pointed at the first guy. Didn't they know a witch's weapon *was* her hands?

Warning whispered along his neck. Something wasn't right.

"Move forward," the Kurjan yelled, shoving the prisoner ahead of him.

Moira slowly stepped forward.

A voice crackled through Jase's earpiece—Realm headquarters was under attack. Adrenaline flooded his veins. He needed to get back to Brenna.

Then the world exploded.

Charges detonated along the gully, throwing rocks into the air. Jase yelled and flew over a jagged edge to land in a cloud of dust.

The Kurjan soldier shot the prisoner in the back several times, turned, and jumped into the helicopter. It rose into the night, firing rounds down at them.

Jase lunged for Moira first, tackling her. Covering her as bullets impacted his back. Conn reached them both, grabbing his vest and Moira's arm to drag them behind a rock.

Sharp edges cut into Jase's arm. He scrambled around for a better view. Panic seized his lungs.

Talen ran into the raining bullets to hoist the prisoner over his shoulder. His body shook with each hard impact as he zigzagged to leap behind a rock. Jase dashed over, ducking low.

He reached Talen just as his brother ripped off the hood.

Unseeing blue eyes were set into a hard-boned face. It wasn't Garrett. Disappointment flowed through Jase until he swayed. Although he already knew, he searched for a pulse. There was none.

"He's human," Talen muttered, wiping blood off his chin.

A human teenager. The Kurjans had murdered a human teenager just to use as a decoy.

The Kurjan helicopter turned around to make another pass. Talen lifted the boy and grabbed Jase's shoulder. "Run."

They ran toward Conn, stopping as another explosion opened up the hillside. Talen shoved Jase toward the gaping hole.

He panicked and pushed back.

"Damn it, take shelter," Talen yelled.

Heat flooded Jase's neck. His lungs seized. "No." He backed away, closer to the line of fire.

Conn jumped in front of him and latched on to his vest. "Follow Moira. Get your ass inside."

Jase struggled in his brother's grip. "Let go." God. He was going to puke. His shoulders vibrated with the need to run. To get the hell away from the open mouth in the rock. "Let go."

Conn reared back and punched him in the face.

Stars exploded behind Jase's eyes.

Blackness fell.

Chapter 18

Jase rubbed his jaw. "How many times did Conn hit me, anyway?" Enough times to have made him miss the rest of the firefight, the rescue, and the return ride to Realm headquarters. It was nearly midnight already.

Dage wiped way the remnants of a bullet hole in his shoulder. "Dunno."

Jase leaned back on the sofa in the main rec room of the lodge, his gaze on his mate. She sat quietly on a guest chair, concern drawing her eyebrows down. "What?" he asked.

She shrugged. "That's quite a bruise."

Conn hit like a jackhammer.

Jase nodded. "I'm fine. Did you manage to keep from burning down the bunker?"

"Yes." She rolled her eyes. "The entire fight was over before we even heard it begin."

Odd, but she sounded almost sorry about that fact.

Dage poked the still healing hole in his shoulder. "We took more casualties than I would've thought. Emma is in the infirmary helping out."

"So they hit from the north as well as the sea." Jase shook his head. "Doesn't make sense. They've lost here before."

"I know. Plus, they were ready for us in Canada. Franco wasn't even there." Dage exhaled slowly. "We need to find Garrett and fast."

Brenna twisted her hands together. "Did you discover the human boy's name?"

Dage's eyes flashed blue through the silver. "Yes. Paul Jacobson—he was a junior at Oregon State—captain of the football team."

Anger heated Jase's blood. "The Kurjans killed an innocent kid just to fool us for two seconds?" Evil bastards.

"Yes." Torment lived in the king's eyes. "I had soldiers take the kid back to his apartment and make it look like a robbery gone bad. At least his family won't have to wonder."

Anger and pain echoed in Dage's tone.

Jase yanked a knife from his boot. "We need to finish this war with both the Kurjans and the demons."

"That'd be great, Jase," Dage drawled. "I mean, considering our forces are at half right now. The last two decades have hurt us. Bad."

Plus, spending so many man hours searching for Jase had taken a toll on the Realm. Guilt and rage mixed inside him until his lungs compressed. "I know."

"What's our next plan?" Brenna asked.

A shrill alarm rent the air.

Jase jumped to his feet in unison with Dage. Then they both ducked as green balls of plasma whipped by their heads.

Dage flipped around, shock on his face.

Brenna gasped and shook out her arms. More weapons shot from her fingers, and the couch erupted into flames.

The speaker set high in the corner crackled. "We have breaches in security tunnels A and D," Talen said. "Kurjan attack teams of three."

Dage leaped for the door and yelled over his shoulder, "Take the perimeter of tunnel A, Jase."

Brenna sucked in air, flames dancing on her wrists. "The escape tunnels? They found the escape tunnels?"

"Yes." It was a trap within a trap. Jase grabbed her hand, ignored the burn, and dragged her outside toward the ocean. Moonlight guided their way. "They knew we'd draw them in and even allow them to disengage the main security system." He should've seen it. The only way to get to Janie was through the escape tunnels.

The mountain lit up with explosions. Shit. A second wave of attack. But his job was tunnel A. He started climbing down the rock wall.

Brenna tugged away. "What in the world?"

"There's a ledge. Trust me."

Her hand shaking, she took his again—this time sans the flames. He helped her down several feet and then pushed her into a small alcove. "You'll be safe here. Try not to blow up the mountain."

She darted forward. "You'll need backup."

"No." He shoved all emotion into a box where it couldn't fuck things up. "I need you safe. Stay here."

Then he backflipped into the air, hitting the ocean in the sweet spot with a minimal amount of splash. Rising to the surface, he scanned the sea. No boat. This squad must've scuba-dived in. Smart.

He lifted himself out of the water and crept behind a rock. The crevice in the cliff could barely be seen by the naked eye. How had they found it? Drawing his knife, he angled close enough to smell fresh earth and then tapped his ear communicator three times so they'd know he was in position.

The screams of a firefight echoed through the night from up above.

A splash sounded, and steam rose from the ocean. Brenna's dark head broke the surface.

Fury ripped through him. Reaching for her arm, he dragged her up to press against the rocks. "I gave you an order."

She met his gaze evenly. "I'm not one of your soldiers."

No, she was his mate. One who'd just plunged into a dangerous sea and found the only safe spot to land by luck. Pure luck. She could've severed her spine, damn it.

His wet ear communicator buzzed. "We took prisoners in Tunnel D to interrogate. Now, we've blocked off Tunnel A—they're on the way out. No quarter," Talen ordered.

Jase cleared his mind and shoved his mate behind a couple of boulders. "Come out, and I'll beat you." Ignoring her outraged gasp, he shifted back into position.

A scrape sounded. He plunged the knife into the crevice and yanked a Kurjan soldier out by the gut. Throwing the guy to the ground, he twisted both ways and sent the head rolling into the ocean.

Pivoting, he sliced the next soldier's Achilles tendon, knocking him down. Twirling, he moved to slash the third soldier in the throat and stopped cold.

The Kurjan held Janie in a headlock, forearm against her vulnerable jugular. He could snap her neck if he just twitched.

"I'm sorry," she whispered.

Jase flashed back to when he'd first met her. She'd had huge blue eyes with such delicate bone structure he'd been afraid to touch her. Until she'd thrown her tiny arms around him and said she'd always wanted to meet her uncle Jase since she'd dreamed about him her whole life.

All four years of it.

Now, she was still frighteningly petite, but the wise eyes of a woman begged him to step out of the way. To let her sacrifice herself for her family.

That he understood.

But he couldn't let her do it. Not even for Garrett, whom he loved more than his own life. So he focused on the Kurjan. "Let her go, and I'll let you live." As a deal, it was a damn good one.

"No." The soldier tightened his hold.

Janie gasped, her eyes widening, her fingers curling around the Kurjan's arm. "Kalin wants me alive, and you know it."

The guy's hold relaxed. "Dead is all right." His voice lacked conviction.

"Dead gets you dead, jackass," Janie hissed, her face turning red.

The soldier's hold relaxed further, and Janie took a deep breath. He focused on Jase. "Move, Kayrs, or I'll break her neck and worry about consequences later."

In the distance, a boat engine flared to life. Jase edged to the side. If he could just get that arm away from Janie's skin, he could take the guy.

A ball of fire suddenly exploded into the rock above the Kurjan. Jase caught Brenna's surprised expression out of the corner of his eye. Splinters cascaded out, one cutting into the Kurjan's cheek. He gasped and stepped back. Jase shot forward and sliced the underside of his wrist, millimeters from Janie's neck.

Janie threw an elbow into the Kurjan's groin. He hissed in pain, sharp fangs dropping.

Jase yanked off the offending arm and tossed Janie toward Brenna. Then he plunged his knife in the Kurjan's gut. Blood spurted over his hand with the burn of pure acid.

Retrieving another knife, Jase cut off his head.

He stood, absolute calm centering him. The final Kurjan crawled across the rocks, trying to fall into the ocean. Jase dropped to his haunches and sliced into the back of the Kurjan's neck. A twist of his wrist, and he decapitated the final soldier.

"Tunnel A—secured," he said.

He wiped the bloody knives off in the salty ocean, stood, and turned around.

Brenna watched him, her face paler than the Kurjans', her eyes wide with shock. No. That was fear.

Brenna smoothed out her expression so Jase wouldn't know how much he'd just freaked her out. Not that he'd killed, but that he'd done so very calmly and with precision. As a killer, he was damn good.

The water bubbled red around their feet, and she fought the urge to vomit.

A bellow from above caught her attention, and she glanced up to see Talen scaling down the rocks. He hit the ground and grabbed Janie in a hug.

Janie hugged him back. "Don't be mad, Dad."

Talen growled low and flipped her around to a piggyback position on his back. "Hold on. We'll talk about it up top—after I tell your mother."

Janie groaned.

Two seconds later, they were headed back up the rock.

Brenna swallowed. Two helicopters exploded, their burned carcasses falling into the ocean. Mere heartbeats later, the boat in the distance blew up. Take that, Kurjans.

Jase watched the debris fall and then moved toward her. She couldn't help but move back. Darn it.

"I told you to stay put," he growled.

Now he was angry? Great. She set her hands on her hips. She'd thrown plasma at the right time, hadn't she? Sure, it had been a fluke, considering she was aiming to the left of the Kurjan. But it still worked. "I thought you might need backup."

"I told you to stay put." His already hard face hardened further.

"You're just repeating yourself."

Wrong thing to say. He ducked a shoulder and tossed her over.

"Hey—" she protested, smacking his back.

"Stop it." One broad hand clamped around her thigh. "Hold on." Impressive muscles shifted as he climbed the rocks as easily as any cougar.

Her head smacked his back several times until she finally grabbed him around the waist to steady herself.

Upon reaching the top, he flipped her over. "Not a sound." Then he listened.

The night had gone silent. Jase tapped his ear communicator.

"What?" Brenna whispered.

His eyes flared, and he pressed a hand over her mouth.

Where was her fire when she needed it? She seemed to be out of juice. Hopefully temporarily.

Then he nodded and released her mouth. "We're clear."

Hope and relief made her sway. "We won? They're all gone?"

He paused. "Yes. We won, and they're all gone."

"Good." For a moment, she'd wondered if the Kurjans would get Janie. "What now?" The second the words left her mouth, she knew they were a mistake.

"Now?" Jase lowered his face to within an inch of hers. "Now we discuss the fact that you disobeyed a direct order."

She opened her mouth to argue, and he held up a hand.

"No." He shook his head. "Don't tell me you're not a soldier. When it comes to battle, when it comes to safety, you'll obey every damn order I give. Do. You. Understand?"

Was he forgetting her gifts? She could make bloomin' fire if she wanted to. Someday she'd be able to control it again. "No."

He stilled. The air vibrated around him, but he didn't move. Slowly, his eyes darkened to midnight. "What did you just say?"

A chill skittered down her spine. She swallowed. "I, ah, said, no."

Just like that, she was over his shoulder again. "Damn it, Jase."

His strides were long and full of purpose. Before she knew it, she was inside their home. The scent of smoke still permeated the air.

Jase set her gently on her feet. "You don't leave this house until you learn that your safety comes before your pride or stubbornness."

"Forget you." Aye, she'd wanted to say the real f-word, but it just hadn't come out. She could keep her dignity and still tell him to stuff it. "You have no clue who I am."

He flipped her around until she faced the wall. Fire lanced through her, and she shot both elbows back into his gut. With a grunt, he grabbed her wrists and pinned them above her head. His impossibly fit body pressed her into the paint.

She kicked back, nailing his ankle.

He bit off an expletive and nudged her legs apart. The hard line of his erection pressed into her butt.

Her nipples pebbled, and she bit back a groan. Desire spiked her blood. Probably the aftermath of battle—of surviving. Yeah, right. It was Jase, through and through. Even though he was being a complete ass, she wanted him. All of him.

He leaned in, and a fang nicked her earlobe. "I'm not a man you want to push, baby."

Oh, but she did. She wanted to push him hard and fast—make him lose control. Make him show her who he really was. Just her. "Don't think you've noticed. I'm a witch, vampire. I could light you on fire."

"You already do." He licked along the shell of her ear. "But you knew who I was, what I am, before you mated me. There's no putting yourself in danger unless I allow it." His free hand slid under her shirt to cup her breast. "And Brenna? I will never allow it."

She'd wanted to know him. The real him. Here he was in full Kayrs fashion. Her eyelids fluttered shut as he flicked the clasp open on her bra. "I'm trained, Jase."

"I'm glad." He ground his pelvis against her ass. "But headfirst into danger is my job, not yours."

She'd never wanted to be on the front lines, nor had she wanted to run into danger. Not in the slightest. But she'd been mated for less than a week, and no way in hell would she allow the vampire to dictate her life. "We each have jobs."

His nimble fingers danced down her belly and zeroed in with ruthless efficiency on her clit. "Think so?"

Her knees buckled, and he pressed her harder into the wall. "Jase—"

"Shhh, baby. Too late to placate me." He slid one finger inside her, even as his thumb teased her clit. The rhythm he set was quick, hard, and just enough to keep her gasping for air.

The hand around her wrists tugged her up on her tiptoes, effectively pushing out her butt. Those dangerous fingers kept playing, holding her right on the edge.

Sparks of need rippled through her sex.

She was so close. So dang close.

"See how well your body obeys?" His voice turned guttural, heated breath brushing her face. "It knows, even if you don't."

She fought back the orgasm looming so close. "I don't take orders from you. Period."

"Come now, Brenna."

She exploded into a million pieces, gasping his name, the waves engulfing her. Her mouth opened and closed. Electrical sensations swept her, and her eyelids fluttered shut. Finally, she came down.

He pressed her clit.

She whimpered, angling away. The aftershocks were too much.

He flipped her around, sliding his hand free. Then slowly, keeping her gaze, he licked off his fingers.

Desire flared awake in her again. Too much, and way too fast. Her knees trembled.

His eyes darkened. "You taste like raspberries and candy. All mine, Brenna. Don't you forget it." Grabbing the back of her head, he slammed his mouth over hers.

Heat engulfed her, hotter and faster than possible. He took the kiss deeper, taking her where he wanted to go. His free hand grabbed her ass and rubbed her against his cock.

She groaned, needing to be filled.

He slowly softened the kiss and then lifted his head. "I have work to do. You want to be here when I get back. Trust me. Don't push me any further." Adjusting his cargo pants, he turned and walked out the front door.

Brenna stood in the hallway, her mouth bruised, and body aching. Oh no, he hadn't.

Fire sprang up her legs, scenting the air with ozone. Oh no! She tried to calm herself, and snuff out the fire. Flames licked along her arms. She clenched her fingers tight, but a small ball of plasma formed on her knuckles.

The ball wavered, morphed, and tripled in size.

Her shoulders shook as she focused.

The ball grew bigger. No! It flew across the room to slam into the wall of windows. The glass shattered, large shards falling. Cold air rushed inside.

She covered her mouth. Well. That'd teach him.

Chapter 19

Garrett Kayrs leaned against the wall, finally understanding why the damn world kept moving. First, the assholes were drugging him. Second, he was on a freakin' boat. A boat. Which explained the carpet. His foot had been smarting all day, and upon removing his boot, he'd discovered they'd taken his tracker out.

Damn it.

But they'd underestimated his nineteen-year-old metabolism. He could finally force the drugs through his system fast enough to get rid of them. His head cleared.

The outside door opened and Kalin strode inside. "The plan is going well."

"You're a moron." Garrett forced a bored look. "Unlock the door and let's end this thing. You die or I die. Either way, stop being a chicken-shit."

Kalin smiled, showing sharp white teeth. "Have to say, I like you, young Kayrs. You might want to be nice, considering we're going to be family."

Garrett maneuvered closer to the bars. "Why are you so intent on this?"

Kalin's eyebrows rose. "You know why. Every species in the world has prophesied Janie's gifts as something extraordinary that will change everything. Whomever your sister mates will gain those gifts."

Maybe. But there was something else. "You like her." Garrett fought the urge to puke.

Kalin's eyes narrowed. "She's a means to an end."

Touchy. "She's more than that to you." Garrett studied the soldier. "You like to kill women, but you saved Janie. That was instinct and not calculation, wasn't it?" Who the hell was this guy? If his one weakness was Janie, how could Garrett use that?

Kalin lowered his chin. "No. That was pure planning for the future. I can't very well mate her and gain her gifts if she's dead, now can I?"

Sounded a bit defensive, now didn't he? Garrett grinned. "All of these oracles, seers, prophets . . . and not one has said what her gifts really are. Sure, she can see the future. So what?"

Kalin shrugged. "I want those gifts."

"No. You want my sister." For whatever reason, the psycho did want Janie. Garrett slid his hands around the bars. "I'll kill you before you get near her. I promise."

"You're a good brother, young Kayrs."

Irritation snapped up Garrett's head. "We are not bonding here, dumbass."

Kalin chuckled. "Oh, I'm fully aware I'll have to kill you and probably soon. But that doesn't mean I don't like you."

The Kurjan really did have a screw loose. "Janie will feel a lot warmer toward you if you let me go."

"Nice try." Kalin shook his head. "I don't want her feeling warmer toward me. The sooner she understands this life, the better." He kept his face stoic, but an underlying stressor lifted his consonants.

The guy did want Janie to like him, but he really didn't want to want that. Garrett's head began to pound. "Has your attack failed yet?"

"The first one failed as per my plan." Kalin picked his fingernails.

Caution whispered through Garrett. "Meaning?"

"The first was a decoy . . . the second included a full frontal assault as well as tunnels A and D." Kalin's grin slid across his lips, slow and sure.

Garrett stilled. "We don't have tunnels A and D."

"Liar," Kalin whispered. "We know all about them—and that

their security will be down after our first, sad and unsuccessful, attempt on headquarters."

How in the hell? Nobody with that knowledge would betray the Kayrs family. "You're wrong."

"Am I?"

Who was the spy? Fury curled Garrett's fingers into fists. He'd kill the traitor himself.

Kalin patiently waited as Garrett worked it out.

Reality hit with the force of a punch. Janie. She hadn't.

Kalin coughed out a laugh. "You should see your face."

Fire heated Garrett's breath. "You bastard."

"Ah, now what kind of talk is that? Your big sister would do anything to save you, now wouldn't she?" Kalin sauntered toward the door. "You may give her hell when she gets here." The door closed with a final *click*.

Damn it all. How could Janie do such a thing? He could handle himself. He was the damn vampire—she was just a human. It was his job to protect her. His spine straightened, his mind finally clear. Time to get the hell off the boat.

Gathering his strength, he punched the wall. Fiberglass cracked and shattered. His knuckles split, and he shoved the pain into a box like he'd been taught.

He might be young and untried, but he'd been trained by the best.

Time to grow up.

The scent of Brenna surrounded Jase as he jogged toward his gym. The woman was a dangerous distraction, and he needed to get a handle on his attraction. He appreciated liking his mate, but his mind couldn't be filled with her. Neither could his heart.

Revenge lived there and would until he'd killed Suri, Willa, and Malco. Especially Malco.

Deep down, where fear resided, Jase wondered why they'd let him live. Until Brenna had brought warmth into his life, every second of freedom had felt like walking through hell. Though instinct whispered it was more than that.

They wanted something from him.

He shoved open the gym door. The scent of burned metal and cotton assaulted his nose. Brenna sure could damage a room.

A Kurjan hung from the ceiling, his arms over his head. Blood dripped down his face, and pain scented the air. Talen stood over to the side, a bloody knife in his hands.

Jase paused. "Where are the other two?"

"Didn't make it." Talen circled the remaining Kurjan. "Guess what? Franco wasn't at the Kurjan headquarters because he's on the run. Apparently Kalin has made a move to rule, and most of the forces follow the psychotic bastard."

Well, it was just a matter of time. Jase nodded. "Any leads on Garrett?"

"This guy was just going to tell me where they're keeping my son." Talen slashed a shallow cut down the Kurjan's torso.

"He's dead." The Kurjan's eyes swirled a bloody red that matched his hair. Most Kurjans had red hair with black tips, unlike Kalin. This guy had clown hair—scary clown hair.

Talen cut again. "He's not dead. Where is he?"

The Kurjan hissed in pain. "Dead. Kalin cut off his head."

Rage flicked across Talen's face. "Now, that's not true."

Jase fought nausea. He'd been tortured too much to be able to calm down. "Listen, buddy. Talen can keep you alive for weeks until you beg for death. Tell us where Garrett is."

Talen focused on Jase, his eyes narrowing. "I've got this, but Dage needs help securing the tunnels again."

Jase opened his mouth to protest and snapped it shut at his brother's stubborn glare. Maybe Talen didn't want Jase to watch any more than Jase did. He nodded. "Call me if you need me."

Making a quick exit, he hurried toward headquarters. The Kurjan's high-pitched screams forced him into a run.

The smell of battle hung over the lodge like a heavy blanket. Smoke, dust, and despair. He yanked open the door and stopped at the sight of Janie and Cara sitting in the rec room. Both had red eyes and noses.

He cleared his throat. "What the hell were you thinking?" Even as the harsh words left his mouth, he wanted to bite them back. Yelling at Janie wasn't going to help anything.

She sniffed. "I did the same thing any one of you would've done."

At twenty-four years old, she was just a baby. An innocent they'd all protected so fiercely. Jase shook his head. "We're not likely to break in the wind, Janet Isabella. You're human, like it or not."

"I'm the freakin' prophesied one," she snapped. "Kalin wouldn't have hurt me."

No, he just would've forced her to mate him. Didn't Janie understand what that meant? One glance at Cara confirmed she knew exactly what it meant.

He sighed, banishing anger. For now. "We'll get him back, Cara. I promise." When he'd been fifteen, he'd lost his parents. The idea of a mother's love and concern was sweet, and he'd protect the woman with everything he had. "Garrett is smart and well-trained."

"So were you," Cara said softly, her blue eyes full of torment. "He's so young."

Yeah, but he was a Kayrs, and he'd survive whatever they did to him. "Right now, Kalin still thinks he has a chance at Janie. So he'll keep Garrett safe as a bargaining chip." Hopefully. Who knew what the crazy butcher would do?

"I know." Cara slipped an arm around her daughter's shoulders. Since Cara was a mate, she hadn't aged, and the two looked more like sisters. "I'm sorry you have to deal with all of this right now, Jase."

His heart thumped. She worried about him? What was it with sweet-hearted females? He was surrounded. "I'm fine. Let's just work on getting Garrett back." He sent his niece a hard look. "Without sacrificing anybody."

Janie pinned him with a stare she'd probably learned from Talen. "It was a good plan. I let them take me to Garrett, and you all rescue us both. Kalin won't hurt me."

If it came down to it, Kalin would kill her before letting her go. "You're remembering the boy from your dreams, not the man he's become." Frankly, the bastard had been a serial killer since he was a teenager. "He's not your friend."

"I know he's not my friend, but I'm the only link we have to finding Garrett, and we need to use that."

Jase shook his head. "How could you tell them about the escape routes?"

She lifted an eyebrow. "I only told them about A and D—those were the least likely to ever be used. Uncle Dage has been planning on filling them in, anyway."

Smart little human, wasn't she?

Jase rubbed his chin. "How did you get word to them?"

"Dreamworld."

Well, shit. "No more dreamworlds, Janet." Jase wondered how he could shut down the worlds.

"No more talk about a trade," Cara said. She glanced at the door. "Where's Talen, anyway?"

"Helping to shore up the tunnels," Jase lied. "He'll be finished soon."

Cara nodded and glanced at her daughter. "Good. I assume he'd like a talk with Janie."

Janie blinked. "Now that sounds like fun."

Jase chuckled and turned toward the far offices, glad he wasn't Janie. "Good luck, sweetheart." He strode through the hallway and shoved open the door to Dage's aboveground office.

The king stood staring out the window.

Jase faltered. "What's up?"

"I failed to see any of this happening."

Jase stepped inside and shut the door. "You can't control your visions."

"I should be able to at least harness them," Dage said thoughtfully. Too thoughtfully. "I didn't see you being taken, Garrett being taken, or Janie giving the fucking Kurjans the blueprints to my fortress."

Jase's gut swirled. Dage in an unpredictable mood never boded well for Dage. For anybody, really. "Janie only gave them intel on the two tunnels you were planning on closing down."

Dage turned around. "How the hell did she know that?"

Jase shrugged. "She's always around and hears everything."

"True." Anger flashed hot and bright in the king's eyes. "So she was willing to give herself to the Kurjan butcher in order to save her brother. As if Garrett would want to live with that."

"She wants her baby brother safe," Jase said softly. "I don't think she thought the rest through."

"No. She thought the plan all through." Dage yanked a knife from his back pocket to toss on the desk. The blade clattered across the wood. "She's not stupid."

"You should probably get this anger out before seeing Janie." Which explained why the king had been staring at the ocean.

"No shit." Dage's gaze narrowed. "You're so great with anger."

Jase flashed his most smart-assed grin. If Dage needed to pick on Jase in order to keep from yelling at Janie, then so be it. "I'm a rock star when it comes to anger, now, aren't I?"

Dage growled low. "You sure you want to do this here?"

Why the hell not? "I'm sure." Adrenaline and anticipation lit through Jase's veins. He and his older brother had been circling each other for months, and it was time.

Talen shoved open the door. "The last Kurjan didn't have a line on Garrett." He glanced from Dage to Jase and then back to Dage. "Now is *not* the time."

"Then get the hell out." Jase kept his gaze on Dage.

Thus he didn't see Talen lunge for him. The air moved, and Talen lifted him against the wall. He impacted with the sound of bricks hitting together. Pain lanced down his spine.

Talen leaned his furious face in close. "My son is probably being tortured by the enemy right now. So if you wouldn't mind forgetting your own problems temporarily, I sure could use some help."

Jase swallowed. He'd tried to convince himself Garrett was fine, but that was unlikely. Reality was a sucker punch tinged with shame. "You're right. I'm sorry."

Talen dropped him.

His feet hit the hard tile, and he tightened his knees to keep his balance. "Do you want me to try with the remaining Kurjan?"

"He's dead." Talen eyed Dage. "You all right now?"

"Yes." Dage rubbed a hand down his face. "I have messages out to every contact we have—even those not aligned with our people. If anybody has a line on Garrett, we'll hear about it."

Jase's hands shook, so he shoved them in his pockets. He'd been lost for five years, regardless of the king's contacts. "Our only good contact is Janie. She can reach Kalin in that weird dreamworld of hers."

Talen rounded on him. "You're not suggesting we trade her?"

"Of course not." Jase glanced at Dage, his mind spinning. Dage was one of the few people on the planet who could maneuver between space and time to end up somewhere else. "You can teleport. Is there any way you could get into Janie's world and find Garrett?"

Thoughts chased across Dage's face before he finally shook his head. "I could probably get into the dream, but I have to know where I'm going to teleport. If Kalin doesn't tell Janie where he is, I won't know where to go."

If Kalin would tell Janie, they didn't need a teleporter. They could go and attack. Jase sighed. "I'm out of ideas."

A quiet knock sounded on the door, and Janie poked her head inside. "I have an idea."

"No." Talen grabbed his daughter for a hug. "Whatever it is, the answer is no."

She leaned back. "We need to do an exchange. Me for Garrett. I'm more valuable to the Kurjans than he is."

Talen shook his head. "You want me to exchange one of my children for the other? I can't do that."

"They won't hurt me." Janie looked toward Dage for support. "We can set a trap for them—as soon as we find Garrett."

"No." Dage backed up Talen. "A trap would still result in gun-fire. It's too risky and not only for you. It's too risky for Garrett. The second Kalin suspects a trap, he'll kill Garrett."

Jase rubbed his chin. "I have a crazy thought."

"We could use crazy," Talen muttered.

"What do you know about Brenna and the winter solstice?" Jase asked Dage.

Dage shrugged. "Just that the Pagurus Comet will be close enough to mess with the atmosphere on a molecular level. Legend has it Brenna will be able to stop time during that moment."

"Stop time?" Jase asked. "Is that possible?"

"Don't know. There are a lot of myths about Brenna, the comet, and the solstice. One says she'll be able to harness the power of the sun and blow up the universe." Dage sighed. "I'm not sure any of them are true."

"Wouldn't she have a clue?" Talen asked.

"Not necessarily," Dage said. "Since she's been so ill, any hints of additional power remained latent. She's been slowly dying for ten years. So who the hell knows?"

"If she's that powerful, do you think she could find Garrett?" Jase asked.

Dage's forehead wrinkled. "I don't know." He grimaced. "In

fact, I don't see how. But maybe you two should start working on the possibility. See what she can do now that she's healing."

Jase nodded and headed for the hallway. So far all she could do was blow things up. Even if she couldn't find Garrett, they needed to get her skills under control before her powers expanded.

Maybe she would be able to blow up the universe.

Chapter 20

Brenna searched for a portion of undamaged tile to spread out the papers. Sitting in Jase's smoldering living room, she punched in keys on the laptop. Who knew there were so many websites dedicated to the comet? And to her?

She should've paid closer attention to Henry about Brenna's Warriors. His website didn't mention her by name, but he was otherwise thorough. With a sigh, she pressed her cell phone to her ear.

"Brenna?" Hope filled his crackly voice.

"Hi, Henry." Not in a million years would she have thought she'd ever call him. "I suppose it'd be silly for me to ask you how you recognized this as my phone number."

"Very silly." Henry snorted. "I've been studying you for over three months—ever since we discovered the comet was coming back. Early belief dictated a millennium would pass before Pagurus flew close enough to mess with matter, and we were wrong. Way wrong."

"I should've paid closer attention to your research." But seriously? A comet?

"That's what I've been trying to tell you." His voice rose in pitch. "But don't worry, I'm prepared. We still have time to mate so I can save you."

She stilled. "Save me? Save me from what?"

"Brenna, for Pete's sake, don't you ever listen?" He huffed out a breath. "The power unleashed will overload you. Your only chance is for your mate to counter the effects, which is why you need to mate a witch. A powerful one."

Panic had her hands seeking some of the papers. "Not true. Conn can counter Moira's powers sometimes. He's a vampire."

"They've been mated for over a hundred years. It took that long for a vampire to learn how to alter matter. You don't have a hundred years." The sound of a computer keyboard tapping filtered across the line. "I'll come to you."

"I mated a vampire." She'd thought it was to save her life. Irony sucked.

Henry gasped like an old man losing at poker. "Tell me you're joking."

"No. I mated Jase Kayrs." Just saying his name spiraled heat into her abdomen.

"Bugger that." Henry sighed loudly. "Well, your only hope now is not to allow the power in. It would've been fun to discover your abilities."

Hope lifted her chin. "I can block the overload?"

"Sure. Especially since you're probably already gaining strength from mating a Kayrs. You have to block the power now. So sad."

"Wait a minute. My sister is an enforcer—she contained my errant plasma balls yesterday." Brenna wondered where Moira had gone—they needed to talk.

"One witch won't be able to help you. Either a mate who can quickly sync with your powers, or a whole barn of witches . . . maybe. That might not even be enough." Henry clicked more keys. "I'm emailing you all the research I've done on the comet and your birth. I wish you had listened to me. Who knows what we could've done on the solstice." The phone clicked.

"Henry?" The damn witch had hung up on her. A second later, her email dinged. Figured he'd have her email address. Her *private* email address. She opened the document and started scanning.

The front door opened and Jase stepped inside. He glanced down and then stomped out a smoldering tile. "How's it going?"

"Great." She perched her glasses up her nose, irritation swirling through her that she still needed them. When would her eyesight return? "I'm learning about the comet and the solstice." Now was not the time to talk about the amazing orgasm he'd forced on her before deserting her.

His eyebrows rose. "Great minds think alike, apparently."

"What do you mean?"

"I'm not sure, but if you're going to have incredible powers for a night, I thought we could find a way to locate Garrett." Jase frowned at the ocean as dawn slowly arrived. "What happened to my window?"

"You pissed me off." Old news. They had more pressing matters to deal with. "How might I locate Garrett?"

"I'm still working the idea out. What have you learned?"

She'd learned that if she tried to harness the comet's powers, she'd probably short-circuit her heart and die, and that was the best-case scenario. Worst case—she'd let off an atomic bomb wherever she stood. "I'm still compiling data."

"Good." Jase sat on the floor and popped his neck. "Can I help?"

"Maybe." The guy was strong and used to have amazing powers. Perhaps he could help her contain the altering matter. She held out her hand and re-formed the oxygen into fiery plasma. She trembled with the effort of containing the matter, but she was finally relearning control. "Can you snuff this out?"

Jase frowned and eyed the weapon. "With my hands?"

"No. With either your own plasma ball or by harnessing the oxygen in the room." If her powers were returning, it seemed likely his would, as well.

He shrugged and zeroed in on the ball.

Nothing happened.

He grunted. "Guess not." Irritation showed in his copper eyes. "There's a chance I'll never regain the ability, Bren. Sad but true."

Yeah, but she needed him to regain it soon. "I won't be able to contain all the power from the comet."

His eyebrows rose. "How so?"

"Too much, too fast." She sighed.

"There wasn't a problem when you were born."

"I know. But I didn't try to harness the comet's power when I was born. I'd like to try now." Without safeguards, she couldn't put the entire world in jeopardy. Who knew? A month ago she was frailer than a human, and soon she might hold humankind in her hand.

The plasma ball zinged toward Jase.

He ducked.

The fire left a fist-sized hole in the front door.

Brenna gulped air. "Oops." Humankind was in for a burning if she failed to learn to control her powers. "Some of the research I read makes it seem like my lack of control isn't merely due to being without power for a decade. Some of this craziness is because the comet is coming closer."

Jase eyed his damaged door. "That makes an ironic kind of sense. Does the research say how you're supposed to contain this new power?"

"Only that my mate should be able to help, if my mate is a witch." She frowned, wanting to give him the full truth. He deserved honesty. "You're not a witch."

"No shit." He pushed off from the floor. "I'll go talk to Conn to find out if he has any tips."

Good plan. "If we can't figure something out, I'll need to go home for the solstice."

"You are home."

She shook her head. "No, I mean closer to the members of the Coven Nine. They're the most powerful witches in existence, and if anybody can help me contain the power, they can." That way maybe she could still try to find Garrett before it was too late.

Jase's chin rose. "We'll discuss the matter after I speak with Conn."

"You can discuss all you want. Talking doesn't change the facts." Ignoring the stubborn vampire, she turned back to the research. There had to be a solution somewhere.

Just as Jase opened the door, Emma Kayrs stepped inside with a sheaf of papers in her hands.

Brenna stood up to meet the queen. "Are those the newest results on my blood?"

"Yes." Emma's eyes widened as she took in the destroyed room and glassless wall of windows. "Your blood is the same."

Brenna coughed. "That's impossible. Look at what I've already done."

"I can't explain it." Emma stepped gingerly over a chunk of ash. "The planekite is just as present in your blood as the poison was five years ago."

Well, that explained the still-crappy vision. "How is that possible?"

"The power from the comet and the solstice," Jase said grimly. "Apparently Pagurus is a bigger deal than we thought."

Darn it. She should've paid better attention to Henry and all of his claims. "Does this mean after the solstice, I'm still going to die?"

"No," Jase growled. "This just means it takes time for a vampire mating to take full effect. You're going to live to see thousands of years. I promise."

That was a promise the vampire couldn't make or keep. "We both were injured, both damaged, when we mated. Maybe we're unable to save each other." She sat back down amongst her papers, her mind spinning. What if on the solstice she could save him for good? If Kane was correct and she would be able to alter matter and unbind a virus, maybe she could somehow help Jase. Help unbind whatever was constraining his natural gifts. Return his powers to him?

Of course, she'd need to heal him without blowing up the world.

Emma sighed and handed the papers to Jase. "I'm still hopeful the mating will help you both. Sometimes it takes more than a couple of days, you two. Give it time."

Time was exactly what they lacked.

Brenna nodded. "I agree." She dusted off her hands. "How are the repairs on headquarters coming along?"

Emma shrugged. "I'm sure they're fine. I've been in the infirmary patching up wounded vampires—who are all cranky but going to mend." Lines of stress darkened the circles under her eyes. "So far nobody has an idea of where Garrett is."

"We'll find him," Jase said softly.

"I know." The queen kicked a piece of ceiling tile out of her way. "I'm going to go check on my sister. Cara isn't holding up very well right now. Understandably."

"Neither is Talen." Jase rubbed a hand through his hair. "Well, shit, none of us are. We have to find him."

Agony flashed in his dark eyes, and Brenna fought the urge to soothe him. He didn't want her help. So she cleared her throat. "What about Jase's blood? Is anything different?"

Emma shook her head. "His blood never changed—although his skills did."

Brenna frowned. "How does that make sense?"

Emma eyed Jase and shrugged. "Don't know. It's not a physical issue." With a sympathetic grimace, the queen disappeared into the early morning.

Brenna sat up. "It's psychological?" She hadn't even considered that possibility.

"So they tell me." His jaw snapped shut.

"Jase, if you can break through your block and help me harness the power, maybe there's a way we can find Garrett." But how? Would she have enough power to become psychic? Reverse time? Send out a missive to the freakin' universe for help?

Her shoulders slumped. "I should've been learning about this entire situation."

"You were trying to save your life." He shook his head. "Don't look back, Bren. There's only forward."

Why did his little nickname for her give her special tingles? God, she was pathetic. He'd made it clear as glass they were friends and had mated to save both their butts. "You're never going to fall in love with me, are you?"

His head jerked. "What?"

Some would call her stupid for shining light on the issue. But it felt brave. "I have to know. Is there a chance?"

He blinked several times. "Brenna, you know I like you—"

She held up a hand. "Good enough." Could she be a bigger moron? So they'd had crazy vampire sex and she'd orgasmed like there was no tomorrow. So little Brenna Dunne had caught one of the most eligible bachelors on earth. So she could tell he was a great guy with a lot to give.

He didn't want to give.

She felt like a pathetic reality-television star who didn't get the guy. But curling up and bawling about it wasn't going to help anybody. It sure as heck wouldn't help find Garrett or help her mutate Virus-27. If she had the chance to save all witches and vampire mates from the damn illness, she needed to do it and stop worrying about her crush. "Forget it. Right now, we need to figure out a way for you to curtail the comet's power." She'd help him get his nephew back safely, and then she'd go home. Alone.

Jase blew out air. "I need to break through my mental block, if that's really what's holding me back."

Admiration welled inside Brenna. The guy didn't want to look inside his own head, but to save his nephew, he'd suffer. What would Jase's love for a woman feel like? Probably all-encompassing and secure. "How do you break through?"

He grimaced. "I go back to Lily."

Chapter 21

Jase took a moment to relax his shoulders before knocking on the prophet's door. She opened before he could knock.

"Come on in." Long skirts swished as she gestured him toward one of the dainty chairs, the scent of strawberries wafting around.

His feet wanted to drag. Yet he forced himself to cross the room and sit. The sound of the door shutting made him jump. His hands shook. This was such a bad idea.

Lily sat across from him and smiled. "You're brave to want to be hypnotized, although I think we should just talk. Your memories are all accessible." Steam rose from a cup of floral tea next to her, and in her long skirt, she looked like a lady from centuries ago. One who shouldn't be exposed to the reality of his life.

He pressed the fine armrests to stand up. "This is a bad idea."

She patted his hand, her skin so pale and delicate. "You can do this."

"I know." How did he explain? "I don't think you should, I mean, you—"

A sweet smile lifted her pink lips. "I've been a prophet for three centuries and during two wars. As such, I've counseled many people who've literally gone through hell." She sighed, her eyes reflecting a weary wisdom she usually hid. "Unfortunately, nothing you say will shock me."

He settled back into the chair and studied the prophet. There was more to Lily Sotheby than he'd seen. "Anything I tell you is confidential."

"I won't tell a soul."

Before that moment, he would've assumed Dage, as king, could get all information from Lily. But now, he doubted it. "If anything I say upsets you, please stop me."

Lily's blue eyes softened. "Everything you say will upset me because I care about you, Jase. We're old friends. But I promise, I can handle the truth."

They might be old friends, but he always felt like a kid in her presence. And something in him, deep down, experienced shame at the torture he'd lived through. As if he'd deserved the pain. No, it wasn't rational—and he was no victim. So it was time to suck it up and deal. "What now?"

"Now you relax."

He barked out a laugh. "No problem." His shoulders hardened to rock.

Lily settled back. "We're going to talk for a while, and you're going to concentrate on breathing in and breathing out. Smooth and easy. Okay?"

"Okay." He breathed in.

"Good. Before the first war started, when you were just a kid, what was it like with four older brothers?" Lily asked.

Jase grinned. "Fun. Lots of fun. We were the Kayrs kids . . . full of fire and trouble. Even Dage was relaxed—well, for Dage."

"Before he was forced to become king?"

"Yes. Before the Kurjans murdered our parents." Jase wiped his wet palms on his jeans. "Dage changed overnight—he had to."

"And he sent you to fight."

"Yes. I was fifteen and old enough." Of course, Jase always had his older brothers flanking him. As war went, he was safe. "Dage has always felt guilty."

"That must be a hard burden for you to bear."

Jase shrugged. "We all have our crosses."

"So true," Lily murmured. "What's your favorite season?"

"Summer—as hot as possible." There was a time he'd raced cars, boats, planes. Anything with speed. His shoulders relaxed as memories assailed him. "Though winter was always good, too."

"What are you afraid to tell everyone?"

The question caught him off guard, and his heart sped up. Concentrating on his breathing, he slowed it down. "I'm afraid everyone will know how crazy I went." One day the rock face had spit out shards, and he'd stuck one in his jugular. Just to end the pain.

"Why?" she asked.

He blinked. "Well, I lost. I mean, they beat me. I went nuts."

"No." She leaned forward, her gaze intense. "You survived, and you won. Regardless of the games your brain created to help you survive."

"I stabbed myself." Suicide wasn't a winning move.

"You didn't die." She shook her head. "Come on. You're a three-hundred-year-old soldier who has killed many times. If you'd truly wanted to die, you wouldn't be sitting here right now."

His lungs seized. "Then, why?"

"I don't know. Maybe it was momentary weakness. Maybe you just needed to do something . . . anything to retain control. But you didn't really try to kill yourself."

At her words, a lump of pain he'd been carrying slowly dissolved. "You must think I'm so stupid."

"No. I think you're brave and still confused. The only way to deal with this stuff is to talk about it, and you vampires stink at talking." She sipped her tea. "No offense."

"None taken."

"Good. The only way to heal is to talk, and to forgive yourself for any shortcomings you think you had." She smiled. "You're well on the way."

Was he, or was he just playing a good game? Part of him wanted to hope, the other part wanted to sink back into plans for revenge. "Thanks."

"I do know you wouldn't have even considered any path other than vengeance before mating Brenna." Lily studied him over the rim of her cup. "Mayhaps you should spend some time with that thought."

He grimaced. "She deserves better."

"Then be better." Lily stood. "Think about everything, and do your homework."

He paused. "Homework?"

"Yes. I want you and Brenna to spend some normal time together doing couple-type things."

Heat flushed up his face. "Um—"

"No. I mean, normal time like furnishing your home or going to a movie." Lily smiled. "Then, let's meet again tomorrow."

Fantastic. He was now one of those guys who met with a shrink every day. "Thank you, Lily." Exiting the room, he ran into Conn. His breath hitched.

Conn paused. "Meeting with Lily?"

God. Now his brother—the ultimate soldier—would think he was some kind of metrosexual. "Yes."

Conn nodded slowly. "She's a good listener."

Jase stilled. "*You've* met with Lily?"

"Sure." Conn hesitated, glancing at the closed door. "Sometimes I have to do something in battle, or see something, and guilt eats at me. So once in a while I talk to Lily."

Jase shook his head. Where had reality gone? "I didn't know that."

"For a while, I didn't want to burden her. I mean, she's so—"

"Dainty." Jase rubbed his head.

"Yeah. That's the word. Dainty." Conn grinned. "But she's tough, and she's good. Has she thrown anything at you yet?"

"Of course not." The woman was a lady.

"Well, hold back, and you'll get a teacup to the head."

Jase snorted. He shifted his feet, finally feeling like a brother again. "We don't gotta hug or anything right now, do we?"

"Shit no." Conn punched him in the arm. Hard. "It's all good."

"How about we move it closer to the wall?" Brenna asked, her concentration on the antique sofa table and matching end tables that had been delivered earlier that day. "I mean, until we buy a sofa to ground the room."

Max Petrovsky easily lifted the table and set it against the living room wall. As a deadly hunter for the vampires, the guy was surprisingly good-natured about moving furniture around the room all morning as he waited for Jase to show up. He turned and glanced at the open wall. "Maybe you should get new windows before you buy more furniture."

Brenna shrugged. "I think Jase already ordered replacement windows." A pleasant breeze wafted in from the ocean, and she took a deep breath. "Though I like the openness." Well, until it rained.

Max eyed the far wall, his odd metallic eyes narrowing. "I think I like the big table over there."

Brenna hid a grin. The king's deadly bodyguard had a thing for feng shui. "Maybe you're right."

Max lifted the heavy oak with one hand to carry it across the room. "When did you say Jase would be back?"

She hadn't. "Soon." Probably.

"Okay." Max loped over to the demolished window and tugged a shard from the top frame. At well over six feet, the hulking soldier came in handy. Humming to himself, he ran his hand along the entire length, dropping glass to the floor. "These might fall on somebody," he murmured.

The front door opened, and he pivoted, instantly on alert.

Brenna stilled. There was the killer with the reputation people whispered about. She turned and smiled. "Hi, Jase. Max was just helping me with the tables."

Amusement lightened Jase's eyes. "Max is actually a great decorator."

Max snorted. "I don't mind embracing my softer side."

Brenna chuckled. There was nothing soft about any of the vampires. "We need more furniture."

"How about we go buy some?" Jase asked.

Was he serious? Brenna leaned against the wall. "Now?"

"Yes." Jase frowned at the missing windows. "We should have replacement glass soon, so we might as well furnish the room."

Her heart pitter-pattered. Jase wanted to go buy furniture with her? Like a real married couple? "What about Garrett? I mean, we can't just leave."

"The best people in the world are working on finding Garrett. The second they have a lead, they'll call us." Jase nodded toward the sofa table. "I like the table on the other wall."

Max shook his head. "Amateur."

"Hmph." Jase surveyed Max. "Are you here to see me?"

"Yes. How was your visit with Lily?" Max asked.

"Good." Jase frowned. "Why?"

"I was being polite. Has she hit you with the ruler yet?" Max absently rubbed his thigh.

Jase grinned. "Not yet, but I'm sure it'll happen. What can I help you with, Max?"

Max prowled toward the door. "I need to collect all of the Degoller Stars from you. The king wants them put away."

Jase stilled. "No."

Max rubbed his chin. "I have an order."

"No," Jase said levelly.

Max paused by the door. "Okay-dokey."

Brenna frowned. "That's it?"

Max shrugged. "Yep. I'm not getting between two Kayrs brothers."

"You're a brother, too," Jase muttered.

"Exactly." Max shoved past Jase to the front porch. "Which means I get to stay out of this one. Thank God," he muttered as he loped down the steps.

Jase turned back toward Brenna. "That was odd."

Not really. Centuries ago, the Kayrs family had taken in Max, making him one of them. As family, Max had wanted to check up on Jase. The hulk had a sweet side. "Are you serious about going furniture shopping?"

Jase shuffled his feet. "Yes, it'll be nice to get away from headquarters for an afternoon."

Yeah, it would. Brenna smiled, her heart lighter than it had been for days. "I do love shopping."

Jase's smile seemed forced. "Ah, me, too."

Brenna snorted. "I'm sure." A vampire shopping for furniture? This was going to be an afternoon to remember.

Jase sprawled on the zillionth leather couch he'd sat on that afternoon. "What's wrong with this one?"

Brenna twisted to see around a tall clock. "That's real leather."

"So?"

"So, one of your brothers married a vegan who will light it on fire if it's in our house." Brenna leaned down and grabbed his hand. "I kind of agree with her, actually. Come on, there's a faux leather ensemble over behind the dining room table I love."

He tugged back just enough to tumble her into his lap, contenting himself with the feel of woman in his arms. "I refuse to sit on any more sofas."

She chuckled and tried to lever herself away from him. "Knock it off."

"No." He buried his face in her neck, inhaling the scent of Ireland. Warmth flushed down his torso, and his jeans became too tight.

The loud clearing of a throat caught his attention. The shop owner peered down his pointed nose. "Sir. I've already asked you twice to stop the shenanigans." He patted his slicked-back hair and nodded toward two human females watching. "You're causing a scene."

The two middle-aged women had been watching Jase since he'd walked into the store, and one kept fanning herself. Maybe she was having heart problems or something. Jase stood and whipped out a credit card with no limit. "We'll take the dining set, the sofa set behind that, the clock, and all of the office furniture my, ah, wife has tagged."

The man straightened, a blush spreading across his face as he was suddenly all teeth. "Excellent. Very good, sir. I'll go write these up." He tripped over a potted plant in his hurry toward the cash register.

Jase shook his head and stood, settling Brenna on her feet. Closing his eyes, he tried to concentrate. Nothing happened.

Brenna elbowed him in the gut. "What are you doing?"

"I'm trying to make it rain in here." He opened his eyes. "But no altering the air for me today." Someday he hoped to regain the skill. Tangling his fingers with hers, he tugged her toward the counter.

She stumbled, glancing at a dining room set in the window. "Maybe—"

"No." God, if he didn't get out of there, he was going to start flashing fangs.

"But—"

That was it. Turning, he yanked her against him and slid his mouth over hers, kissing her hard. Heat roared between his ears and down his spine to pool in his groin. Releasing her and leaning back, he studied her flushed face. "Somebody so sweet shouldn't be so damn sexy," he rumbled.

Twin "ahs" came from the women behind the potted plants.

Brenna grinned. "You just can't behave."

"If you cared about me, you'd set this place on fire." He was only half-joking.

Her eyes sparkled, while her smile slid away. "I do care about you. Probably too much."

The temptation to slide into such honest sweetness grabbed him around the heart.

The owner cleared his throat. Again. "For an additional ten percent, we can deliver your furniture today."

Jase kept his gaze on his woman. "Somebody will pick it up later today." He turned and flashed his teeth. "Be nice to them. They're not nearly as polite as I am."

The guy paled.

Jase signed, accepted his card, and bulldozed Brenna out of the store before she could change her mind. "You promised me ice cream if I bought you the dining room set."

She slipped her small hand into his and pointed down the sidewalk. "There's a place down there." As they passed teenagers on skateboards, joggers with yapping dogs, and little old ladies with puffed hair and brightly colored purses, Brenna snuggled into his side. "It feels weird to be doing normal stuff."

A kid dressed in all black careened a skateboard by the elderly ladies, grabbing a pink purse and angling away from Jase.

Jase manacled the kid by the throat, lifting him several feet as the board crashed into a parking meter. "Give it back."

The kid's eyes widened, popping out. He held the purse away, and the woman reached for it. "Bad boy." Tucking it to her ample chest, she smiled at Jase. "Thank you, young man."

"Yes, ma'am." Jase smiled and dropped the kid. He ran across the street.

Brenna sighed. "Now that's normal for us."

Jase looked up at the ice cream sign. "Let's get a snack, and then we need to get home. We should have news on Garrett."

Reality just wouldn't stay away, no matter how much he wanted to pretend.

Chapter 22

Garrett eyed the wires lining the wall. He'd broken through the first few layers, but the explosives were well set. Blowing up the boat held a certain appeal, but he'd like to jump off first.

The outside door opened, and Kalin appeared. He eyed the damaged walls and exposed wires. "You're about to blow yourself up." He held a latte cup in one hand.

Garrett frowned. "You drink lattes?" For some reason, he'd figured the butcher only drank blood and sucked on dead things.

"Sure. With soy milk. That cow's milk is full of hormones." Kalin mock-shrugged.

Who the hell was this guy? "I figured I'd cut the blue wires."

"Interesting." Kalin took a gulp of the steaming brew and hummed in appreciation. "You'll be dead in seconds if you cut all the blue wires. Or the red. Or the green."

Garrett eyed the wires. "That leaves yellow."

"Nope. Those, too."

So the release was in a pattern. One he had no clue how to decipher. "How extensive is the blast?"

"You'll only kill yourself." Kalin leaned against the far wall. "The boat may sink, but we'll all survive. So, young Kayrs, I wouldn't cut a wire, were I you."

He might survive the blast so long as his head remained attached to his body. Garrett rubbed his chin. Might as well take advantage of the calm Kurjan. "What's your plan, anyway? I mean, your best-case scenario. You mate Janie, and what?" Not that there was a chance in hell Janie would mate this asshole.

Kalin shrugged. "First, I figure out what the big deal is with her powers, then I use them. Subsequently, we have many, many sons with power . . ."

"And you rule the world?" Was this a comic book, or what? "You know that's crazy, right?"

"It's not a bad plan, really. Our scientists are working on a cure for our aversion to the sun. Someday, I'll live in the Caribbean." His eyes swirled purple through the bright green. "Once I take care of the vampires and the lowly shifters, I'm taking out the demons."

"Isn't this the part where you let loose with your evil laugh?"

Kalin flashed a grin. "You're a smart-ass, Kayrs."

Like he'd never heard that before. "I'm realizing that you're going to be my first kill."

"Oh no, I'm not. I may not have your sister's psychic powers, but there's a moment coming up soon where somebody is headless, and it might be me. Or not. Either way, you're not present."

"Who is?" Garrett moved closer to the bars.

"Ask your sister."

Oh, he would. First second he got off this stupid boat. "I take it your plan didn't work?"

"No." Kalin sighed. "The vampires repaired the security system faster than we'd hoped, and we didn't get Janet out fast enough. Lost six good men, too."

"You shouldn't have sent them up against my family."

"I still have you, now don't I?" Kalin took another drink.

For now. Garrett cocked his head. "Are you really a serial killer?"

Kalin grimaced. "I do enjoy a good hunt."

"You hunt women—even human ones. Easy prey." Garrett's gut clenched.

"Well, a guy does need a hobby."

Several loud thunks echoed from up above. What the hell? Slivers of pain pierced Garrett's brain.

Kalin lifted his head. "Damn it." Throwing his latte on the carpet, he yanked the door opened and ran upstairs.

Garrett pressed his temples, dropping to one knee.

The air filled with tension until oxygen held weight. His back trembled. What was going on?

Fear made his ears ring. His vision blurred.

His fangs dropped.

Gunfire shook the boat. Shit. If they sank, could he get out?

The boat pitched. Men screamed. Boots thumped on the stairs.

Reality swam out of focus. Had they somehow drugged him again? Explosions shattered his mind. His stomach lurched. Stumbling to the corner, he puked up the sandwich they'd fed him earlier.

The boat rocked, and he slammed into the bars. His shoulder cracked. Pain blurred his vision. He bit through his lip to keep from crying out.

Okay. Dropping to his knees in front of the wires, he struggled to focus. Uncle Conn had spent years teaching him about bombs and detonation. The multicolored wires spread out in every direction.

The room spun, and he coughed out a laugh. Damn, he needed to focus. Sticking his pinkie in his ear, he swirled it around. Nope. No blood. Why did his brain hurt so bad?

A high-pitched shriek ripped through the night. Were his people attacking? Boots thumped down the stairs, and the door flew open.

Fear nearly knocked him down. On the other side of the bars stood a demon. White hair, black eyes, plenty of silver medals on his right breast. A soldier.

Garrett snarled and rose to a fighting stance.

The demon smiled.

Brutal images of death flashed behind Garrett's eyes. He staggered back, his stomach revolting again. Drawing a deep breath, he tried to focus and fight through the pain.

His nerves misfired, shrieking agony into his central nervous system. Blood dripped over his upper lip from his nose. Red hazed across his vision.

The demon drew a glowing green gun from a side holster.

Garrett settled his stance. If he was going to die, he was going to face the bastard shooting him.

The demon pointed the gun and fired at the lock. The door flew open.

Garrett backed away from the open doorway, measuring the

demon's arm span. They were about the same height, but the demon was much broader through the chest. For now. Give Garrett a century or two, and he'd take the guy.

"Walk on your own, and I'll stop the pain, Kayrs," the demon said, his mangled vocal cords marking him as a purebred.

The guy knew his name. The horrible images disappeared form Garrett's mind. The pain ebbed to a low throb.

Demon or not, outside the bars was much better than inside, near the explosives. So he nodded. His hands shook, so he wiped them down his pants. He reached the doorway, and the demon flipped him around to zip-tie his wrists.

The cord cut into his flesh, and he bit back a snarl.

The demon leaned in, his breath heated. "Walk quietly, and I won't explode your brain. Fuck with me, and you'll never think clearly again."

Garrett nodded again. The best place to attack would be topside, where he could jump into the ocean. "Where are we going?"

"My people have been looking for you. Let's just say we have plans." The demon shoved him toward the open doorway.

The thought of the hell his uncle Jase had gone through almost stopped Garrett from moving. His ears rang, and his heart raced into battle mode. God. What was he going to do?

Brenna frowned at the new configuration of the living room. "I'm not sure."

Jase groaned and dropped into an overstuffed chair, eyeing his half-finished bowl of Chunky Monkey on the end table. "We've been moving furniture for two hours. The moon is high, the night is dark, and I'm finished."

"You're on your fifth bowl of ice cream. If nothing else, you need to burn calories." With a snort, Brenna flounced past him. Well, she tried.

He shoved out a foot to trip her. Arms windmilling, she plummeted toward him, where he easily caught her. "Are you calling me fat?"

She righted herself, shoving against his chest. "If the tight jeans fit . . ."

His fingers instantly found her rib cage.

"Nooooo." She struggled, giggling, fire dancing on her arms.

Whoa. He'd forgotten about the fire and stopped tickling her. "Relax, darlin'."

She sucked in air, and the fire swished out. "I'd be so upset if we burned up our new furniture."

Pleasure filled him at her use of the word *our*. "We should probably break it in."

Delight filled her pretty eyes as she maneuvered to straddle him. "Last time we played in this room, I broke all of your windows."

"Our windows."

She lifted a shoulder. "Maybe."

Playing hard to get, was she? He kept her gaze, slowly unbuttoning her shirt. Feminine knowledge filled her eyes and provided a natural challenge. Even so, he forced himself to go slow, to stay with the fun they'd had all afternoon. "I enjoyed shopping with you."

A dimple flashed in her left cheek. "No, you didn't. You wouldn't even share your ice cream."

"I did share." He smoothed the shirt down her arms.

"Only the first cone." She slid her hands along his chest, humming softly.

"Well, then." Reaching for his spoon, he pressed it against her pink mouth. "I'll share now."

Her tongue flicked out at the melting ice cream, and he fought a groan. Even playful, his witch was beyond sexy. "Happy now?"

She licked her lips. "No."

His cock flared to life and tried to punch through his jeans. "You're a hard woman to please."

"You should try harder." Her lids half closed.

"I really should." So he dumped the bowl over her chest.

She burst out laughing and glanced down at the Chunky Monkey covering her bra and skin. "You didn't. That's so cold."

Yeah. Her pretty nipples had sprung right to attention. "My apologies." He couldn't help the grin. Was this what happiness felt like? He'd forgotten.

She dug both hands through his hair. "Clean up your mess, Kayrs."

"Of course." He leaned in and licked the ice cream from her skin. The woman tasted even better than the dessert. So sweet.

She breathed against him, her heart clamoring beneath his mouth.

A nip of a fang shredded her bra. "I'll buy you a new one," he whispered, dipping to capture a nipple.

"Fair enough." She shoved him away to rip his shirt over his chest. Her eyes softened, and her fingers glided along his scars. "You truly are a beautiful man." Leaning forward, she kissed the jagged scar above his heart.

She'd done that once before, and he'd felt her touch to his soul. "I'm nowhere near beautiful, Bren."

She leaned back and frowned. "You are missing something."

What? He glanced down. "Huh?"

"Aye." Clutching his shoulders, she shoved her torso into him and rubbed herself along his chest. Wetness instantly coated his skin. With a saucy grin, she leaned back. "Now who's sticky?"

He glanced down at the mess on his chest. "You're going to clean that up."

"With pleasure." She licked along his pecs and up his jawline to nip at his ear. Then her fingers dug into his ribs.

He jumped, unsettling her. She tickled harder. He chuckled, lifted her with one hand, and ripped off her jeans.

"Smooth." She reached for the button on his jeans and yanked it free. The disc flew into the far wall. Shimmying down his lap, she tugged the material free when he lifted his butt. Then she straddled him again, nude as could be.

Ice cream had pooled along her collarbone, so he obliged her by licking her clean. She chuckled and tilted her pelvis along his engorged shaft. She was wet and ready, and he couldn't help but grin. They'd always been so intense, the sudden playfulness intrigued him. Even so, nothing could've prevented him from lifting her by the hips to settle down onto his cock.

Her eyes widened as he slowly lowered her, allowing her tight sheath to accommodate his size.

Finally, her butt hit his thighs.

He blew out air, fire flashing through his balls. Control. He needed to keep control or this would be over way too quickly.

She sighed softly, her inner thighs pressing against his legs.

Then her fingers dug into his ribs again.

He jumped, his cock scraping her internal walls. The need to pound roared through his blood. "Stop that."

"No." Leaning forward, tilting her body, she tickled him harder.

So he lifted her and then dropped her along his shaft.

She gasped, her eyes widening. "I do like that." Pressing her knees into the couch, she lifted herself and then dropped back down. He groaned, and she grinned, full of fun. The sprite did it again.

His control snapped. Grabbing her hips, he turned and flattened her on the couch, thrusting hard. Her legs wrapped around him, her hands dug into his biceps, and she met each thrust with one of her own. The smile remained on her pretty face.

He grinned back, pounding harder, the need to come shoving every other thought from his head.

Gliding his finger along her lips, he shoved it inside her heated mouth. She sucked, the feeling shooting straight to his dick. Then, he removed his finger and drew a wet trail between her breasts, over her abs, along her mound . . . to twirl around her clit.

She arched against him, her eyes widening, her body thrown into an orgasm that gripped him tighter than a vise. Seconds later, his balls drew tight, and he erupted.

Seconds, minutes, maybe a lifetime later, he finally relaxed against her. Their upper chests stuck together. He laughed and picked her up. "Back to the kitchen, my ice cream fiend."

She sighed and tucked her face into his neck.

Home. Jase held her close and wondered. Could this be home? He set her on the counter and reached for paper towels to clean their chests. Then he carried her toward the bedroom so he could get dressed.

She lay on the bed, her eyes sated. "Where are you going?"

"I need to lock the gym but I'll be right back." He should work out, but he'd rather grapple in bed some more with Brenna. "I promise."

She stretched like a lazy cat. "I'll be here."

"I'll hurry." And he would.

Jase all but jogged out of the house, his heart lighter than it had been in years. The moon guided his way, soft and bright. He had to lock the gym just in case some of the younger kids got curious. There were too many weapons in there to play with.

He'd reached the pathway before Conn bellowed his name. Something in the tone chilled him to the bone. He turned and broke into a run without thinking, halting in front of his brother. Heavy boot steps echoed, and he pivoted to see Dage running toward him.

"What?" he asked.

Fury lit Dage's eyes. "We have confirmation that a squad of demons found the Kurjans. They've taken Garrett."

Chapter 23

All thought and sound screeched to a stop in Jase's head. His vision narrowed to a tunnel. His heart rate actually slowed. "No."

"Yes." Dage pushed inside the lodge and slid open a keypad. A hidden door opened to reveal a large armory. "We traced the message to the warehouse district in Seattle."

Jase yanked a vest over his head. "Why did the demons take Garrett?"

"Doesn't matter." Dage tied a knife sheath to his leg.

Jase stilled. "They'll want a trade. They want me."

"I said it doesn't matter." Dage tightened his bulletproof vest. "You're staying here to guard headquarters."

"No, I'm not." Jase reached for a knife long enough to decapitate a demon in one slice. "I spent five years with them. Five years learning how to counter their mind attacks. You need me."

"I can't afford you right now," Dage said grimly. "Sorry."

Conn grabbed Dage's arm. "Jase is right. We need all the help we can get countering their attacks. Somebody has to keep a clear head."

Dage stepped into Conn's space. "Jase hasn't had a clear head in five years."

Jase cleared his throat. "I'm standing right here, assholes." He slipped the knife along his leg. "I know I've been on edge, and that

I screwed up last time. But I'm dealing, and I'm focused. Plus, I'm an excellent decoy considering the demons want me back."

Dage turned his head. "Why? Why do they want you so badly?"

"Willa wants me." Just the words burned down his throat. The fucking female demon had tried to seduce him more times than he could count, and he'd almost fallen into her trap. "Her brother probably just wants me dead."

"If you screw this up, I'll kill you myself—and no bringing the Degoller Stars," Dage muttered. "Everyone else is arming themselves underground. We meet at the helicopters in ten minutes." He turned and jogged toward the doorway. "Take a moment and say good-bye to loved ones. This is going to get ugly."

Conn grabbed another gun and pierced Jase with a look. "Don't make me regret backing your play. If you do screw up, Dage won't get the chance to kill you before I do." Without another word, he turned and ran into the night.

Jase swallowed. Two death threats in the span of a minute. Not a bad night, all in all. While he wanted to bring the decapitating stars, he understood Dage's insistence on adhering to the treaty. Those stars killed vampires as easily as demons. He headed into the night, turning toward his home. What was left of it, anyway.

He found Brenna sitting on a bench overlooking the tumultuous sea. Moonlight glinted off her hair, bathing her like a goddess. The moment hurt. His chest ached.

"So you're going to fight demons," she said softly.

"Yes."

She shook her head. "Do you think you're ready?"

Hell, no. He'd never be ready. "Yes."

She stood to face him, her head not reaching his chin. "If I asked you not to go?"

His mouth opened but no sound emerged.

She nodded. "That's what I thought."

"I have to go. It's Garrett." Surely she understood.

"Yes, I know." She reached up and palmed his jaw.

Everything in him wanted to lean into her touch. To lose himself in her. So he remained still. "I'll return by dawn."

"You'll save Garrett. I'm sure of it." Her gray eyes glowed with an ethereal glimmer in the moonlight. For the first time, he saw the lineage of witches in her. Powerful, beautiful, feminine witches who harnessed the moon.

"I know." He brushed a kiss on her nose.

She swallowed. "Will this obsession ever be over? Even after you find Garrett?" Her small shoulders steeled as if for a blow.

"No." He frowned. "Not until the last one is dead. No more demons."

"That's what I thought," she murmured and stepped back. "Stay safe, Jase."

He hesitated and then nodded. "Moira is staying to help secure headquarters. You stick with her squad." Without waiting for an answer, he turned and jogged around the house to the street. Something had just happened with Brenna, but he couldn't figure it out. The words had felt like good-bye.

He shook his head, breaking into a full run toward the landing areas. There would be time to fix things with Brenna after he got Garrett back. A familiar rage welled up from his gut, and he ruthlessly shoved fury down. Anger wouldn't help him now. He'd learned young that killing with cold efficiency kept him alive. That was what he needed now—because there was no doubt he'd kill tonight.

He reached the head helicopter and jumped in the back next to Conn. Dage piloted while Talen sat in the front. "Go," he said, shutting the door.

The bird lifted into the air. Talen nodded for him to slip on earphones and waited until he complied. "Three copters, attack formation. You're shield, Jase."

Jase nodded.

"Kane and Amber are in helicopter two for shields." Kane's mate, Amber, had a natural ability to shield from demon attacks, and Kane had slowly learned the skill from her. "The last helicopter will come in from the sea, blasting as we land."

Jase took a deep breath. As a plan, it was risky. But it was all they had. "Do we know Garrett is on location?"

"No." Talen turned back toward the front windshield. "I also don't like how we traced the message. Kane said the message was well secured, and he had to go through several servers, but still. Might be a trap."

Jase leaned forward. If it was a trap, they were prepared. "The key to countering a demon attack is to let it in." Which explained why he'd gone so nuts.

Talen turned his head. "Let it in?"

"Yes. Let the images in, let the pain in, and make it yours. If it's yours, no matter how devastating, it can't kill you. It can't decapitate you. Enjoy the pain." He'd give anything not to have to admit that.

Serious eyes filled with sorrow as Talen studied him before turning back to the night. He exhaled. "Fair enough."

They flew low, hugging the treetops, the ocean glinting to the left. Jase closed his eyes, resting his head against the wall. What was up with Brenna? He was losing her, and part of him wondered if he'd ever had her. Their mating was unconventional, but he'd come to rely on her in the short time they'd been together.

Could she rely on him?

Her plan to head back to Ireland for the solstice didn't sit well. He needed her close and safe on his continent. The witches couldn't protect her like he could.

Within an hour, his head started to ache. His eyes slowly opened. "The pressure in the air has changed."

"No shit," Talen muttered.

"Don't forget to let the pain in and ride it." Jase leaned to look at the trees spinning by. How many demons were down there? Enough to affect the atmosphere just by existing. Anticipation slithered down his spine.

The helicopter set down in a darkened alley. Jase jumped out, sprinting into a fast jog behind Talen. They maneuvered through alleys, keeping to the shadows, until they reached a chain-link fence. He scaled it easily, landing quietly on the other side.

The industrial park was silent, but the thrum of power rode the wind.

"Heat signatures in Building 4A near the wharf," Kane said through the earpieces.

Talen gave the go-ahead, and Jase sprang into action.

The demons hadn't realized they'd been compromised, or the pain would have started.

He peered around an outbuilding at the innocuous warehouse

and lifted his assault rifle. His finger itched with the need to fire. So he took several deep breaths, filling his lungs with the scent of salt and ocean.

Talen cut him a glance. "You okay?" he mouthed.

Jase nodded. His knees vibrated, wanting to run and attack.

"Everyone is in position. Fire in the hole," Dage ordered from the other side of the building.

The night lit up with fire.

All four walls of the building exploded outward. They couldn't risk harming Garrett, so the charges had been placed to open and not destroy.

A slam of energy hit Jase from the south. He grabbed Talen's arm and pointed to a gray outbuilding that was big enough for one room. "In there," he mouthed. Then he ducked low and ran toward the back.

Talen followed, guns in hand. The sounds of battle echoed behind them with shrieks of pain and gunfire. Smoke filled the air.

Reaching the back door, Jase nodded.

Talen yanked it open, and Jase darted inside.

Three men in full soldier uniforms stood in attack formation, guns out. Maps lined the walls, and a table in the center was full of battle plans. Debris, containers, and bricks were scattered throughout the space.

Jase dove to the side and rolled, coming up firing.

Talen did the same.

Jase hit one demon, while the other two ducked behind metal containers.

The breath in Jase's lungs heated. He recognized one of the soldiers. A high-up officer in Suri's army, the guy had helped torture Jase more than once. He growled low, rage sharpening his vision.

Talen scrambled to the north and jumped the other guy, hitting him in the head three times. The demon hit the floor, unconscious.

Jase ducked under a volley of bullets and reached the one he'd shot. Removing the long blade, he decapitated the bastard with one hard slice. Turning, he slid between two containers.

Images of death filtered through his head along with a piercing pain. He smiled, his fangs dropping. Opening his mind, he allowed the terror to take hold. Bile rose from his gut. He sucked in all the demon energy he could reach. The pain slowly dissipated, digging somewhere deeper than his physical being. Something to worry about later.

He lifted up, facing the remaining soldier. "I remember you."

The demon smiled, his black eyes morphing to purple. "I remember you, too."

Talen staggered into view, his knife at the throat of the demon slowly regaining consciousness. "Stop the attack, or he loses his head."

The mind attack ebbed.

Blood dripped off the knife in Jase's hand. "Where's my nephew?"

The demon frowned. "Not here. Why would you think he's here?"

Fucking demons always lied. Fury ripped down Jase's torso, and he stalked closer. "Last chance. Tell me where he is."

The demon's silver medals matched his hair. Had he earned some of those by torturing Jase? By breaking him? The bastard shook his head. "I don't know where he is."

Jase darted forward.

"*Cineri gloria sera venit,*" the demon chanted.

Jase stopped cold. Confusion hazed his vision. His gun lowered.

"Jase?" Talen growled, angling to the side.

No sound would come out of his mouth, no matter how hard Jase tried to speak. His legs weakened.

The demon chuckled. "You didn't think we let you live for the hell of it, did you?"

Dread weighed down Jase's limbs. He coughed, fighting to speak. "Can't move."

Talen sliced off the head of the soldier he was holding, throwing him to the ground and reaching for Jase.

"*Cineri gloria sera venit.*" The remaining demon hissed. "Now, you kill. *Nunc.*"

Jase pivoted, his gun rising to point at Talen. Oh God. He fought his own hold, but it was absolute. What in the hell? He tried to growl, but nothing came out. His legs trembled with the need to turn away, but they remained in place.

His brain wasn't controlling his body.

Talen's eyes widened. "Jase. You can beat this. Dig deep." Even so, Talen slowly drew a knife from his pocket.

Jase slid the safety into place.

"*Nunc,*" the demon said.

The safety clicked off with a flick of Jase's finger. His shoulders shook as he tried to fight the command to kill.

Talen dropped to the ground and threw the knife. The long blade embedded itself in the demon's eye. The soldier grabbed the handle, screaming.

The mental hold on Jase disappeared. Roaring, he turned and tackled the demon.

"Wait, Jase," Talen yelled. "We need him for information."

A roaring filled Jase's head. Blood covered his vision. Rage heated him until he couldn't breathe. Yanking out his knife, he slammed it into the demon's neck, piercing all the way to the floor. Spitting venom, he twisted right and then left.

The demon's head rolled away.

Jase lifted up, bellowing. He'd kill them all. Pivoting, he ran toward the door.

Talen stopped him, both hands against his chest.

Jase threw his brother to the side, yanking open the door.

Talen's tackle came from behind and thunked Jase's face against the asphalt. A firm hand grabbed his hair, lifted, and slammed his forehead back down.

Stars exploded behind his eyes.

Then, he slid into the safe blackness of unconsciousness.

Chapter 24

Even though the demon was holding back his power, Garrett's brain hurt like it was swelling against his skull. He swallowed blood from biting his tongue. The steps to the top wavered, and he had to concentrate not to trip.

Gunfire echoed through the night.

He reached the top of the boat, and fresh air slapped him in the face. Cold and pure, it tempted him to breathe deep. Two men grappled near the bow.

The demon shoved him in the ribs. "The raft is over there."

A second demon shot a Kurjan and knocked him into the water. The demon jogged over. "The boat will detonate in three minutes."

"Good," the first demon said. "Let's get out of here."

A small splash sounded, and a large hand gripped the railing before a man vaulted over. Water sprayed. He swung at the other demon, knocking the guy to the ground.

Hope filled Garrett. While the guy wore a mask, he obviously wasn't a demon.

The demon holding him shoved him harder toward the stern. "Move, kid."

Garrett slid across the wet floor, tightening his knees for balance. "Untie my hands, and I won't fall."

"Don't care if you fall." The soldier grabbed his arm and yanked.

"Now that's just not nice." Garrett pivoted and kneed the guy in the nuts. The demon hissed in pain. Garrett crashed his forehead on the guy's nose.

Cartilage cracked.

Instant pain ripped into Garrett's brain. He cried out, going blind. A punch to the face sent him ass-over-teakettle back down the stairs. His face landed first, followed by his legs.

The pain in his nose compounded the agony in his brain, and he rolled over.

With a hard *thump*, the demon landed next to him. The bastard groaned as he hit. Garrett scrambled to the far wall, tugging uselessly with his wrists.

Long legs came into view as the man dressed in black jumped into the room, slamming the door shut. He was dripping wet, and a mask still covered his face.

The demon lifted his head, and the tall guy slammed a flak boot into his jaw. The demon slumped unconscious.

Using the wall for balance, Garrett stood. Who was this guy? Green eyes stared out of the mask, and sharp fangs dropped low. A vampire? "What the hell?"

The guy grabbed Garrett's elbow and swung him around. A quick snip, and his hands were free.

He pivoted. "You're a vampire?"

"Partly." The guy ripped off the mask to reveal a hard face with dark hair. A scar lined the side of his face.

Gunfire pattered through the night.

The guy turned and eyed the exposed wires in the cell. "Hmmm." Grabbing the demon by the armpits, the guy threw him with a fierce grunt. The demon hit the wires and kept going.

"Duck." The vampire tackled Garrett to the carpet.

The world detonated.

Heat flashed a second before smoke filled the cell.

Garrett turned his head to view the gaping hole in the wall. Moonlight glinted off the churning waves outside.

The boat pitched.

The vampire hauled Garrett up by the shirt and tugged him to the opening. "Jump and swim north. I have a raft waiting."

A body hit the water from the above deck. Garrett's gut clenched. "Thanks, but I'll just—"

The guy knocked him into the water.

He went under, swallowing salt. Sputtering and swearing, he shoved to the surface and smacked his head on the bottom of the boat. The guy splashed next to him and yanked him free.

"Listen, kid. If you want to live, you'll follow me to the fucking raft." Turning, the guy dove under the surface.

Garrett paused and eyed the ocean. He couldn't see the shore, and the boat would explode soon. Taking a deep breath, he slipped a knife from the throat of a floating body and then dove to follow his dubious rescuer.

He kept pace, keeping track each time the guy readjusted his course.

The night stilled. A second later, the boat exploded with a ball of fire billowing out. Garrett sucked in air and dove several feet down to avoid being hit by raining debris. The ocean surface lit to a bright orange above him.

He swam under the fire until it no longer glowed. Shooting to the surface, he sucked in oxygen and glanced back at the burning embers. No shouts of pain or gunfire remained.

"This way, kid," the guy whispered.

Garrett searched again for the shore but could only see darkness. He slipped the knife into his jeans and swam toward the voice. A small raft bobbed in the swelling waves, while his new friend hung on the edge.

A man leaned over the side. "It took you long enough, Zane."

The guy nodded. "Kayrs? Get the hell on the boat."

Garrett's mind spun. "Zane? Janie's Zane?"

"That's me." Zane grabbed the back of Garrett's shirt and yanked up, while the guy in the raft tugged.

Garrett flopped over and scrambled to sit with his back to the other side. The guy helped Zane up, and the two instantly started rowing away from the remnants of the boat.

"What the fuck took you so long?" the other guy asked.

"Shut up, Sam." Zane shook out his wet hair, keeping his rowing rhythm. "You try to maneuver in between a Kurjan and demon fighting to grab the trophy."

Garrett growled. "I'm not a trophy."

"You are tonight, sport." Sam grinned, his green eyes glowing in the darkness.

Similar bone structure and the same color eyes. "You two brothers?"

"No," Zane snapped. "I don't have family."

Now why did that sound like a lie? Garrett shrugged. "Whatever you say, man."

Zane growled.

Sam tapped his ear. "There's a lot of chatter about a firefight in Seattle tonight. I think the Realm boys took on Suri's soldiers."

Zane snorted. "That's unfortunate. The prize was on a boat in the Pacific."

Garrett sat up. "Who won?"

Sam shrugged. "Don't know, but all hell broke loose. Even the human cops are headed to the scene."

Garrett relaxed his shoulders. His people knew how to fight. If the humans were involved, his family was already long gone. "What about Suri?" Uncle Jase really wanted to kill Suri.

"He wasn't in Seattle," Sam said. "Your people attacked one of his main bases, though. He'll be hurting."

"My people?" Garrett eyed the two. He'd known Zane was part vampire, but nobody knew what else. Gut feeling? The guy was a shifter—one who didn't align with the Realm. "Who exactly are you, anyway?"

"I'm the guy you owe," Zane said.

Maybe. Maybe not. "How did you find me?"

Sam grinned. "Contacts, young man. It always comes down to who you know, now doesn't it?"

Zane shook his head. "Shut up, Sam."

Garrett tried another tack. "What do you want with my sister, anyway?"

Zane's eyes flashed fire. "I want your sister to stay the fuck out of the war."

"Have you met my sister?" Garrett snorted.

Zane sighed. "Yes. Well, kind of."

"She's not staying out of the war." In fact, hadn't Janie said the end would come down to her, Kalin, and Zane? Garrett jerked his head up. "Did you kill Kalin?"

"No. He and a demon were going at it, and I only had a second to save your ass. I'm sure he got free—he's too smart to die on the boat." Zane frowned, the moonlight casting dark shadows across his face. "But our time is coming."

Lights glowed from a distant shore. Garrett stiffened.

Zane held out a hand. "No need to dart away. I'm not keeping you. This time."

Yeah, like he'd trust some wacko Janie only met in dreamworlds. "Gee, I appreciate that." Garrett yanked out the knife, twisting the blade to catch the light. "I'd hate to have to kill you after the kind rescue."

Sam grinned at Zane. "I really like this kid."

"You should meet his sister," Zane muttered. Then he pointed to a lighthouse about a mile away. "Can you make that lighthouse?"

Garrett nodded. "Sure."

"Okay. There's a disposable cell phone duct-taped to the northern side. Get there, call your people, and stay out of sight until they pick you up." Zane stopped rowing.

Garrett tucked the knife way. "Um. Well, thanks."

"Not a problem." Zane eyed the distance. "Get going now before the sun comes up and you're easy to spot."

Garrett fell back and over the edge, making a small splash. He grabbed the boat and hauled himself up to face Zane. "Saying I do owe you. What do you want?"

Zane pierced him with that odd green gaze. "I want you to keep your sister out of the war for as long as possible."

Garrett shrugged. "That was my plan anyway."

"Good." Zane shoved him in the shoulder, and he splashed back into the ocean. "And don't fuck up my great rescue here by getting caught. Speed to the phone and call for help." Oars hit the water again, and the raft quickly moved out of sight.

Garrett bobbed in the sea for a moment, his gaze on the waning moon. With a shrug, he turned and put all his strength into swimming around the lighthouse. He took several passes until he was sure nobody waited for him.

Then he swam to shore and yanked out his knife.

Still nothing. So he walked around the lighthouse until he found the cell phone. Grabbing it, he dialed one of the public numbers, just in case, and asked to be transferred.

Several transfers later, a female voice answered.

His throat nearly closed, and he felt like a little kid again. "Mom? It's Garrett."

Jase's ears still rang from Talen knocking him out. What the hell was it with his brothers beating on his head lately? Guilt made it hard to move. He'd pointed a gun at Talen, and might've shot him. What kind of trigger had the demons put into his brain?

Was he a danger to his family now? What if the trigger was activated again?

He sat in a cozy relaxation room in the main lodge. The window was wide open, letting the scents of sea and fish into the room.

Kane shook his head, staring at a printout. "I don't know how we missed the trigger."

"You missed it because I haven't dealt with everything that happened." Jase's hands closed into fists on his bloody jeans. "The Latin words he spoke sounded familiar, but I don't know what they mean."

"It's the sound that matters," Kane said absently. "There's only one thing to do. We have to hypnotize you."

"I know." Dread compressed Jase's lungs. "Have we gotten anything from the demon we brought back?" Dage had captured one of the soldiers after the raid.

"Not yet, and frankly, you don't need to worry about it." Kane pierced him with a hard glare. "Talen said you didn't shoot him when ordered."

"No, but I wanted to. Or rather, my body wanted to."

Kane nodded. "That's good. The trigger isn't set as deep or as well as they thought." He turned and sat on the matching sofa. "Why don't we get rid of that trigger for good?"

"Sounds like a plan." Jase took a deep breath. "I'm ready."

A knock echoed on the door, and Dage poked his head in. "How's it going?"

"Just started," Kane said.

Jase rubbed both hands down his face. "Any news from the prisoner we took from Seattle?"

"Not yet." Dage eyed Kane. "You going to hypnotize him and delete the trigger?"

"That's the plan," Kane said.

"See if you can make him be not such an ass." Dage shut the door.

Jase grimaced. "He's pissed."

"No. He's worried." Kane reached over his head and dimmed the lights. "You've been out of control twice lately, and both times could've gotten you killed."

Jase settled his shoulders. "Let's get rid of that trigger so I can go hunt demons."

"Damn it, Jase." Kane blew out air. "Fine. Count down from ten."

Dage poked his head in again. "Just got word—Garrett called. Seems he's safe. We leave in five minutes, so suit up."

Jase stiffened, his gaze flashing to Kane's concerned one. "I guess we'll do this later."

Jase leaned out the door of the helicopter as the waves undulated below him. Even after being damaged, he was the best sniper around. Especially when shooting from a moving vehicle. Conn aimed out the other side, while Dage piloted the craft low and tight. Two other helicopters flew close, one holding the landing party, which included Talen and Kane.

Dawn was breaking just in time, and light glinted off the lighthouse. Peaceful rocks tumbled from the building to the shore. Nothing moved on the land.

Jase ignored his unease and kept watch through his scope.

The first helicopter landed, and Talen burst onto land to find his son, sweeping wide. Kane protected his back as they ran for the structure. Moments passed. Finally, both men emerged from the damaged door, and Kane sent the negative sign.

Damn it. Where was the kid?

Movement from the ocean a few yards back caught Jase's eye. He narrowed his scope to focus. Slowly, Garrett's dark head emerged from the deep. Then his eyes, and his smart-assed grin.

Jase jerked his head, and Conn looked. He tapped a communicator to relay the kid's location.

Smart. Very smart. Garrett had done exactly what they'd trained him to do.

The kid swam to shore and had barely made it when his father yanked him up for a huge hug. The relief crossing Talen's broad face made Jase's shoulders relax. When had Garrett gotten so damn big? He stood as tall as his father.

Kane tugged him away for a hug.

Jase tapped his ear communicator. "Get on the helicopter, and get the hell out of there. We'll hug at home."

Dage snorted into the microphone. Conn flashed him a grin. Relief and triumph swirled in his green eyes.

Jase nodded. Yeah, they'd finally won one. He needed to get his arms around the little shit. Thank God Garrett was all right.

The trip home took too long, and Jase began to worry about what Garrett had gone through. Had they tortured him? The helicopters set down at the landing site simultaneously, and he jumped out to find his nephew.

Then he had to step back as Cara Kayrs ran past him, full-bore for her son.

Garrett caught her, laughing, getting her sweatshirt wet. "Mom, I'm fine."

Cara laughed and cried at the same time, patting his arms, his back, checking him out. "Are you hurt? Did they hurt you?"

Garrett shook his head, looking down over a foot at his mother. "No, honest. I'm fine but hungry. Man, I'm hungry." He glanced up as Janie sprinted into view, and fire leapt into his eyes.

Jase paused. Sometimes he forgot about the predator beneath the kid's good humor. Garrett was every inch his father's son.

But he loved his sister, and he caught her when she launched herself at him. He closed his eyes, hugging her tight. Then he whispered something in her ear.

Janie stiffened, and then relaxed, hugging him. She whispered something back, and even Jase could hear Garrett's low growl as he set her down.

Enough. Jase moved forward.

Garrett caught his eye and grabbed him in a wet hug. A salty, wet hug. "I was worried about you," Garrett said.

Jase smacked him on the back and levered away. "Worried about me?"

"Yeah. I was scared you'd be reliving everything because of me. I'm so sorry." Garrett's odd gray eyes sobered.

Jesus. Something in Jase's chest thumped. Family. They killed you every time. "I'm fine. I was seriously worried about you."

Garrett shrugged. "I'm good. No torture, and I escaped, but I didn't get to kill anybody." He frowned.

Good. Jase wasn't ready for Garrett's first kill.

Dage clapped an arm around his nephew's back. "Good job with waiting in the ocean. Let's go debrief you."

"Hell no." Cara yanked her son's arm. "He gets checked out by the doctors, then he gets food, then he can be interviewed, and then we're having a welcome-home celebration."

The king wavered and looked like he wanted to argue, but even he wouldn't mess with an angry mother. Finally, Dage nodded. "Of course."

Garrett allowed his mother to lead him away, yet turned and gave his sister a look. Man, what Jase wouldn't give to be a fly on the wall for that conversation. Apparently Garrett had been informed that his sister tried to sacrifice herself for him.

Family.

Janie Belle Kayrs sat on the bar, swinging her foot back and forth in the small game room, a beer in her hand. Her younger brother paced by the pool table after having been checked out by doctors and given a pizza.

They had the room to themselves, since their mother was currently setting up a party for Garrett in the large game room.

"You might as well let it out," Janie said.

Garrett turned, fire flashing in his eyes. In that moment, he looked exactly like their father, and Janie couldn't help smiling.

"I am so pissed at you," Garrett growled.

She wanted to tell him not to swear, but since he was technically an adult, and he'd been captured by evil, the time had passed to try and raise him. But she was still his older sister, and he needed to remember that. "So?"

He stilled, pivoting to face her. "So? Did you just say *so?*"

"Of course you're angry. But you did what you had to do, and I understand that." She adored her younger brother and hated to know she'd worried him. But if she'd had a chance to save him, how could she not?

Red climbed into his face. "You will *never* try to sacrifice yourself for me again. Got that?" His voice shook.

If she didn't know him, he'd probably look scary. Really scary.

But she'd burped him as a baby, and he didn't get to try vampire in-timidation tactics on her. "Don't go getting all Kayrs-male on me, asshat. I understand you're upset, but you don't need to yell at me."

Aqua flashed through the metallic gray of his eyes. Man, he was getting pissed. He leaned back against the pool table, his hands denting the wood. "I am a vampire. Although you're crazy, you're still a human. I don't die. You do. So, I protect you." He spoke slowly and through clenched teeth.

Janie's temper began to stir. "I'm five years older than you, and I'm a psychic."

"So?" He lifted a Kayrs eyebrow.

Pride filled her at how tough and strong he'd become. "The Kurjans want me alive. They're fine with you dead. So trading myself for you was a smart, tactical move."

"Did you let the Kurjan butcher take your blood?"

The words caught her off guard, as no doubt they were meant to. She inhaled quickly, forcing herself to meet her brother's furious gaze. "Not exactly."

"Explain."

"Don't be getting all bossy with me." Damn it. She hadn't wanted anybody to know.

"Janie—"

"Fine. No, I didn't *let* Kalin drink me. But, in a dreamworld, one time he did bite me. So yes, he has my blood, and I can't keep him out of the dreamworlds any longer." Her face heated.

Garrett's eyes narrowed. "How did he get close enough to bite?"

She smoothed her face into surprise and shrugged. "I don't know."

"If you lie to me again, I'm telling Dad."

Damn it. She cleared her throat. "I bit him first."

Shock widened Garrett's eyes. "You what?"

"I needed to be able to yank him into the dreamworlds whether he liked it or not, and taking his blood gave me that power." Why didn't everybody understand she had a job to do? A fate to fulfill?

"You're fucking kidding me." Garrett launched himself from the table to tower over her, even though she was sitting on the tall bar. "You bit him. You took a Kurjan's blood. You're crazy."

"Stop swearing." God, if he told their father, Talen would have a heart attack. "I took Zane's, too."

Garrett stepped back, his face paling. "Tell me he didn't take yours."

Janie bit her lip.

"God damn it all to fucking hell." Garrett scraped both hands down his face. "I should've killed him. Shit. I should've killed them both."

Janie frowned. "Huh?"

"Zane rescued me from Kalin and the demons trying to take me." Garrett's shoulders settled.

Warmth flushed through Janie so quickly she swayed. Zane had put himself in danger to save her little brother? She hadn't heard the full story yet. "Did Zane say anything about me?"

Garrett growled. "Yeah. He said to keep you the fuck out of the war."

That sounded like Zane. "What did he smell like?"

Incredulousness flashed across Garrett's face. "Like a guy who'd climbed in from the ocean. What else?"

She shrugged. "I don't know. Any idea what he is besides vampire?"

"My guess is some sort of shifter. A graceful, dangerous type." Garrett turned for the doorway.

"You can't tell about the blood," Janie said softly.

"I have to." Garrett kept his broad back to her. When had he gotten so big?

"Why?" she whispered. "Knowing will only keep Dad up at night, and there's nothing he can do about it."

Garrett glanced over his shoulder, suddenly looking years older. "Fine. But you tell me every time you meet with either one of them, and what happens."

She nodded, jumping down from the bar. "It's a deal."

Chapter 25

Brenna waved at her sister as she hustled into the main room of the lodge. "Garrett!" She scrambled around the sofa to grab the kid and hug him. "Thank God."

He returned the hug with one hand, awkwardly patting her back. His other hand held a sandwich. "I'm fine, Aunt Brenna."

"Good." For the first time in days, she could finally breathe. She leaned back to study him. He'd been home for almost twenty-four hours and had been checked out head to toe by the doctors. His eyes were clear, and his body relaxed. He really was fine. She hugged him again.

He laughed.

Then she released him and wiped away a quick tear. Cara stood to her right, so she grabbed her in a hug.

Cara hugged back. "He's really okay."

"I know." Brenna studied her friend. "Though you look fried."

"It's been a tough one." Cara smiled over at her mate. "Talen can finally relax."

Brenna grinned and spotted Jase over in the corner. A purple bruise lined his jaw, and dark circles cut under his eyes. She maneuvered around family to reach him. "Are you all right?"

"Yes." He ran a hand down her arm, a small smile playing on his face as he watched Garrett. "Twenty-four hours of hypnotism with Kane is like getting hit with bricks for three days."

"You let Kane hypnotize you for that length of time?"

"Yeah. That was the only way to reach the trigger implanted by the demons—they thought I'd kill family on command." Jase lost the smile.

"You wouldn't." She slipped her fingers through his, even though she knew she shouldn't. "Did Kane find the trigger?"

"We think so. It's a simple matter of deprograming, and since he understood the Latin commands, he thinks he got them. Of course, he wants to double-check several times over the next week." Jase shrugged and glanced down. "I've missed you. How are things?"

"Good." She cleared her throat. "I, ah, actually need to talk to you."

"Okay." Giving a nod to his brother, Jase led her outside and into the darkening night. They walked along the ocean cliffs toward his house.

Deep shadows played across the sea, and Brenna took a moment to appreciate the tones. She hadn't painted in much too long. "I'm going home tomorrow morning."

He stopped. "No, you aren't."

"Yes." She lifted her head and wandered her fingertips along his bruise.

He closed his eyes and held still, as if the gentle touch could somehow heal him. "We already discussed this."

"No. I tried to discuss, and you just ordered."

"I need you to stay." He opened his eyes and slid his hand under her chin. Lowering his head, he brushed her mouth with his.

His lips were firm and so warm. Her heart breaking, she opened her mouth. He swept in, gentle and demanding. Need spiraled inside her, encompassing every nerve ending. She sighed deep in her throat.

He released her to place soft kisses along her jaw to nip her ear lobe. "We can work this out, Bren."

"I need to be with the Coven Nine during the solstice tomorrow night." She tilted her head back to allow for better access.

"You don't need to harness the power because you're going to block it," he murmured, tracing the shell of her ear.

Desire slammed through her to pound in her sex. As a witch, she could block any power from entering her body by creating imaginary but absolute shields. Shielding was the easy part. Allowing fire inside and then controlling it? That was the hard part. "I want to harness the power." Who wouldn't?

He leaned back. "That's too dangerous and you know it."

She shrugged. "I want to take the risk."

He slid his hands down to grip her ass and tug her against him. His cock pulsed through his jeans, and her thighs softened. "Then Moira, Conn, and I will help you to harness it."

The fact that he hadn't just ordered her to shield herself warmed her heart. "You think I should give it a try?"

"I would. We can try training later. But it'll be difficult to duplicate the kind of power that's likely to come from the comet." He grinned, and the charming Jase she used to know finally showed up.

She returned the smile. "I used to have such a crush on you."

He licked his lips. "Really, now?"

"Yes." Her cheeks heated.

"What did you fantasize about?" Teasing, the man was downright dangerous.

She laughed. "You name it."

"I will." He swept her up and strode along the cliffs toward his home. "Have you noticed we haven't properly christened the bed?"

She snuggled closer into his chest, her hand over his heart. Was it possible their mating could actually work out? "I have noticed that. But, well, we've slept in the bed."

"Ah, baby. Our bed won't be properly christened until you scream my name in it at least three times." He leaned down and captured her mouth, his tongue sweeping inside.

She broke away. "Three times? Not sure you have that in you, vampire."

He laughed, the sound freer than it had sounded since they'd mated. "That sounds like a challenge."

" 'Twas definitely a challenge." She leaned up and bit his earlobe—not so gently.

He growled and made short work of the hallway to the bedroom. "You owe me a new living room."

She shrugged. "For better or for worse—" Then she stopped. Blast it. They weren't married. They were just mated. Of course, for vampires mating meant more than marriage. So much for silly dreams of walking down an aisle. She swallowed. "Get your own living room back into shape."

"*Our* living room." He set her on her feet, both hands threading through her hair. "You taste like hope and sunshine." His mouth took hers again.

She pressed her palms against his hard abs, marveling at his strength. When he kissed her, she couldn't think. Hell, she didn't want to think. But sometimes reality needed to exist. She pushed away. "Jase, I'm not sure—"

He frowned and challenge lightened his eyes. "Not sure about what?"

"This." Her knees were flush against the bed. How could she explain that he'd break her heart if she let him?

"We're mated."

"I know." Even though her brain was telling her to run, her body moved closer into his heat.

"You don't want me?" His eyebrow rose.

"Of course I want you." She rolled her eyes. The man could probably scent her arousal. "But, well, I want more." There. She'd said it.

"So do I," he said softly, gripping her chin with his thumb and forefinger.

Her heart slammed against her ribs. Her childhood crush was actually coming true. "You do?"

"Sure." He kissed her again. "Give me a chance. I could make you happy."

"I want love." Sometimes a girl just had to spell things out for a vampire.

He nodded. "I know. So do I. All I can promise is that I'm open to anything and everything we could make. I have strong feelings for you, Brenna, trust me."

She did trust him. Could strong feelings become love? They'd only been mated less than a week. But she loved him—regardless of the time line. "I need to think."

"Hell no. No thinking." He dove in again, all passion, all determined male. Somehow her shirt hit the floor. "Let me show you." His talented mouth wandered down her neck to lick her collarbone. "Your skin is like marble. So smooth, but the right friction warms it right up."

One of her fantasies had been Jase seducing her. As if he knew, his thumbs brushed across her nipples through the bra. Electricity zipped to her sex. She bit back a whimper. "So responsive." He un-snapped the bra and slid the straps off her arms. "With the prettiest pink nipples."

Dipping his mouth, his abrasive tongue scraped across one nipple. She gasped, clutching his head. "Jase—"

"The way you say my name—it's so sexy." He slipped his hand inside her jeans to run along her hip. Her skin bunched, and her ab-dominal muscles contracted.

He released her and stepped back.

Cold air made her clench.

The heat in his eyes made her shiver.

"Take off your jeans, Brenna."

Her hands trembled on the top snap. "I thought you were seduc-ing me."

"Seduction is about control." His chin lifted. "Now lose the jeans."

She unbuttoned the pants and shoved them down her legs. "Take off yours."

"No. You take them off."

Intrigue leapt through her on the heels of lust. Seduction was about control? He was turning it over to her. The thought blasted her. Feeling powerful, feeling feminine, she unsnapped his jeans.

His jaw twitched.

Aye. His cock pressed hard against his zipper, straining the teeth. She smiled and slowly released him.

He blew breath through his tight lips.

Sliding gracefully to her knees, she tugged his jeans and briefs to his ankles. He groaned low in his chest as his cock sprang free. A deep purple bruise marred his right thigh.

She leaned in and kissed the wound.

His thigh muscle clenched beneath her mouth. She smiled and licked her way up. His hand dropped to her head.

She shook it off. "Don't bug me."

"Yes, ma'am," he said, widening his stance.

Just how long could he maintain control? She gripped the base of his cock, once again marveling that they fit together somehow. The vampire gods had been very generous with the youngest Kayrs brother.

Taking her time, she licked from the base to the tip.

His hand dropped to her head again. "Brenna—" A warning. Without question, a warning.

Feminine power flushed through her. Humming softly, she took the tip in her mouth. Her jaw protested, so she breathed deep and tried to relax. He was so damn big.

The fingers in her hair clenched, sending erotic tingles down her spine.

She took him deeper, gripping him tighter.

He made a sound between a growl and a moan. Sexy and male. So she did it again.

The room tilted as he drew back and yanked her up. His mouth found hers the same time he tossed her on the bed. Stretching out on top of her, he held her face still, kissing her hard.

She kissed him back, wrapping her legs around his hips.

He broke away. "No." Reaching back, he unhooked her legs. One hand slid beneath her, and he flipped her over onto her stomach.

She protested and moved to sit up.

A hard slap to her butt halted her motion.

"Hold still." He rubbed the abused area.

Fire and need crashed right to her sex, which throbbed. She tried to slide her knees beneath her to get some leverage.

The second slap echoed around the room.

She cried out, sensations bombarding her.

"I said to hold still." He bent down and bit her left buttock, right above the marking.

An orgasm bore down on her, and only the third slap to her butt kept ecstasy at bay. She shifted against the bedspread, her body on fire.

He licked up her spine, his cock brushing her thighs. Rolling her to her side, her rear to him, he lifted her thigh and plunged inside her with one hard stroke.

She gasped and pressed back against him.

The sensations were more erotic than she could've dreamed. He slid his arm under her waist and flattened his palm against her chest. He pushed down as he thrust up, the powerful muscles in his chest shifting against her shoulder blades.

Going on instinct, she dug her fingernails into his thigh.

He stilled. Tension spiraled through the room. The second his control snapped, freedom rushed through her.

He plunged out and back in, thrusting with incredible strength. Holding her tight, he pounded harder, until her entire body flared into exquisite need.

Sharp fangs embedded in her neck, and she exploded.

She cried out his name, her eyes sightless on the far wall, her fingers clutching the sheets. Waves roared through her. His hold tightened as he came.

Slowly, the fangs retracted and he withdrew. Turning her over, he covered her. He tangled his fingers in her hair and placed a soft kiss on her nose. "Everything will work out, Bren. Trust me."

Chapter 26

An hour after christening the bed with Jase, Brenna sat on her new chair gazing at the three people currently trying to blow her mind to bits. Moira, Dage, and Jase all sat on the sofa, sending powerful vibes her way. "This isn't fun, and I'm tired."

Moira rolled her eyes. "It's not supposed to be fun, and you can sleep later. Now, we're going to hit you with power again, and I want you to block it completely."

"But I don't want to block the power from the comet, I want to use it." She eyed Jase. "I can feel vibrations from you. I mean, when you send out power, I can actually sense it. Can everybody, or is it just me since we've mated?"

Jase shrugged. "Dunno."

Dage glanced at his brother. "I can sense power, but I can't feel it."

Brenna could sense *tension* between the brothers. At some point, they were going to explode if they didn't talk it out. "Maybe you two should spend some time figuring it out."

"We're fine." Jase kept his focus on her. "Block, Brenna."

So he was back to bossy Jase again. While she wanted to tell him to stuff it, she really needed to practice in order to harness the power from the comet and the solstice. "Fine."

They'd practiced for hours, and now she could decipher the individual energies. Moira's was fiery and feminine, a hard hit with an aftershock. The king's was smooth and deadly, yet ruthlessly contained. He didn't want to harm her.

Jase's was the most interesting in that his energy came in bursts of controlled power, with masculinity and passion throughout. She hoped the passion came from the fact that they'd mated. If he could throw power, maybe he could control the elements again soon.

She imagined great shields of steel rising between her and the three immortals.

"Nicely done," Jase murmured, pride filling his eyes.

"Excellent," Moira agreed, her shoulders relaxing.

"Good enough." Dage stood and assisted Moira up. "The power from the comet will be different from our individual power, so only Jase can train you on that. You can block Moira and me, but you can't take our power in. It's impossible. Jase is a different story, but good luck with him."

Brenna frowned. "I don't understand."

"You can take my power into your system," Jase said quietly. "The same way we should someday be able to use each other's gifts." He stood and escorted Dage and Moira to the door. "Thanks for the help."

They nodded and left quietly after Dage leaned down and murmured something to Jase. Jase shut the door and leaned back against it.

Brenna stretched her legs onto an ottoman. "You and your brother need to have a heart-to-heart before one of you explodes."

"Something to think about another day." Strong and graceful, Jase prowled toward her, sitting on the ottoman and placing her feet on his lap.

"What did Dage whisper to you?" she asked.

"Nothing." Jase's eyes veiled. The tension in his neck said otherwise.

"Tell me."

He exhaled. "The demons have doubled the bounty on your head, and changed it to dead or alive. They just want you taken down."

Fear and anger crashed into her stomach. "Because of the solstice?"

"No." His jaw snapped shut. "Because of me."

She slowly nodded. "They won't get me."

"I know." He flipped off her shoes and ran nimble fingers along her arch. "Now, I'm going to send power your way, and I want you to draw it in."

She bit back a moan at the wondrous foot massage. "I'm confused. You can send power my way, but you can't control the elements? How is that possible?"

He stilled, gaze raking her. His eyebrows slashed down. "Your ankle hurts."

She started. "Um, yeah. I twisted it earlier when we were moving furniture." A dull ache continued to pound through her tissues. Then she tilted her head. "You can feel that pain? I mean, since we mated?"

"Yes." Gingerly, he swept his hand along her injury. The pain instantly disappeared.

"No way." Brenna leaned forward and poked her ankle. "You took away the injury."

"Mates can do that usually." His grin showed relief and charm. "Dage always takes away Emma's headaches."

"Oh." Now Kane's plan for Brenna to mutate the virus somehow made more sense. "So, if I can weaken the virus, maybe vampires can remove the virus from their mate's chromosomes."

"Exactly." Jase's breath caught. "We hoped something like that would work on your illness, too. I have an idea—try to center yourself."

"All right." Digging deep, she forced calmness through her body. A tingling glide of power poured through her blood, inside her veins, roaring among her tissues. Her lungs expanded, and her brain relaxed. "Oh God." Her eyes opened wide.

Jase blew out air, his hold tightening. "I think I felt it."

Tears filled Brenna's eyes. A song sang through her body—a song of healing and ultimate health. "I felt that . . . like you took a little of the poison." The mating had worked, and maybe someday he'd be able to completely expel the poison from her system. "Is it in your blood?"

He nodded and closed his eyes. The sense of vampire healing vibrated off of him in waves. Several minutes later, he relaxed and opened his eyes. A smug grin lifted his lips. "I know I was only able to take a tiny bit, but I got it. There's hope."

Gratitude slashed through her along with love. "Thank you." There really weren't any other words.

"Of course. Soon I'll be able to mess with the elements again. Just think what a power couple we'll be." Good nature filled his eyes. "I hate to push you further, but we need to train. Let's see what you can do now."

"Okay." Brenna centered herself. "Send energy my way, and I'll see if I can draw it in."

He grinned and soon a warmth slid along her skin. She drew the heat in, her lungs expanding. Going on a whim, she focused on the air molecules around them. Droplets instantly fell to the floor.

She gasped in surprise. "I changed the elements with your power." Her grin even felt happy.

He smiled back. "That's amazing. If you can do it, maybe I can, too." He eyed the droplets on the floor and concentrated.

Nothing happened.

He sighed. "Well, it might take more time. But I think I'll get it." Then he shoved heat her way mentally. "Take the warmth and try to cool it off. Imagine ice cascading around the heat."

She nodded. The power from the comet would most likely be hot. Concentrating, she tried to imagine ice around the mental heat sent by Jase. The heat slowly cooled. She sighed and leaned back, her hands trembling. Damn, enough for the night.

"Good." Jase rubbed her other arch. "You're getting too tired, and I don't want to overload you." A knock sounded on the door, and Jase turned, his body stiffening. "Come in."

Janie Kayrs opened the door, her eyes huge in a pale face. "I'm sorry to bother you."

Jase's shoulders went back. "You had a vision, Jane?"

"Yes." Her gaze flicked to Brenna and back. "It was hazy and surreal, but I saw the demons take Brenna. Somewhere dark and in the earth." Janie blanched. "I'm so sorry, but I really wanted to warn you."

The handsome vampire who'd rubbed Brenna's feet disappeared to leave a stone-cold killer in his place. "Thanks for letting us know."

"Of course." Janie paused, her hands clasped together. "The witches have a book based on the Prophecies of Arias, right?"

Brenna lifted her chin, her mind spinning. "If we do, that'd be top secret. How do you know about it?"

Janie nodded, her eyes darkening. "I had another vision about the book—it's full of prophecies regarding the current war. I need that book, Brenna."

Brenna kept her expression neutral. It was treason for her to talk about the hidden library owned by the Coven Nine. "I don't know about any such book, but if I did, and if you wanted to see it, I'd contact my people to determine if it were possible."

"Thank you," Janie murmured. "Sorry again about the frightening vision."

The poor woman didn't have a choice with the visions, now did she? Brenna forced a smile. "It's better to have the information, and I appreciate your letting us know. Get some sleep, Jane." The woman rarely seemed to rest.

Jase waited until his niece had nodded and shut the door behind her before focusing on Brenna. "We need to up your security."

Wait a minute. She was a witch just coming back into her powers. "No, I—"

"Don't argue with me." He reached down and pulled her up. "It's late, we've trained enough tonight, and we're getting some sleep. Tomorrow we'll fight about security and safety."

Brenna stumbled along with him toward bed, her ears ringing. How in the heck could she get through to him when he went cold like this? She shivered, hugging herself. Sometimes she didn't know him at all.

Jase kicked the sheet off his legs and struggled to force the dream into nothingness. He'd wanted to leave Brenna in bed and go for a run, but she'd asked him to stay. Feeling like an ass for the way he'd shut her out earlier, he'd stayed in bed. He'd slid into the dream he most hated within an hour.

Underground again, he found himself in the cell formed of rock and earth. A small window up above let in meager light, and dripping water echoed in a cadence guaranteed to drive him crazy.

He glanced down at his wounded, gaunt body. Burns and cuts marred every exposed inch of skin. Heated blood coursed from his ears, nose, and eyes from the most recent mental attack.

The rock wall morphed into a face. Long, sober, it was a familiar face. "You need to kill him," the face said. "Kill them both."

Jase coughed up blood, shock weighing down his limbs. The face talked. "Suri and Melco will die. I promise."

The face spit out rocks. "No. It has to happen now. Their plans will destroy the world, not just you. Before the solstice . . . make it happen. The young prophet's vision is true . . . they'll kill your Brenna. They will take your witch, and they'll kill your family. Trust me. It's now or . . . it's hell forever."

Did he say solstice? Jase tried to shove to his feet and stumbled against the wall. "This isn't real." Digging deep, he forced himself to wake up.

His heart pounded, and his sweat soaked the sheets. Brenna lay on her side next to him, sleeping quietly. The moonlight caressed her smooth skin. In sleep, she looked so young and at peace.

Careful not to wake her, he slid from the bed and buried his head in his hands. The dream was another mind-fuck, but the sense of urgency wouldn't leave him. Nothing was going to happen before the solstice, but it was time to end this. Janie's visions were never wrong. If he didn't kill the demon leaders, they'd kill Brenna.

He stood and slipped into the closet to don jeans and a shirt. Grabbing his boots, he crept out of the room, grabbed supplies, and left the house. A quick jog took him to a back entrance to the main lodge. Thank God the tunnels in the underground headquarters weren't fully repaired yet, or the prisoner would be too far down to reach.

But aboveground? The demon was fair game.

One guard manned the control room. "Hi, Chalton," Jase said, smoothing his face into calm lines. "I came to see the demon."

Chalton wore his customary frown. "Dage wanted the guy on ice until the morning." He reached for a phone.

Jase was on him before he could dial. Tucking his arm under Chalton's neck, he slowly tightened the hold until Chalton flopped like a fish, shooting elbows back. "Sorry about this," Jase muttered. He would've never gotten close enough had Chalton not trusted him. "Really sorry."

Grabbing the zip tie from his pocket, he fastened Chalton's hands behind his back, then secured him to a post in the corner. Even if the vampire woke up, he wasn't going anywhere.

Jase hit a button to unlock the door and jogged down the steps to reach the cell.

The demon lay on a cot, staring at the ceiling. He turned and stood, black eyes filling with purple.

Jase slipped his gun from his waist. "Where's Suri?"

"Fuck you." The garbled tone proved the soldier was purebred demon. The silver hair was a good clue and matched the row of many medals across his uniform.

"Not interested." Jase shot him in the gut.

The soldier doubled over with a muffled *oof*. Straightening up, he grimaced. With a grunt, the bullet dropped out of his flesh to ping on the cement floor.

Images of death and destruction ripped into Jase's brain, followed by slice after slice of pain. He smiled.

The demon's eyes widened. "What the hell?"

"Your attacks don't affect me." Not true, they still hurt like hell. But he could deal and still function. "Years of countering them, I'm afraid."

The soldier lifted his chin. "You're the youngest Kayrs brother."

"Sure am." Jase pointed the gun at the soldier's head. "We haven't met, have we?" Many of his torturers blended together until they all looked like Malco.

"No. Not my thing." The demon brushed dirt off his medals. "Though I could definitely have broken you."

"You're still welcome to try." Jase shot him in the cheek.

The demon's head twisted, and blood sprayed. He growled and turned back to face Jase. The bullet dropped out of his flesh, and the hole slowly closed. "That all you got?"

"No." Jase unlocked the cell door and stepped inside, drawing his knife. The idea of torture turned his gut, but he needed answers to stop the people who'd kill his family. There wasn't a question in his mind that the demons would come after Brenna just to hurt him. They'd tortured him for fun, but he'd torture for necessity. Unlike the demons, he'd get no pleasure from the act. "That was just foreplay. Now we get to the good stuff."

It took nearly three hours to break the demon. Finally, Jase wiped the blood off his blade and returned to the control room. Chalton sat in the corner, fury in his eyes.

Jase paused. "I said I was sorry."

"Unbind me, asshole."

Jase grimaced. "Not quite yet. You'll call Dage, and I need a head start."

Chalton eyed him from head to toe, eyes widening.

Jase groaned and glanced down at the massive amount of blood covering his clothing. Some was his from the demon's mental attacks—his nose had bled for hours. But most belonged to the demon.

Chalton growled. "Is he dead?"

"Unfortunately." Jase hadn't intended to kill him, but the guy was stubborn.

"Did he give you the information you wanted?"

"Yes." The prisoner had finally given up the demon stronghold in Nevada, but he hadn't been able to confirm how long the leaders would be on site. Most would be leaving within the day, apparently. Time was too short. "I'll send word back in a couple of hours for somebody to release you."

"I'm going to kick your ass, Kayrs," Chalton growled.

"You're probably gonna have to stand in line." Jase exited the room, shutting the door tight. Chances weren't great he'd return from the demon stronghold, but at least he'd take out the leaders there. The demon he'd tortured had confirmed that the demons had plans to attack the vampires on the solstice.

So was the dream a coincidence or some odd vision? Chances were a coincidence. Visions had never plagued Jase, unlike nightmares. Those would always find him.

The moon was dropping low in the sky, and soon dawn would arrive. He'd be on his way before then but first needed supplies and fresh clothes.

Opening his front door, he stopped short at the sight of Brenna sitting in the moonlight with a sketchbook in her hands. Several drawings surrounded the spot where she sat on the floor near the open wall.

She looked up, shock filling her face as she scrambled toward him. "Is that your blood?"

"No." Heat filled his lungs—an odd sort of panic. "I'm fine."

She frowned and fingered his wet sleeve. "I don't understand."

He pulled his arm away, not wanting demon blood to touch her. "Why are you up?"

She stepped back. "I woke up and you weren't there. Where were you?"

He shrugged and avoided her gaze. "I have work to do, but I'll be home later." Turning, he headed for the armory off the kitchen to change.

She followed him. "Jase, what's going on?"

"Nothing." Why did she have to be awake, damn it? "Everything is fine. Go back to sleep, and we'll celebrate your birthday later."

She ignored his offering and grabbed his arm. "Did you torture that demon?"

He shook her off and yanked the bloody clothes off his body. "I did my job. You knew it wasn't pretty." Grabbing combat gear, he quickly suited up.

Brenna lifted her chin. "You're going after the demons."

"Yes."

"By yourself?" she asked, edging toward the door.

He grabbed her shoulder. "Yes." Lowering his head toward hers, he gave her his fiercest expression. "You're not to call anybody. Understand?"

Fire flashed into her eyes. "Aye, I understand. I'm to let you go off on your suicide mission without lifting a finger."

"Yes." He tugged a bulletproof vest over his head.

She wrapped her arms around her waist, hugging herself. "What about the solstice tonight?"

He paused. "I'll be back."

"If you're not?"

"Then Moira and Conn will help you." The disappointment in her eyes cut through his heart like a sharpened blade.

"I need you."

The words slashed deeper than her expression.

"I'm sorry, Bren." And he was—with everything in him. But this was his last chance to get Suri and Malco before they disappeared again. "Please understand."

"I do. I fully understand." She turned and headed into the kitchen. "I'm going home. Don't try to contact me again."

He stood in the armory, indecision halting his movements. For years he'd dreamed of this moment, he'd planned for it. Not even for Brenna could he give up his need for revenge. "I'm sorry."

"Me, too," she whispered, slowly moving out of sight. Out of his life.

He turned and grabbed another knife, shoving all emotion away. If he survived, he'd bring her back.

Doubt filtered through him, and he shook it off. One battle at a time. For now, he needed to grab the Degoller Stars from his gym. It was way too late to fight fair. Slipping out the door, he ran under the cover of darkness to his gym.

Stepping inside, he stopped short at the sight of Dage leaning against a far wall. Rage had lit the king's eyes a vibrant blue, cutting hard lines in the sides of his mouth.

Jase swallowed, his anger rising. "Chalton freed himself."

"Yes." Dage twirled a star in his hand. "You killed the demon."

"I plan to kill several more." Jase eyed the two remaining stars on the top shelf.

His older brother waved a hand, and locks engaged on the large door. "I don't think so."

Temper heated Jase's lungs, even as he measured the holes in the metal from Brenna's fireballs. Not one was big enough for him to jump through. "Unlock the doors."

"Fuck you, Jase." Dage threw the star, and the weapon stuck in the far wall.

A roaring filled Jase's ears. "Fuck you, King."

"Ah, there's the anger I've been looking for." Dage angled closer, his voice softening to a deadly tone. "No more brave stoicism, huh?"

Jase's fingers clenched his hands into fists. "You don't want to do this."

"Oh, but I do." The king stepped close enough to hit. "Let's talk about that anger, shall we?"

"I'm angry at the demons, which is why I have to go. Now." Panic had Jase stepping back.

"No, you're mad at me. It's time for you to stop being such a chicken-shit and deal with it." Dage angled to the side, effectively blocking Jase's way to the exit.

"I'm not mad at you."

"Well, I'm pissed as hell at you." The smile the king flashed lacked humor.

"I know. I've been a pain since I got back, and as soon as I take care of the demons, I'll work on the attitude." Jase tried to shove down the anger, but fury rose up like furious insects finding a hole in the surface.

"No. I'm pissed because I spent half my life training you, and you failed. You allowed the fucking demons to capture you, and then you let them almost break you." Fire crackled along the king's arms.

"What?" Jase stepped back, the sense of betrayal chilling him. "You think this is my fault?"

"Hell, yes."

Jase saw red. He jumped for the king, slamming him to the ground, not even registering the relief sliding across Dage's face.

He punched with full strength into Dage's jaw, trying to reach the floor.

Dage's head slammed against the concrete, and he reared up, throwing Jase into the door.

Pain lanced down his spine. He came out swinging, going for blood.

Dage caught him with an uppercut, not holding back. Jase flew back into the wall, knocking the stars to the ground. His vision wavered. In his entire life, Dage had never tried to hurt him.

Until now.

"This is your fault, King," Jase growled, circling his brother, fury burning him from the inside. "You sent me to fight as a kid, and then sent me to the demons. You're more king than brother." He swept out a foot and nailed Dage's knee.

Dage pivoted, swinging wide to break Jase's ribs. "I thought you could handle it. I was wrong."

Jase punched Dage's sternum, satisfaction lifting his chin when bones shattered. "I handled it."

The king's fangs dropped low. "Bullshit. I should've sent one of the women." He kicked Jase square in the jaw, sending his head crashing back.

Jase growled and lost all control, arms swinging.

Dage met each hit, each kick, with one of his own.

Heavy fists pounded on the door.

They ignored them, both looking to draw blood.

All of the rage, shame, and fear Jase had been living with rolled through him, strengthening his hits. The agony flowed out of him inch by inch. Blood sprayed, bones shattered, and emotions ruled.

The pounding on the door got louder, and a drill sprang into action.

An hour passed. They both fought as if they had nothing left. Finally, Jase knocked his bloodied brother to his knees. Gravity yanked him right down, and he kept going until he lay prone. Blood poured from his body in several places.

He coughed up blood. The ball of fire that had been living in him disintegrated. Gone for good.

Dage slid onto his back, his broken bones rattling. "Feel better?"

Jase tried to see out of his swollen eyes. "Yeah. You?"

"Much." Dage wheezed out air.

Jase didn't know what organ to heal first. "Are we going to be all right?"

"Yes. Of course. We just needed to exorcise the demons. Ha-ha." Dage coughed, the sound echoing like death. "Are we all right?"

"Yes—we've always been all right. I've just been angry." So angry sometimes he couldn't even think.

"That's what I figured." Dage groaned. "You blew up my spleen."

"Sorry." Jase's lung collapsed. "Ow."

"Tell me now. Everything," the king wheezed, the drill continuing outside.

So he did. Lying in blood next to his damaged brother, Jase let loose the truth. His fears, his pain, his guilt.

Dage listened quietly until he wound down. "I missed you."

Jase sighed. "I missed you, too."

The door flew open. Talen, Kane, and Conn ran inside, panic on their faces.

Dage chuckled and then groaned. "Our rescuers."

Jase opened one eye. "The see, hear, and speak monkeys." His laugh made him groan with agony.

Kane dropped between the two, his fangs slashing into his wrist before he stuck it to Jase's mouth. Talen did the same with Dage.

"I'll get Max. We need more blood," Conn said, turning and running from the building.

Kane's blood exploded down Jase's throat. "What the hell?"

Jase swallowed. "We had a disagreement."

Kane lifted one eyebrow. "Is it settled?"

Jase exhaled. "Yeah. It's settled." And it was. For the first time since being rescued, he felt whole. He turned his head to view his battered and bruised older brother.

Then he smiled.

Chapter 27

Brenna punched in keys on her laptop, muttering to herself. She'd only been gone a few days, and already the Dublin economic plan needed tweaking. The plane banked to the left, and she took a moment to say good-bye to the life she might've had.

"See ya, asshole," she said into the clouds. Within thirty minutes of Jase's heading off on his suicide mission, she'd packed and secured a plane ride home. Small private plane with six empty rows and a bedroom in the back. Being one of the Coven Nine often had its perks.

"Asshole," she muttered again. "*Trust me, Brenna.*" He'd whispered the words, and she'd believed them. Aye, her heart freakin' ached. A real, deep-in-the-chest hurt. She'd known better than to fall for him. Two hours into the flight, and she wanted to cry, but Jase Kayrs didn't deserve her tears.

Green danced along her arms, and she ruthlessly shoved it back. Setting the plane on fire would be disastrous.

Even now, as the solstice neared, energy heated her blood.

Power. Untapped and absolute.

She'd reach home just in time to watch night arrive. She fingered the pendant around her neck with its dangerous bug. Midnight was her hour, and she'd be ready. At that time, she'd cure Virus-27.

A scrape sounded from behind her. She stiffened. The two pilots were in the cockpit, and she was the only person on the plane.

Something shuffled.

Reaching for a knife in her laptop case, she slowly stood and turned.

Jane Kayrs slid outside the bedroom, one eyebrow raised. "You going to stab me?"

Brenna slid the knife back into the bag and eyed the young woman. "What are you doing here?"

Janie tugged down her sweater and moved to sit in the chair facing Brenna's. "They took the guards off me since Garrett is home, and this was my only chance to get free." Wise blue eyes twinkled. "I thought we'd make a break for it together."

Brenna shook her head. "You're in danger, and you know it."

"I'm always in danger," Janie said softly. "It's my job to end this war, and I can't do that under the heavy mantle of security. Surely you understand."

Janie had the petite, fit frame of a normal twenty-four-year-old woman, and the stunning eyes of a centuries-old soul.

Brenna sighed. "What's your plan?"

"I've been having constant visions regarding the Prophecies of Arias, and the current war. I need to read that book." She paled even more. "Something is in there, but I don't know what."

Brenna patted her hand. "I'll see what I can do, but if the book exists, no non-witch has ever seen it."

"Understood. Plus, I need to meet Zane in person and try to talk him into ending this war. My visions have always shown the moment to come down to us and Kalin, and it's time." Janie slid her hands down her frayed jeans. "It is so time."

Brenna recognized love when she saw it. Why did the sensation have to hurt so much? "You don't even know who or what Zane is. What makes you think he's one of the good guys?"

"He saved Garrett, didn't he? That goes a long way to convincing me we're on the same side."

"Doesn't mean you won't get your heart broken."

"Like you did?" Janie sighed. "Uncle Jase is confused, but I can tell he loves you."

Brenna rolled her eyes. "He's not confused, he's just obsessed. So you think I should've stayed?"

"Hell, no." Janie grinned. "You have to stand up to those vampires, or you'll never get anywhere. You made the right move."

"I didn't leave for a move." Brenna shook her head. "I left for good."

"If you say so." Janie leaned back. "You know he'll come after you."

Would he? If he did, what then? More empty promises? "I don't think so, Jane." Brenna glanced at her watch. "Great timing on revealing yourself. If we head back now, I won't arrive home in time to prepare for the solstice."

"That was the goal." Janie reached to open the refrigerator and drew out a beer. "I'll contact Zane when we're closer to Ireland and come up with a plan."

The woman was crazy. "You don't think I'm going to let you meet with Zane, do you?"

Janie smiled again. "Yes, I do. By the way, happy birthday."

Brenna snorted. "Thanks so much."

Janie frowned, dropping the unopened can. "Something's happening."

The urgency in her tone made Brenna sit up straight. "What's happening?"

An object clipped the left wing, and the plane rocked. Fire danced along the metal. Another explosion echoed from the right wing.

Panic curled Brenna's hands around the armrest. "Secure your seat belt." She slid her belt into the buckle as Janie did the same. An alarm blared through the cabin.

The pilot shoved open the cockpit door. "We've been hit. Brace yourselves for impact, because we're going down."

"When you call in, let them know Janet Kayrs is on board." Brenna shoved down panic as the plane dropped several yards. Her stomach rose to her throat. She grabbed the knife from the bag and tossed it to Janie. "Be ready when we land."

Janie caught the handle and nodded, her eyes wide.

Brenna opened another compartment and drew out a gun. The plane twisted, and she bashed into the window. "Where are we?" she yelled over the alarm.

"Over the Mexico desert," the head pilot bellowed back.

Brenna clutched the gun, keeping the barrel pointed away from Janie. "Who's in the desert?"

Janie's hands turned white on her jeans. "Well, it's probably too hot and sunny for Kurjans, and most shifters like the cold, same with vampires."

Brenna nodded, her mind spinning. "That leaves witches and demons. Could be either." Had she been stupid to disregard the CRAP group? They'd been organizing for years—maybe they had a presence all over the world. Of course, maybe the Kurjans did have a presence in the desert. She turned toward the front. "Are you two armed?"

"Of course," the pilot yelled. "Get ready to hit."

Outside the window, the red of the desert grew larger and closer.

"I'm going to put down as close to the rock formations as possible," the pilot yelled over the alarm. "Head for shelter." He slammed the door shut.

"If we survive," Janie muttered, her face devoid of color. She reached out to hold Brenna's hand. "Is the safety on the gun?"

"Yes." Brenna tightened her hold.

The plane tilted, and she bit back a scream.

The refrigerator opened, and drinks spilled out. A beer bottle shattered, sending liquid spraying.

Brenna eyed Janie, her stomach tightening. The woman was human and wouldn't survive most injuries a witch could heal from. "Janie, press your cheek against your knees." Maybe there was some way Brenna could shield Janie from injury. At least she could block her niece from any projectiles.

Janie nodded and dropped into the crash position.

The alarm suddenly cut off. Instant silence filled the cabin. The first bump was gentle, and Brenna began to relax.

Then the plane slid sideways, spinning around. She screamed, dropping her face to her legs. Janie's hand tightened on hers. Momentum slapped her cheek against the armrest.

Something exploded outside, and heat flared through the cabin. *Oh God, Oh, God, Oh God.*

Metal cracked, thundering in protest. The plane rocked, lifting up and slamming back down. A bottle hit Brenna in the arm, slicing her skin. Unfastening her seat belt, she moved to cover Janie from harm.

The plane pitched, and she flew into the woman. The chair ripped from the floor, sending them flying into the door of the cockpit. They hit the ground with a loud thump.

Then everything stopped. No sound, no movement . . . only the smell of smoke. Brenna lifted herself off Janie, running her hands along her niece's limbs. "Are you all right?"

"No." Janie shoved hair off her face. "Shit, no. You?"

"No." At least they weren't dead. Brenna unbuckled Janie's belt. "We have to move fast."

Gunfire echoed, and a cry of pain filtered under the cockpit door.

Panic heated Brenna's lungs. Her eyes met Janie's wide ones. She tilted her head toward the knife, and Janie nodded.

Brenna released the safety on the gun and stood to face the door. Inching forward, she unhinged the lock. "Stay behind me." Taking up a firing stance, she slowly toed the door open.

A full contingent of demon soldiers faced the doorway, guns out. Crap. "Hide in the bedroom, Janie." Brenna grabbed for the door and slammed it shut. The metal was instantly ripped out of her hands to go spiraling into a series of red rocks.

The closest demon smiled. Power cascaded around him, but he held it in check. "Come out of the plane, please."

Janie inched behind Brenna toward the bedroom.

"Both of you," the demon said. "I'd rather not rip into your brains, but I will if you don't move. Now."

Brenna took a deep breath, eyeing the squad of five. She couldn't take all of them. So her hands rose. "I'm the only one in here."

Images of dead animals shot into her head followed by a slash of agony. She bit her lip. Janie hissed in pain behind her, the knife clattering to the ground. The images and pain dissipated.

The demon shook his head. "That was a warning. Come out, both of you, now."

"Fine." Brenna paused long enough for Janie to reclaim the knife and hide it. "We're coming out." She allowed the gun to rotate on her finger harmlessly, and the first demon took it.

The guy in charge quickly bound her hands along with Janie's, leading them through a series of rock formations. Brenna yanked back. "Our pilots."

The demon shoved her back into motion. "Your pilots didn't make it."

Nausea rose from her belly. She hadn't even asked the names of the two witch pilots. Her people were dead because of her. "I'm going to cut off your head myself."

The demon chuckled. "I've heard good things about witches in bed . . . that you're hotter than feline tigresses."

Yeah, but she'd been mated. If any other male touched her besides Jase, he'd blow up with a fierce allergic reaction. "Sounds like a date, handsome. Why don't we get to it right now?"

He leaned in and smelled her. "Oh my. Mated a vampire, did we?" He tsked his tongue. "Now why would I keep you alive?"

"You tell me. You brought down my plane." She glanced behind her to see Janie doggedly moving along.

"I'm following orders, witch. You mean less to me than the dirt over there." The demon led them around another group of rocks to waiting helicopters. Brenna stopped short. The demon laughed. "You didn't think we brought your plane down where we planned to keep you, right?" He grabbed her hair and dragged her to the closest bird, tossing her in.

Brenna scrambled over to the edge as Janie landed next to her. How in the hell were they going to get out of this one?

She eyed Janie, who glanced down at her boot. Okay. Their hands were tied, but they had a knife.

She nodded. Time to plan.

Jase winced as his rib snapped back into place. He sat, leaning against the wall of his training building, trying to heal.

Dage groaned as his nose re-formed. "Not the face."

Jase grinned. "Your nose looks like a pancake."

The cartilage slowly slid back into alignment. "Not now."

Jase sucked air into his healing lungs. "I'm sorry about everything."

"Me, too." The king rolled his neck. "I fully plan on taking out the demons, just so you know. But when we go in, we go in fast and smart. No more losses."

Jase nodded. His brother was right. "I understand."

A bone cracked, and Dage winced. "Does Kane think he got the trigger in your brain?"

"Yes." Well, Kane said he'd hoped—but hope was all they had. "At least now I understand why they let me live."

Dage nodded. "Yeah. Though there's a lot of chatter that Willa wants you back. Sounds like a psycho bitch."

"She is." Jase grimaced as blood slid down his throat. "She

killed humans to give me blood—making me think we were allies. I didn't know about the human women until I'd been drinking for weeks."

Dage shook his head. "That's twisted."

"Yeah. She tried to convince me that mating her would save us both." He shivered and fought down nausea. "I considered it." The confession almost made him puke.

"But you didn't go through with it. Thank God." Dage curled his lip. "I'd hate to have to kill one of my brothers' mates."

"She won't stop coming." Jase sent healing cells to the back of his left eyeball. "The woman is obsessed and pure evil. If Suri hadn't nearly cut off my head and buried me, she would've hidden me forever." And the woman had a very loyal set of guards. Maybe someday she'd take down her brother and lead the demons.

"The fact that the demons attacked the Kurjan boat the other night pleases me." Dage cracked his knuckles. "I'm not pleased Garrett was the prize, but I like our enemies turning on each other."

"That beats them becoming allies," Jase said.

"The demons will never ally with the Kurjans." Dage shook his head. "But they usually leave each other alone. Now, Kalin will retaliate against the demons—he has to."

"So we sit it out and let them fight?" Jase frowned.

"No. But the weaker they are, the easier it'll be to take them down." Dage cleared his throat. "Have you discovered anything new about Brenna and the solstice?"

"No. Just that she'll be infused with power. Kane wants her to figure out how to cure Virus-27. Maybe find a way to make the virus release its hold on individual chromosomes."

"Is it possible?" Dage asked.

"Shit if I know. Though, well, I doubt it. Brenna's power seems to be in the form of fire. Nothing subtle there." Although the pretty woman was very subtle, her power was not.

"Yeah. That's what I thought." Dage nodded. "It'd be cool if she could somehow harness the power into an energy source. Something long-lasting."

"I wish I understood more about it—even Brenna is in the dark."

"Well, she's just been trying to survive the last decade."

Jase grimaced. "Yes, and her power is returning because of the comet. What happens when the comet leaves?" Would Brenna still be vulnerable to the poisoning again? "Her blood isn't any different than it was before we mated."

"Give it time."

Jase nodded. "I will." Now that he had his brain on straight, he'd give Brenna all the time she wanted. He needed to go apologize to her. The hurt in her eyes earlier still made his gut ache. Trying to balance himself with his healthier hand, he moved to stand.

"Where you going?" Talen asked from his position near the door.

"Need to talk to Brenna," Jase muttered, his eyes swimming. Just how much internal damage had Dage inflicted, anyway? He glared at the king.

The king grinned.

Talen snorted. "Your mate boarded a plane nearly two hours ago—bound for Ireland. Dumbass."

Jase swayed. Damn it. "She actually left me?" An unexpected hurt sliced through his chest.

"Of course she left you." Talen shook his head. "Now get off your ass and go get her back."

Jase nodded. "Yeah. Good plan."

Dage stood and groaned as he clutched his ribs. "Wait a minute. If you don't want her, let her go. Bren deserves it."

"I do want her." Jase tried out his healing ankle.

"She deserves more," Dage muttered.

She did deserve more. Jase stilled, flashes of pretty Brenna filtering through his mind. His heart finally relaxed. The idea of living without her hurt more than anything he'd ever felt. "I love her, Dage."

The king smiled. "It's about time—go get her."

Jase nodded. "I'm gonna have to grovel."

"Hell, yes." Talen opened the door. "Maybe I'll come and watch."

Conn slid into view, his eyes a wild green.

Jase paused, his gut clenching. "What?"

"Brenna's plane went down over Mexico. The pilot called in an attack." Conn grabbed Talen's arm. "Janie was on the plane."

Talen shook him off. "What do you mean, Janie was on the plane?"

Conn shrugged. "When the pilot called in, he reported Janie was there. I don't know anything else."

The world stopped spinning and narrowed to the moment. Jase stood up straight. "How long ago?"

"Ten minutes." Conn eyed his watch. "I have teams ready to go—wheels up in five minutes."

Jase paused, glancing at Dage. "The demons have a base in the Nevada desert." A fact he'd learned from torturing the demon earlier. He rubbed his head, his mind spinning. "If the plane went down in Mexico, they're probably not there any longer."

Dage nodded. "We'll take two copters to Nevada, and the other two will hit Mexico just in case." He loped into an uneven jog. "Let's suit up."

Jase sprinted to keep up, his ankles and wounded legs protesting. Drawing on fear, drawing on fury, he shoved the pain into a box to be opened later.

The Realm had missiles at headquarters to take out anyone who came too close. It made sense other species would have the same.

But over the Mexican desert?

He shook his head. Could be the Kurjans, or it could be a rival shifter clan. But deep down, where terror liked to ferment, the truth lived.

The demons had Brenna.

Chapter 28

Brenna stumbled down the stairs toward the cell. The rocks above her pressed in. God. How had Jase survived living for five years in a rock cell? She bit her lip as power coursed through her. Now wasn't the time to burn the demons. Soon, though.

Janie crashed into her back, and Brenna's face smacked the rock wall.

"Oops," the demon guard said. He opened a door and shoved her inside. She hit the ground and rolled, her hands still tied.

Janie landed next to her in a heap. "Asshole," she muttered, swinging her legs around to sit. Dust billowed up from the hard ground.

The door slammed shut.

Brenna eyed Janie. The woman had been silent during the two-hour helicopter ride until they'd landed in the middle of what looked like the Nevada desert. "Are you all right?"

"I'm fine." Janie took a deep breath. "The guard took my knife. Now, I'm wondering if I should meditate and call Zane and Kalin. Let Zane's people and the Kurjans converge on the demons here."

"Then what?" Brenna asked.

"That's why I haven't quite called." Janie looked over her shoulder and started rubbing her zip tie on a shard of rock. "I'm not sure what would happen next. Maybe I'll just call Zane."

How odd to be able to meditate and cast your thoughts across the earth. "Our pilots called in the attack. The vampires and my people should at least have an idea of where we are."

"The vampires are your people now, too." Janie's binds released. "Hell, yeah."

Brenna sent fire down her arms to smolder on the zip ties. They burned apart.

Janie grinned. "Show-off."

"I've been practicing control. Thank goodness it's finally paying off." Brenna stood and peered at the new lock in the door. "How do you feel about fire?"

"Love fire." Janie leaned closer. "Could you melt the lock?"

"Maybe. Or maybe just throw a plasma ball into the rock wall and see what happens." Brenna scratched her head. While she wasn't sure why the demons wanted her, she knew why they wanted Janie. Her niece wasn't going to be forced to mate anybody on her watch. "We need to make a move, I think."

Janie nodded. "Okay. Door or wall?"

"Let's try the door first." Brenna shoved her pinkie in the lock, and sent fire into the metal. Her finger burned. "Ouch," she hissed, yanking her hand free.

Janie frowned and leaned down. "It didn't work."

No kidding. "Okay. Back up." Pushing Janie behind her, Brenna slowly formed a green plasma ball in her hands. It wavered, glowing, gathering power. Then, swinging her arm back, she threw it at the wall.

The plasma hit with the sound of a bat cracking, burrowing a foot in before fluttering out. The smell of burning ozone and scattering dirt filled the room.

"Nice job," Janie said, leaning around Brenna. "Hit it in the same spot, and we might get all the way through."

Brenna nodded and put her hands together.

The door opened, and pain cut into her head. The demon guard pointed a gun at Janie. "Come with me, witch."

Brenna shook her head, biting her lip at the pain. "I think I'll stay here."

The instant attack dropped her to her knees. Janie fell next to her.

Brenna's eyes filled with tears.

The demon grabbed her arm and dragged her from the cell,

locking the door. "When I ask you to come, you come." He yanked her to stand, and the attack stopped. "Understand?"

"I'm going to burn the heart from your chest," she hissed, her vision wavering.

"Sounds like fun." He poked her in the back with the barrel of a gun, prodding her along. They wound through tunnels, twisted to and fro, until she finally lost all sense of direction.

He knocked on a door set into rock. The door opened, and he pushed her inside a plush bedroom with a sitting area. Motioning to a floral chair, he shoved her down.

She sat with a plop, her hands catching on the wooden arms.

Yanking out zip ties, he secured her wrists on the arms. "We wouldn't want you throwing fire, witch." Whistling a tune from the roaring twenties, he sauntered from the room.

Brenna glanced around. A large bed took up the corner with one of her paintings above it. A silhouette of two people making love, she'd painted it several years ago. The blue of the background still wasn't quite right.

The door opened, and Willa glided inside. Female demons were notoriously tiny, and this one more than most. The muted light caught on her silvery hair, making it nearly glow. In contrast, her black eyes seemed fathomless. She moved toward a bar on the opposite wall and poured herself a drink.

Brenna tested the ties. They were tight.

Willa turned around, long skirt swishing. "So we meet again, witch."

Brenna forced a bored expression. "Good thing, because I want my painting back." The painting had disappeared from a Dublin museum about a decade ago.

"Finders, keepers." Willa took a deep drink of the brew. "Jase Kayrs admired it so often while in my bedroom in Scotland."

"Your bedroom is in the earth?" Brenna snorted. "Your people hide you, do they?"

Willa flashed her teeth. "I like the earth. So did Jase. That man can kiss, can't he?"

Brenna smirked. "Jase never kissed you."

"The hell he didn't. Grabbed my ass and shoved his tongue as far down my throat as he could." Willa's hand slid along her side, her face flushing. "He was amazing. Every time."

Brenna bit back a gag. "So how did you fall short?"

"Excuse me?" Black eyes flashed.

"Gee, Willa. I slept with him once, and he planted the huge old Kayrs marking on my ass. You had five years with him—hungry, weak, and desperate. Yet you couldn't clinch the deal?" Brenna tapped her foot on the Persian rug. "Pathetic."

Willa snarled, and waves of pain shot through Brenna's eyes into her brain. She gasped, her vision disappearing. Only darkness remained.

Slowly, the attack stopped. Willa sipped her drink. "That old marking on your ass really has ruined everything, now hasn't it?"

Great. Pissing off the psycho demon was a wonderful idea. Brenna took a deep breath, thankful she could see again. "I really don't know what you mean."

"Well, I can't mate him now, even after I kill you." Willa sighed.

That was true. Matings were forever, and there were no do-overs for the vampires. Brenna concentrated on sending energy to the bottom of her hands. If she kept the power low, could she hide the plasma? "Jase would never have mated you."

"Maybe, maybe not. But that means he doesn't get to mate anyone else." Willa pouted out her lip, looking about sixteen. "He'll trade himself for you, and then I'll teach him what a mistake he made. Of course, you'll die, too. He'll get to watch that one."

"If you trade me, you can't kill me." The woman was nuttier than Brenna's aunt Dottie's cobbler.

"Oh, we'll do a double-cross at the trade." Willa frowned. "Or I'll trade you and then take you out from a distance with Jase watching." She clapped her hands together. "Yes. That's a much better plan."

Whoa. Brenna needed to get out of there. "Does Suri know you've made a move here?"

"No. My brother doesn't see the big picture." Willa sighed. "Malco does know, however. He'll do whatever I want." Her sly smile made Brenna want to puke. "Jase knows Malco. I think Malco blinded Jase for a week once."

Fury cascaded up Brenna's spine, and green danced along her arms. She snuffed it out.

Willa stared thoughtfully over her glass. "I heard you lost your powers. Something about a poisoning."

"They're coming back." Brenna smiled sweetly. "Since I mated Jase."

A knock sounded at the door, and the guard brought in Janie. "Are you sure about this?" he asked Willa.

Willa nodded and gestured toward the other guest chair.

The saliva dried up in Brenna's mouth. "What are you doing?"

The guard shoved Janie into a chair and zip-tied her hands.

"Well, it's been fun." He disappeared through the doorway.

Willa blew out air. "So you're the famous Kayrs psychic?"

Janie eyed Brenna and then Willa. "So you're the crazy bitch who failed at getting my uncle Jase naked."

Willa smiled. "Yes, well, you're his punishment for that."

"Punishment?" Brenna tried to lean forward.

"Yes. I don't need two of you for the trade, so Jase's lovely niece here dies for his transgressions." Willa set down the glass. "Since she's a human, I can make her brain explode through her ears."

Janie paled. "What's plan B?"

Brenna struggled against the ties. "Wait a minute. Don't you know who she is?"

"Yes, I do." Willa held her hands out toward Janie. "In fact, my people are split whether she should be put down or allowed to mate. My brother wants her put down, and I agree."

"But she's prophesied to change the world." Panic had Brenna seeing red.

"We like the world the way it is," Willa patiently explained. "Don't worry. I'll give you the chance to tell Jase all about her death. How fun will that be?"

The chick was seriously nuts. "No—wait. Blow my brains instead."

Willa wrinkled her nose. "I'd rather kill you with Jase watching." She pointed at Janie, and Janie cried out in pain.

Brenna struggled against the bindings, kicking out her legs.

Janie hissed, and blood shot from her ears.

Fire lanced down Brenna's arms, and her ties smoldered away. She leaped across the room to tackle Willa into the bed. They rolled over, and Brenna punched the demon in the nose.

Willa howled and grabbed her face.

Icepicks attacked Brenna's mind, and she yanked away, her brain weeping.

Willa kicked her in the chin, and she hit the carpet.

Enough of this shit. Brenna drew deep for power, forming a plasma ball in her hands.

Willa slowly turned and wiped blood off her mouth. Images of brutalized people shot into Brenna's brain. Pain cascaded down her spine.

She threw the plasma at Willa.

Willa jumped out of the way, and the fireball zipped over Janie's head to crash into the wall. Janie yelped and teetered on the chair.

Shit. "Sorry, Jane." Brenna leaped to her feet, forming more plasma.

Willa ran toward the door, and Janie tripped her with a foot. The demon slammed headfirst into the wall. She turned around, gasping, and yanked a double-edged knife from her boot.

"Go near my niece, and I'll burn you alive," Brenna warned, fire dancing down her arms.

A plasma ball zinged to hit the painting above the bed. Crap. She still didn't have control.

Willa gasped. "You're burning your own painting?"

"I never could get the blue hues right." Brenna angled closer to Janie. She had to be careful not to hit Janie with fire.

Willa clutched the knife and inched toward Janie.

Brenna threw a ball, hitting Willa square in the chest. The weapon lifted the demon, hurling her at the wall above the door. She dropped with a loud thump. Snarling, she lunged at Janie, knife out.

Brenna's fire fizzled out.

Janie twisted at the last second, taking the cut to the shoulder.

Brenna jumped across the room and tackled Willa, arms punching. The demon wrapped her legs around Brenna's torso and flipped them over, plunging with the knife.

Brenna turned her head at the last second, and the knife sank into the stone. "You bitch." She grabbed Willa's arm and yanked her off.

Willa crab-walked back to lean against the bed. "I don't need weapons against you, witch." Lifting her head, she sent out vibrations of energy that cut through the oxygen with a hiss.

A hot poker split Brenna's brain in two. Janie's shriek of pain drowned out Brenna's sob. God. Lightbulbs exploded behind her eyelids. Images of death filled her mind while pain reached for her soul.

Gasping, she forced her eyes open.

Janie's high-pitched cry chilled down Brenna's spine. She was a witch and a member of the Coven Nine. No fucking demoness was going to ruin her brain. Her hand shaking, she yanked the knife from the floor.

Willa smiled, sending pain tinged with mental poison to cut through Brenna's cerebellum.

"Nice try." Brenna flew across the room, landing on the demoness. Using all her strength, she plunged the knife in Willa's throat.

Shock filled Willa's eyes, and she fell to the side.

The images and pain disappeared.

Grunting, Brenna straddled the demon and twisted first right and then left. Blood spurted up to burn her face and neck. Willa's head rolled free.

Sliding off the body, Brenna turned her head and retched into the corner. The smell of death and vomit made her puke harder.

God. She'd killed.

Slowly, she turned to find Janie staring wide-eyed at her. "Are you all right?" Janie asked.

"No." Brenna staggered to stand. The room pitched. Sparks shot from her fingertips to start the bedspread on fire. She dashed forward and yanked it to the ground, stomping out the flames.

Then, grabbing the bloody knife, she stumbled toward Janie to cut the zip ties. "We have to get out of here."

Janie nodded and slipped an arm around Brenna's shoulders. "Lean on me."

The door flew open, and Malco stood on the other side. He took one look at the scene. "Willa!"

Brenna shoved Janie behind her and tried to gather plasma.

The demon backhanded her across the face, and she flew into the wall. Darkness wavered over her vision. She shot out, aiming for his gut. He punched her in the cheek, and stars exploded behind her eyes.

She dropped to the bloody ground, unconscious.

Chapter 29

Jase narrowed all fear, all focus, to the battle at hand. The second the helicopter touched down, he leapt out and ran for hell.

Talen set the charges and told everybody to get low.

Jase ducked behind a large rock, his rifle out and ready to shoot.

Dage grabbed his shoulder. "You cover the entrance."

"You'll need me—I can shield more than most of you." The idea of heading into the earth made his head spin and his legs weaken. "Brenna's down there, Dage. I have to go."

Dage eyed him, indecision crossing his still bruised face. "All right. But the second panic sets in, you move topside."

"I will." His gut churned like he'd just fallen out of a plane. Brenna was down there. He didn't have a choice. God, please let her still be alive. Janie, too. The thought of the demons hurting either woman filled him with a rage he thought he'd banished. For now, he'd dig deep and use it. They'd turned him into one cold bastard, and now they'd regret it.

The front entrance exploded out. Debris, rock, and a demon's head flew by. Jase swallowed and released the safety on his gun.

Dage turned and ran toward the burning hole. Jase steeled his shoulders and followed.

Charred rock surrounded him, and the scent of burned flesh slid down his throat to land in his gut. Tendrils spread out, and he gagged.

Then he froze.

He flashed back into survivor mode and stopped feeling. His thoughts narrowed in focus, his muscles relaxed. No emotion, no doubt, no humanity remained.

As a vampire, as a warrior, he often had to dig deep to find humanity. Now, easily and with a hint of relief, he let it slide away.

He ran downstairs with rocks falling all around him, on him, cutting into his flesh. The pain he welcomed. Lifting his chin, he waited.

The first mental wave from the demons below sliced into his brain, and he sucked it deeper. Deeper into his mind, deeper into his soul. They'd taught him not only to deal with agony but to enjoy it. Sad but true.

So, he took the pain deeper, and turned agony into strength. One he'd shove down their gullets until they choked.

Dage growled low and stumbled.

Jase grabbed his shoulder and leaned in. "Take in the pain and twist it. You're the damn king. Do it."

Dage sucked in air and nodded. "Got it."

Maybe he did, maybe he didn't. Either way, his brother would survive.

They reached the bottom of the stairs to face two pathways. Instinct and vibrations told Jase where to go, and he kicked an opening in the rock in front of him to reveal a third corridor. "I've got this one. Check in every five minutes."

His brothers nodded, and headed down the other ways.

Good. The most power came from this direction, and it was time. Time to take back what was his. His mind flashed to Brenna, and he tripped. Damn it. Shoving any thought of her into the back of his brain, he ran full-bore into the darkened passageway.

The walls morphed around him, reaching for him.

So he welcomed their presence and increased his pace.

Two demons rushed out of an alcove, and he attacked them like a man possessed, firing into their chests. One knocked the gun from his hand, and he reached for twin knives in his belt.

He plunged the blades into the demons' necks, shoving until steel met rock. One demon hung in place, eyes wide. "Been preparing for this, assholes."

Following the first demon to the ground, Jase twisted right and left until the head rolled free.

The other guy sent out a wave of devastating images and pain. Jase smiled and tilted his head to the side. "That all you got?"

The demon's eyes widened. Then he jerked away from the wall and lunged at Jase, the knife still embedded in his throat.

Jase pivoted and reached for the handle while grabbing the demon's hair and yanking down. The demon's spine split apart, and he cried out, falling. Jase straddled him and quickly decapitated him before sliding the blade free.

Wiping the blood on his shirtsleeve, he ran down the corridor toward the vibrations of power. The sound of gunfire and dying men filtered behind him, but he couldn't worry about the fight. He needed to find Brenna.

The brand on his hand pulsed with angry demand, an odd reassurance that she was still alive. He'd know if she'd been killed.

He followed the twisting and turning corridor, somehow knowing it led to the leaders. For five years he'd studied them when his brain still worked. The passageway narrowed, the rocks reaching for him. "Later," he muttered to the suddenly morphing faces. The ground rumbled above him. So many layers and tons of earth ready to fall on his head.

Damn it. He had to hold it together.

The scent of oranges chilled him through. Willa. He paused and then turned a corner to see a door in the rock. The scent came from the other side. The idea of walking into any room of Willa's splashed bile up his throat. Had Willa gotten hold of Brenna and Janie?

Tightening his grip on the knife, he kicked open the door.

The smell of blood and death slammed into him. Panic shoved him inside. Blood covered a white rug, and Willa's head faced him, eyes wide. Her body lay several feet away. Willa was dead.

He exhaled, glancing around the room. Emotions slid in—he was glad he hadn't had to kill a woman, and he would've ended her.

Small vibrations of energy centered him. Brenna's energy. She'd been in the room.

Had she killed Willa? Regret filled him. Brenna shouldn't have to kill.

Damn it. No emotions.

He shook his head and once again tried to focus. Turning, he followed the corridor farther down until reaching another door. Dark energy, ruthlessly held in check, slid under the doorway. Malco.

Jase forced emotion into nothingness and planted his boot near the doorknob. The door opened to reveal a large cell with rock walls and floor. One miserable lightbulb hung from the ceiling, swinging back and forth.

Malco held Janie against his chest, a jagged-edged knife to her vulnerable throat. Brenna lay facedown over in the corner.

Jase's heart clutched hard.

Janie's eyes widened until the black iris banished all the blue. "She's knocked out—not dead."

"Yet," Malco said, his lip curling. He stood well over six feet, pale face, black eyes, and white hair. A purebred monster. "Took you long enough to find me."

Jase lowered his knife to his side. "Let them go. I'm the one you want."

"In due time." Malco eyed the long scar along Jase's jaw. "Remember when I gave you that pretty memento?"

"Somewhat." Jase forced a shrug. His nightmares were filled with the days of getting tortured until he wanted to die. But some memories brought dark pleasure. "You wanted so badly for me to beg." He tilted his head to the side, studying the man who couldn't quite break him. "Yet I never did, did I?"

"Oh, you would've begged." Malco drew Janie up to her tiptoes, and she leaned her head back against his chest as he pressed the knife closer. "But Suri thought you were too close to breaking, and it was time to let you go."

By nearly decapitating him. "Five years, and you couldn't do it, asshole." A small trickle of blood ran down Janie's pale throat, and Jase bit back a growl, angling to the side. "Where is Suri, anyway?"

"He had personal business." Malco shrugged. "Figured I could handle you."

"You never could before," Jase murmured. The bastard held Janie tight—no way to throw an elbow or a punch. He glanced down at Brenna's back, which moved as she breathed. Thank God.

An odd electric blue glow filtered along her arm. He frowned, squinting, and the glimmer disappeared. The damn solstice would occur in minutes, and he had to get her conscious and ready to block the power, if possible. But under the circumstances, maybe blocking would be impossible. If so, he had to figure out a way to help her, maybe by taking some of the power himself. As her mate, he should be able to siphon from her.

His grip relaxed on the knife handle. "How about you stop hiding behind the little human and face me? It's about time we did this, don't you think?"

"Soon enough." Malco lowered his nose to Janie's hair and took a deep breath. "The human smells like life." Then he smiled. "*Caeca invidia est.*"

Jase's head jerked back. His body went still. Panic flushed through his lungs. He couldn't move.

Malco laughed. "I figured you hadn't found that trigger. The others, sure. But we made sure one was buried deep enough even Kane couldn't find it."

Jase bit his tongue, trying to move his arms. They remained at his sides.

Malco flashed sharp incisors. "Kill the witch, Kayrs."

The knife wavered in his hand, but Jase's body pivoted and moved toward Brenna. Dropping to his haunches, he grabbed her shoulder and flipped her over. A dark purple bruise cascaded along her right cheekbone. His hand trembled as he traced the wound with his fingers.

"Put the knife to her breast," Malco said softly.

Jase fought his body, but his arm lifted until the edge of the knife pressed above Brenna's heart.

Damn it. He had to control this. Sweat broke out on his brow, and his shoulders shook. How the hell had Kane missed this trigger? Now he couldn't even command his own body. There had to be a way.

"Uncle Jase, don't—" Janie's voice stopped with a gasp of pain.

Jase turned his head to see Malco's knife set a millimeter in Janie's skin. Her eyes filled with tears. God, if Malco dug any deeper, he'd cut her jugular.

"Back to the witch." Malco nodded toward Brenna.

Jase's body obediently turned back to the task at hand.

Brenna's eyelids flew open. Her pretty brown eyes focused and then widened. "Jase?"

He loved her. He needed to tell her. But when he opened his mouth, no sound emerged.

She glanced down at the knife that had torn through her shirt. "Um, Jase?"

"Kill her, Kayrs," Malco said.

Panic filtered across Brenna's face, followed by calmness. She looked him right in the eye. "Don't even think of following that asshat's orders."

Jase's head jerked back. Asshat?

Brenna's hand slid along Jase's arm to reach the hand holding the knife handle. "You control your body, and you control your life. Let go of the knife."

He tried to unfurl his fingers, but his entire body remained still.

Brenna smiled. "I love you, Jase. Always have and always will, no matter what happens."

Love. He felt it, too. Alive, mysterious, and somewhere deeper than his body. A growl rumbled up from his gut. He had to let go of the knife before he shoved it through her breastbone.

"This is touching." Malco sighed loudly. "Kill the bitch. Now."

Wrong words to say. Brenna was as far from a bitch as possible. Jase fought his body, his instincts, his own muscles, and yanked away. Gasping for breath, he glared at the weapon still in his hand. They didn't own him—they never had.

With a battle cry, he stood and threw the knife across the room. Keeping his muscles tense, he reached deep into his own mind and shattered a wall.

Blinding pain cascaded across his skull along with the sound of breaking glass.

Jumping up, he swirled around to face his enemy. "Trigger gone."

Malco snarled. "Pity. Guess I'll have to kill you all." Lifting his chin, he sent out a brutal wave of agony and images to slam into their brains.

Brenna cried out behind Jase.

Jase drew in the pain, forming a shield around the images. "That all you got?"

"No." Malco yanked the knife across Janie's throat.

Chapter 30

Jase froze, the world narrowing to that second in time. His niece's head dropped back as her jugular sprayed blood. Way too much blood.

Malco tossed her across the room and lunged.

Jase registered the sound of Janie hitting the far wall before Malco plowed into his stomach, throwing them both against the rock. Shards ripped down, cutting into his face and neck. Rage he had no intention of controlling roared through him, tightening his hands into fists. The first punch shot into Malco's solar plexus, and Jase aimed for the stone behind him.

Malco exhaled, slapping both hands against Jase's ears.

Brenna yelled Janie's name and scrambled to the prone woman.

It was too late. Everything in Jase knew it was way too late for Janie. His heart hurt. How was he going to tell Talen his daughter was dead? And Cara?

The demon grabbed Jase's still ringing ears, pressing in while leaning down and keeping his gaze. The black eyes swirled to purple, and the demon chanted in Latin. Words Jase had never heard before.

Pressure compounded behind Jase's eyes. His arms went slack. Nails poked holes in his brain, and a sucking sound filled his ears. Lights flashed, and his stomach revolted. Then blackness covered his vision.

The room tilted, and he dropped to his knees. Blind and helpless.

Brenna's anguished cry filtered through the pain. "Janie," Brenna yelled. "God, wake up."

There was no waking up for Janie Belle Kayrs. Jase stopped fighting the pain and blindness. He'd trained for this moment, and if it was his last, he'd go out swinging. There was no way on earth he'd allow Janie's killer to breathe for one more day.

Losing himself, losing any humanity he'd tried to keep, he allowed the pain to turn him into the creature they'd wanted. His eyes flashed open, and the nails in his mind slid away.

Malco's eyes widened.

Jase smiled and punched straight up into the demon's groin. Malco released him, leaning over with a pained *oof*. Jase sprang into the air to clamp his thighs around the demon's head and twist. Vertebra popped, and they plunged to the hard ground.

Straddling his enemy, Jase punched both fists into Malco's face. His breath centered, his mind cleared, and he battered bones and flesh almost rhythmically. Blood flew into his cheeks, burning like cigarette ashes. Malco tried to punch back, and Jase himself levered up, bringing his knees down on the demon's biceps with a force that broke bones.

Malco cried out in pain, his skull shattering.

Jase grunted, panting with the effort, his torso straining as each punch landed harder. He'd been training for five years for this moment, and yet he felt nothing. The demon's skull crushed into bits beneath his hands, the man losing consciousness.

"Damn it, Jase," Brenna yelled.

He kept hitting, the sound of flesh hitting wet flesh surrounding him.

"Jase?" She yelled louder.

He slowly turned his head, not halting his motions. His witch held her hands over Janie's throat, blood coating them.

She stretched and kicked his knife toward him. Green fire danced along her arms and through her hair. "Finish him and get over here."

The knife tumbled end over end toward him, finally landing near his foot. Blood coated his palm, and the handle slipped from his grasp when he reached for it. Stopping his movements, he wiped his hand down his chest. Grabbing the knife, he lifted it over his head and plunged the blade into Malco's throat. The demon didn't even move. Jase twisted both ways until the head was severed. Staggering to his feet, he kicked Malco's head across the room.

Then he turned and lurched toward Brenna.

She had both hands over Janie's throat, but it was too late. Janie's blue eyes stared sightlessly at the ceiling, her body lax in death.

Reaching Brenna, he placed a hand on her shoulder. "Let her go, Bren." Fire burned his palm, and he released her.

She turned her head, tears in her eyes. "Jane can't be dead."

"She is," Jase said woodenly. "Now get up. We have to get out of here."

Brenna slowly leaned back, her hands sliding to her knees. "Do something."

"There's nothing to do." He ignored the burn and hauled Brenna to her feet. They had mere minutes until midnight. "There's still fighting going on, and we have to get you topside before the solstice. Let's go."

Brenna pivoted and grabbed his shirt with both hands. "You don't get to go numb. Not now and not here." Her palms scorched through his bloody T-shirt to burn his chest.

He shrugged her off, his mind wanting to clear. With a low growl, he shoved all emotion back down. "Move."

She stepped back, blood on her face, her eyes wide with tears. "No. Janie's dead, but we're not leaving her."

They had to go. If Brenna would only leave with Janie, then he'd have to carry his niece out. He bent and slid both hands under Janie's still body.

That one touch destroyed him.

Memories flashed through him so quickly, he dropped again to his knees. The first time he'd met her—she'd only been four years old. Big blue eyes, wild hair, so fragile and breakable, he'd been scared to death to touch her. Yet she hadn't given him a choice. She'd launched her tiny body at him, fully expecting and trusting he'd catch her. And he did. Then she'd patted both small hands against his face and smiled, showing a gap in her front teeth.

From that second on, she'd been family. A girl he'd protected as she'd grown into a woman he'd trained.

But it hadn't been enough. Not nearly enough.

He'd failed.

Sorrow burst through him with a gale's force, and tears welled in his eyes. They flowed unchecked down his face, mixing with blood and dirt. He hadn't wanted to feel this—he hadn't wanted to feel anything. As he looked down at her delicate bone structure, he finally broke.

The rock walls morphed into faces around him. Faces he'd spent so much time with years ago. They shook their heads, eyes sad and full of recriminations. He'd let the demons win. They'd killed Janie, and they'd won.

He'd lost.

Brenna tried to cool the fire along her skin, reaching out to rub Jase's shaking shoulders. His grief popped the oxygen and made the air too heavy to breathe. The rocks rumbled around them, pieces falling down. They really did have to get aboveground.

She could feel the moon rise.

The power of the comet as it careened by the earth.

Power undulated around her, through her, trying to get in. She held it at bay. Barely. "Jase?" she forced out.

He didn't move. His head was down, his eyes slowly closing. Damn it. Allowing him to stay numb would've ruined him for all time—she knew that. But this? Maybe this was worse. Her heart broke for him. For the entire Kayrs family.

Flames danced on her skin in colors of aqua and green. She stepped away from Jase to keep him from being burned. Energy rippled through her veins, through her muscles, to vibrate along her flesh.

Entrancing and intriguing, the power tempted her.

God, it tempted her.

But she couldn't contain so much by herself—not after a decade of weakness. Even so, she touched the pendant around her neck. Could she beat the virus?

An explosion rocked the world outside, tilting the room, and she fell back against the wall.

Jase stood with Janie in his arms, his shoulders slumping. "Follow me out."

Sparks danced inside Brenna's skin. God. It was too much. A

fireball careened from her hand and slammed into the doorway, tumbling the door inward, and making rocks fall to block the way. Shit.

Jase paused.

There was no way out now.

Taking a breath, Jase placed Janie back on the floor and prowled over to the mound of rocks. "We need to dig out."

Power and the sense of life filtered through Brenna. She slowly turned to eye the dead woman on the ground. Wait a minute. Just how powerful could she become? Carefully, she made her way over to Janie, opening her senses on the way.

No filters, no shields, no safety.

It was a long shot, but Brenna was willing to take it. She turned her hands over, palms out, allowing the universe in. The virus would have to wait.

Jase chucked a rock aside, turning to glance her way. "What are you doing?"

"Nothing," she murmured, trying to concentrate.

Jase bounded up. "Brenna, no. Stop it."

She turned toward him as a myriad of different hues sprang up along her exposed skin. Tons of colors, all vibrant and alive. "I may be able to bring her back."

Jase tucked his chin, grief filling his copper eyes. "No, sweetheart. You'll just harm yourself. Stop. Now."

"No." She allowed a sad smile to lift her lips, the sensation hurting. "I have to try. It might work."

Anger and regret flashed across his strong face. He stood and prowled toward her. "I can't let you do this."

"You can't stop me." Her voice deepened, the sound resonating and not completely her.

"I can." His hand closed into a fist. "Don't make me. Please."

Energy and strength coursed through her from her head down to her toes. Energy she drew in and reshaped to make it her own. "Step back. I don't want to burn you." Fire crackled along her legs, sounding like a campfire deep in the woods. The sensation pricked her nerves, burning and stinging. Yet, she kept drawing it in.

"If I have to knock you out, I will." His face was set, the expression hard. But emotion and pain swirled in his amazing eyes. "Stop it, now."

"No." God. The pull of power was too addictive, too necessary. She couldn't stop now even if she wanted to—which she didn't. She might actually gain enough power to bring Janie back. The woman had only been gone for minutes, and surely it was possible. Untold power felt like something too wonderful to name—even though it kind of hurt. But in a good, too tempting way. "Go dig us out."

He swung.

She stepped back and swept out an arm. Fire lanced out, forming a living wall between them. He lifted his chin, anger tightening his lips to a white line. "Drop the fire. Now."

"No." She spread her arms, and the wall surrounded her and Janie. Jase couldn't get in unless she allowed him passage.

He growled and slid a hand into the fire. The scent of burning flesh filled the room.

"Burn all you want. I'm not stopping." Brenna shook her head, the power fuzzing her brain, her emotions washing away. Knowing full well the risks, she allowed them to disappear. She allowed the power to turn her into somebody else—somebody who might be able to heal Janie. To bring a human back from the dead, Brenna had to turn into something new. Something dangerous and probably something that couldn't last.

Sparks flew around the room. The earth rumbled below them, while thunder filled the night above them. Loud enough to be heard so deep in the earth.

The rhythm of the wind, the strength of the storm, the life of the earth filled her, surrounded her, lifted her higher than she could've imagined. A song erupted down her spine, a new song, a melody she could only feel. Too high and strong to be heard, it wove through her skin and flesh, tightening in a universal truth.

She was more powerful than the earth, sharper than the truth. More everlasting than reality—stronger than death.

Her hands vibrated, a wild dark blue dancing along her fingers. Turning, she knelt and placed both hands across Janie's throat.

Tendrils danced from Janie to tickle through the blue. Brenna tipped her head to the side but couldn't see anything. Yet something, a presence of a sort, reached for her hand. Was it Janie's soul?

"Stay in there," Brenna whispered, pressing harder against ripped flesh and damaged tissue.

The earth trembled, rumbling deep with the hint of violence.

Something unnatural was happening, and the earth would object. That was fine. Brenna could fight the planet if necessary. Potent power filled her, entranced her, drugged her.

She felt the exact second the comet drew close.

Forcing the energy into her hands, she pressed Janie's soul back into her body. Blood squirted, the vessels quickly mending before flesh drew together.

Janie gasped, rearing up, her eyes wide.

Brenna fell back. Holy crap.

Janie clutched her neck, wheezing in air. "What . . . happened?"

"You died." Brenna lurched to stand and waved the fire wall down.

Jase rushed forward to yank Janie up in a hug. Tears slid down his face. "I can't believe it."

Brenna's lungs heated and compressed. Uh-oh. She backed toward the demolished doorway, struggling to breathe. The sky bellowed a warning loud enough to be felt as well as heard. The ground shook. Rocks fell from the ceiling in large chunks.

Her body filled with energy and insurmountable power. She tried to shove it out, but it was too late.

Way too late.

Chapter 31

Jase settled Janie on the ground, her back to the rock. Faces morphed around him. Some familiar, some new. Had they missed him? He shook off the odd question, accepting the strangeness of his captivity. The faces had helped him to survive, to not be so alone. His brain had done what it could to keep him from going completely crazy.

Brenna backtracked to the far wall, her eyes wide and an unfathomable black. Her hair cascaded around her, curling as if she'd been electrocuted.

She was beautiful.

And dangerous as hell.

Flames danced on her skin, along her neck, even deep in her eyes. Panic lived there, as well. Then resignation.

Oh, hell no. The woman wasn't giving up. He shook his head, fighting to be heard above the rumbling earth. "Dig deep, Bren. Fight the power. You used it, you owned the bitch. Now let it go."

Crimson spread along her high cheekbones, and her eyelids half-closed. Ecstasy and pain raced across her face. "Caaan't contain it," she gasped.

"You can." He dodged to the side to avoid a falling boulder. They needed to get out of the ground before the tunnels collapsed. "Find the ice."

"There's . . . no . . . ice," she hissed out, grimacing. "Too much . . . too hot . . . step back. Now."

"No." He moved closer to her, heat singeing his arms and face. So much heat.

The fire wavered around her and crackled. She cried out, pain washing her face white.

Janie cried out from behind him, scrambling out of the way as rocks pummeled down.

Male voices echoed from the hallway as boulders were tossed aside. Talen and Conn shoved inside, bloody and bruised. But alive.

"We have to go," Talen growled, running to help his daughter stand and half-carry her into the hall. "Now."

"Go," Brenna shouted above the shaking earth. Regret twisted her lips, and tears made steam rise on her face. "Get out. Now."

Jase shoved Conn into the hallway after Talen and Janie. "Go. We'll be all right."

His brother turned and eyed Brenna. "I'll stay with you."

"No." Jase shook his head. "I can't worry about both of you."

"But if she blows, you'll both be buried."

"I know. Go home to your witch, Conn. I'll take care of mine." Jase couldn't be responsible for his older brother's death if this went the wrong way. His only chance to save Brenna lay in total concentration. "You have to go and make sure our brothers don't try to come back down here." They would, and that would be disastrous. The Kayrs men needed to get clear.

"I'm not leaving you."

"You are. I need you to trust me." Jase fought to keep his face clear and confident. His older brother had always stood between him and danger, but that time had passed. "You have to help Talen get Janie out of here—it sounds like you'll need to dig out, and time is running short. Janie is the only human, and she definitely won't survive an explosion. The rest of us have a chance. Get going. Please."

Conn studied him as debris rained around them. Finally, with a nod, he grabbed Jase in a hard hug.

Emotion choked Jase's throat, and he clasped his brother tight. "I'll see you topside."

Conn levered back, his eyes glazed. "Topside." Then he turned and followed the path Talen had taken.

Jase nodded and took a deep breath. Good.

Brenna's eyes filled with more tears. She grabbed the pendant around her neck. "I can't focus the energy into the virus. I'm trying, but—"

"Stop worrying about the virus. Concentrate so you don't blow up." Panic swept through his limbs along with a fierce determination.

She cried out, pain scenting the air. "Please, go. Now."

He shook his head. "I won't leave you. So you'd better control this."

"I can't." She winced as fire cut into her jugular, highlighting her veins in bright red through her pale skin. "Too much."

The fire was burning her. Jase stepped closer, his skin sizzling. Taking a deep breath of the heated air, he forced calmness through his nerves. The wall inside his mind had shattered, and he'd taken control. The last vestiges of his captivity, of his torture, had disappeared by his own effort. For years they'd tried to break him, but he was stronger than they'd imagined.

"You failed," he bellowed to the morphing rocks.

Brenna tilted her head. "What?" she yelled through the smoke.

He settled his stance and opened his hands. "Hold on, baby." He could do this. It was time to reclaim his life, to be who he wanted to be and not who the demons had tried to turn him into. He was Jase-fucking-Kayrs, and he controlled the elements.

Brenna's mouth opened in a silent scream as the fire started to consume her.

Jase peered into the raining debris to individual oxygen molecules. Digging deep, he commanded them to alter their state.

Water dripped through the air.

Exhilaration swept him. It was as if a missing limb had suddenly been returned. Power rushed through his veins in an electric arc.

Brenna screamed, and he narrowed his focus. Water splashed over her, quickly turning to ice. Steam rose with a sharp hiss all around her. The fire fought him, and he pushed back with as much strength as he could without harming Brenna. The ice might sharpen and stab her, so he kept a tight rein on the power.

Life and power hummed in his blood. A feeling he'd missed.

The ice cracked, and he added another layer. More steam rose.

The fire turned blue, fighting him. Brenna's eyes widened and then closed.

He sent another layer. "Dig deep, Bren. Find calmness," he yelled. Maybe she could hear him through the ice and fire, maybe not.

The fire burned brighter. With a crash, shards of ice shot out, one piercing his jaw.

Pain flashed down his neck.

The fire was snuffed out, having spent all its energy throwing off the ice.

Brenna dropped to the ground, her hand going to her chest. She gasped, swallowed, and opened her eyes. Panic flashed across her face, and she lunged for him, her hands pressing on his wound.

"I'm all right." He grasped her bloody hands and tugged her in for a quick hug, while sending healing cells to his screaming neck. The skin began to stitch together with a painful pull. The room tilted and the floor split. Jase took Brenna's hand, trying to shield her head, and yanked her into the hallway. "Run, baby. Time to run."

He turned and smashed into Conn. "What the hell?" Behind Conn stood Talen, Kane, Dage, and Max, all dirty and bloody.

Conn smacked his shoulder. "We got Janie and the wounded to safety and came back for you."

Dage gave him a look that said *Duh.*

The huge wave of emotion that engulfed him caught him up short. They were his brothers, and he should've known they'd never leave him underground. He nodded, his throat clogging. There weren't words, really.

The rocks exploded, sending fire toward Conn. Jase waved his hand, and a wall of ice blocked the flames.

Conn grinned through grime and blood. "Awesome."

Yeah. It was.

Dage growled. "Let's go before this whole damn thing collapses."

Jase yanked Brenna close and nodded. "Run."

Brenna sat on a stone bench watching dawn begin to lighten the day. The ocean churned below, dark and mysterious. She'd been debriefed by the king and her people as soon as the helicopters had touched down. A medical examination showed that mating Jase as well as pulling in the comet's power had cured her of the poisoning, which she'd already known. Still, it was nice to have medical confirmation. Oddly enough, she still needed to wear glasses. Apparently the damage to her eyes couldn't be countered. However, for the first time in a long time, she knew she'd live a long life. Finally finished, she'd headed to Jase's home for a quick shower. The house stood behind her lacking its windows.

It might've been a happy home for her. But some things weren't meant to be.

Jase had stayed with her underground when she was sure to blow up. More than that, he'd risked his own life and sanity to save her. But when it had come down to it, he'd chosen revenge over helping her. A man in love didn't make that choice. Although he was an honorable man and would fulfill his duties, she didn't want to be a duty, and she didn't want him to sacrifice for her. She owed him, and she'd make this easy on him.

Spreading out her fingers, she watched aqua flames dance on her skin. The comet had passed, as had the solstice, but some power remained. Much more vibrated through her veins than she'd ever had, even before she'd been poisoned. Unfortunately, she needed time to regain control.

She sensed Jase before he prowled into view. The early light flitted across his angled face, highlighting shadows and strength. Tucking his hands into faded jeans, he leaned against the trunk of a massive pine.

"How are you?" he asked, his voice a deep rumble.

A shiver wound down her spine from the husky tone. "I'm fine."

"Good. Sorry we missed your birthday."

"I'm glad it's over."

He eyed the ocean. "How's your control?"

"Marginal, but I'll get it." This polite talk was giving her a headache. "I'm sorry I couldn't cure the virus."

He turned, his eyes cutting through the morning. "You did something better. What you did, saving Janie . . ."

"I know." Sometimes life took odd twists.

"Thank you." His hair was growing out, and she wondered if he'd let it go shaggy like when he was younger. The relaxed look worked on him. "Kane thinks the triggers are out of my brain for good now."

"I'm glad."

"So you don't need to worry any longer."

"I'm leaving tomorrow." She extended her legs, stretching the tendons. The Kayrs men were honorable to the core, and Jase would try to be a good mate. But they'd mated for convenience, and for survival, and she wouldn't hold him to honor. "Maybe when a cure is found for Virus-27, we'll also figure out a way to negate matings." The idea of him mating somebody else cut deep.

"No." His instant grin flashed white teeth.

"Don't be difficult," she sighed. "I don't want to stay."

He pushed off from the tree. "That's unfortunate, because I'm not letting you go."

Now that sounded like a Kayrs male, didn't it? She shook her head. "You already let me go."

"I was wrong." He stood with his feet braced, tall and indomitable. "And I was coming to get you."

She'd been treated like a duty her entire life. She deserved better. "I owe you for saving my life, but that's all you get. You don't get me."

"Ah, Brenna. I already have you." His voice dropped to a tone that licked along her spine and softened her sex. "Fight me all you want, but you won't win. You're not going anywhere."

Anger tickled the base of her neck, and flames danced on her skin. She stood, trying to keep her voice level. "You might want to rethink that. Some of the comet's power remained." The need to challenge him rose hard and fast in her. He thought he could treat her like a duty and dictate her life? Not a chance in hell.

"You want to fight? We'll fight. You throw fire, and I'll throw ice." He sounded like he was discussing the latest football scores. "But you're staying here, and you're staying with me."

Panic flushed through her. She turned for the house. "I said, no." A hard wind smacked into her chest, halting her progress. She flipped around, fury crackling over her skin. "You don't want this."

"Oh, but I do." He angled closer to her, a predator on the prowl.

Fine. Extending her fingers, she shot three hard plasma balls at his face. One casual sweep of his hand sent the wind carrying them out to sea.

Brenna dropped her hand and side-armed a ball at his leg. The plasma hit hard, knocking him back a step.

He growled and lunged for her.

She yelped, hands up in defense. Her palms burned through his shirt, shredding the cotton. He grabbed her, ice washing along her skin.

Thank goodness. She hadn't meant to burn him. "I'm sorry."

The corners of his eyes crinkled. "I've always thought you were hot."

God. That charm would be the end to her. "Let go of me."

"Not going to happen." He slid his arms around her waist. "Ever."

Tempting as sin, he was. She shook her head. "I want love."

"You have it."

Her heart lurched, and she searched for calmness. "The real kind."

He grinned, flashing a dimple. "I love you with everything I am, with everything I'll ever be, and with every hope I could ever dream."

Now that was just sweet. She wanted to fall into the dream, but reality always returned. "What about Suri?"

"I don't love him at all." Jase pulled her closer, into his hard body.

"You know what I mean." The man had left her once to chase revenge, just when she'd needed him.

Jase leaned back, his gaze serious. "You come first, no matter what."

This was too good to be real. She shook her head to keep sane. "No."

"Yes."

She bit her lip. "What about revenge?"

"I still want it—and I want Suri dead." Jase's hold tightened. "But I won't leave you when you need me, I promise."

Dreams didn't come true like this. "Jase—"

"I'm damaged, and I'm determined to kill." Regret twisted his lip. "But I'm all yours, baby. The good and the bad."

Well, now. "No, you don't understand."

"I do understand. What's more, I love you. Completely. Please stay."

The words rang with truth, and her heart thumped hard. If she wanted him to accept her for herself, she could do no less for him. She needed him, and she wanted to be there every day to help him fight his demons. Who knew? Maybe they'd actually win. "All right."

He lifted an eyebrow. "And?"

Her smile broke free. "I love you, too."

His smile beat hers. "In that case"—he released her and dropped to one knee—"how about we do this right?"

She stopped breathing. "Right?"

"Yeah." He pulled out a platinum diamond solitaire surrounded by intricate Celtic knots. "This reminded me of you. Consider it a late birthday present." He slipped the ring on her finger.

The morning light flickered across the amazing stone. She blinked.

He grinned. "Marry me."

"You're supposed to ask." She grinned. A Kayrs didn't ask, but the thought was amusing.

"Would you do me the incredible honor of marrying me?" he asked softly.

The man was full of surprises. "Yes." She rushed him, and he caught her, falling back with a laugh.

A golden cuff instantly fastened around her left wrist, the magic metal re-forming to a tight fit. She frowned. "What in the world?"

"My brothers and I each have a cuff from childhood—they attach to our mates, too." Jase rolled her over, pressing her into the ground.

"Take it off."

"Nope. It stays on." He tangled his fingers in her hair.

Desire warmed her torso. "My sister doesn't wear a cuff."

"I think it's on her ankle." Jase captured Brenna's mouth in a hard kiss. "Though maybe you could convince me to take it off . . ."

Brenna had finally found her home. Who knew it'd be with a wounded, scarred vampire? "Not a problem, Kayrs." Hooking her ankles at his waist, she kissed him with all the love she'd held back until now.

Chapter 32

The king of the Realm finished securing the ancient cuff links at his wrists, his mind focusing on fifteen other matters at once. A rustle sounded by the doorway of his bedroom, and he turned.

The world silenced.

The blue of Emma's dress was stunning, yet it didn't come close to the beauty of her eyes. His mate had pinned her dark hair up and left her delicate throat bare. His fangs wanted to drop low and bite. Quite possibly the smartest woman he'd ever met, she still held a kindness in her that humbled him every day. Her determination to cure Virus-27 concerned him because he understood obsession.

She was his.

Dage eyed the gold cuff wrapped around her upper arm. "What made you decide to wear the cuff?"

She flashed a smile. "The bride requested we all wear the cuffs since Jase refuses to remove the one from her wrist."

How odd. He and his brothers were all mated. Happily mated to incredible women. Dage forced a smile to hide his concern and took a swig from his ever-present grape energy drink.

Emma lifted an eyebrow. "What's wrong?"

He gave a sheepish smile and tossed the can in the garbage. "Everyone is happy for the moment. Just waiting for the other shoe to drop."

"I thought a real clodhopper dropped earlier this morning?" She removed a clutch sitting on the dresser.

"Good point." He lifted a jewelry box from his tuxedo pants and flipped the lid open.

She gasped, reaching for the beautiful necklace. "The stone is beautiful—what is it?"

"Red diamond." He'd searched the globe for the rare stone, and it had taken two years to broker the sale. "Its beauty isn't close to yours."

She grinned. "Charming, King. Very charming."

Well, a guy liked to try. "Thank you, love." He turned her and quickly fastened the necklace, turning her back around. "Now, that's pretty." Of course, he was talking about her smooth skin, but the jewelry wasn't bad, either.

She smoothed down his lapels. "Did you tell your brothers about the offer?"

"Yes." Now wasn't the time to discuss this.

She tightened her hold. "Did you tell Jase?"

"No." Dage ran his palms down her toned arms—such delicate bones to protect. "I figure we'll inform him after the honeymoon."

"Tell him now." Emma shook her head. "No more protecting him for his own good. He deserves better."

When his little scientist was right, she was right. "I'll talk to him today after the wedding."

"Good." Emma fingered the diamond pendant at her throat. "Do you think the demons really want a truce?"

"I don't know. We took out Willa and Malco, so Suri is scrambling. He also knows Jase will find him sometime, so maybe he really does want a truce." The demon leader had called to offer negotiation that morning. "He seemed to think he could get the Kurjans to the table." Ending the war would be the best thing for the Realm—for Janie. But first Dage had to convince his brothers to end the war. Damn. He had to convince himself.

Emma pursed her lips. "Considering the timing, it's probably a trick."

"What timing?"

"Janie. The Kurjans want her alive, the demons want her dead, and countless other species want her, too. She'd an adult . . . and something is coming."

Dage exhaled slowly. Sometimes he forgot the human woman he'd married had been a psychic even before they'd mated. "I feel it, too. Something is coming."

Emma took his hand and led him to the door. "But today we celebrate. Our family is strong and whole. Let's go pick up Talen and Cara and worry about the rest tomorrow."

Three centuries ago, the king had learned to enjoy the good days to the fullest, because they rarely lasted. But this woman? She lasted. No matter what happened, they'd last. So he took her hand and followed her toward the chaos that was a family gathering. "I love you, Emma," he whispered.

She turned, surprise in her eyes. Then she smiled. "I love you, King."

Talen watched his mate try to make the gold cuff fasten to her wrist. The cuff's magic lay in the mating bond, and his had been damaged the second she'd been infected with Virus-27. So far, the virus had weakened her and messed with their mating bond by slowly unraveling her chromosomal pairs. She was currently somewhere between a vampire mate and a human. Safe for now.

But they had to figure out a way to stop the damn things from unraveling.

"There," Cara said triumphantly, nearly dislodging one of several potted plants on their dresser. "I used tape."

He forced his lips to curve and mask his fury at the virus. "You look beautiful." And she did. Her hair was down around her shoulders, and she wore a blue gown that matched her eyes. Almost. Her eyes held a luminosity no fabric could duplicate.

"We're all wearing blue. Brenna's a bossy bride," she said.

Yeah. She'd insisted the brothers wear tuxedos. Talen belonged in a tuxedo as much as a Doberman belonged in high heels. But any sacrifice was worth it if Jase had found some peace. Maybe even happiness. "Jase is doing better, right?" he asked, tucking a weapon beneath his jacket.

The little empath grinned. "Yeah. Jase is on the mend, so stop worrying."

Thank God. "I don't worry. I fix."

"Right. Speaking of which, your temper has seemed rather dormant considering your daughter gave the Kurjans info on our tunnels and tried to sacrifice herself for her brother." Cara slid gold earrings into her ears.

Talen sighed. "She did what any of us would do to save family. The idea of either Janie or Garrett in danger makes my gut hurt, but they're well-trained, and they're smart."

Cara snorted. "You increased security on them both."

Well, of course he had, right after he'd increased security on Cara. "I don't know what you mean, mate."

"Hmmm." Cara shook her head. "What do you think of the demon leader's offer to end the war?"

"It's a good strategic move, considering we took out several of his lieutenants this year." Talen kept his voice calm and his face bland. As the strategic leader of the Realm, he'd end up between Dage, who'd want to end the war, and Jase, who'd want to kill Suri first. But that was a problem for another day. So he stepped into his mate and backed her into the wall. "We have a few minutes here."

A pretty blush covered her cheekbones, and she batted at his tie. "Knock it off. Emma and Dage will arrive any minute to take us to the main lodge."

"No." He wrapped his hands around her waist and lifted her until they were eye-to-eye.

"Yes." She slid her palms over his shoulders, a feminine smirk on her lips. "If you smudge my makeup, the bride, who is a rather powerful witch, will throw plasma at you."

He'd been burned before. So he covered Cara's mouth with his, taking one simple taste to assure him of their future. To assure him they'd beat the virus, beat the demons, destroy the Kurjans, and find peace for their children. Releasing her, he smiled at the bemused look in her eyes. "How long do we have to stay at the reception?"

"We have to stay until the speeches and cake." Cara fixed his tie. "But I have a feeling you and your brothers will start celebrating, so my guess is we'll be home around dawn."

That's what she thought. They needed time alone, and he needed her. "We'll see about that, little mate."

Max Petrovsky hated tuxedos, he hated social functions, and he hated wearing boxers. "The boxers are too much."

His mate glanced up from securing a pretty anklet around her ankle, her foot on a kitchen chair. "I read boxers increase sperm count. You want to have a baby, right?"

"I'm a damn vampire and have more sperm than you can imagine." By all that was holy. It took centuries for vampires to have kids, as it should. They lived forever usually. He and Sarah had only been mated for a short time, and kids would come someday.

"Did you just swear at me?" Sarah's brown eyes sparkled.

"Ah, no." He tugged on his tie. "I would never swear at you." Jeez. He shuffled his size-eighteen feet. "I'm sorry."

She sauntered toward him, the sweetest woman he'd ever met, to straighten his shirt. "You're forgiven."

He relaxed his shoulders. Yeah, he was the king's bodyguard, more like a brother, and he was known as the most dangerous hunter in existence. But one woman could reduce him to nothing if she wanted.

Good thing his Sarah had a kind heart and would never hurt anybody. Well, usually. Max grinned at the little teacher. "I heard you almost skinned Garrett Kayrs along with two of his friends yesterday in class."

Sarah chuckled and fixed his tie. In her heels, she stood over six feet tall, still several inches shorter than he. "Those three. Too much energy, too much intelligence, and way too much testosterone. They used the main computer as a dating site—and Garrett arranged to meet a much older woman from Toledo. She agreed to send him a plane ticket, of all things. Thank goodness I caught them first."

"What did you do?" Max asked.

"I made them write essays about true love and how to respect women." Sarah bit her lip. "You should've seen Garrett when he got to the part of the assignment that required him to write a poem." She threw back her head and laughed, the sound free.

Max smiled. "You're a mean one when you want."

"Thank you." Her grin was stunning. "I'm going to miss those boys after this year when they head off to college."

"You've taught them well, *Milaya*." Pride filled Max. He slipped a finger between her breasts and tugged the blue material away.

She slapped his hands. "We don't have time to play."

There was always time to play. So he dropped his mouth to her neck and traced her beating pulse with his tongue. She sighed and pushed him while angling her head so he'd have better access. He nipped just under her jaw.

She sighed, sliding her hands around his waist. Then she stiffened and drew back. "Why do you have a gun?"

He frowned. "I always have a gun."

"We're going to a wedding." She shook her head.

Well, yeah. But they'd all be armed—even the groom would have a weapon somewhere. "Sweetheart, we're at war. I'm always armed."

"No." She lifted the gun free of his waistband, turning it over.

He didn't like seeing a weapon in her hands, and his heart rate increased. So he gently removed the gun and placed it on top of the refrigerator. "We'll just leave this here."

Her sweet smile made him feel like he'd already won a war. "Thank you," she breathed.

He nodded. Of course, he had another gun along his leg and three knives hidden on his body. He was a bodyguard to the king, after all. "You know I'm a soldier, right?"

"Sure." She patted his butt. "But this is a family wedding where your brother is finding happiness. No guns."

Had she met his family? "If you say so." He'd accepted a long time ago that even though they weren't blood, the Kayrs brothers were his family. The idea filled him with warmth. "Weddings aren't always safe."

Sarah rolled her eyes. "Of course they're safe. Don't worry—this will be a relaxing, fun time."

God. Sometimes he just loved her optimistic view of life. They were walking into a wedding room filled with vampires, witches, and shifters. It'd be a miracle if nobody got shot. So he smiled and gathered his mate close. "You're right. This will be perfect." He'd make damn well sure of it, just to keep his Sarah happy.

Kane leaned against the fireplace, his gaze implacable on the blond beauty trying to look innocent across the room. "What did you do?"

She lifted a creamy shoulder. "I have no idea what you mean."

So they were going to play it that way, were they? He set his scotch on the mantle. "When was the last time I spanked you, Amber?"

His mate lifted her chin. "Last week, when I organized the protest against the group doing animal testing on nail polish."

"No." He prowled closer to her, appreciating the fire that flashed into her gorgeous eyes. "I believe the protest was fine. It was your breaking and entering the facilities and putting yourself in danger that guaranteed my palm print on your ass." He'd always planned to mate a logical easygoing doctor or scientist. Thank God Amber had blasted his plan to hell. The woman was a planet-protecting vegan with spirit. Which was fine, so long as she kept out of danger. "You know to be careful."

She lifted her chin. "Careful is for wussies."

Damn. Not one inch of her was afraid of him. He couldn't help the slow smile. "Those countermoves you learned from Conn were damn good." She'd nearly taken out his knee before he'd flipped her over it.

"I know." She smoothed her hands down his tuxedo jacket. "I'm a pacifist, but I have no problem knocking you out next time you try it."

"Tell me. Now." He didn't need to go into more detail. The woman could always read him.

Her grin was all imp. "I just made sure one of the caterers learned veal is bad."

He didn't want to know. He really didn't want to know. "Tell me you didn't mess with the menu Brenna wanted."

"I didn't. Brenna would never want veal." Amber's eyes widened. "You really need to learn to relax."

With her as a mate? There was no relaxing. He tugged on a strand of her curly hair. "You promised to have fun today and not mess with anybody."

"I always keep my promises."

Uh-huh. "Did you hear the demons called and want to negotiate a truce?"

"No." She stilled. "Do you think they mean it?"

"I truly don't know." He brushed a thumb along her smooth jaw. "I like the idea of peace."

"Me, too." She grabbed his lapels and yanked him down for a hard kiss. "If we stopped fighting the demons, we could spend more time and resources fighting the virus."

Exactly. There was no question Virus-27 needed to be cured before more mates were infected, and Kane would love to spend all his time working on science instead of strategy. The idea of his mate being susceptible to the damn bug kept him up more nights than he could count. "I'm sure once everything settles after the wedding, we'll sit down and figure out the right path."

"Do you think Jase will want peace?" Amber asked, snuggling closer.

"Yes and no." Kane slipped a hand down her bare back. "I'll need to talk to Conn to figure out where we'd hold negotiations. This would be a military act."

"So long as we find peace."

Kane nodded, his hand dipping lower. "I love this dress."

His wild vegan tilted her chin and smiled into his eyes. "I love you. Let's go to the wedding."

Conn paced the wall of windows of their house, his hands in his pockets. The sun glittered off the ocean waves. What a perfect day for a wedding. He needed to relax and put himself into party mode.

Moira swept into the room. "Sorry I'm late."

"You're fine." He turned from the window and nearly swallowed his tongue. Talk about an understatement. "You're gorgeous, *Dailtín.*"

She smiled, her green eyes lighting up. "Brenna made us all wear blue dresses, and I thought mine needed some sparkle."

Yeah. Shimmering, sparkling, sexy-as-hell dress. "I totally agree." He tugged his hands free. "Where's your weapon?"

She lifted her chin, power dancing along her skin. "Which one?"

"You keep looking at me like that, and we're never gonna make it to the wedding." He wanted to tease her, but damn, he might be serious. Getting her naked and beneath him was far too appealing.

Delight flashed across her face. "While I love the thought of grappling in bed all day, your baby brother is marrying my baby sister. Our families would break down our front door looking for us."

Now that was the truth. He studied his witch. "You're the most beautiful thing I've seen in three centuries."

Her smile slid to sweet. "Aren't you charming today."

"Just thankful." And he was. Thankful for her, for his family, for the fact that Jase was healing. Life held promise again. "I'd be lost without you, Moira Dunne-Kayrs. Sometimes I forget to tell you that."

Her expression softened, and she approached him, hands flattening on his chest. "What's going on?"

He grinned. "I give you a compliment, and you ask me what's up?"

"No. I can feel something is up. You're thoughtful—and wary." Curiosity and understanding commingled in her eyes. "Is it the offer from the demons?"

He lifted his chin. "Maybe. You know how in battle, you can feel an opponent switch their approach?"

"Yes."

"I feel like we should be looking over our right shoulders." The instinct didn't make sense, but it was one he trusted. "Something's coming."

"Aye. Something's coming." Moira slid her dress up her right thigh to reveal a gun tucked securely in place. "But not today. Today is for love and family."

He glanced at the clock. "Love, huh?"

She let her skirt fall and backed away. "No. No time. No."

"Oh, my little Irish beauty." He stalked her, steering her toward the wall. "You know I don't like that word."

Blue danced on her skin, and she formed a plasma ball, her eyes lighting with fun. "Don't make me blow you up."

"You throw that, and I'll be inside you within minutes." God, he hoped she threw. One thing he knew without question was his witch couldn't resist a challenge.

She kept retreating. "Blast it. We need to get to the wedding—you know that. Stop moving, damn it."

"Moira, I'm going to have you before we leave this house. Easy or hard, it's going to happen." He loved the fire that lit her eyes as well as the dare that lifted her chin. "So stop moving and kiss me."

Predictably, his woman threw the plasma.

He caught the fire and fizzled the flames out between his fingers. Then, with a grin, he lunged for his mate.

Chapter 33

Brenna smoothed down the Irish lace, appreciating the centuries of women who had worn the dress before her. Love and hope lived in the soft fabric. She stood in the small room of the lodge while the sun played across the ocean outside. She smiled at her older sister. "Moira, your hair needs work."

Moira grinned and sat at the vanity to fix her hair. "Sorry I was late. 'Twas totally Conn's fault."

Aye. Brenna didn't need a road map. "I figured."

Moira turned. "Tell me you're happy."

"I'm happy." Brenna smiled as she realized the truth of the statement. "I love him."

"Good." Moira patted wild curls into place. "Life as a Kayrs mate isn't easy, but it's well worth it. They're good men."

"I know." Brenna nodded. "Jase likes me for me, and not for who the world thinks I should be."

Moira laughed, her eyes sparkling. "That does sound familiar, you know. The world thought I should sit on the council and dictate policy. Only Conn knew that I belonged on the front lines dealing with witches misusing magic."

"I like sitting on the council." Glancing at the quiet street outside the window, Brenna leaned toward her sister. "Janie had a vision regarding the Prophecies of Arias and thinks she needs to read the book to end the current war."

Moira blinked. "What did you tell her?"

"Just that the book didn't exist, and if it did, I'd need to go through the proper channels to gain her access. But we should get her access, don't you think?"

"Yes." Moira slipped her feet back into the heels. "The book is in an ancient language, and I have no idea what it says. Do you think she'll be able to decipher the pages?"

"Maybe." Brenna touched up her makeup. "She deserves a chance to try."

The door burst open, and Deb Stewart swept inside with the bouquets, her dress swishing. "Everyone is seated."

Brenna reached for her arrangement of bluebells and green rosemary. "Everyone getting along?"

Deb grinned. "I didn't say that. Your sisters are all in blue, as are the Realm mates, but everyone chose different blues."

"That's fine." Brenna stretched her calves in the high heels.

"Yeah, I know. But some of the shifters wore blue, too." Deb laughed. "And the younger Realm vampires are seriously flirting with a group of female wolf shifters out of Washington, and their Alpha is glaring."

"Their Alpha is Terrent Vilks, and he's an ally," Moira said, reaching for her bouquet.

Brenna sighed. "Yeah, but Terrent is over-the-top protective of his pack."

Deb nodded. "I think he's with a very pretty shifter who knocked over a row of baskets?"

Brenna laughed. "Yes, Maggie is his mate, and she's a bit . . . um . . ."

"Clumsy as hell," Moira said flatly. "But we love her anyway. Speaking of shifters, have the lion shifters arrived?"

"Yes." Deb patted her hair back into place. "Jordan and Katie were already busy chasing two energetic seven-year-olds around. Those cougar twins are just too cute for words."

"I can't wait to catch up with everyone," Brenna said. "But, we do need to tell Garrett to watch out for the wolf cheerleaders. Terrent won't let Garrett seduce one of those girls."

"Seduce?" Moira coughed. "Garrett wouldn't know how to seduce a sure thing. The kid is cute, but *seduce*? I don't think so."

Brenna glided toward the door. They'd better get a move on before all hell broke loose. "Garrett is a Kayrs who recently survived battle with both Kurjans and demons. He's a hero, and he has the vampire's charm. Plain and simple."

Moira frowned. "Good point. Let's get him occupied before the wolves declare war on us, too."

Brenna chuckled. "Here I thought my wedding day would be calm."

"To a Kayrs?" Moira shook her head. "Your life will never be calm. But let's go get married."

Brenna waited until her family and friends took their places before sliding her hand through her father's arm. Doctor Dunne smiled down at her, and she nudged him. "Two daughters mating vampires, huh? You okay?"

Her father grinned. "My girls have found love and adventure. Of course I'm happy." The music started, and he escorted Brenna into the main room of the lodge, which had been turned into a wedding venue for the day.

Brenna almost stumbled at seeing Jase. He stood up front with his brothers, a solid wall of strength and family. The scar on his face spoke of suffering, while the love in his eyes promised a future. A good future. She smiled, and his eyes flared.

So much power came with love from a man like that. She could handle it, and she could handle him. Sure, he was wounded, but he loved her. She felt the warmth of his love even across the room. As a mate, she could feel inside his skin.

She belonged there.

As she crossed the room, she ignored the young vampires, the giggling shifters, and all of their family and friends. Her only focus was on Jase Kayrs, the man she'd mated for survival and had ended up loving. She reached his side, and she tucked her arm through his.

When he dropped his head to press a gentle kiss on her forehead, she finally found her place in a crazy universe.

Jase headed for the bar after dancing for a while with Brenna. The ceremony had been beautiful, but not nearly as lovely as the woman who was now his wife. She'd hustled off to take more pictures with her sisters, and he needed a drink. His brothers beat him there, and shot glasses were filled. He knew family, and he knew peace. It was a rare moment to feel both, and he took the time to just appreciate life. He glanced at the wall of vampires, his heart warming. "Thank you for not giving up on me."

Conn slammed a hand down on his shoulder with a force that would've killed a human. "We're brothers."

That pretty much said it all.

"What now?" Kane asked, his intelligent gaze on the partygoers.

Dage sipped his drink. "Now we figure out what the demons really want."

"They want Janie," Talen said, his low growl a direct contrast to the smile he sent across the room toward his mate. She smiled back, her shoulders relaxing.

Jase nodded. "Yeah. That's what I think, too."

"They can't have her." Conn poured another round of shots while Max reached for more pretzels.

Jase eyed Garrett while he danced with a young witch. "How's Garrett doing, anyway?"

"Fine." Talen popped pretzels into his mouth. "He is unsure whether he should be grateful to Zane or whether he should've killed him."

Sounded about right. Jase eyed Dage. "Have we found Zane? Might be a good ally."

"No. My guess is he's part of one of the warring shifting clans in Iceland. They're brutal but well-funded," Dage said. "I'm not sure if we want him for an ally."

"We don't," Talen said flatly. "Next time, we kill him. We don't need some vampire-shifter getting into Janie's dreams. Period."

Jase nodded. "I agree." Brenna caught his eye, and he straightened. "If you think the war will really end, I'd support negotiations even with the demons." Not that he wouldn't get revenge someday. But for now, his family and people needed safety.

Dage nodded. "I appreciate that."

"I'd bet my left arm the demons don't really want peace," Jase said quietly.

"I agree," Dage said just as quietly. "Let's worry about that tomorrow."

Good plan. Jase smacked his brother on the back. "For now, I'm going to dance with my mate." Stalking across the room, he swept her up just as the band belted out a new song. He twirled his bride around in a fast dance, enjoying the delight flashing across her classically lovely face. He'd been dancing for centuries but had never felt so free. The music slowed, and he tucked her close.

She snuggled in with a soft sigh. "I'm glad you're not on fire about this treaty business."

He slid a hand to her lower back, spanning her waist. "Peace would be good for the Realm." If he could keep Garrett and his buddies away from a war, he'd negotiate in a heartbeat. Unfortunately, he knew Suri. Being tortured for years tended to give insight into the torturer. If Suri was offering peace, there was a huge price. Chances were, Dage would refuse to pay.

"So you won't kill him?" Brenna asked softly.

"I'll kill him." Even if they found peace, a time would come when he and Suri would meet again. Destiny was ongoing, and fate could take eons. But in the end, they'd be fulfilled. "I'm in no hurry." He eyed Garrett and a pretty wolf-shifter trying to slip away. Terrent Vilks was immediately in the vicinity, pointing them both to the cake table. Jase laughed. Nice try, Garrett.

Brenna glanced up. "What's so funny?"

"Young love." Frankly, his money was on Garrett. The night was early. He glanced down at his stunning witch. "Our love."

Brenna smiled. "Did you think we'd end up like this?"

"No." He tucked her close. "At my lowest, when I'd been tortured for so long, and Willa made her offer, I almost considered accepting her as a mate just to get out of hell. Until I looked up and saw your painting."

Brenna tightened her hold. "My painting grounded you?"

"No. It made me think of you, and you saved me." He tilted her head back, needing to explain. "You *are* kindness, class, and beauty. I knew if I ever had a chance to experience any of those things, I had to say no. So I did."

A soft smile curved her lips. "You're saying we saved each other."

"Yes." He closed his eyes and moved to the music. He'd never doubted fate, and he'd never been worried about destiny. Perhaps there was a bigger plan in place, perhaps not. Either way, he'd found his path home to the one woman who would always be his. She'd healed him, and he would protect her forever. In fact, she'd made him believe in forever. The brand pulsed on his hand in agreement. He glanced down at the Kayrs marking, finally understanding what it meant.

Forever had teeth, and when it was right, it sank in. "I love you, Bren. Forever."

Epilogue

Janet Isabella Kayrs knew better than to dance all night in three-inch heels, but she'd been having so much fun, she'd forgotten to change her shoes. As she slid into bed, she tried to flex away the pain. Cramps escalated up her calves. Good thing she'd had plenty of wine, or it'd hurt worse. Her head spun. Yeah. Plenty of wine.

She breathed deep, sliding into the misty world between dreams and reality. There was a time she'd controlled the world, and now she needed to learn how to reclaim the power. For tonight, she drifted away and wandered inside the now empty ballroom.

Zane entered from the ocean side, his footsteps echoing in the empty room, his gaze taking in the remnants of the party. "Who got married?"

She glanced down at her heels and slipped them off. This was her dream, and her feet deserved a break. "My uncle Jase married Brenna Dunne."

"Ah." Zane brushed flowers off the bar. "Did you have a date?"

She tilted her head. "Maybe."

"Hmm." He moved closer, his gaze on her shimmering blue dress. "You look beautiful."

So did he. In faded jeans and a dark T-shirt, Zane was the most handsome man she'd ever seen. Deadly angles made up his face, which highlighted eyes a deep green. Deeper than any river she'd ever seen. "Thank you."

He traced a knuckle down her face. "Your birthday is coming up soon. What do you want?"

Heat flared through her at the gentle touch. She sighed at the approach of her twenty-fifth year. As a child, she'd known that was the year fate would be met. "I want to win."

Zane nodded. "Me, too."

"Speaking of which, thank you for saving Garrett."

"Not a problem." Zane's eyes darkened. "Now you owe me one."

Was that a fact? She was damn tired of waiting for destiny, and twice as tired of waiting for Zane. So she stepped into him and tilted her head. "What exactly do you want?"

His nostrils flared. "Don't play, Janie Belle."

She kept still. "What in the world makes you think I'm playing?" Her frown narrowed her focus. "I've always known how this would end, and I've never considered it a game."

"None of us knows how the war will end." His lip twisted as his hand slid around her neck. "We know the players, but do you really know who wins? Are we together or on opposing sides?"

"Together." Heat cascaded off him, even in the dreamworld. But no smell. She'd always wondered about his scent.

"Is that your heart or brain talking?" His lids dropped to half-mast. "What do you really know?"

"I know the good guys." She kept her face set in honest lines. Was it possible to have fallen in love as a child? To have known her destiny since she was four years old? "Without a doubt, I've always known the Realm wins. So you might want to get on board."

"Ah, Belle. You don't know the final outcome, and there are no true good guys in this war." His fingers tightened on her nape. "I'd like to think you've never lied to me."

"I haven't."

"Then tell me the truth. Tell me about your vision. You owe me."

Yeah, she did. "Why did you save Garrett?"

"Because he's your brother, and I could." Zane lowered his head closer to hers. That close, she could see tiny flecks of darker green in his irises. His lips covered hers.

Warmth flushed through her along with an intriguing edge of need. She'd never felt it with anybody else. Only Zane. Her knees weakened and her spine tingled. He swept inside her mouth, taking claim.

She'd always known he'd stake a claim. He lifted his head, and the desire swirling across his strong face gave her strength.

He licked his lips. "Now talk."

The man was right—she did owe him. The need to trust him, to have him trust her, became stronger than the desire to be strategic. "The end to the war comes this year, when I'm a quarter of a century old. You, Kalin, and I end up in the same place at the same time. At least one of us doesn't make it out."

"At least one?" Zane asked.

She closed her eyes and exhaled. "My feeling is only one of us will be left standing." Frankly, she'd never truly believed it would be her. "I've always hoped you lived, Zane."

He made a noise low in his gut. "Don't be sweet. Please, don't be sweet."

She couldn't help the smile as she opened her eyes. "You didn't think this would be easy, now, did you?"

Please read on for an excerpt from Rebecca
Zanetti's brand new Dark Protectors novel!

VAMPIRE'S FAITH

The Dark Protectors are Back!

Vampire King Ronan Kayrs wasn't supposed to
survive the savage sacrifice he willingly endured to
rid the world of the ultimate evil. He wasn't supposed
to emerge in this time and place, and he sure as hell
wasn't supposed to finally touch the woman who's
haunted his dreams for centuries. Yet here he is, in an
era where vampires are hidden, the enemy has grown
stronger, and his mate has no idea of the power she
holds.

Dr. Faith Cooper is flummoxed by irrefutable proof
that not only do vampires exist . . . they're hot
blooded, able to walk in sunlight, and shockingly
sexy. Faith has always depended on science, but the
restlessness she feels around this predatory male
defies reason. Especially when it grows into a hunger
only he can satisfy—that is if they can survive the evil
hunting them both.

CHAPTER 1

Dr. Faith Cooper scanned through the medical chart on her tablet while keeping a brisk pace in her dark boots through the hospital hallway, trying to ignore the chill in the air. "The brain scan was normal. What about the respiratory pattern?" she asked, reading the next page.

"Normal. We can't find any neurological damage," Dr. Barclay said, matching his long-legged stride easily to hers. His brown hair was swept back from an angled face with intelligent blue eyes. "The patient is in a coma with no brain activity, but his body is... well..."

"Perfectly healthy," Faith said, scanning the nurse's notes, wondering if Barclay was single. "The lumbar puncture was normal, and there's no evidence of a stroke."

"No. The patient presents as healthy except for the coma. It's an anomaly," Barclay replied, his voice rising.

Interesting. "Any history of drugs?" Sometimes drugs could cause a coma.

"No," Barclay said. "No evidence that we've found."

Lights flickered along the corridor as she passed through the doorway to the intensive- care unit. "What's wrong with the lights?" Faith asked, her attention jerking from the medical notes.

"It's been happening on and off for the last two days. The maintenance department is working on it, as well as on the temperature fluctuations." Barclay swept his hand out. No ring. Might not be married. "This morning we moved all the other patients to the new ICU in the western addition that was completed last week."

That explained the vacant hall and nearly deserted nurses' station. Only one woman monitored the screens spread across the desk. She nodded as Faith and Dr. Barclay passed by, her gaze lingering on the cute man.

The cold was getting worse. It was early April, raining and a little chilly. Not freezing.

Faith shivered. "Why wasn't this patient moved with the others?"

"Your instructions were to leave him exactly in place until you arrived," Barclay said, his face so cleanly shaven he looked like a cologne model. "We'll relocate him after your examination."

Goose bumps rose on her arms. She breathed out, and her breath misted in the air. This was weird. It'd never happen in the hospital across town where she worked. Her hospital was on the other side of Denver, but her expertise with coma patients was often requested across the world. She glanced back down at the tablet. "Where's his Glasgow Coma Scale score?"

"He's at a three," Barclay said grimly.

A three? That was the worst score for a coma patient. Basically, no brain function.

Barclay stopped her. "Dr. Cooper. I just want to say thank you for coming right away." He smiled and twin dimples appeared. The nurses probably loved this guy. "I heard about the little girl in Seattle. You haven't slept in— what? Thirty hours?"

It felt like it. She'd put on a clean shirt, but it was already wrinkled beneath her white lab coat. Faith patted his arm, finding very nice muscle tone. When was the last time she'd been on a date? "I'm fine. The important part is that the girl woke up." It had taken Faith seven hours of doing what she shouldn't be able to do: Communicate somehow with coma patients. This one she'd been able to save, and now a six-year-old girl was eating ice cream with her family in the hospital. Soon she'd go home. "Thank you for calling me."

He nodded, and she noticed his chin had a small divot—Cary Grant style. "Of course. You're legendary. Some say you're magic."

Faith forced a laugh. "Magic. That's funny."

Straightening her shoulders, she walked into the ICU and stopped moving, forgetting all about the chart and the doctor's dimples. "What in the world?" she murmured.

Only one standard bed remained in the sprawling room. A massive man overwhelmed it, his shoulders too wide to fit on the mattress. He was at least six-foot-six, his bare feet hanging off the end of the bed. The blankets had been pushed to his waist to make room for the myriad of electrodes set across his broad and muscular chest. Very muscular. "Why is his gown open?"

"It shouldn't be," Barclay said, looking around. "I'll ask the nurse after you do a quick examination. I don't mind admitting that I'm stymied here."

A man who could ask for help. Yep. Barclay was checking all the boxes. "Is this the correct patient?" Faith studied his healthy coloring and phenomenal physique. "There's no way this man has been in a coma for longer than a couple of days."

Barclay came to a halt, his gaze narrowing. He slid a shaking hand through his thick hair. "I understand, but according to the fire marshal, this patient was buried under piles of rocks and cement from the tunnel cave-in below the Third Street bridge that happened nearly seven years ago."

Faith moved closer to the patient, noting the thick dark hair that swept back from a chiseled face. A warrior's face. She blinked. Where the hell had that thought come from? "That's impossible." She straightened. "Anybody caught in that collapse would've died instantly, or shortly thereafter. He's not even bruised."

"What if he was frozen?" Barclay asked, balancing on sneakers.

Faith checked over the still-healthy tone of the patient's skin. "Not a chance." She reached for his wrist to check his pulse.

Electricity zipped up her arm and she coughed. What the heck was that? His skin was warm and supple, the strength beneath it obvious. She turned her wrist so her watch face was visible and then started counting. Curiosity swept her as she counted the beats. "When was he brought in?" She'd been called just three hours ago to consult on the case and hadn't had a chance to review the complete file.

"A week ago," Barclay said, relaxing by the door.

Amusement hit Faith full force. Thank goodness. For a moment, with the flickering lights, freezing air, and static electricity, she'd almost traveled to an imaginary and fanciful place. She smiled and released the man's wrist. "All right. Somebody is messing with me." She'd just been named the head of neurology at Northwest Boulder Hospital. Her colleagues must have gone to a lot of trouble—tons, really—to pull this prank. "Did Simons put you up to this?"

Barclay blinked, truly looking bewildered. He was cute. Very much so. Just the type who'd appeal to Faith's best friend, Louise. And he had an excellent reputation. Was this Louise's new beau? "Honestly, Dr. Cooper. This is no joke." He motioned toward the monitor screen that displayed the patient's heart rate, breathing, blood pressure, and intracranial pressure.

It had to be. Faith looked closer at the bandage covering the guy's head and the ICP monitor that was probably just taped beneath the bandage. "I always pay back jokes, Dr. Barclay." It was fair to give warning.

Barclay shook his head. "No joke. After a week of tests, we should see something here that explains his condition, but we have nothing. If he was injured somehow in the caved-in area, there'd be evidence of such. But... nothing." Barclay sighed. "That's why we requested your help."

None of this made any sense. The only logical conclusion was that this was a joke. She leaned over the patient to check the head bandage and look under it.

The screen blipped.

She paused.

Barclay gasped and moved a little closer to her. "What was that?"

Man, this was quite the ruse. She was so going to repay Simons for this. Dr. Louise Simons was always finding the perfect jokes, and it was time for some payback. Playing along, Faith leaned over the patient again.

BLEEP

This close, her fingers tingled with the need to touch the hard angles of this guy's face. Was he some sort of model? Bodybuilder? His muscles were sleek and smooth—natural like a wild animal's. So probably not a bodybuilder. There was something just so male about him that he made Barclay fade into the meh zone. Her friends had chosen well. This guy was sexy on a sexy stick of pure melted sexiness. "I'm going to kill Simons," she murmured, not sure if she meant it. As jokes went, this was impressive. This guy wasn't a patient and he wasn't in a coma. So she indulged herself and smoothed his hair back from his wide forehead.

BLEEP

BLEEP

BLEEP

His skin was warm, although the room was freezing. "This is amazing," she whispered, truly touched. The planning that had to have gone into it. "How long did this take to set up?"

Barclay coughed, no longer appearing quite so perfect or masculine compared to the patient. "Stroke him again."

Well, all righty then. Who wouldn't want to caress a guy like this? Going with the prank, Faith flattened her hand in the middle of the guy's thorax, feeling a very strong heartbeat. "You can stop acting now," she murmured, leaning toward his face. "You've done a terrific job." Would it be totally inappropriate to ask him out for a drink after he stopped pretending to be unconscious? He wasn't really a patient, and man, he was something. Sinewed strength and incredibly long lines. "How about we get you out of here?" Her mouth was just over his.

His eyelids flipped open.

Barclay yelped and windmilled back, hitting an orange guest chair and landing on his butt on the floor.

The patient grabbed Faith's arm in an iron-strong grip. "Faith."

She blinked and then warmth slid through her. "Yeah. That's me." Man, he was hot. All right. The coming out of a coma and saying her name was kind of cool. But it was time to get to the truth. "Who are you?"

He shook his head. "Gde, chert voz'mi, ya?"

She blinked. Wow. A Russian model? His eyes were a metallic aqua. Was he wearing contacts? "Okay, buddy. Enough with the joke." She gently tried to pull loose, but he held her in place, his hand large enough to encircle her entire bicep.

He blinked, his eyes somehow hardening. They started to glow an electric blue, sans the green. "Where am I?" His voice was low and gritty. Hoarse to a point that it rasped through the room, winding around them.

The colored contacts were seriously high-tech.

"You speak Russian and English. Extraordinary." She twisted her wrist toward her chest, breaking free. The guy was probably paid by the hour. "The jig is up, handsome." Whatever his rate, he'd earned every dime. "Tell Simons to come out from wherever she's hiding." Faith might have to clap for her best friend. This deserved applause.

The guy ripped the fake bandage off his head and then yanked the EKG wires away from his chest. He shoved himself to a seated position. The bed groaned in protest. "Where am I?" He partially turned his head to stare at the now-silent monitor. "What the hell is that?" His voice still sounded rough and sexy.

Just how far was he going to take this? "The joke is over." Faith glanced at Barclay on the floor, who was staring at the patient with wide eyes. "You're quite the actor, Dr. Barclay." She smiled.

Barclay grabbed a chair and hauled himself to his feet, the muscles in his forearms tightening. "Wh—what's happening?"

Faith snorted and moved past him, looking down the now-darkened hallway. Dim yellow emergency lights ignited along the ceiling. "They've cut the lights." Delight filled her. She lifted her voice. "Simons? Payback is a bitch, but this is amazing. Much better than April fool's." After Faith had filled Louise's car with balloons filled with sparkly confetti—guaranteed to blow if a door opened and changed the pressure in the vehicle—Simons had sworn vengeance.

"Louise?" Faith called again. Nothing. Just silence. Faith sighed. "You win. I bow to your pranking abilities."

Ice started to form on the wall across the doorway. "How are you doing that?" Faith murmured, truly impressed.

A growl came from behind her, and she jumped, turning back to the man on the bed.

He'd just growled?

She swallowed and studied him. What the heck? The saline bag appeared genuine. Moving quickly, she reached his arm. "They are actually pumping saline into your blood?" Okay. The joke had officially gone too far.

Something that looked like pain flashed in his eyes. "Who died? I felt their deaths, but who?"

She shook her head. "Come on. Enough." He was an excellent actor. She could almost feel his agony.

The man looked at her, his chin lowering. Sitting up on the bed, he was as tall as she was, even though she was standing in her favorite two-inch heeled boots. Heat poured off him, along with a tension she couldn't ignore.

She shivered again, and this time it wasn't from the cold.

Keeping her gaze, he tore out the IV.

Blood dribbled from his vein. She swallowed and fought the need to step back. "All right. Too far, Simons," she snapped. "Waaaay too far."

Barclay edged toward the door. "I don't understand what's happening."

Faith shook her head. "Occam's razor, Dr. Barclay." Either the laws of physics had just changed or this was a joke. The simplest explanation was that Simons had just won the jokester title for all time. "Enough of this, though. Who are you?" she asked the actor.

He slowly turned his head to study Dr. Barclay before focusing back on her. "When did the shield fall?"

The shield? He seemed so serious. Eerily so. Would Simons hire a crazy guy? No. Faith tapped her foot and heat rose to her face, her temper stirring. "Listen. This has been fantastic, but it's getting old. I'm done."

The guy grabbed her arm, his grip unbreakable this time. "Did both shields fail?"

Okay. Her heart started to beat faster. Awareness pricked along her skin. "Let go of me."

"No." The guy pushed from the bed and shrugged out of his gown, keeping hold of her. "What the fuck?" He looked at the Foley catheter inserted into his penis and then down to the long white anti-embolism stockings that were supposed to prevent blood clots.

Faith's breath caught. Holy shit. The catheter and TED hose were genuine. And his penis was huge. She looked up at his face. The TED hose might add a realistic detail to a joke, but no way would any responsible medical personnel insert a catheter for a gag. Simons wouldn't have done that. "What's happening?" Faith tried to yank her arm free, but he held her tight.

Dr. Barclay looked from her to the mostly naked male. "Who are you?" he whispered.

"My name is Ronan," the guy said, reaching for the catheter, which was attached to a urine-collection bag at the end of the bed. "What fresh torture is this?"

"Um," Faith started.

His nostrils flared. "Why would you collect my piss?"

Huh? "We're not," she protested. "You were in a coma. That's just a catheter."

He gripped the end of the tube, his gaze fierce.

"No—" Faith protested just as he pulled it out, grunting and then snarling in what had to be intense pain.

God. Was he on PCP or something? She frantically looked toward Barclay and mouthed the words security and Get the nurse out of here.

Barclay nodded and turned, running into the hallway.

"Where are we?" Ronan asked, drawing her toward him.

She put out a hand to protest, smashing her palm into his ripped abdomen. "Please. Let me go." She really didn't want to kick him in his already reddening penis. "You could've just damaged your urethra badly."

He started dragging her toward the door, his strength beyond superior. A sprawling tattoo covered his entire back. It looked like…a dark image of his ribs with lighter spaces between? Man, he was huge. "We must go."

Oh, there was no we. Whatever was happening right now wasn't good, and she had to get some space to figure this out. "I don't want to hurt you," she said, fighting his hold.

He snorted.

She drew in air and kicked him in the back of the

leg, twisting her arm to gain freedom.

Faster than she could imagine, he pivoted, moving right into her. Heat and muscle and strength. He more than towered over her, fierce even though he was naked. She yelped and backpedaled, striking up for his nose.

He blocked her punch with his free hand and growled again, fangs sliding down from his incisors.

She stopped moving and her brain fuzzed. Fangs? Okay. This wasn't a joke. Somebody was seriously messing with her, and maybe they wanted her hurt. She couldn't explain the eyes and the fangs, so this had to be bad. This guy was obviously capable of inflicting some real damage. His eyes morphed again to the electric blue, and somehow he broadened even more, looking more animalistic than human.

"I don't understand," she said, her voice shaking as her mind tried to make sense of what her eyes were seeing. "Who are you? Why were you unconscious in a coma? How did you know my name?"

He breathed out, his broad chest moving with the effort. The fangs slowly slid back up, and his eyes returned to the sizzling aqua. "My name is Ronan Kayrs, and I was unconscious because the shield fell." He eyed her, tugging her even closer. "I know your name because I spent four hundred years seeing your face and feeling your soft touch in my dreams."

"My—my face?" she stuttered.

His jaw hardened even more. "And that was before I'd accepted my death."

ABOUT THE AUTHOR

REBECCA ZANETTI has worked as an art curator, Senate aide, lawyer, college professor, and a hearing examiner—only to culminate it all in stories about Alpha males and the women who claim them. She is a member of RWA, has won awards for her works throughout the industry, and has a journalism degree with a poli-sci emphasis from Pepperdine University as well as a Juris Doctor from the University of Idaho.

Growing up amid the glorious backdrops and winter wonderlands of the Pacific Northwest has given Rebecca fantastic scenery and adventures to weave into her stories. She resides in the wild north with her husband, children, and extended family, who inspire her every day—or at the very least give her plenty of characters to write about.

Please visit Rebecca at www.rebeccazanetti.com.

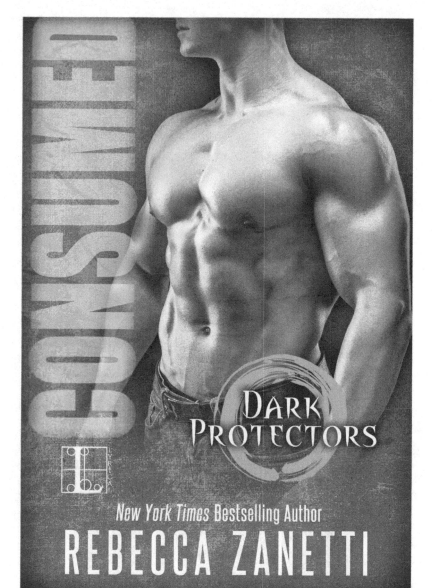

CONSUMED

DARK
PROTECTORS

New York Times Bestselling Author
REBECCA ZANETTI

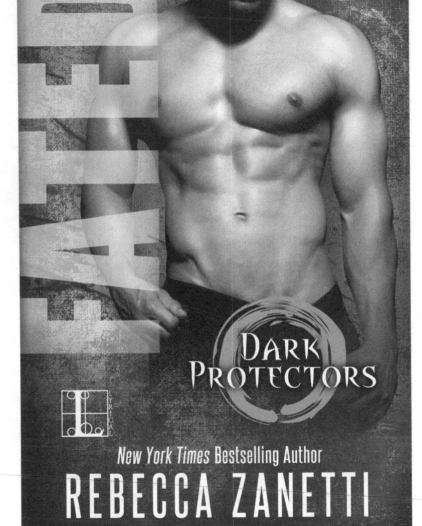

DARK
PROTECTORS

New York Times Bestselling Author
REBECCA ZANETTI